By William Dietrich

WILLIAM DIETRICH

THE BARBARY PIRATES

AN ETHAN GAGE ADVENTURE

HARPER

An Imprint of HarperCollinsPublishers

HARPER

An Imprint of HarperCollins*Publishers*
10 East 53rd Street
New York, New York 10022-5299

Copyright © 2010 by William Dietrich
Excerpt from *Blood of the Reich* copyright © 2011 by William Dietrich
Map by Casey Greene for Springer Cartographics LLC.
ISBN 978-0-06-156807-7

First Harper digest printing: April 2011
First Harper premium printing: April 2011
First Harper hardcover printing: April 2010

HarperCollins® and Harper® are registered trademarks of HarperCollins Publishers.

Printed in the United States of America

Visit Harper paperbacks on the World Wide Web at
www.harpercollins.com

10 9 8 7 6 5 4 3 2 1

To Mateo and Selena Ziz,
who were just the right age to contribute to this tale!

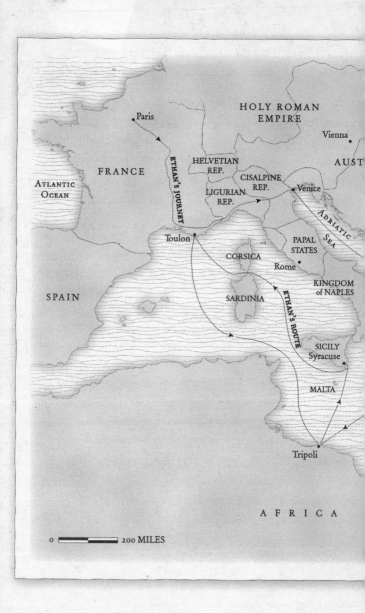

PART ONE

CHAPTER 1

After I trapped three scientists in a fire I set in a brothel, enlisted them in the theft of a stampeding wagon, got them arrested by the French secret police, and then mired them in a mystic mission for Bonaparte, they began to question my judgment.

So allow me to point out that our tumultuous night was as much *their* idea as mine. Tourists come to Paris to be naughty.

Accordingly, I was hardly surprised when a trio of savants—the English rock hound William "Strata" Smith, the French zoologist Georges Cuvier, and the crackpot American inventor Robert Fulton—insisted that I take them to the Palais Royal. Scientific luminaries they may be, but after a hard day of looking at old bones or (in the case of Fulton) marketing impractical schemes to the French navy, what these intellectuals really wanted was a peek at the city's most notorious parade of prostitutes.

Not to mention supper in a swank Palais café, a game or two of chance, and shopping for souvenir trifles such as French perfume, silver toothpicks, Chinese silks, erotic pamphlets, Egyptian jewelry, or ivory curiosities of an even-more ribald nature. Who can resist the city's center of sin and sensuality? It was even better, the scientists reasoned, if such entertainment could be attributed to someone as discreet and shameless as me.

"Monsieur Ethan Gage *insisted* on giving us this tour," Cuvier explained to any acquaintance he met, reddening as he said it. The man was smart as Socrates but still retained his Alsatian provincialism, despite his rise to the summit of France's scientific establishment. The French Revolution has replaced breeding with ability, and with it traded the weary worldliness of the nobility for the curiosity and embarrassment of the striving. Cuvier was a soldier's son, Smith from agricultural stock, and Fulton had been sired by a failed farmer who died when he was three. Bonaparte himself was not even French but Corsican, and his generals were tradesmen's offspring: Ney the son of a cooper, Lefebre a miller, Murat an innkeeper, Lannes an ostler. I, sired by a Philadelphia merchant, fit right in.

"We're here to investigate revenue sources and public sentiment," I said to reinforce Cuvier's dignity. "Napoleon is keeping the Palais open in order to tax it."

Having resolved after my recent calamitous visit to America to reform myself, I suppose I should have resented the presumption that I was expert at negotiating the notorious Palais. But I *had*, in the spirit of social and architectural inquiry, explored most of its corners during my years in Paris. Now, in June of 1802, it remains the place Paris comes to be seen or—if one's tastes run to the scandalous or perverse—safely invisible.

Smith—recently fired from his canal-surveying job in England, and frustrated by the lack of recognition for his rock mapping—came to Paris to confer with French geologists and gape. He was a surveyor built like an English bulldog, balding and thick, with a farmer's tan and the bluff, ruddy heartiness of the ploughman. Given Smith's humble origins, English intellectuals had paid absolutely no attention to the rock mapping he'd done, and the snobbery rankled. Smith knew he was more intelligent than three-quarters of the men in the Royal Society.

"You're more creative for not being stuck in their company," I suggested when Cuvier brought him to me so I could serve as interpreter and guide.

"My career is like the ditches my canal company digs. I'm here because I'm not sure what else to do."

"As is half of London! The Peace of Amiens let loose a tide of British tourists who haven't come over since the revolution. Paris has hosted two-thirds of the House of Lords already, including five dukes, three marquesses, and thirty-seven earls. They're as transfixed by the guillotine as by the trollops."

"We English are just curious about liberty's relation to wickedness."

"And the Palais is the place to study, William.

Music floats, lanterns glint, and a man can lose himself amid roving minstrels, angular acrobats, bawdy plays, amusing wagers, brilliant fashion, smart talk, intoxicating spirits, and swank bordellos." I nodded to encourage him.

"And this is officially tolerated?"

"Winked at. It's been kept off-limits to the French police since Philip of Orleans, and Philippe Egalité added the commercial arcades just before the revolution. The place has since weathered revolt, war, terror, inflation, and the conservative instincts of Napoleon with hardly a stammer. Three-quarters of Paris's newspapers have been shuttered by Bonaparte, but the Palais plays on."

"You seem to have made quite a study."

"It's the kind of history that interests me."

In truth, I was out of date. I'd been away from Paris and back in my homeland of America for more than a year and a half, and my frightful experiences there had made me more determined than ever to swear off women, gambling, drink, and treasure hunting. True, I'd been only partly successful in these resolutions. I'd used a grape-sized glob of gold (my only reward from my Trials of Job on the western frontier) to get a stake in St. Louis card games. There had been the distraction of a frontier barmaid or two, and a hearty sampling of Jefferson's wines when I finally reported back to the President's House in Washington. There he heard my carefully edited description of France's Louisiana Territory and agreed to my idea of playing unofficial American envoy back in Paris, trying to get Napoleon to sell the wasteland to the United States.

So I had a thimbleful of fame and a dram of respectability, and decided I should finally live up to both. Admittedly, I couldn't resist embroidering my military exploits when I was given trans-Atlantic passage by an American naval squadron headed for Europe to protect our shipping from the Barbary pirates. It was convenient to me that the bashaw of Tripoli, a pirate king named Yussef Karamanli, had declared war on the United States the year before, demanding $225,000 to make peace and $25,000 a year in tribute. As so often happens in politics, Jefferson—who had argued against a large military—was using five frigates built by his predecessor, Adams, to respond to this extortion with force. "Even peace may be purchased at too high a price," my old mentor Benjamin Franklin once said. So when Jefferson offered me a ride on his flotilla, I accepted, provided I was able to get off in Gibraltar before any fighting could start.

I needn't have worried. The squadron commander, Richard Valentine Morris, managed to be at once unqualified, timid, and procrastinating. He brought his wife and son along as if going on Mediterranean vacation, and was two months late setting sail. But his congressman brother had helped Jefferson win the presidency over Aaron Burr, and even in young America, political alliances trump inexperience. The man was a connected idiot.

My own war stories during the voyage convinced half the officers I was a regular Alexander, and the other half that I was a habitual liar. But I *was* trying, you see.

"You're some kind of diplomat?" Smith tried to clarify.

"My idea is that Bonaparte sell Louisiana to my own country. It's emptiness the French have no use for, but Napoleon won't negotiate until he learns if his French army in St. Domingue, or Haiti, defeats the slaves and can be moved on to New Orleans. I have a connection to the general here, Leclerc."

I didn't add that my "connection" was that I had tupped Leclerc's wife, Pauline, back in 1800, before she'd joined her husband in the Caribbean. Now, while Leclerc fought yellow fever as well as Negroes, my former lover—who was also Napoleon's sister—was reportedly learning voodoo. You can get an idea of her character from the debate in Paris on whether it was she, or Napoleon's wife, Josephine, whom the Marquis de Sade used as inspiration for his latest depraved pamphlet, "Zoloe and Her Two Acolytes." Bonaparte resolved the issue by having the author thrown into prison for either possibility. I read the book to monitor the debate and spark erotic memory.

So I'd made my way from Gibraltar to Paris, living on a modest American government allowance and pledging to finally make something of myself, once I figured out what that something should be. The Palais, Gomorrah of Europe, was as good a place to think as any. I bet only when I could find an unskilled opponent, consorted with courtesans only when need became truly imperative, kept myself in physical trim with fencing

lessons—I keep running into people with swords—
and congratulated myself on self-discipline. I was
pondering whether my talents could best be harnessed for philosophy, languages, mathematics,
or theology when Cuvier sought me out and suggested I take Smith and Fulton to the Palais Royal.

"You can talk mammoths, Gage, and show us
the whores as well."

I was the link in our quartet. I was deemed an
expert on woolly elephants because I'd gone looking for them on the American frontier, and there
was more excitement in Europe about animals that
aren't around anymore than those that are.

"The elephants' *extinction* may be more important than their former *existence*," Cuvier explained
to me. He was a pleasant-looking, long-faced,
high-domed man of thirty-three with arched nose,
strong chin, and pursed lower lip that gave him the
appearance of constant deep thought. This accident
of nature helped his advancement, as so often happens in life. Cuvier also had the fierce seriousness
of a man who'd risen by merit instead of odd luck
like me, and his organizational flair had put him in
charge of the Paris zoo and French education, the
latter task striking him as the more thankless.

"In any system the bright shine and the dull
yearn only to escape, but politicians expect educa-
tors to repeal human nature."

"Every parent hopes their unexceptional child is
the teacher's fault," I agreed.

Cuvier thought that I—without rank, income,
or security—was the enviable one, dashing about
on this mission or that for two or three govern-

ments at a time. Even I have trouble keeping it straight. So we'd become unlikely friends.

"The fact that we're finding skeletons of animals that no longer exist proves the earth is older than the Biblical six thousand years," the scientist liked to lecture. "I'm as Christian as any man, but some rocks have no fossils at all, suggesting life is not as eternal as Scripture suggests."

"But I thought a bishop had calculated the day of Creation rather exactly. To October 23, 4004 B.C., if I remember right."

"Claptrap, Ethan, all of it. Why, we've already cataloged twenty thousand species. How could they all fit on the Ark? The world is far older than we know."

"I keep running into treasure hunters who think the same thing, Georges, but I must say their abundance of time makes them balmy. They never know when they belong. The nice thing about the Palais is that there's never any yesterday and never any tomorrow. Not a clock in the place."

"Animals have little sense of time, either. It makes them content. But we humans are doomed to know the past and looming future."

Smith was a bone hunter, too, and theories were rife about what kinds of ancient calamities might have wiped out ancient animals. Flood or fire? Cold or heat? Cuvier was also intrigued by my mention of the word "Thira," which I'd read on medieval gold foil unearthed during my North American adventure. A particularly evil woman named Aurora Somerset had seemed to think the scroll had some importance, and Cuvier told me Thira, also known as Santorini, was a Greek island of great interest to European mineralogists because it might be the remains of an ancient volcano. So when "Strata" Smith came over from London, anxious to talk rocks and see strumpets, it was natural we all be introduced. Cuvier was excited because Strata concurred with his own findings that fossil bones of a particular kind were found only in certain layers of rock, and thus could be used to date when that rock was laid down.

"I'm using the exposures in canals and road cuts to begin drawing a geologic map of Great Britain," Smith told me proudly.

I nodded as I've learned to do in the company of savants, but couldn't help asking, "Why?" Knowing which rock was where seemed a trifle dull.

"Because it can be done." Seeing my doubt, he added, "It could also be valuable to coal or mining companies." He had that defensive, impatient tone of the bright employee.

"You mean you'd have a map of where the seams of coal and metal are?"

"An indication of where they might be."

Clever. Accordingly, I agreed to organize our trip to the Palais, hoping that after a night of drinking Smith might let slip a vein of copper here or pocket of iron there. Maybe I could hock word of it to stockjobbers or mineral speculators.

Fulton, thirty-six, was my own contribution to our foursome. I'd met him upon my return to Paris when we'd both waited fruitlessly for an audience with Bonaparte, and I rather liked that he seemed even less successful than I was. He'd been in France for five years, trying to persuade the revolutionaries to adopt his inventions, but his experiment at building a submarine, or "plunging boat," had been rejected by the French navy.

"I tell you, Gage, the *Nautilus* worked perfectly well off Brest. We were underwater three hours, and could have stayed six." Fulton was good-looking enough to be a useful companion when looking for ladies, but he had the fretfulness of the frustrated dreamer.

"Robert, you told the admirals that your invention could make surface navies obsolete. You may be able to keep from drowning, but you're the worst salesman in the world. You're asking men to buy what would put them out of work."

"But the submarine would be so fearsome as to end war entirely!"

"Another point against you. Think, man!"

"Well, I've a new idea for using Watt's steam engine to propel a riverboat," he said doggedly.

"And why would any man pay to fuel a boiler when the wind and oars are free?" Savants are all very bright, but it would be hard to find common sense in a regiment of them. That's why they need me along.

Fulton had been far more successful painting lurid circular panoramas for Parisians on great city fires. They'd pay a franc or two to stand in the middle rotating, as if in the conflagration themselves, and if anything is better testament to the peculiarity of human nature, I can't name it. Unfortunately, he wouldn't take my advice that the real money was not in steam engines that nobody really needed, but rather in frightening pictures that made people think they were somewhere other than where they were.

My idea, then, was this. We'd have a lads nights out at the Palais Royal, I'd pump the savants for information on lucrative veins of coal or why medieval knights with a taste for the mystical and occult might have jotted down "Thira" on gold foil in the middle of North America, and then we'd see if any of us could come up with something that could be sold for actual money. I'd also continue working on reformation of my character.

What I wasn't counting on was the need to bet my life, and the French secret police.

CHAPTER 2

Horror we can habituate to. Defeat can be accommodated. It is the unknown that causes fear, and uncertainty that haunts us in the hollow of the night. So my resolution to reform myself was weaker than I knew because the truth was that I hadn't sworn off women entirely. After the agony and heartbreak I'd experienced on the American frontier, I wanted to reestablish contact with Astiza, a woman I'd fallen in love with four years before during Napoleon's Orient campaign. She'd left me in Paris to return to Egypt, and after the heartbreak of my latest adventure, I began writing her.

If she'd declined to renew our relationship, I'd have understood. Our time together had been more tumultuous than satisfying. But instead I got no answer at all, despite her promise that we might one day find ourselves together again. Of course Egypt was still recovering from the British expulsion of the French the year before, so communication was uncertain. But had anything happened to my partner in adventure? I did manage to contact my old friend Ashraf, who said he'd seen Astiza after her return to Egypt. She'd been her usual mysterious self, reclusive, troubled, and living in near seclusion. Then she abruptly vanished about the time I returned to Europe. I knew it would have been more surprising to hear she'd settled into domesticity, and certainly I'd little claim on her. But to not know nagged at me.

Which is how I led my companions into the wrong bordello.

It happened this way. The Palais Royal is an enormous rectangle of pillared arcades, its courtyard filled with gardens, fountains, and pathways. We ate at an outdoor café and gawked at the trollops who costumed themselves as the most prominent socialites of the republic, in between the trio's tediously learned arguments on bone classification and the merits of screw propellers. I showed them where Bonaparte used to play chess for money as an artillery captain, and the arcade where he'd met the prostitute to whom he'd lost his virginity as a young soldier. Yonder was the club where foreign minister Talleyrand once spent 30,000 francs in a single night, and nearby was the shop where Charlotte Corday bought the knife with which she stabbed Marat in his bath. Sodomites with plumage as elaborate as the whores walked the Street of Sighs arm in arm, given that such love has been decriminalized by the revolution. Beggars mingled with millionaires, prophets preached, cardsharps prowled, and the perversely pious sought out chambers where they could negotiate sexual whippings to the most precise calibration of penance and pain. We descended into the cellar "circus," where couples danced amid "nymphs" posing in diaphanous clothing, and pretended to study with an academic's objectivity the complex's forty-four statues of Venus.

As we circulated, Cuvier was persuaded to try his hand at the new game of "21" that Napoleon had helped popularize, Smith sampled varieties of champagne with a pub crawler's endurance, and Fulton studied the acrobats' use of leverage.

He had to be dragged away from a fire-eater. "Imagine if we could invent a dragon!"

"The French wouldn't buy that, either."

I guessed this group was as happy looking at the prostitutes as hiring them. Given that half the Palais' amusements were technically illegal—French kings had issued thirty-two decrees against gambling since 1600—it was my full intention to keep us out of trouble. Then I heard, while leading our little squad through a dim arcade of shops and descending stairways, a female voice call my name.

I turned to see Madame Marguerite, or, as she preferred to be called, Isis, Queen of Arabia. She was a bordello manager of entrepreneurial ambition whom I'd encountered before I reformed. "Monsieur Gage! You must introduce me to your friends!"

Marguerite operated one of the more ostentatious brothels in the Palais, a warren of vaulted caverns under a crowded gambling salon. Its decor was Oriental, and the courtesans' filmy costumes were inspired by feverish European fantasies of the seraglios of Istanbul. By rumor you could sample hashish and opium there, while imagining yourself master of a harem. It was costly, decadent, illegal, and thus quite irresistible. It was also no place for esteemed savants. My instinct was to hurry by, but Marguerite rushed out to block us, my companions bunched up nervously behind as if we were at the entrance to the maze of the Minotaur.

"Hello, Isis," I said warily. "Business going well?"

"Brilliantly, but how we've missed our Ethan! We'd been told you'd disappeared in America. How heartbroken were my concubines! They wept, thinking of you at the mercy of Red Indians."

Well, I had spent money in the place. "I'm back, my hair still attached, but newly reformed," I reported. "Celibacy is good for character, I've decided."

She laughed. "What an absurd idea. Surely your friends don't agree?"

"These are savants, men of learning. I'm just showing them about."

"And there is much my girls can show. Collette! Sophie!"

"I'm afraid we can't stay."

"Is this the Arabian place?" Cuvier interrupted behind me, craning to look. "I've heard of it."

"It looks like an Ottoman palace in there," said Smith, squinting through the doorway. "The architecture is quite intricate."

"Do you really want to be seen entering?" I asked, even as Marguerite seized my arm with enthusiasm. "I *am* responsible for your reputation, gentlemen."

"And we in this house are mistresses of discretion," our hostess assured. "Esteemed savants, at least experience my décor—I work so hard at it. And it's so fortuitous we meet, Ethan, because my assistant inside was just asking about you!"

"Was she now?"

"It's a man, actually. He plays the role of Osiris." She winked.

"I'm not of that taste."

"No, no, he only wants to talk and wager with you. He's heard of your gambling skills and says you'll want to bet for the thing you most desperately wish to learn."

"Which is?"

"Word of your Egyptian friend."

That startled me, given my puzzlement about Astiza. I'd never mentioned her to Marguerite. "How could this Osiris know that?"

"Yes, come in, come in, and hear his proposition!" Her eyes gleamed, her pupils huge and waxy. "Bring your friends, no one is looking. Share some claret and relax!"

Well, it was against all my resolutions, but why would a stranger know about my long-lost love in Egypt? "Perhaps we should take a look," I told my companions. "The scenery is worthy of the theater. It's a lesson in how the world works, too."

"And what lesson is that?" Fulton asked as we descended into Marguerite's grotto.

"That even looking costs money." Isis pulled us into the welcoming chamber of her seraglio and my savants gaped at the "Arabian" beauties on parade for inspection, since their costumes combined would be about enough to account for one good scarf. "This won't take a minute," I went on. "Go on to the rooms just to be polite. Fulton, buy a girl a glass and explain steam power. Smith, the auburn-haired one looks like she's got all kinds of topography to map. Cuvier, consider the anatomy of the blond over there. Surely you can theorize about the hourglass morphology of the female form?" That would keep them occupied while I learned who this Osiris was and whether he knew anything but rubbish.

The savants were so content to pretend it was all my idea that Marguerite should have given me a commission. Unfortunately, she was tighter with a franc than my old landlady, Madame Durrell.

"And which fancy would *you* care to tickle, Ethan?" the brothel keeper asked as the girls dragged the savants into a chamber tented with gauze curtains. Negro servants brought tall brass Turkish pitchers. Candles and incense made a golden haze.

"I've adopted rectitude, I said. 'Be at war with your vices,' Ben Franklin used to tell me. A regular bishop, I am."

"A bishop! They were our best customers! Thank God Bonaparte has brought the church back."

"Yes, I heard they sang a Te Deum in Notre Dame at Easter to celebrate the new Concordat with Rome."

"It was delicious farce. The Kings of Judah above the entrance are *still* headless, ever since the revolutionary mobs mistook them for French kings and knocked their tops off. It's like a stone monument to the guillotine! The church itself, which the Jacobins designated a Temple of Reason, is in wretched disrepair. The Te Deum was the first time the bells had rung in ten years, and none of his generals could remember when to genuflect. Instead of kneeling, the rabble presented arms when they elevated the host at consecration. You could hardly hear the Latin for all the snickering, whispers, and clatter of sabers and bayonets."

"The common people are happier the Church is back, which was Napoleon's point."

"Yes, the country is drifting to the old ways: faith, tyranny, and war. No wonder the mob has voted overwhelmingly to make him first consul for life! Fortunately, my kind of business thrives in every political climate. Be they royalist or revolutionary, cleric or marshal, they all like to tumble." She raised a flute of champagne. "To desire!"

"And discipline." I took a swallow, eyeing the girls wistfully. The savants seemed to be chatting away as if this were the Institute—trollops can pretend fascination with anything, it seems, even science—and the air was heady with hashish and the aroma of spirits. "I tell you, it feels good to abstain," I continued doggedly. "I'm going to write a book."

"Nonsense. Every man needs vice."

"I've sworn off gambling, too."

"But surely there is *something* you would wager for," a male voice interrupted.

CHAPTER 3

I turned. A swarthy, hawk-nosed man in the getup of a sultan had entered the antechamber. His eyes were predatory and his lips thin as a lizard's, giving him the reptilian guise of an inquisitor, or one of my creditors. His turban was decorated with an ostrich feather of the kind the soldiers had collected in Egypt, by shooting the dim-witted beasts that ran wild there. He didn't really look Arab, however, but French. We all like to pretend.

"May I present Osiris, god of the underworld," Isis/Marguerite introduced. "He's a student of Egypt like you."

The man bowed. "Of course I haven't found treasures like the famed Ethan Gage."

"Lost everything, I'm afraid." People always hope I'm rich, in case I might share. I disabuse them as quickly as I can.

"And left Egypt before the campaign was over, did you not?"

"As did Napoleon. I'm American, not French, and I control my own life." This wasn't quite true, either—who does control his life?—but I didn't want it implied I'd scuttled.

"And would you care to wager that life?"

"Hardly. I've been telling the Queen of Arabia here that I've reformed."

"But every man can be tempted, which is the lesson of the Palais Royal, is it not? All have something they long for. None are completely guiltless. Which is why we congregate, and never judge! We may admire the righteous, but we don't really like them, or entirely trust them, either. The most pious are crucified! If you want good friends, be imperfect, no?"

My companions, I realized, had been led by their consorts out of sight. The savants were either bolder or drunker than I thought. Which meant that I was suddenly quite alone. "Nobody's more imperfect than me," I said. "And just who are you, Osiris? Do you procure?"

"I assist, and learn. Which is how I can offer a wager to tell you what you want to know, and you don't have to bet a sou to win it."

"What do you think I want to know?"

"Where the priestess is, of course."

Astiza was a priestess of sorts, a student of ancient religion. I felt a jolt of memory.

"She still touches your heart, I think. Men call you vain and shallow, Ethan Gage, but there's spark and loyalty in there as well, I'm guessing."

"How do you know about Astiza?" I was aware that with the absence of my companions, two new men had materialized in the shadows, bulky as armoires. They now guarded the brothel door. And where was Marguerite?

"It's my fraternity's business to know what men wish to know." And he drew from his robe that symbol I'd encountered before on the neck of my enemy in North America: a golden pyramid entwined with the snake-god Apophis hanging from a chain: the crest of arms, of sorts, of my old nemesis the Egyptian Rite. The last time I got entangled with this bunch it was for torture at an Indian village, and I automatically stiffened and wished for my longrifle, which of course I'd left at home. This Osiris seemed snakelike himself, and I felt dizzy in the smoky musk of the room. It smelled of hashish.

"You're part of the Rite?" The Egyptian Rite was a renegade group of corrupt Freemasonry founded a generation before by the charlatan Cagliostro, and which had been plaguing me since I won a medallion in a Paris card game four years before. I'd hoped I was done with them, but they were persistent as taxes.

"I'm part of a group of like-minded people. Pay no attention to rumor. We're reformers, like you."

"Can I see the emblem?"

He handed it to me. This one was heavy, perhaps solid gold. "Try wearing it, if you like. I think it conveys a sense of power and confidence. There's magic in what one puts on."

"Not my style." I hefted it, considering.

"I respect your pledge against gambling, Monsieur Gage. How inspiring to encounter reform! But please don't be alarmed by this symbol. I'm offering alliance, not enmity. So I propose a simple riddle, a child's puzzle. If you answer it correctly, I will take you to Astiza. But if you answer it incorrectly, your life will be mine, to do as I say."

"What does that mean? Are you the devil?"

"Come, Monsieur Gage, you have a reputation as a master of electricity, a savant. Surely a child's game doesn't daunt you?"

Daunt me? I was holding in my hand a symbol of what, as far as I knew, was a cabal of snake worshippers, sorcerers, perverts, and conspirators. "And what do *you* risk?"

"The priceless information I hold. After all, you've staked no money."

"Nor have you! So if you want to play riddles, we *both* must play. Your purpose against my life, Osiris." That should give him pause. "If I win my riddle and you lose mine, you must not only send me to Astiza but explain once and for all the business of your odd Rite. What are you eccentrics really after?" I'd remembered a puzzle Franklin had told me once, and decided to try it on him.

He considered, and shrugged. "Very well. I never lose." He held up a minute glass.

My blood was up. "Start the sand, then."

"My riddle first. Two condemned men are at the bottom of a sheer pit that can't be climbed, and are scheduled for execution at dawn. If they could reach the lip of the pit they could escape, but even with one standing on the other's shoulders, they cannot reach that high. They have a shovel to tunnel, but to dig far enough will take days, not hours. How can they escape?" He turned the timer.

I watched its hiss of grains and tried to think. What would old Ben have advised? He was a font of aphorisms, half of them annoying. *Buy what you have no need of and soon you will have to sell your necessaries.* True enough, but what fun is money if not to squander?

Confinement? *They that can give up essential liberty to obtain temporary safety deserve neither.* That was no help either. The sand was piling up at the bottom of the glass and Osiris, or whatever his name really was, was regarding me with amusement. *We get old too soon and wise too late.* Well, that certainly applied to me. Sand, sand, draining down . . .

But that was it! Sand! "They tunnel," I announced, "but only to obtain sand to pile on one side of the pit. When it is high enough, they stand on it to reach the well's lip."

My riddler slowly clapped his hands. "Congratulations, Monsieur Gage, your reputation for a modicum of wit is not entirely undeserved. It appears I'm to take you to Astiza."

"And explain the goal of your bloody Rite as well, perhaps. You had your turn, so now it's mine. You must make a statement. If your statement is false, I will take all your possessions. If it is true, I will require the truth of who you really are and what our game really is."

"You are posing an unwinnable dilemma, Monsieur."

"That's the challenge, isn't it?" I turned the glass, and the sand began hissing again.

Osiris considered, watching the seconds pour out as I had. Then he smiled, a slit in a cruel face. "You will take all my possessions."

Now it was my turn to nod in grudging acknowledgment. "Well played."

"I turned your dilemma on its head. If you take all my possessions, that makes my statement true. But if it is true, you cannot take my possessions, which requires a false statement. And yet without taking my possessions, my statement is false, so I don't owe you the truth either. You must release me of either obligation."

"You would make a Franklin man."

"And you, an Egyptian."

Weren't we the complimentary pair? "So, will you take me to Astiza as you promised, even if you won't tell me all I want to know?"

"Yes. But she's not here in Paris, Monsieur Gage. Nor in Egypt, either, I'm afraid. But no matter. As your riddle was double-edged, mine was as well. Had you lost, your life would have been mine, as you promised. And though you've won, your life is still mine—I will take you to Astiza, but I will have to take you in a roundabout way." He nodded to his hulking companions. "Your presence is imperative in Thira, you see, where we will go en route to your lover. There's a secret we need found. I hope you're flattered we need your insight. But if not, I brought these companions to ensure you'd come along."

"I'm sorry, Ethan," Marguerite called from behind one of her spangled curtains. "These are not men to trifle with! They threatened to hurt me! I had no choice but to lure you down here! It was you or me!"

Have I mentioned I have bad luck with women? The door was blocked by ogres and behind me was a subterranean seraglio. I tried to think of a plan. One of the doormen lifted manacles.

"Then I have no choice either." I once might have hesitated to use force, given my naturally affable personality, but I've learned the rascals of this world thrive on good men's indecision. I whipped Osiris's pyramidal medallion as hard as I could across his face, making him curse and reel. Then I kicked the nearest of his troglodytes in the cockles, bending the bastard like slamming the leaves of a book. The other tried to charge but collided with the first two, and so I had time to aim and hurl the damn trinket at a bank of candles.

The only plan I'd been able to come up with was to set us all on fire.

CHAPTER 4

W ax tapers went flying as the heavy gold ornament and chain sliced into the pretty array, flame arcing like fire arrows. Osiris, or whatever his real name was, stumbled back against his trolls with a curse and a snarl, blood flowing through the hand clutched to his cheek. He reached for a hidden pistol with the other, but as silk curtains ignited from the scythed candles, I toppled Ottoman lamps on the floor. Oil spilled, and before he could draw and shoot, I hopped back through a gush of flame.

Smoke bloomed behind me as the fire flared, and my would-be captors cried out and retreated. Madame Marguerite was screaming. In seconds I'd turned her little anteroom into a merry inferno, and as I retreated deeper into the brothel smoke rolled against the ceiling. The trollops behind me began shrieking as well.

So I'd set fire in front and had stone walls to my

back. Not ideal. And where the devil were my savants? "Georges! Robert! William!"

"Here!" I heard Fulton shout. "Damn it, Gage, what have you done now?"

I found him coatless but otherwise presentable, a half-dressed strumpet crawling away on her hands and knees. My, she had a fetching bottom. "I was just explaining the process of adding oxygen to my *Nautilus*," the inventor said, coughing, "when all the shouting started. Cuvier and Smith are insensible, I'm afraid. They drank from those Turkish vessels, and I think there's something in the wine." He looked past me at the lurid light coming from the room from which I'd retreated, the smoke orange in its glow. "By Zeus and Jupiter, Ethan, have you been drinking, too? I believe you've started quite the alarming fire."

"It was the only way I could prevent being manacled by the henchmen of that madman Osiris," I explained hastily. "He's of the Egyptian Rite, a nasty bunch I've encountered before." To emphasize the point, shots sounded and bullets buzzed through the smoke to ping against the stone walls of the cellar. I dropped, yanking Fulton down. "Best to stay low. Most men shoot high, and there's less smoke at the floor."

"Very informative, Gage. Unfortunately, as near as I can tell, the only door out is on the other side of your inferno."

"It's true I didn't have time to entirely think my plan through. But the bonfire is rather like the panorama you painted, don't you think?"

There was a whoosh as more curtains caught.

Settees sprouted flames as if they were logs on a Christmas fire. Heat pulsed like a throbbing heart.

"Considerably hotter."

We retreated back another room to where Cuvier and Smith lay blearily, drugged and hacking. Three other half-naked male patrons and their prostitutes were crawling about, all of them bawling in terror. "Surely there's a back door," I said, trying not to join the panic. I grabbed a trollop and shook her. "You! Which way out?"

"She bricked it up to control us!"

Well, damnation. I still didn't have a clue where Astiza was, either. When I finally perfect my character, I'm going to conduct a more placid life. "Unless we can find a great deal of water, it seems I've cooked us," I conceded.

"Or we can re-create that door," Fulton said grimly. "Where did they brick up the second entrance?" he asked the girl.

"It's two feet thick of heavy stone," she wailed. "You'd need a day to break it!"

Fulton looked at me with exasperation. "What's below us?" he asked me.

"How the devil would I know? Smith's the rock man."

"And above?"

"A gambling salon, I think. We're in the cellar foundation of one wing of the Palais."

"Then that's the solution! To the tent! We go for the keystone, Ethan!"

I had no idea what he meant but followed his lead still deeper into the bordello, thankful to get farther from my fire. In another room was an erected tent of the Arabian type, piled with cushions and carpets to make a desert fantasy. Stout poles that reached nearly to the vaulted stone ceiling held the fabric up.

"Those are our battering rams," the inventor said. "Our only hope is to bring the ceiling down on top of us."

"Start a collapse? Are you mad?"

"Would you rather cook? If we can drop the floor of the gambling den, we can crawl out."

I glanced upward. "But the stonework looks sturdy as a castle."

"Which you didn't consider before setting us ablaze, did you? However, the ceiling will be thinner than the walls, and every fortress has a weak point. Now wrap the tent and some of the pillows round that pole there, like a giant torch. Smith, Cuvier!" He slapped them into some semblance of stuporlike action. "Find water, or at least wine! No spirits that might ignite! Hurry, if you don't want to roast! Ethan, go stick this matchstick into your fire and set it aflame!"

"Then what?"

"Carry it back to me."

Not having a better idea, I advanced toward the inferno. The gunshots had ended; presumably because Osiris and Isis had the sense to flee out the main door. My ten-foot-long "torch" caught like a match and I retreated from the heat with the end of the tent pole blazing, Fulton helping me swing it up against the ceiling. "The keystone in this vault looked weakest," he said, panting, letting the flames roar up against the central part of our roof. There the vault met at a central stone, the compression keeping the entire building steady. We squinted as bits of flaming fabric rained down. "We need to imitate quarrymen and use heat and cold to crack it."

"I can hardly breathe," I wheezed.

"Then work faster!"

The flare of silk and cotton burned out against the stone overhead just as Cuvier and Smith came dragging in a jar of liquid. Fulton grabbed it, swung, and hurled the water or wine—I was never sure which—against the heated ceiling, cool liquid against hot stone.

There was a snap, and cracks appeared, bits of rock spitting out. The keystone at the arched ceiling's center was fractured.

"Now, now, the other tent pole! Hurry, before we pass out!"

I understood. I took a second pole, not yet burned, and rammed it against the stone highest in the ceiling with all my might. More rock rained down.

"Harder, harder!" Fulton shouted, helping me bang against the ceiling.

"Blazes, this is hard work," I gasped, wondering what we were supposed to do if the ceiling truly gave way on top of us.

"Get the whores to help!"

As smoke swirled and the main fire licked toward us, the girls joined our battering, aided slightly by the woozy zoologist and drugged canal surveyor. Grunting, we rammed like pistons, driven by the energy that comes from fear and desperation. Finally there was another crack and the central stone suddenly plunged down, hitting the brothel floor with a bang. A girl shrieked and jumped aside. There was a dark gap overhead, the ceiling's domed vault leaning in toward nothing.

"More, more, before we're consumed!"

The fire's heat kept rising. We rammed like maniacal besiegers and more stones began to drop and bounce, the women shouting warning as each came down. We could hear yells of confusion from the gambling hall above. Finally there was a grumble of grinding stone and cracking wood, building to a roar.

"Back, back, toward the fire!" We retreated out of the way as the ceiling suddenly caved, the vault collapsing of its own weight. Its crash shot out a cloud of dust. As it did so, there was a crack of beams and the casino floor above parted and gave way as well. A shaft of light broke in like a ray of heaven, even as splintered wood, gaming tables, chips, and playing cards plunged and fluttered into the new crater. Two or three stunned gamblers tumbled with it, dropping into our little cook pot as we cheered.

As blessed air rushed in, the fire behind bellowed.

"Up," I gasped. "Climb the beams before the fire consumes them!"

We came out of the column of smoke like a hive of demons, the naked women black as coal, the stumbling savants drunk and punchy, and the swallowed gamblers screeching from their little preview of hell. Fulton leaped clear like a devil-king, singed but triumphant. We'd broken free!

I crawled out on the casino floor, eyes streaming, as patrons stampeded this way and that. Despite the confusion I had the presence of mind to salvage a coin or two.

French fire wagons had pushed to the door of the bordello and salon and were beginning to pump water into the hole we'd made. Beyond, a bleeding Osiris and half a dozen of his henchmen were crouched in the garden shadows in case by some miracle we might emerge. What did he truly want? What did he know about Astiza?

I pointed to Fulton. "There are our enemies."

"*What* enemies?" He was hacking and wheezing. "I thought we came to be entertained."

"I'm never entirely sure what's going on myself. But we need a way out of the Palais. He meant to seize me, one way or the other, and drug you."

"But how do we get out of his place? We can't outrun them with Cuvier and Smith half sensible and a thousand people between us and the street. Can we fetch the police?"

"They don't come here. If they did, they'd arrest us with that other lot and sort it out later. We might be strangled by our cellmates. And any scandal won't help our causes with Napoleon."

Water began to spout from the leather fire hoses as the fire brigade pumped fiercely. A chain of people were passing water in buckets from a Palais fountain to the copper tub mounted on the back of the fire wagon. It was a splendidly modern idea, although it didn't seem to be making much progress against my fire.

"I'd propose a larger fire wagon and a horse-driven pump," the inventor observed. "Or perhaps steam. But at least the authorities are trying."

"That's it! We'll seize a fire wagon."

"Are you serious? We won't be arrested, we'll be shot. And they need it for the fire."

"They've no weapons, and Madame Marguerite deserves a few more flames for trying to entrap us. Look, more engines are coming, more than the fountains can feed, and that one there is simply waiting in line. We'll pretend we're dashing to get more water. Once we get past the men who tried to manacle me, we'll give the fire wagon back."

"It's hardly bigger than a chariot!" Indeed, the two-wheel contraption was not much wider or longer than a field gun and hardly looked capable of putting out a campfire.

"We'll have to squeeze." And, collaring the dazed Cuvier and Smith, we charged. Fulton un-twisted the hose loose from a wagon's brass spigot while I heaved our two friends into a tub they didn't really fit into. Their displacement slopped water over the rim. Then I seized the reins and, to cries of protest, lashed the two engine ponies out into the park and tables of the Palais. Diners scat-tered, prostitutes ran, and chess pieces went flying as we careened through the cafés. Then we were dashing pell-mell down the palace's quarter-mile central courtyard, smashing aside chairs and bat-ting lanterns as we made for the main entrance, which was an arched carriageway leading to the street beyond. Osiris saw our charge and ran to in-tercept us. Behind him, still hunched in pain and waddling as he hurried, was the man I'd kicked.

I rode them down.

I'd dealt with the Rite before, and they'd haunted

my life like a recurring nightmare. I didn't know what Osiris wanted and didn't care, I only wanted to break free of his breed once and for all. So I balanced on the wagon and shook the reins as if flapping a blanket, horses stampeding, Fulton roaring as he hung on, Cuvier and Smith moaning. The riddler fell under my team. We bounced as we hit him, swerved, and skewed through the gate, hub scraping. I heard a shot and dared not look back.

We clattered out onto the broader rue Saint-Honoré, Palais patrons protesting behind us, pedestrians scattering ahead. The immense Louvre was a cliff in the dark. Paris is a mess of traffic at the best of times, delivery wagons blocking lanes and horses backing and pissing, so we came up against some trucks and carts, our horses getting tangled in their harnesses. Giving up the reins, I hauled our party from their perch. "Now, now, run!" We had to hide!

And that was when a languid man with black cane stepped in front of us with an air of utter authority. He held up his hand and said simply, "On the contrary, I command you to stop, Monsieur Gage."

"Stop?"

"I'm afraid you're all under arrest." Around us materialized a dozen gendarmes. We'd run from Egyptian Rite to the Paris police.

"By whose orders?" I tried to bluster.

"By those of the first consul himself, Napoleon Bonaparte."

CHAPTER 5

A rrest?" I had to think fast. "We were simply trying to escape some thugs who sought to trap us in a fire." I glanced back to see if Osiris was staggering after us, but saw no sign of him. "And fetch water. These men are esteemed savants."

Fulton was gray with smoke and rock dust and Cuvier and Smith were drugged and swaying. Our clothes were torn and our dignity shredded.

"Monsieur Gage, it is not your escape you're being arrested for."

How did this policeman know me? "For what, then?"

"For consorting with the English while on a French diplomatic mission for Talleyrand in North America," he said coolly. "You violated your instructions from the French government—not surprising, perhaps, given your service to the British against French forces in the Holy Land in 1799.

To which we could add corruption of the morals of esteemed savants. For conspiring in prostitution, which does, after all, remain illegal. For your colleagues' illicit consumption of drugs imbided in a brothel. For arson, for promotion of a riot, for destruction of property, for the running down of pedestrians, for theft of a fire wagon, and for the fouling of traffic."

I licked my lips. "I can explain all that."

"Unfortunately, it is not me you are to explain to."

"And you are?"

"Ah." He bowed. "Minister of Police Joseph Fouché at your service." His eyes were sleepy but watchful, his mouth set in an expression of skepticism, and his posture light but alert, like a fencer poised for a match. He was the kind of man who seemed unlikely to believe anything I had to say, which wasn't a bad place to start. He was also extremely able and dangerous. He'd found the conspirators who tried and failed to blow up Napoleon with a keg of gunpowder on Christmas Eve, 1800, executing key royalists and using the excuse to send a hundred French anarchists to the Seychelles Islands.

"Fouché? You bother with tourists like us?"

"Monsieur, I bother with everyone, everywhere, at all times. Including the murderer of a prostitute some four years ago . . ."

"I had nothing to do with that!" I'd once been unjustly accused, and had some notoriety because of it, but I thought Napoleon had put that issue to rest. "I warn you that I know the first consul myself." I drew myself up. "I'm a hero of the French victory at Marengo, and of the Treaty of Morte-fontaine. I also represent President Jefferson of the United States."

"Yes. I would prefer simply to imprison and guillotine you, but Napoleon still thinks you might be useful. Just how, after nearly setting yourself on fire, I can't imagine." No hint of humor crossed his face. "I understand you've been attempting to see the first consul for some time. Your blundering has now won you that opportunity. The meeting will not have the agenda you intended, however."

The trio behind me was trying to follow all this with dazed bewilderment. "At least let my friends go," I said. "This was all my doing."

"Your friends, Ethan, are the only reason I am saving you." He snapped an order. "Lock them all up before they trample someone else."

This was not the way I'd intended meeting Bonaparte, given that I fancied myself as a diplo-mat. He *did* have a habit of seeing people on his own time and at his own advantage. As we were herded into a waiting prison wagon it occurred to me that it was highly coincidental that the French minister of police, considered by many the most feared and powerful man in France after Napo-leon himself, happened to be waiting at the gates of the Palais Royal just as I'd made a thorough fool of myself. Did the mysterious Osiris or treacherous Marguerite have some connection with the equally mysterious Fouché?

"Ethan, what the devil?" Fulton asked as the door clanged shut. We started with a lurch.

"It's all part of our visit," I said vaguely. "We're off to see Bonaparte. You did want an audience with him, didn't you?"

"Not as a criminal! I told you we shouldn't have stolen the fire wagon."

"You should feel complimented. We've been arrested by Fouché himself."

"For what?"

"Me, mostly."

The other two savants were still drugged and groggy about our arrest, and I knew I'd have to ask Bonaparte for the favor of releasing them, putting me in his debt. In short, the first consul had saved my appointment with him until I was dependent on his mercy. I suppose such tactical maneuvering was the reason he was ruler of France, and I was not.

Our wagon, with only tiny windows for air, wound through the streets of Paris in the darkest hour of the night. By peering out the openings I could occasionally discern a landmark in what was still a sprawling, medieval mélange of a city in recovery from the revolution. Its population had dropped a hundred thousand to just over half a million, thanks to the flight of royalists and an earlier economic depression. Only under Napoleon was the economy reviving. I guessed our destination from our westerly direction.

"We're going to his château of Malmaison," I predicted to the others. "That's good news. No one you know will see us."

"Or see us disappear," muttered Cuvier, who was beginning to regain his wits.

"Malmaison? Bad house?" Smith translated.

"A neighborhood name in memory of an old Viking raid, Bill. Probably your ancestors."

"Bah. They sacked England, too. And came from France, the Normans did."

Paris as always was a hodgepodge of palaces, crowded houses, vegetable plots, and muddy pasture. The only people I saw at that predawn hour were some of the thousands of water carriers who laboriously carry buckets to homes from the city's inadequate fountains. The average Parisian makes do with a liter of water a day, and one of the reasons Bonaparte is popular is because he's beginning to remedy the shortage.

My companions finally dozed.

From Paris's crowded center we passed into its greener periphery, then through the Farmers-General enclosing wall built by Louis XVI to combat smuggling. We crossed the bending Seine and entered the sprawling suburbs of villages, estates, and hunting preserves. Somewhere off to the south was Versailles, I guessed.

Finally, an hour after dawn, we came to the first consul's new home west of the city. Since seizing power just three years before, Napoleon had lived at the Luxembourg Palace, the Tuileries Palace, and was spending upward of 1.5 million francs to ready the old château of Saint-Cloud. Meanwhile, he liked to get away from the city to this estate Josephine had bought while he was in Egypt. He'd been infuriated by her purchase at the time, but had since warmed to Malmaison's country charm.

We followed a high stone wall to an iron gate

guarded by soldiers, and after a word from Fouché passed into a gravel lane between two rows of linden trees. When we were finally let out, stiff, unkempt, and hungover, I saw evidence of Josephine's sweet taste. If her husband's eye was for grandeur—how he loved a military review—Josephine's was for beauty.

Malmaison is a pretty château in the French style, with yellow stucco, pale blue shutters, and a slate roof. Its long rectangle is only a single room in width, meaning that light floods through from windows on both sides of its public spaces. Ornamental trees are planted in trim green boxes, and a riot of flowers grows up to the sills of the windows, cut to fill countless vases inside. We could hear birdcall from the park.

"We're here to see the first consul," Fouché announced to some potentate in braid, sash, and black patent slippers.

"He's already out by the pond. He never seems to sleep. This way."

We stepped through a room with Roman columns and peeked left and right. The dining room had frescoes of Pompeii dancers, which made sense because Josephine was an avid fan of the recent excavation of that ash heap. Roman antiquities filled the shelves. On the other side of the entry was a billiard room and beyond it a rather opulent drawing room with expensive embroidered chairs, the arms decorated with winged Egyptian goddesses. It was homage to Bonaparte's adventure at the pyramids. Two large and melodramatic paintings flanked the fireplace.

"Odysseus?" I guessed.

"Ossian," Fouché replied. "The first consul's favorite poem."

Then into a grand music room with harp, piano, and portraits of constipated-looking French ancestors, the morning sunlight pouring on warm wood like honey. The marble eyes of Roman generals followed us with opaque gazes.

"There's a meeting room upstairs draped with fabric as if the occupants are in an oriental campaign tent," the policeman said. "The furniture is carved with Egyptian deities and Nubian princesses. It's all quite imaginative."

"A little fevered with the furnishings, isn't he?"

"Bonaparte believes even a chair can sing his praises."

Smith turned slowly about. "This isn't like a British prison at all," he marveled blearily.

"The French like to tidy up."

We left the home again by glass doors and followed a gravel path toward a pond fed by a small river. Butterflies flitted in Josephine's little paradise, sheep cropped to keep the grass down, and peacocks strutted. We were nearing the decorative lake when a gun sounded.

"*Napoleooon!*" We heard a woman's protest, coming from a window high in the apartments behind us.

She was answered by another shot.

We passed through trees and came to a cluster of a dozen aides, officers, and groundsmen, proof that the great are seldom alone. One servant was reloading a fowling piece while Napoleon hefted another, squinting at some swans swimming and flapping at the opposite end of the water. "I purposely miss," he told the others, "but I can't resist teasing Josephine." He aimed and fired, the shot hitting the water well short of the birds. The swans erupted again.

"*Napoleooon, please!*" her wail came.

"There's swan shit everywhere," he explained. "She has too many of them."

Fouché stepped forward. "It's the American Gage," he announced. "He's made trouble, as you predicted."

CHAPTER 6

Bonaparte turned. Again he exhibited that electrical presence, that firmness of command, which inspired and intimidated. The shock of dark hair, the bright gray eyes, the oddly sallow skin for a soldier of Corsican descent (a slight yellow tint, which I wondered might hint at some malady), and the tense energy were all there as I remembered. He was thicker than when I'd last seen him almost two years before—not fat, but the leanness of youth was gone. Napoleon had the mature muscle of a thirty-two-year-old soldier dining at too many state banquets. His hair was combed forward in the Roman style to cover a hairline already beginning to slightly recede, as if he lived and aged faster than most men. His gaze was calculating, yet amused.

He pretended surprise to the French scientist. "You, too, Cuvier?"

"First Consul, I don't even remember what happened. We were following Gage. I lapsed into un-consciousness and awoke in catastrophe . . ."

"Yes, I quite understand. I've met the Ameri-can myself." He shook his head and then glanced with slight distaste at Fouché, as if wishing he didn't need the policeman. But of course he did, if he wanted to stay in power. "Savants with your abilities should think twice before enlisting Ethan Gage as a guide to depravity. No man attracts more trouble. Or gets out of it so frequently." Now he looked directly at me. "The last time we met, you crawled out of a pond at Mortefontaine with your hair almost on fire. I sent you on to America to get you away from my sister. What did you learn there that is useful?"

I blinked, trying to summon coherent thought. Was I a prisoner or a diplomat? "Louisiana is almost unimaginably large and unimaginably dis-tant," I said. "It is full of fierce Indians and desired by the British. Unless you have an army to hold it, it's more liability than asset. I suggest you sell it to the United States to keep it out of English hands." I turned. "Sorry, Smith."

The geologist blinked. "I really have no opinion. It's a long way from my canals."

"I *have* an army, in St. Domingue, if Leclerc doesn't lose it to disease and those damn blacks," Napoleon said. "What would your nation do with Louisiana?"

I shrugged. "Jefferson thinks everyone should be a farmer, if it can be farmed."

"And can it?"

"Eventually it is empty of trees, like the steppes. The weather is terrible. I don't know."

He sighed. "At least you don't tell me what you think I might like to hear. That's the only reason I didn't shoot you long ago, Gage. And these savants are experts at bones and rocks?"

"Yes, First Consul. We went to the Palais Royal on a lark and were lured into a brothel. We entered simply to study its interior décor, and then a fire broke out . . ."

"Which you set. Fouché's report got here before he did. I know more about what went on there than you do. I asked about your friends, Gage, not your stupidity."

"Fulton is . . ."

"Yes, yes, I know all about his damn plunging boat. He might have crept up on the British navy but could never catch it."

"With additional money for improvements . . ." Fulton began eagerly.

"Enough, I said!" It was a military bark, and Fulton's mouth snapped shut. "You, Gage, were trying to learn something of an old lover, am I correct?"

Fouché had clearly been spying on us, if he hadn't arranged the entire affair himself to embarrass me. I took a breath. "You remember Astiza, First Consul. You were going to shoot both of us outside the Tuileries."

"Women." He glanced back at the château. "Josephine is mucking up our estate with her damned swans, which I have threatened to shoot, but she pleads, and so I relent, so there is more shit, so then I take out my guns, and eventually we reconcile . . ." He smiled a moment at a private memory. "Women by natural order should be the property of men, but the reality is that we're slaves to them, are we not?"

"I don't think even Josephine would call you a slave, First Consul."

"Well, *you* are indentured to *me*. I gave you two hundred dollars and clear instructions and yet you spent much of your time in North America with the British, just as you did in the Holy Land. Are you their spy, Gage? What are you doing with this ditch-digging Englishman, Smith? What is it about Smith's grasping nation of pirates and tinkerers that makes you find their company so appealing?"

"Pirates and tinkerers?" Smith protested.

"It is Paris I came back to, First Consul," I interrupted. "I ended up fighting the English couple I met in America, not allying with them. They were part of the same perfidious Egyptian Rite I kept warning you about at the pyramids. Now I've encountered it in the Palais Royal as well. I declare it's a conspiracy you should fear. And what the British taught me is that it would be easier for you to sell Louisiana than to lose it."

"Hmph." Napoleon sighted at the swans again, but didn't fire, handing the gun back to a servant. "Well, I have a new mission for you now, and if you help, then maybe I'll consider your arguments about a sale, which should make Jefferson happy." He addressed my companions. "You were arrested, gentlemen, thanks to the impetuousness of Ethan

Gage here. The man is a brilliant imbecile. But you are about to have an opportunity for clemency and a quiet expurgation of this incidence of whoring and drug-taking. I want you to take ship for the Greek island of Thira and investigate a peculiar rumor."

"Thira!" Cuvier exclaimed.

"Your presence as savants should help blind the Ottomans to your true task, which is to sound out Greek patriots about the idea of revolt against the Turks. We have lost Egypt and the Ionian Islands, and the damnable British are refusing to evacuate Malta as required by our new peace treaty. Yet Greece as an ally would be a thorn to Istanbul, Austria, and the English, and a rose to us. All we need is a steady ally, and I have one in mind, a scholarly firebrand named Ioannis Kapodistrias. You're to meet him, under the guise of an archaeological mission, and see if French help could instigate a revolt."

"Didn't you try that in Ireland?" I reminded, undiplomatically.

"It will work this time."

"And *what* archaeological mission?" If I sounded wary, it was because I associated the trade with trick doors, collapsing tunnels, and near drowning. Pyramids and temples have a way of pinching in on you, I've found.

Fouché answered. "As minister of police, it's my responsibility to keep an eye on all factions that represent a possible threat to the state, including the Egyptian Rite. One of my investigators learned that you'd been asking your scientific associates in

Paris about the island of Thira at the same time these renegade Freemasons were acquiring books and maps on it."

"But all I know of Thira is the name."

"So you say. Yet what a remarkable coincidence that so much attention is being paid to an obscure rock on the Aegean Sea. And you, Ethan Gage, return from America after association with the British and seek out the American inventor Fulton, the British surveyor Smith, and a French expert on ancient cataclysms. How conspiratorial! The idea of using a bordello as cover was really quite ingenious."

"It was Madame Marguerite who lured us."

"Come, Gage, we know each other too well for you to play the fool with me," Napoleon said. "This charade of bumbling confusion is all very amusing, but you insert yourself in every mystery and conspiracy there is. Nor do I think your esteemed friends would associate with a rake and wastrel like yourself unless there was advantage to be gained. You meet the Rite in the bowels of the Palais Royal, start a fire, initiate a riot, run down your competitors, and pretend to ignorance? All of us know you must be in pursuit of what's been long rumored."

"First Consul!" Cuvier cried. "I swear I know nothing about his plotting!"

"Of course not," Bonaparte said mildly. "Gage is using you. Using all of you. He's a devious rascal, a master of intrigue, and if he were French I've no doubt Fouché would have recruited him to the police long ago. Is that not true, Minister?"

"Even now I do not fully understand his motives and alliances," Fouché admitted.

I, of course, had not the slightest idea of what was going on, and was trying to decide if I should be proud or insulted by this new description of me as brilliant, devious, and a master of intrigue. All I'd seen was the word "Thira" on a scrap of golden foil in the middle of the American wilderness—a Norse Templar artifact, according to my late companion Magnus Bloodhammer—and nothing else. Still, if the police were so smart, maybe I could learn something from them.

"I'm also looking for Og," I tried. That was written on the foil, too, before Aurora Somerset made a mess of the whole thing. She was the reason I'd sworn off women.

At that word, Fouché stiffened and looked at me warily. Cuvier, too, stared curiously. But it was Napoleon who'd gone white.

"What did you say?" the first consul asked.

"Og." It sounded silly even to me.

The first consul glanced questioningly at my three companions, and then addressed the others. "I think Monsieur Gage and I need a moment alone."

CHAPTER 7

We walked fifty paces from the group and stopped by the pond shore, out of hearing from anyone else. "Where did you hear that word?" Napoleon asked sharply.

"In America."

"America! How?"

I sighed. It was the first time I'd even tried to relate what really happened, and I didn't expect anyone to believe me. "You may remember a Norwegian named Bloodhammer who visited Mortefontaine when we celebrated the treaty between France and my own country," I began. "He found a place in the Louisiana Territory, far beyond the frontier, which had Norse artifacts." I decided not to mention anything more about the bewildering site. "One was a gold metal sheet, encased in a rotting shield, which had writing that bore that word. It stuck in my mind because it was so odd."

"What else did it say?" Bonaparte looked disturbed, almost queasy.

"The inscription was in Latin, which I can't read. I could only make out a few words and then a fight broke out and the foil was destroyed. It happened in a struggle with a British woman from the Egyptian Rite, actually—quite a long story." No need to mention I'd been her lover. "Just as I was telling you, I was fighting the British, not spying for them."

"So you don't know what it means?"

"No. Do you?"

He frowned, looking out across the pond. The cluster of aides and police were looking at us curiously from a distance, envious of my sudden intimacy with their leader. "Gage," he finally asked quietly, "have you ever heard of the Little Red Man?"

At the mention of that curious French legend I had the odd feeling I was being watched from an attic window of the pretty château. I turned, but there was nothing to see, of course: its small rectangular dormer windows were dark and blank. Josephine had withdrawn inside as well. "I've heard rumor. Everyone has."

"Do you believe in the supernatural?"

I cleared my throat. "I've seen odd things."

"The Little Red Man is a gnomelike creature dressed and concealed in a red hooded cloak. His face is always in shadow, but he is short and bent with long brown fingers. Sometimes you can see the gleam of eyes. Watchful eyes. Disturbing eyes that know far too much."

"All France knows the tale, but it's only a story."

"No, he is real. He first appeared to Catherine de'Medici, and by reputation lives most commonly in the attic of the Tuileries Palace that she built. He appeared to French royalty on occasion, usually in times of crisis. To me it was just a fable as well, the kind of myth to amuse children. But then I saw him in Egypt."

"General!"

He nodded, lost in remembrance. "I've never been so frightened. It was shortly before the Battle of the Pyramids. He came into my field tent at the night's darkest hour, when I'd exhausted all my aides and was the only one still awake. I'd just heard of Josephine's infidelities and was beside myself with rage and sorrow, and couldn't sleep."

I remembered in Egypt when Junot related to me his unhappy task of informing the general of his wife's unfaithfulness, revealed by pilfered letters that had been sent from France.

"A doctor would say it was hallucination, of course. But the creature spoke of the future in a deep, sly voice with a tone I've never heard before or since. He was not of our world, Gage, but as real as your three savants standing by the pond over there. And then he began to prophesy."

That day in Egypt, Napoleon had seemed possessed.

"Later I had similar visions in the Great Pyramid—you'll remember when I lay in the sarcophagus? But troubling ones as well! In any event, the Little Red Man promised me at least ten years of success to accomplish what I need to accomplish, which is why I was so confused by my loss to you and that obstinate Sidney Smith at the siege of Acre. I was not supposed to lose! But I didn't lose, in the end, because my defeat ultimately directed me back to Paris to take charge here, thanks to your Rosetta key. The Little Red Man had known after all."

So was I some blind instrument of fate, setting in motion events I didn't understand? "What has this got to do with Og?"

"The creature said I should seek its ruins, because a machine of great power was at stake. If it fell into the wrong hands it could disrupt my destiny."

"Ruins where?"

"I've ordered research into just that question. Gog and Magog, it seems, are referred to in the Bible, and are sometimes interpreted as lands at the ends of the earth. Og itself is a Celtic reference to a distant, powerful kingdom. I wonder if there was some common, root language."

Magnus had believed in long-ago civilizations and forgotten powers.

"This machine had something to do with Og, I was told. The Little Red Man said he'd warned French leaders at critical times before, and that I must remember that word because I would hear it again someday. I remembered the sound of it— Og—because it was so odd, but I hadn't heard it spoken again until now." He stared. "By you."

Despite myself, I felt a shiver. "I don't know any Little Red Man."

"But you do find ancient things, and fate keeps bringing us together. You're an agent of destiny, Ethan Gage, which is why I've remained intrigued by you. I've told no one of Og, and very few of the

Little Red Man, and yet you bear that word. You, the wayward American."

"It was simply written down. I'd no time to make sense of it."

"Sense! Sometimes I think I'm as lunatic as my brothers." Napoleon's odd family was, of course, the source of endless gossip in Paris. The more he tried to elevate his relatives to positions of responsibility, the sharper the public witticisms in cataloging their faults.

"My elder brother Joseph only wants to be rich, and he's loyal enough," Bonaparte confided. "But Lucien is venal and jealous, and Jerome is reportedly smitten by some ship-owner's daughter in Baltimore. Baltimore!" He said it as if it were a barbarian fiefdom. "I forced Louis to marry Josephine's daughter, Hortense, this last January, but Louis doesn't really like women and Hortense loves one of my aides. She spent the night before her wedding weeping."

Why he confessed all this to me I don't know, but men sometimes tell me things because they figure me inconsequential. Of course the actual Paris gossip was more malicious than *that*. Napoleon's brother Lucien had started a rumor that Napoleon forced the marriage of Hortense and Louis because Napoleon, her stepfather, had impregnated her himself in his desperation to father an heir. Hortense's marriage, so the gossip went, would legitimize a potential successor. Certainly Hortense was heavy with child, but who made it, and when, was open to speculation. I was wise enough not to ask.

"You're not a lunatic," I said sympathetically,

to ingratiate myself. I can be a shameless courtier. "You just bear the weight of rule."

"Yes, yes. Ah, Gage. You cannot imagine how carefree you are, floating free of responsibility!"

"But I'm trying to influence the future of Louisiana."

"Forget Louisiana. Nothing is going to happen with Louisiana until the situation in Haiti is resolved. The blacks fight on and on." He scowled. "And now you bring back memory of the gnome! He came into my tent past all my guards. His cloak dragged on the sand, making a track like a snake's." His voice was hollow, his eyes distant.

"But we don't know where Og was."

"Yes we do. Og is a word scholars associate with Atlantis."

"Atlantis?" Hadn't the gold foil borne that word as well? "And where is *that*, exactly?" I'd heard of it, of course—Magnus Bloodhammer had talked of it in America, savants had debated its geography, and we'd even speculated it was the source of mysterious copper mines in the wilderness—but I wasn't sure of the details.

"Atlantis is Plato's story—a fabulous kingdom named for Atlas that was destroyed in some upheaval. Legend has that it was advanced and sought to assert its influence over the entire world. The common belief is that it was distant, like Og, perhaps. Beyond Gibraltar, what the Greeks called the Pillars of Hercules."

"So what has Og to do with Thira?"

"Perhaps because they are not far apart after all. My geographers tell me there's a place on the coast of Greece also referred to as the Pillars of Hercules. In Egypt, my savants mentioned Thira as the source of a cataclysm great enough to have spawned the Atlantis story. What if that island was the fabled kingdom? Or what if its destruction sank an Atlantis nearby?"

Sank Og? Which perhaps came from a language that might have been used by half-mythical beings, I thought, remembering my earlier adventures. Of godlike creatures named Thoth or Thor, whose footsteps I'd followed. Again there was this speculation about our mysterious forebears, remembered now as gods or legends. Where had we, or our civilization, really come from?

"It is simply myth," Napoleon continued. "Or is it? What if this Og/Atlantis really existed, and left something behind that evil seeks? In recent decades there has been frantic research into the legends of the ancients, driven by the popularity of Freemasonry and new archaeological discoveries. Some artifacts have even been found." He meant the Book of Thoth I'd pilfered, I was sure. "So what else is out there? Why is this Egyptian Rite so persistent in its search? I believe nothing, and yet I can't afford not to believe. These are things that might decide battles, dynasties, or wars. And so, once again I am face-to-face with you."

I swallowed, remembering Thor's hammer: a myth that had almost fried me alive. "You want me to determine the truth of these rumors?"

"There are reports speculating that there are secrets to be found on Thira, an island of no political significance."

"My colleagues think it has geologic significance."

"Which is why you're here instead of in jail. Come, let's confer with the others—but not a word about my Red Man. If you speak of this day, I'll have you shot."

"Secrets are my specialty."

He glanced skeptically, but what choice did he have? We were two rascals in expedient partnership. We walked back to rejoin the group, Napoleon's hands clasped behind his back as if to control his own intensity. My three scientific colleagues were regarding me with new respect after my quiet tête-à-tête with the first consul.

"We were discussing Plato's fiction of Atlantis," Bonaparte explained to the others.

"Except some scholars believe it might have been real," Fouché amended. He had the sleepy watchfulness of a cat, his mind calculating truths and evasions like a warehouse full of ledger clerks. "And that it might have left something behind."

"Which, however unlikely, you are to investigate," Napoleon now told us briskly, rubbing his hands together as if to shake a chill. "The rumor is that this object may have been left on this island. Yet if I send a military expedition to Thira, it will set off a war with the Ottomans I don't need. But a party of savants? Who cares what scientists do? With luck you can slip in and out without being seen. If not, you're simply on a mission to explore an old volcano. They'll think you're harmless eccentrics."

"*What* object?" Cuvier asked.

"This will interest Fulton," Fouché said. "The

rumor is that a terrible weapon from ancient times may still exist, or at least the knowledge of how to build it. The nature of this weapon isn't clear, but speculation is that the nation who gets it first will control the Mediterranean, and perhaps the world."

"You mean it's some kind of ancient war machine?"

"Yes."

"I'd like to see that." Fulton was as drawn to machines as I am to women.

"When we learned the Egyptian Rite was seeking a meeting with Ethan Gage, we knew we had to act. It's imperative that we learn the truth of these rumors before something monstrous falls into the wrong hands."

"What, English hands?" Smith challenged.

"I'm speaking of this cult, which seems to have an agenda counter to all civilized nations. While we'd have preferred not to include you, Monsieur Smith, this is not a French-English rivalry—it is union in a greater cause. Besides, Gage gave us no choice after his expedition dragging you to the wicked Palais. Now, I'm afraid, you must briefly cooperate with the French government in this hunt for knowledge. We are at peace, after all."

"But my business is in Britain!"

"My information is that you're quite unemployed."

"Not to the point of wanting to go to Greece!"

"We are your new employer."

"And if I refuse?"

"Then we'll confine you as a spy until this

matter is sorted out. Cooperate, and you may advance your geologic career. We know your work has been ignored by the Royal Society."

"Wait just a minute," Fulton said. "I may be interested in ancient machinery, but I've no interest in this Thira, or Og, either!"

"You do if you want French interest in your peculiar idea for a steamboat," Napoleon said. "You've exhausted our patience and budget with your ridiculous *Nautilus*, but if you help us with this, we'll give your new contraption a fair look."

"Oh."

"And you, Cuvier, will accompany these men as a French patriot to provide this quartet with Gallic logic and purpose. You will be the expedition's leader and purser. Unless you prefer disgrace, dismissal from the Institute, and loss of the education ministry?"

"I wish only to reclaim my honor, First Consul. We savants have a reputation, even if Gage does not. I apologize for associating with riffraff, but perhaps good can come of it."

"And me?" I asked, not happy that no one was objecting to the "riffraff" description.

"According to Madame Marguerite, who is secretly in *our* employ, this Osiris fellow you ran over promised to take you to your lost love Astiza," Fouché said. "He wanted to take you to Thira, too. The woman must be there, or at least you might find a clue to her whereabouts. Do this errand for France and we'll send you on to the Egyptian lady. If not, you can go back to the United States to explain that your efforts to persuade us about

Louisiana came to a complete failure and that our Caribbean army will soon occupy New Orleans. You will be banned from France, blamed for abject diplomatic failure in America, and forced to find a real job."

I swallowed. The prospect of actual work does daunt me. "So all we have to do is go to Thira, talk to this Greek fellow, and poke about for an ancient weapon?"

"*Find* an ancient weapon. Or at least bring back word of it before Ottoman soldiers, foreign spies, pirates, rebels, bandits, or the Egyptian Rite get to it first. Consider it a holiday from normal duties, gentlemen. A boy's adventure."

Sleepless, gritty, sore, and frightened, we numbly assented. What choice did we have?

"But how are we to find this weapon?" Cuvier asked.

Fouché took out a small velvet bag. "Before our troops were forced out of the Ionian Islands, one of our officers made purchase of a relic, a ring, from a distressed noblewoman. She said it was forged late in the fifteenth century. It was oddly fortuitous; the man said the duchess was quite beautiful and quite enigmatic. Some contend the ring was made by Templars themselves. When my agents heard about it, I decided to acquire it. I think you'll see why."

The ring had a flattened section like a miniature seal, and we saw immediately that it bore the word "Thira." In the background was a domed building with part of the dome missing, as if someone had taken a bite, like a crescent moon. In the foreground was what looked like a stone sarcophagus meant to bury the dead, with its lid open. A man in robes and a medieval cap appeared to be climbing into the coffin, as if it were a bath. Or perhaps he was climbing out.

"What does it mean?"

"No one knows," the policeman said, "but it obviously refers to the island. Why would Templars forge this of such an obscure place? Thira is little more than a cinder. This Greek patriot you will meet may find this useful in helping you."

"Perhaps that's where the weapon is," I said, studying the piece. "He's climbing in to get it." Compared with the medallion I'd carried in Egypt, this one seemed plain enough.

"Then you're to do the same. Look at its reverse."

I turned the ring to inspect the flattened part that would be against the skin. There was another dome, this one quite normal, and inside it the letter "A."

"What does that mean?"

"We have no idea. Deciphering this object will keep you occupied on your trip to Thira. The essence, gentlemen, is speed. Go swiftly, go silently, and go ahead of any pursuit."

"Pursuit?" I always hate that.

Cuvier rubbed his weary face. "At least we can study the volcano. Maybe we will be lucky enough to have it erupt."

"Wouldn't that be a treat," I said drily.

"Good!" Napoleon said. "Now—who wants a shot at my swans?"

CHAPTER 8

Napoleon promised we could accomplish our mission in a month or two. And indeed, with Europe in peace and the roads mostly dry in high summer, we made our way overland from Paris to Venice in a mere two weeks, traveling south through France and then east across the new Cisalpine Republic that Napoleon had created after his victory at Marengo. I saw no evidence we were being followed. Of course our enemies, if they hadn't given up, might guess exactly where we were going, given that Osiris, Marguerite, and Fouché all seemed more aware of what was going on than we were. Our quest was probably about as secret as a failure of contraception in the ninth month. On the other hand, perhaps we'd discouraged the Egyptian Rite or Fouché had delayed them, and the entire trip would be a holiday lark.

While my companions were less than happy at

being drafted and blamed me for Bonaparte's coercion, they were also excited about traveling at
French government expense. Cuvier had been en-
trusted with our allowance, though like all pursers
he was hard to persuade to spring for the nobler
vintage of wine or choicer haunch of meat. "I have
to account for your consumption at the end of all
this," he'd grumble, "and I'm damned if I know how
to explain to the ministry why this wheel of cheese
was necessary over that one—which is cheaper and
a hundred grams heavier, as well."

"I thought you French put food above art, or
even love," Smith said.

"But when it comes to expenditures, our accoun-
tants have the taste of the English."

I didn't complain. I was aware that I was riding
in a coach, with no assignment but to get somewhere, when so many people were not. We'd pass
long rows of peasants scything at dusk, or stable
boys mucking out horse stalls with sunburned
shoulders, or a maid parting a sea of chickens that
closed up behind her as she left a trail of scattered
grain. I thought how different, how safe and how
dull, to be tied to one place and have one's days
dictated by the turn of the seasons. I'd walk to
stretch in the evenings, eating a piece of fruit, and
if I came upon a boy who seemed smart or a ma-
demoiselle who was pretty, I might show them my
longrifle and even help by shooting a crow out of a
tree. They treated such a diversion like magic, and
me like an exotic visitor from another world.

The savants were apprehensive but excited.
They'd see a geologically dramatic island at the

edge of the Ottoman Empire, dabble in political intrigue, and maybe make an archaeological discovery or two. Certainly our mission was more thrilling than academic meetings. The truth was that I still had some reputation as a hero, and the scholars hoped a little of my dash might rub off. I couldn't blame them.

We settled into roles: I the not-entirely-trusted-yet-redoubtable guide, Cuvier our paymaster and skeptical supervisor, Smith the make-the-best-of-it dogged Englishman always ready to shoulder more than his share of luggage or responsibility, and Fulton our tinkerer, who proved fascinated by every waterwheel and canal lock. The inventor helped pass the time by sketching out schemes to improve the suspension of our coach, all of which the driver dismissed as impractical or too expensive.

We also discussed, from boredom, the need to rewrite the history of the world.

"What we know is that rocks have been laid down and worn away over eons," Smith said. "But how? By catastrophe, like a volcano or great flood, or the patient erosion of wind and rain? And why all that fuss at all, before we humans even appeared in Creation? What was God's point?" He picked up rocks at every way station, marked their type on his map of France—the stones all looked the same to me, but he told them apart like a drover picks out his cattle—and then tossed them out the coach window.

"We also know that there were many creatures alive on earth that no longer exist," Cuvier said, "many of them gigantic. Did Creation start with more variety and greater grandeur that has since been thinned and shrunken by time? That seems a peculiar kind of progress. Are we the pinnacle of Creation, or its shrunken fruit? Or have animals actually changed from one kind into another, as suggested by Saint-Hilaire? I find his proposal ridiculous for any number of reasons, not the least of which is that we have no idea how such a mutation could occur."

"He told me that odd idea in Egypt," I put in, cradling my longrifle between my legs. It wasn't just nervous habit; I'd been robbed on the stage before. "More interesting to me is the question of how civilization got started, and whether marvelous things were once known and then forgotten after the fall of the Roman Empire. Some of my acquaintances have suggested that myths of the ancient gods actually refer to early beings who somehow taught mankind how to grow, build and write, and by doing so lifted us out of the mud. The Egyptian Rite thinks the knowledge of such ancestors, if relearned, could provide terrible power. I've seen some things to make me suspect they might be right."

"What things?" Cuvier asked. He'd brought a red-leather notebook and pen to record our discoveries, a tin officer's field kit with scissors, comb, and toothbrush, and a combination clock and compass in a copper case. He'd write down our remarks and mark our direction with every entry, as if no one had ever mapped the highway before.

"A book that caused nothing but trouble. And a tool, a hammer, that was even worse."

"And now we're off to find an ancient weapon," said Fulton, "with Bonaparte, Fouché, and those lunatics in Madame Marguerite's bordello curious about it, too. Why Napoleon is so anxious about forgotten weapons, when he won't give a proper hearing to my modern ones, is beyond me." He was amusing himself by taking apart his own pocket watch for the pleasure of putting it back together, but kept losing sprockets and springs when the coach went over bumps, making us have to look for them on the vehicle's dusty floor. Cuvier took care to keep his own compass-clock out of the inventor's reach.

"It's human nature to see the flaws in what you have and perfection in what you don't," I said. "Besides, buying your submarine or steamboat means uncomfortable change, Robert. Sending us on a treasure hunt to conspire with a Greek patriot risks nothing."

"Except us," Smith said. "It's the man on the lip of the canal who wants it dug deeper, not the man at the bottom."

"The man at the lip will argue he can see farther, and better measure the necessary depth," Cuvier said.

"And the one at the bottom should reply that he's the one who can weigh the rock and soil, and count the blisters."

¤ ¤ ¤

At Venice we ferried across a limpid lagoon to that fabled, crumbling wedding cake of a city that was still buzzing from Bonaparte's brief occupation in 1797. French troops had torn down the gates of the Jewish ghetto (many Jews had enlisted in Napoleon's army as a result) and ended a thousand years of Venetian independence with a flurry of decrees declaring republican ideals. The revolution had been brief, since the Treaty of Campo Formio had given the city to Austria a few months later, but the ghetto hadn't been reestablished and the population was still debating the merits of the frightening freedoms the French had promised. They discussed as well contrary warnings that French reform ultimately meant tyranny. Was Napoleon promise or peril? Was he liberator, or lord?

I was tempted to linger in the city by the decadent beauty of Venice: the mysterious twisting of its fetid canals, the iceberg majesty of its sinking, leaning houses, the rhythmic song of its lyrical gondoliers, its arched, weather-stained marble bridges, its baroque balconies pouring out cascades of flowers, and its dark-haired beauties weaving through the pillars at the periphery of Piazza San Marco like duchesses at a dance, their silks shimmering like butterfly wings. The queen city of the Adriatic rang with bell, song, lush opera, and echoing church choir, and smelled of perfume, spice, charcoal, urine, and water. Sunlight burned on the wavelets, and candles beckoned when it was dark.

But I'd reformed, I reminded myself, and thus resisted the temptation to peek at pleasure, indulgence, and wickedness. Instead, I begged my companions for just enough time to hunt down a fine Venetian rapier in an armory shop, given the reputation of Italian cutlery. A Venetian sword was renowned for its slim and supple balance and elegant curved guard, and yet it carried a shave more weight and sturdiness than its French counterpart.

"All the best duelists have one," I justified.

A naval cutlass would be more practical for alley fighting, but the rapier was elegant to the feminine eye, giving me a certain swagger. I felt dashing when I buckled one on and studied myself in the store's cracked antique mirror, deciding I looked quite the courtier. So I spent twice the money I should have, and learned when I tried to walk that the weapon banged so annoyingly on my thigh that I eventually took it off and tied it across my back like Magnus Bloodhammer's old ax, lest I tangle my own legs. This was the new nineteenth century, I reasoned, and I assumed that in the unlikely event I actually *needed* a weapon as antique as a rapier, I'd have warning enough to unstrap, unsheathe, give it a whet and a polish, and get into some kind of proper stance. Besides, I still carried my habitual tomahawk and longrifle, the latter marred by an annoying crevice in the stock where Cecil Somerset had broken his sword in my last adventure. The gun was so banged about that it retained little of its original elegance when forged in Jerusalem. Still, it shot well, and I looked like a little arsenal with everything strapped on. Women eyed me with wary interest behind their splayed fans, wondering just what kind of rogue I might be, and men edged around me in narrow lanes as if I were balmy as a butcher. Venetians are used to all sorts of visitors, but whispers began about Ethan Gage, the frontier American. That secretly pleased me.

Given that we were adventuring into Ottoman territory, my companions tolerated my weapon shopping by doing their own. We enjoyed the excuse to acquire manly accoutrements.

Cuvier, after a period of perplexity, settled on a pair of brass-and-silver dueling pistols in a rosewood box. They'd be deadly enough within ten paces.

Bluff and hearty Smith went for something entirely more formidable, a wicked blunderbuss—Dutch for "thunder gun"—which fired a spray of balls from a barrel just fifteen inches long. The piece was short enough to be concealed under a coat or cloak. When Smith tried it out from the quay at the harbor, its stunning report sent up clouds of pigeons at San Marco two hundred yards away. "It kicks like a mule but bites like a bear," he reported. "Just the thing to make a boarding party think twice."

I expected Fulton to pick out a similar firearm, perhaps an even more complex and mechanical-minded one like a nine-barreled musketoon, designed for fighting from a foretop and rarely used because it had the alarming habit of kicking so powerfully that it could knock its user out of the rigging. That seemed the kind of design problem that would challenge the inventor, and I pictured him fixing braces and pulleys to hold his torso against the recoil. But no, Fulton became intrigued with the unlikeliest of instruments, a scuffed and dusty Scottish bagpipe he found in a market stall.

"*That* will make our enemies run," I said good-naturedly. "I've heard the pipes, and it sets dogs howling. Invaders stayed out of Scotland for a thousand years because they couldn't stand the noise."

"That fire-eater in the Palais gave me an idea," Fulton replied. "I can't play this, but I can play *with* it. What if it could spit fire? Something to tinker with as we sail south." He pressed the bag and got a wail. "Or entertain us."

I'm rather tolerant of lunatics, which is why I know so many of them.

We paid for our purchases, the inventor blowing a wheeze or two on his Scottish pipes while we winced, and then the savants said we must press on.

"We hurry so science can find more time," Cuvier explained. "Thira is a depository of time. We need time to explain the mysteries of our planet because nothing makes sense without it. Time, time, time."

"Most people don't sensibly fill the time they have already, Ben Franklin would say."

"I said *science*. The human mind is imprisoned by our brief concept of history, Ethan. The globe becomes ever more complicated and all our explanations have to be crammed into a few thousand years, like a sprouting boy with shoes three sizes too young. But if the earth is older than we think, then all kinds of new ideas become possible."

"What kind of ideas?"

"That if the world wasn't always as it is, then it mustn't always remain this way, either," Smith put in. "Perhaps we're only a chapter in a longer tale. That we men are not the reason for existence, but just players in a bigger drama we don't understand."

"People won't like that, William. We like to think history begins and stops with us."

"Then why did God leave us clues that it didn't?" the Englishman said.

"Well, surely if the rocks are *that* old, we've time enough for supper on the piazza before getting to them, eh?"

"Fouché and Napoleon told us to hurry. The Venetians are looking at us oddly. Looking at *you* oddly."

"Fouché and Napoleon don't have blisters on their backsides from hurrying hundreds of miles to one of the loveliest spots on earth. The thing to do when people look at you, gentlemen, is to look back, particularly at the pretty girls!"

It was also necessary to relax, I continued, because we hadn't yet found a Venetian captain to take us where we needed to go. Venice had been at odds with the Turks for the better part of three hundred years, and Ottoman waters swarmed with pirates. The Greeks were under the thumb of Muslim masters who referred to their peasant subjects as *rayah*, or cattle. No Venetians were anxious to go to such an unpromising dot on the sea as Thira. The captains we'd talked to kept quoting fares more suitable for sailing to the moon. So we'd prowl the docks tomorrow, I promised, meanwhile finding a table in Campo di San Polo. My companions, as seduced by Venice as I was, finally assented. Stars came out, and piazza musicians, and jugs of wine. As we toasted our progress so far, my companions began to tipsily eye the parade of Italian lovelies in the same hungry way I was. Like Odysseus, we'd been sidetracked by sirens—and my own miscalculation that any enemies must be behind or ahead.

We were well in our cups when who should sashay by but one particularly delectable and tawny beauty, hair high as a tower, dress cut to the outermost precipice of her bosom, and skin as flawless as a flower petal. I hoped for a wink or even a word of invitation, but instead she reached tantalizingly to the hem of her dress, gave us a glimpse of ankle, and impishly plucked something from her skirts. Was it an apple? She held the thing to our tavern torch for a moment and it sparkled like a pixie's wand, and then she rolled it in our direction with the sweetest of smiles.

"Is this Italian custom?" Smith said, belching from drink, as the object stopped between our chairs.

"If so, she bowls with the grace of Aphrodite," Cuvier slurred.

"What is it, Ethan?" Fulton asked, looking in curiosity at smoke drifting up from the smoldering sphere. "A festival invitation?"

I bent to look under the table. "That, my friends, is a grenade."

CHAPTER 9

I don't know why beauty disap-
points so regularly, but I daresay
women usually don't pitch bombs in my direction
until we've been acquainted for an hour or two.
This one was galloping away before I could even
say hello, and her sole purpose seemed to be to
shred our lowest and most vital extremities. With
the instinct that comes from being misunderstood
so frequently in love, I scooped up the smoking
grenade, looked wildly about, and pitched it into
the only depository I could spot—our tavern's
brick oven.

The resulting explosion, which coughed out a
spray of brick, bread dough, charcoal, and fragments of rotisserie duck, could still have lacerated
our top halves if I hadn't tackled my comrades into
a heap, our table toppling over as a shield. We were
enveloped in a cloud of brick dust, but fortunately

the oven had absorbed the worst of the blast and the patrons we shared the place with escaped with just a fright.

"It's the Egyptian Rite!" I cried, my ears ringing and my brain addled by the explosion. "To the horses!"

"Ethan, we're on an island," Cuvier said, coughing. "We have no horses."

"Aye." I shook my head and blurrily saw caped men entering the other side of the Campo, dressed in black and brandishing things that glinted in the dark. One was waving his arm to direct the others. "To the gondolas, then!"

"I don't think they're giving us bloody time," Smith said.

We picked ourselves up, grabbed our scattered weapons and bags, and bunched to run as the strangers charged toward us. People were screaming, I realized as my hearing returned.

Then there was a roar that made everyone in the piazza jump and Smith slammed backward against the half-ruined oven. He'd fired his blunderbuss, packed with eight balls, and three of the attackers went sprawling. Bullets ricocheted like fleas in a bottle. The other scoundrels yelped, ducked, and broke toward cover.

"By thunder, Englishman, there's a naval broadside!" Cuvier cried.

Agreeing that our rock hound had set a good example, I took up my longrifle and aimed for the man who seemed to be the leader. I stilled my breath, aimed to lead him as he sprinted for the shadows, squeezed, and fired. He went down, too, skidding on the cobbles, and I was rewarded with cries of dismay.

"Always load before dinner," I said.

"And with a blunderbuss, it doesn't matter much how much you drink during it," Smith said, and burped.

We retreated, me halfheartedly clawing at the rapier strapped to my back and cursing that I hadn't bothered to carry it on my hip after all. The good thing about swords is you don't have to load them with powder and ball. The bad is you have to get damnably close to people trying to kill you. Now bullets came our way, making a smacking sound as they chewed into wood and stucco. We ran faster.

At the Giuffa Canal we didn't hesitate. A gondola was sweeping by with a paying client, its gondolier warbling a song, and so we sprang like pirates, crashed aboard, and pitched the poor passenger overboard.

"For your own safety!" I called as he splashed into the dirty water, his hat drifting away like a little raft.

Then I finally got my rapier clear and pointed at the gondolier's throat. "The Grand Canal! Don't worry, there's a tip in it for you!"

Our helmsman looked goggle-eyed at my blade. "Should I sing, signor?"

"Save your breath for the stroke. We're rather in a hurry." As he began powering us down the canal, I turned to the others. Smith was already swabbing out his blunderbuss and pouring in fresh powder. "Cuvier, get out those pretty pistols of yours and shoot the rascals when they reach the canal. Fulton, please don't play a song."

"They put a hole in my bagpipes, damn it."

"Then invent something else." I tried to remember the city's confusing spaghetti of canals. "We'll go to San Marco harbor and see if we can buy our way onto a ship out of here."

"My God, who was that woman?" Smith asked, his hand trembling slightly as he tamped down a fresh fusillade of shot. Killing is a jolt, especially the first time.

"Not one to flirt, I guess. It's a bet she's working for our enemies. I think we're in a race to the secret of Thira, which means that I'm afraid we shouldn't have tarried after all. I expected better of Venice. Especially after the price of our inn."

"I see something following us," Cuvier said, peering back into the dark. There was a flash as his pistols went off, blinding us to whatever he had aimed at. I couldn't believe he'd hit a thing with his popguns, but we heard a *wang* of ricocheting lead, and a yell.

"By mastodon tusks, they work!" he cried. "We're quite the dangerous men!"

We swept past a curve and back into darkness, then squirted out of the small canal into the broad one that makes a sweeping "S" through the city. It's a canyon of grand mansions four and five stories high, candles and lanterns gleaming behind tall windows to reveal aged munificence within, the leftovers of glittering empire. I saw centuries-old tapestries, crystal chandeliers, brocaded curtains, and white, moonlike faces peering out in curiosity at our noise. We sculled under the Rialto Bridge, lovers strolling its arched promenade, and headed toward the city's main harbor and the anchored ships off the Piazza San Marco. Domes and towers loomed up against the stars, and the sound of opera floated across dark water.

"I think we discouraged them," Smith ventured, looking back.

"I'm afraid I must disagree, Monsieur Smith," Cuvier replied, pointing ahead with one of his pistols, the ramrod jutting from its barrel because he was reloading. "Our pursuers seem to have a lot of company."

A line of gondolas was sweeping down to intercept us from the canal ahead, blocking our intended escape. We spied enough gleaming metal to fill an armory. There was a ripple of flashes and spouts of water kicked up around us as the reports of the shots echoed off the buildings. Chips of wood flew off our gondola, and our helmsman froze.

"I'll skewer you if you try to jump!" I warned him, my rapier aimed again at his throat. "Steer into that side canal there, before they get off another volley!"

We turned into a small channel that cut across the island by a different path. Maybe we could lose our pursuers in the liquid labyrinth that was Venice. This narrow tributary was dark, the houses seeming to lean in. Only the water gleamed.

A lantern appeared behind as the gondolas in pursuit followed us. We could hear the furious thrashing of their oars. I fired my rifle again at the lead boat and its light danced, but didn't go out. Someone fell into the water, and more guns fired back. Bullets pinged off the stonework and we involuntarily flinched. "Wish I could see to aim for their gondolier," I muttered as I reloaded.

"Please leave us out of this, signor," our own said with quavering voice. Realizing he was a logical target, our gondolier was driving us with more ambition than customary. Dark buildings zipped by as if he were powered by Fulton's steam. Shutters were banging open as occupants leaned out to see what was going on, but everything was in shadow. What they observed was a parade of racing phantoms, our nearest pursuer less than fifty yards behind. The occasional twist or low bridge prevented either of us from getting a clear shot.

Bells began ringing, but no authorities came to our aid.

"I've got an idea," said Fulton. He was eyeing a gondola unwittingly coming the other way, beginning to drift as its gondolier paused in confusion at the echo of shots and our own maddened pace. As we passed them the inventor reached out and neatly snatched the scull from the confused boatman, leaving him to drift into the path of our pursuers. Fulton clambered to the bow of our boat.

"What's your plan?"

"Wait for me on the far side of this bridge."

The bridge was a low arched stone one, typical for the city. As we came to it, the American suddenly thrust the oar down, planted it on the bottom of the shallow canal, and vaulted himself onto the roadbed above. We slid under him, and I ordered the gondolier to halt on the bridge's far side. The boat skewed as we stopped and then slowly backed toward Fulton. Meanwhile the inventor had jammed the pole of his captured oar into the stone railing he had just jumped over, and was prying. "I wish I had a fulcrum." Then there was a grunt and a crack.

We heard curses in three languages as the lead gondola of our pursuers collided with the one we'd left drifting. There was a cry and another splash. Then our assailants came toward us again, and Smith, Cuvier, and I readied to give a volley.

"Wait for my command!" whispered Fulton, who had hidden behind the balustrade.

The enemy boat was speeding for the bridge, pistols and swords pointed at us in a bristling hedge that just caught the starlight.

Then, with a groan, the stone railing gave way. Blocks as heavy as anvils were levered off the bridge lip by Fulton and fell just as the gondola was passing underneath, crashing into the vessel and snapping it to pieces. The occupants tumbled into the water.

The inventor, oar still in hand, leaped from the other side of the bridge to a water-washed porch and scrambled toward our boat. "Fire at the next one!" he ordered.

I liked his cool head.

So when the second attacking gondola came out of the gloom, slowing at the sight of comrades thrashing in the water, we let loose a volley: Cuvier's two pistols, my rifle, and Smith's blunderbuss all went off at once. There were screams, more oaths, and the second pursuing boat tipped as dead and wounded spilled into the canal.

"Now, now, go for the harbor!" Fulton cried as

he jumped aboard. Our gondolier sculled as if he were on fire.

"Nice work, Robert," I congratulated.

"It's all in the leverage. Archimedes showed how it could be done. 'Give me a lever and a place to stand and I will move the earth,' the old Greek said."

"Clever bastard, wasn't he?"

At the next bridge, where the canal narrowed because of the structure's abutments, Fulton had us stop while he wedged the extra oar at an angle widthwise across the canal behind us, just at water level where it could catch a gondola's bow. "That will block the rest until they chop it away," he said. "It may give us enough time."

Then we hurried on, our gondolier panting.

"Being with you is proving to be consistently dramatic, Monsieur Gage," Cuvier said, in order to say something. He was getting quicker, I noticed, at reloading.

"Bloody exciting," Smith agreed. "Who are those devils?"

"Egyptian Rite, I assume. Or their hired merce-naries. Anxious, persistent, and hostile. Lucky they didn't cut us off."

Finally we broke from the narrow canal and glided out into the broader lagoon. The domes of the Basilica were a geometric symphony against the sky, and moored gondolas bobbed in the light chop. But how to find a ship in the middle of the night?

Then a lantern glowed in the stern of a xebec.

"Here, here! This is the one you want!"

CHAPTER 10

Our gondolier sculled briskly toward the Turkish vessel, anxious to get rid of us.

Its Muslim captain, brown as leather and whip-quick, beckoned us closer. His sleeveless vest revealed muscle worthy of a skilled topman, and his dark eyes were lively as a rug merchant's. "Row to the other side of my vessel, away from the city! Yes, come to Hamidou! I heard shots and suspect you need quick passage, my new friends!"

We rounded the stern and drifted close to the other side. Half a dozen other sailors with close-cropped beards lined the gunwale, dressed in bloused trousers, bright sashes, and in some cases, turbans.

"Gage, these are Muhammadans," Cuvier objected.

"And we need to go to Ottoman waters."

"Yes! I will take you where you wish to go for

half what these Christians would charge you," the entrepreneur promised. "No ship is swifter, no passage cheaper, than my *Mykonos*. But you have money, my friends?"

"Yes, and we need to leave now."

"Then you need Hamidou! Dragut is the best sailor on the Adriatic and the Aegean. Look at my little arrow here. Fifty feet long, narrow and shallow, able to slip anywhere. My sails are black, so we move like a phantom."

"Do you know the island of Thira?"

"Of course! I was almost born there! And for two hundred francs, we leave at this moment. For three hundred, we leave an hour ago!" He laughed. "The Christians will charge you three times that to go to Turkish waters. They are afraid of pirates. But I have nothing but friends!"

"And why are you quite so cheap?" asked Fulton, with Yankee skepticism.

"Because I go to the Aegean anyway. I take you to Thira, trade at nearby islands, and then pick you up to bring you back." He nodded. "I, Hamidou Dragut, vow it!"

"You're a Turk?"

"I am Greek, I am a Turk, I am whatever you want me to be. I sail with all faiths. Do not hesitate! Look—do you see the gondolas? They are looking."

I climbed the side of the hull and looked across the deck of his ship at Venice. Craft had emerged from the same canal we had and were sculling toward the moored gondolas, searching.

"There are more of them than there are of you," the captain said.

"We're hoping to slip in and out of Thira before anyone much notices."

"Then Hamidou is the man for you! I am a ghost. Invisible. A good smuggler."

"Not smuggle. Simply arrive and depart without official interference."

"Thira is a small island, with small bureaucrats. A word, a coin, and you will be secret enough. I know everyone. All are my friends."

His gaze flashed from one to the other of us looking for belief with the energy of a man who is used to doubt, because he doesn't worry too much about truth or principle. In other words, I knew the type and recognized his usefulness. "This Dragut looks like just the rascal we need," I told the others.

"Trustworthy?"

"Expedient."

We boarded, coins were counted out, and Dragut's men sprang to quietly raise anchor and sails. The crew hauled on the lines in the dark with the surety that comes from long practice. None objected to our sudden nighttime departure, once they saw money. Even as the pursuing gondolas hunted along the shore, we drifted from Venice before first light blushed in the east, not daring to set a lantern. The water hissed under our keel, a dawn breeze carrying the smell of the city, and then the sails stretched as the wind freshened, rigging creaking. The boat leaned, came alive, and settled into rhythm. The city's lamps began to fade behind us, disappearing with the last of the stars.

We collapsed into sleep.

◘   ◘   ◘

I awoke at midmorning and inspected the craft we'd hired. Our xebec had two main masts and a mizzen, lateen sails, a dozen light cannon to ward off thieves, and a high, graceful poop we savants could relax on while the half-dozen Muslims worked the ship. There was a simple cabin below that Hamidou said we could share with him but which was too low to stand in. His crew slept on the open deck, and below a main-deck grating was the hold for sails, supplies, and cargo. Long, narrow, and shallow-drafted, it was ideal for poking in and out of the tight harbors of the Mediterranean.

The city had disappeared, and we were alone on the sparkling Adriatic. "Good morning!" Hamidou greeted. "I will get you to Thira two days faster than any captain in Venice!"

We ate a breakfast of couscous and lamb—the crew's leftovers from the night before—and took stock. The nice thing about a scrape with danger, I decided, was that we four savants had developed the fellowship of shared peril. We had the exhilaration that comes from escape, and the camaraderie that comes from relying on each other for our lives.

I, with my rifle, tomahawk, and sword, was considered the veteran. I'd been in battles, and this granted me an assumption of competence and courage. It's why men work hard to become dangerous.

Smith, cheerful at this opportunity to see more of the world than the bottom of a canal ditch, took

an avid interest in the working of the Islamic ship
and a dedication to cleaning his blunderbuss. He
fired it once for the sailors, the kick punching him
backward, and its roar made them jump and cry in
wonder and delight. The bullets kicked up a spray
on the sea.

Fulton had sewn a patch on his wounded bag
and was fitting metal tubes to extend the pipes,
half filling the bag with seawater and squirting it
at Cuvier in a spray he adjusted by tinkering with
the nozzle.

"You're constructing a fountain?" the Frenchman asked.

"I'm making a dragon. I need to find some oil
on Thira."

Cuvier, when not recording expenses and compass readings in his journal, proudly showed his
new pistols to Hamidou Dragut. The pair had a
fine time with mock duels, pacing the length of
the xebec before turning and firing with clicks of
hammers, like boys.

"These pistols are as pretty as a houri!" our captain exclaimed. "This is good, because death should
be elegant. I would be kissed by weapons like these,
or the American's pretty sword, and bleed happily.
You are gentlemen of taste and refinement."

The truth was that we felt cheerful. There's
thrill in cheating danger. We were swashbucklers,
out for scientific fame. Bonaparte's required journey was a diversion to a Mediterranean where all
colors are brighter, all meals slower, all evenings
more languid, all women more mysterious, and all
cities more ancient. The wind was warm, and the

limoncello liqueur we bought was ambrosia from the islands, sweet and sharp as honeyed ice.

For me, the conversation with Napoleon about his Little Red Man had ignited a hundred memories and unanswered questions. I remembered Bonaparte's bold stay alone in the granite sarcophagus of the Great Pyramid, lying like a dead man and emerging from its dark chamber with hallucinatory visions. I'd been embroiled in a deepening puzzle ever since—first the medallion and the pyramid, and then the Book of Thoth in the tunnels of Jerusalem and the City of Ghosts. Magnus Bloodhammer had dragged Norse myth and North America into the tangle, and all this musty legend pointed to some ancient beginnings forged by strange god-men with powerful knowledge, long forgotten and only half rediscovered. There were secrets that had been anxiously sought by conquerors from Alexander to the Crusaders, and a weird, dark history that interwove with our more conventional one. Each time I thought the mystery had finally slammed shut, another door would open. Each time I thought the Egyptian Rite was out of my life, it would unexpectedly reappear. Each time I thought I'd fought or tunneled my way to some final conclusion, yet another quest became necessary. It was dangerous as the devil, and I grieved for the friends I'd lost along the way, but it was also as intoxicating as a temptress or a chest of gold. I was becoming the master, I realized, not of electricity as my mentor Franklin might have hoped, nor commerce as my father desired, nor even war as Napoleon might instruct, but of a story with snakelike twists that hinted where we'd come from. It led back into the fog when time began. While Smith and Cuvier looked to rocks for the answer, I was the scientist of myth, the investigator of the improbable. Fate had woven me a career out of fable.

Dragut was curious, of course, why four European scholars (I benefitted from their company by being lumped with them) would want to coast round the Peloponnese of Greece and fetch up at a rocky island on the rim of the Aegean. Thira had no city, no commerce, and no ancient ruins of any note. "They are poor and pious, on an island the devil made," he said. "It is one of those places in the Mediterranean where nothing is."

"We study the history of the earth," Smith told him. "Thira is dramatic."

He shrugged. "I allow it is steep. But what need of history?"

"Men learn from the past."

"Men are slaves to the past, always trying to correct old errors. Trust in Allah, my friend."

"I trust you to sail this ship safely to where we want to go."

"Yes! Put your faith in Hamidou, too! I will surprise you!"

We caught a northwesterly *maestro* wind off the continent and surfed down the windy Adriatic, quickly passing the Austrian possessions of Dalmatia and then, as the breeze fell, coasting by Croatia, tiny Montenegro, and the western coast of Greece that was controlled by the Ottoman Empire. The wind gradually gentled, the sea a saucer of sparkle. Castles crowned rocky headlands, pastel villages lined aquamarine bays, and bulbous church steeples served as navigation marks between reefs and islets. The blue of sea and sky deepened as we sailed south, clouds sweet as cream.

The seven Greek islands of the new Septinsular Republic, created when the Russians and Turks ejected French troops three years before, slid by like high green jewels: Corfu, Kefalonia, Ithaca. It was one of the leaders of this tiny experiment, charismatic Count Ioannis Kapodistrias, whom we were to secretly meet on Thira. There was cloud at the summit of Kefalonia's Mount Ainos as we breezed by, and I could smell the pine from its shore. It beckoned like a green paradise, but we had no time to tarry. We were going to a place dry and largely treeless, and more like Creation when the world began.

CHAPTER 11

Thira, that Greek island that the Venetians call Santorini, rises sheer from the blue Aegean like a wall of jagged chocolate, its volcanic cliffs topped by white-washed villages that cling to the crest like frosting. Thira is actually an archipelago of half a dozen islands, the broken remnants of an ancient crater. We sailed into its caldera drunk from wind and the dazzling sunlight of the Aegean, all colors brighter, all edges sharper, the babble of our sailors foreign, our mission misty, and my scientific companions as anticipatory as if they were on holiday. We were in legendary Greece, cradle of democracy, edge of the Ottoman Empire, in a place that looked as if it was created yesterday and could be remade by an explosion tomorrow. Our destination island was a crescent that enclosed a seemingly bottomless bay four miles wide by six long. Across this bay was the smaller island of Thirassia that represented, Smith told me, the opposite side of the old crater wall. In the harbor's center was a small, low, rumpled island as pocked as the moon. It was smoking.

"This is what the world looked like when it began," Cuvier said. "Rock and water."

"Look at the strata of those cliffs, Georges!" Smith exclaimed. "Eruptions laid down like rows of bricks! We can read them like a book!"

"What shelter this would be for a navy," Fulton added. "Cliffs you could cuddle under."

"Or the worst lee shore," Dragut said. "There are days when the *meltemi* blows that you do not want to be in here, my friend. It can be an evil place."

"Evil? I can see the blue domes of half a dozen churches from here."

"Christian churches are no shield against the devil when Satan awakes."

"And mosques no shelter from an earthquake. Bad things happen to all of the pious, Dragut. The solution would be to use science to warn of disaster."

"No, worse things happen to nonbelievers, like savants and French revolutionaries. And no one can warn about the will of God. I put my faith in Allah."

"Cuvier," I interrupted, "you described this as one of the oldest places in the world, but I'm not sure what you meant by that," I said.

"Oldest and newest," the scientist said. "Old in that it's like our planet's beginning, raw and mostly treeless. New in that when that isle in the center belches, hot new rock comes out. The island destroys and remakes itself."

"It seems an odd place to hide anything you want to keep."

"And a forbidding place if you want to keep treasure hunters away."

We made for a small harbor at the base of the island's cliff, the little port cast in shadow this morning by an escarpment hundreds of meters high. Fishing boats bright as toys bobbed by the rubble quay, their gay colors a contrast to the grim rust, brown, and gray striations towering above. The shoreline was so steep that Dragut could bring his xebec right to the short jetty. We hired donkeys for a slow, sure-footed trek up a switchback trail etched into the face of the somber cliff, the animals bristly, ears twitching, and their clop steady as we swayed. The route had no railings and was slick with manure, the donkeys blinking against the flies. Smith kept making us stop so he could peer at different clumps of ugly rock, as if willing the soil to speak. The cliff looked mute to me, and the view out to the other side of the vast bay was across an unnerving gulf of air. I was anxious to get off the precipitous trail.

At last we gained the top and had a better understanding of the geography of this peculiar island. Thira's western edge was a crescent of steep cliff, its houses perched at the rim of the crater ridge like nests of birds. To the east of this scimitar the island sloped more gently down to the sea in a broad fan. There the ground was divided by stone fences into pasture, vineyards, and cropland, all of them brown in midsummer. It looked to me that little had changed since Odysseus roamed. Around was Homer's wine-dark sea, spotted by whitecaps, the wind cooling us after the stillness beneath the cliffs.

"Imagine this slope of land continuing from the sea upward to a peak over what is now the central bay," Smith said, using the sweep of his hand to fill the void. "It would be an immense mountain, visible for a hundred miles. A cone, like Etna. And then a cataclysm even worse than the one that consumed Pompeii and the peak disappears! In its place is a volcanic crater, hundreds or thousands of feet deep, filled with the sea. That crater is what we just sailed across."

"But the bay is a league in extent," Fulton marveled. "What kind of force would turn an immense mountain into such a hole?"

"What indeed," the geologist said. "While Gage searches for ancient weapons, Cuvier and I are going to be exploring what really drives the world."

"And what is that?"

"Nature herself. Imagine if we could harness her more fully!"

◘   ◘   ◘

Our arrival at such a small island could not go unnoticed, but the Ottoman constable seemed more confused than suspicious about it, especially after Dragut offered that we would pay any special immigration fees the portly Turk might invent. We had French documents with colorful stamps the man couldn't read, and surveying instruments he didn't understand. Both helped make our mission seem official, or at least important, while at the same time so technical as to be incomprehensible. We said we were making measurements for the French Institute—possibly true—and that our findings were anticipated by the Sublime Porte in Istanbul, which was a cheerful lie. The fat functionary took his coins and wandered off to make a report by slow mail to authorities on the mainland. By the time it reached anyone with the rank to make a decision about us, we'd be gone.

Dragut went down to his ship for what he said would be a quick trading run to a neighboring island. "I will come back to collect you, I promise! Trust Hamidou!"

We meanwhile found lodging in a vintner's house in the village of Megalochori, a rendezvous set up by Fouché's agents. Here we were to secretly meet the young doctor whom Napoleon thought might someday lead the Greeks to independence from Turkey: handsome, charismatic Count Ioannis Kapodistrias. When Russia and the Turks set up the Septinsular Republic on the obstinately Christian Ionian Islands, the eloquent Kapodistrias became one of the tiny republic's two chief ministers. He was only twenty-five, but had the magnetism of a Napoleon or Nelson. By force of personality alone he'd persuaded rebels on Kefalonia to stay within his tiny new nation, and was reportedly guiding it to a constitution based on liberal principles.

Now he was hoping to lead a wider revolt, and chase the same rumors that we were.

While we waited for Kapodistrias to make contact, Cuvier and Smith began surveying the ancient caldera from the cliff rim, trying to calculate the cataclysm required to make it. Fulton wandered off with his bagpipes, saying he wanted to experiment with oils to fill the instrument, and sketch the workings of the island's windmills. I practiced my fencing against imaginary opponents, worked on temperance by hiking to island vintners for what I told myself was only a judicious tasting, and kept a celibate distance from island women who reminded me of my half-Greek Astiza, dark-haired and olive-skinned. Was I supposed to find some clue about her on this island?

It was a lazy idyll, for one dazzling Mediterranean day.

And then as I walked the trail on the cliff edge at the end of the second day, congratulating myself again on self-discipline, I saw two corsairs sailing into the vast bay at sunset, their sails the color of dried blood. They flew no flag or banner and made no sound, but their decks were crammed with men. Was this Ioannis Kapodistrias, bringing a small Greek army with him? Or Ottoman soldiers, come to catch him or us?

Or some other menace entirely?

Their approach triggered every self-preservation instinct I had.

I hurried back to where we were staying to announce we might not have time to wait for our rendezvous, or Dragut, either. We might have to hide.

Fortunately, our Greek patriot was already there.

◘   ◘   ◘

Kapodistrias came cloaked and shielded with a broad hat, slipping in quietly from wherever he'd been sequestered here in Turkish territory, since he could be arrested for this trespass. His entourage consisted of only two bodyguards, and he carried no weapon. But once he cast his cloak off with a whirl, he impressed us immediately. The minister was a lean and handsome doctor with cheekbones that could have been chiseled out of Athenian marble. He had a voice that would give credit to the ancient orator Themistocles. Like many of the most able men, he was also refreshingly modest.

"I'm afraid I had no fleet to come with," he said with a slight frown after I described the new ships. "No navy, no army, no diplomatic passport, and no time. Are you sure it isn't a routine cargo or ferry to this island?"

"It looked like armed men to me. Did the Turks get word you're here?"

"Possibly. But it might be pirates, too. In any event, our meeting must be brief."

"Maybe it's the gondola men," Smith said. "We seem to be drawing enemies wherever we go."

"Gondola men?"

"We were attacked in Venice by a fleet of gondolas. A beautiful woman threw a bomb at us, and a Muhammadan captain charged us two hundred francs to escape. Gage here says there's some kind of cult called the Egyptian Rite pursuing the same legends we are."

"By the saints: for a quartet of intellectuals, you attract quite the excitement."

"Just Ethan. He finds trouble wherever he goes."

Kapodistrias looked at me warily, as if uneasy that he'd been caught up with my dubious luck. "It's imperative no one knows I was ever on this island. You realize that if my people did not possibly need French help someday, I wouldn't have come at all?"

"Then help us with our mystery and we'll investigate while you depart," Cuvier said. "And tell Napoleon how you helped us. He can be a powerful ally."

"A sensible suggestion from a famed naturalist," Kapodistrias said. "I'm honored to meet Georges Cuvier, and have read of your important work organizing nature. You must know, however, that I fear France as much as I admire it."

Cuvier nodded reluctantly.

"The French soldiers behaved poorly when they occupied our islands."

"They were young men, far from home."

"And not well disciplined. However, the revolutionary ideals that the officers brought were like a bolt of lightning. For the first time, every Greek dares dream of freedom from the Turkish yoke, of standing firm as we did at Thermopylae and Salamis. We don't know if salvation will come from Russia, France, or Britain, but our tiny republic in the Ionian Islands is just the start of our hope. All of Greece deserves to be free."

"Then we're friends," Cuvier said. "Bonaparte wants an independent Greece as counterweight to Turkey, Russia, and England. But the British have driven us from Egypt, the Russians have driven us from your own islands, and the English admirals dream of making the Mediterranean their own little lake. Napoleon asked us to sound out Greek sentiment for independence through you, but also to get your help investigating rumors of a secret on Thira that might benefit both of us."

The Greek's look was cautious. "Buried cities and ancient weapons."

"Is it true at all?"

"Old stories. I'm glad your Englishman is enthralled by rocks, because there's probably little else on this poor island. It's a shattered volcano, home to a few poor fishermen and farmers. But stories persist, as stories tend to do. There's a rumor that this island has a gate to Hades."

"Hades!"

"I think that legend comes from literal truth. You can burn your hand in the vents of steam on that island in the harbor. This island was old, and hot, when Pericles built Athens. It has Venetian castles, Doric temples, prehistoric tombs, and stories of people who lived when religion and witchcraft were one. Pile up three thousand years of history and the web of legend, prophecy, superstition, and lies becomes as thick as the weavings of the mythical Arachne. Who knows what's true and what isn't in a place like this? Idols were their gods, and fable their science."

"Sometimes the two intersect," Cuvier said quietly. "I've seen drawings from Bavaria of an ancient reptile with wings like a bat. It too is extinct, I hope, but it looks as if it could have flown from the gates of hell. Perhaps our medieval iconographers drew from nature."

"And there's really a Greek rumor that the ancients had some kind of powerful weapon?" Fulton interrupted to clarify. "If true, it could instruct modern inventors like me. And Ethan here is our expert on ancient mysteries and hidden powers."

"Is he now? Hidden powers? I would like some of those." There was a twinkle in the Greek's eye.

"Count Kapodistrias, the French helped my own nation win independence," I said. "Greece will most likely need help as well. Napoleon can be a good friend or a deadly enemy. If we carry back word that you're a friend to the ideals of the revolution, it will open the way for possible partnership—not conquest—in the future. In return, is there anyone in Thira who might help us with these old legends? The rumors have reached as far as Paris, and our charge is to determine their truth before greedier and less scientific people come here instead."

He looked at me shrewdly. "Yes, a curious group. You have the look of an opportunist, your friend is a mechanic, and then we have scholars of rocks and bones. One Frenchman, two Americans, and an Englishman. Why did Napoleon send *you*?"

"Out of hope the Ottoman authorities would find us odd and inconsequential."

"And why did you agree to go? Besides your rocks?"

"We have legal problems that Monsieur Gage caused in Paris," Cuvier said. "This mission for Bonaparte will erase them, so we're doing what we have to do—that's the way the world works. Are you not obligated yourself to the Russians and Admiral Ushakov?" It was Ushakov who'd thrown the French off Corfu.

Kapodistrias nodded. "All men are in debt. All right, then. The missive I received from your agent said *you* have a clue for *me* that might help us find this secret."

I took out the ring with its picture of dome and grave, with a man climbing out of the sarcophagus. "Do you recognize that building?"

"A church, perhaps. There are two dozen on this island alone."

"Look at the dome. It's broken, or half completed."

"Ah." He looked carefully. "But of course. Agia Theodosia! The Compromise of the Cannon!"

"The what?"

"The church and a Venetian fort rose in concert in the village of Akrotiri, faith through one gate and the state through another. But then artillery evolved, and as its guns were installed it became apparent that Theodosia's dome was blocking the field of fire. The Venetian officers said the church should move, and the Orthodox priests said the fort should give way to God. It was proposed that the dome be lowered, but the monks refused even that—opinions are held strongly in Greece. Finally an impatient Venetian Catholic fired a cannon ball through the Greek Orthodox cupola, and threatened to destroy the entire church. Instead, the fathers reluctantly carved out a slice of the dome to allow the sighting of the gun toward enemies that, in the end, never came. The original dome architecture has since been restored, but the story of the 'bitten dome' is well known. There's no other church in Thira this ring could refer to."

I imagined the dome with a scoop out of it, one side concave, and admired the compromise. I think everyone should get along.

"Where is this church?"

"Not far—two kilometers, perhaps. But we had better hurry. If Ethan Gage is correct about those approaching ships we may be in a race, gentlemen, for the gate of Hades. And in that case, you will have to race alone."

"What do you mean?"

"It's too coincidental we have all arrived at the same time. I will direct you to the church and wish you well, but I must not be caught with you. Do you have a ship of your own?"

"Gone to a neighboring island but promising to return."

"Then look to your weapons and your wits, and hope your captain hurries."

CHAPTER 12

The village of Akrotiri, on the southwestern arm of Thira's crescent island, looked like a scrabble of stucco dice stacked on a grassy slope. It culminated in the modest ruins of a small Venetian fortress, half dismantled by the Turks more than a century before. What had once been some lordly fiefdom was now a ruin, on a lonely island at the edge of a decaying empire. Next to the fort entrance was a Greek Orthodox church, and it was here Kapodistrias led us under a half-moon. Akrotiri was still except for the bark of a dog or two, and in the silvery light looked empty and timeless, the peeling brown and white houses seeming to grow out of its geology like angular rocks. We, on the other hand, made far too much noise. Our weaponry clanked. Our boots tramped. In a hundred yards we gave away more evidence of our presence than a tribe of Dakota would while galloping through Saint

Peter's. Fulton had insisted on bringing his bagpipes, and every once in a while they would let out
a wheeze, low groan, or odd sloshing.

"Please don't play," I said.

"I've a different kind of song, inspired by our
night at the Palais Royal. This the French navy
might actually buy, if I can set things on fire."

I wondered if we were at the right place at all.
Thira, like all of Greece, is dotted with churches
of plain, whitewashed stucco topped by faded blue
domes, as ubiquitous as stables and not a great
deal fancier. The windows are tiny, the doors
stout planks of weathered wood, and the interiors
without pews—Greek worshippers stand before
God. Was this nondescript place a door to a fabled
weapon?

It was night, the church locked, and so
Kapodistrias—who seemed to be enjoying his
moment of skulduggery—rousted the village priest
from his cell next door and convinced him that
Greek patriotism required the opening of doors
for us.

"But why?"

"We're looking for the gate of Hades, Nikko."

"And why would you seek such a thing? Are you
devils?"

"We're friends of Greece."

"But why are you at Agia Theodosia?"

"An old signet ring has told us to look here. These
men won't be but a moment. They are men of science, patros, who want to understand the past."

"The past is best left in the past. That's what the
past is for."

"No, Greece will learn from them."

He reluctantly unlocked the door. "Wait here." He went ahead to light some candles, and then came back. "You'll see. This is a poor church in a poor village. There's nothing here."

The Greek pulled him aside. "Then let them see for themselves."

We passed through the anteroom, or narthex, and on into the main nave, lighting more candles on their manoualia stands. The structure was small and, compared with a Catholic or Protestant church, sparser of furniture and richer in decoration. My stable analogy had been too hasty. There was a primitive but grand picture of Jesus in the dome overhead, ready to uplift or condemn. Hanging below was an elaborate brass chandelier called a horos, and beyond it was the most decorative part of the church, a polished brass dividing wall consisting of a grilled gate flanked by enameled panels of angels and saints. By custom, only the priests passed up the steps and through the gate to the altar in the sanctuary beyond. The succession of spaces reminded me of the ancient Egyptian temples I'd seen: a penetration to the holy.

"The church seems rather small," Cuvier said. "What are we supposed to be looking for?"

"A sarcophagus. I don't see one."

"In the sanctuary, perhaps?" asked Fulton.

Smith went up to the gate and tried it but it, too, was locked. "All I see is an altar.

"Where's the priest?"

We looked around.

"Kapodistrias is gone, too," Cuvier said. And

indeed, we realized the Greeks had not followed us inside but instead closed the main door behind us, leaving us alone. If we were to discover the gate of Hades, it seemed, we were on our own.

"Gage, is this a trap?" Fulton asked.

I tried the church door. "It's been locked or braced from the outside. Maybe they're trying to give us time to explore undisturbed."

"Or maybe Kapodistrias doesn't trust the French after all," Cuvier said.

"He just can't share the risk, I think, and endanger his republic. But I'd feel better if Hamidou was waiting for us. I wasn't expecting those new ships, with all those men."

"What if Ottomans are following us? We should flee, too," Fulton said. "This place isn't like Fouché's ring at all."

"We've come more than a thousand miles. Let's at least see if anything's here. There's a bar—let's lock the door from the inside, too."

Unfortunately, except for the Byzantine decoration typical of the Greek religion, the nave was barren. It took about as long to search as my purse, which is to say almost no time at all.

"There's nothing here," Cuvier said, rather obviously. "Ethan, I agree with Robert. We should retreat."

"Absolutely. Just as soon as we check the sanctuary."

"But that's locked."

"Which is all the more reason to enter it. Gentlemen, I have some experience in this kind of thing and I've found the more difficult it is to get into a place, the more it pays to do so. People are always sticking things in hidden cellars or sealed attics or armored armoires, hoping the rest of us won't have energy enough to peek. Why keep anyone out unless there's something to find?"

"Because it's sacred?" Smith ventured.

"Well, that, too."

I went to the grilled wall that separated the nave from the altar sanctuary. Three steps led up to it, and painted icons were on either side of the gate. Jesus looked disapprovingly at me from one side, and Mary—seeming as skeptical of me as some of the other women I'd dallied with—frowned at me from the other. Saints and angels stood guard, too, looking no friendlier. I eyed the keyhole. "Cuvier, bring me one of your pistols."

"For heaven's sake," Fulton said, appropriately. He set his bagpipes down, the instrument making a soft buzz as he did so, and hopped up the steps beside me. Out came a set of wiry steel instruments. "There's no need for a gunshot, which will only jam the lock. I made a study of these mechanisms as a boy and found that patience can open most anything." He began fiddling with the lock. "I don't make a habit of this, but there's utility in being able to manipulate a keyhole. Of course there's nothing to see, as you can tell by looking through the bars, and if the village catches us doing this we'll be stoned as sacrilegious heretics, or worse."

"I just want to make sure this sanctuary isn't the front porch to Hades."

"Do you smell any sulfur?"

"Let's take that as a good sign."

"And no lightning bolts for trespass yet, either," Smith added.

The inventor had the gate open quick as a thief, and we gingerly passed into the sanctuary, feeling we were trespassing on divinity itself. There was a wooden cabinet to one side with a chalice and other instruments of worship. A censer to provide scented smoke hung nearby. In the middle was the altar itself, draped with a tapestry. There was a cylindrical container and gospel on top, and a processional cross and gilded fans behind.

"What's the coffee urn then?" Smith asked innocently.

"A tabernacle, you Protestant heathen," Cuvier said. "It's where they hold the sacraments."

"Ah. Could it have a clue then?"

"To get to Heaven, not Hades."

I bent and walked the stone floor, looking for a crack or pull indicating a way downward. There was nothing I could see. The coin and Kapodistrias's advice seemed a dead end.

Outside, dogs began barking again. Someone was coming.

I stood, considering. Then remembering a temple in Egypt, I decided to take a closer look at the altar by lifting one corner of its cloth and peering underneath.

"Is that allowed?" Smith asked.

"We're not even allowed on this island," Fulton replied.

Aha. The altar was not made from a wooden table but a stone box, I saw. I stepped back. It was the length and width of a man. "There's our sar-cophagus."

"Where?" Cuvier asked.

"It's the altar. They hide it by covering it. Their altar is a grave, if you can believe that. Take the tabernacle off there and set it aside."

"I will not. I'd fry in hell."

"I thought you French revolutionaries don't be-lieve anymore."

"Didn't. I went to the service at Notre Dame."

"Well, I'll do it, then. I'm damned anyway, de-spite my reforms." Feeling oddly queasy, I lifted the holy objects off the altar and placed them on the preparation table to one side. Surely God wouldn't mind for a moment or two. Smith helped me fold the altar cloth—we tried to be careful—and we re-vealed a stone sarcophagus similar to the one cast into the signet ring. The lid overlapped the box. When I tugged, it seemed cemented in place.

"I think we'd better pry," I said.

"You can't be serious!" Cuvier wasn't used to trea-sure hunting, which generally involves a fair amount of burglary, desecration, demolition, and dust.

"The coin shows a man going in or out. I know it seems callous, but if we've got the right church we need to peek inside. If we hurry we'll have it boxed up and things back in place in time for ser-vices."

"You'd better. I think there's a crowd forming outside." We could hear barks, voices, and bumps on the church door.

"But how are we going to get the lid off?" Smith asked.

I looked at Fulton. "Robert, you're the one who pried that railing off the bridge."

He swallowed. "I had an oar."

"Those iron candle stands look sturdy enough to me." I took out my tomahawk and began chipping at the joint between lid and box, heedless of the damage it was doing to the edge of my blade. "Fetch one and we'll jam it in this crevice I'm making." They hesitated. "Quickly, lads, we've come this far! Probably nothing to see but bones, and nothing wrong with that, is there? We'll all be fossils soon enough."

So we hammered a wedge point into the junction between box and lid and used a sacred manoualia, the candle stand, as a lever and one of the stiff choir chairs as a fulcrum. I was sweating at the thought of what the locals would think if they stumbled in on us, but in for a penny, in for a pound. Someone started hammering on the church door. "Smith, take your blunderbuss into the narthex and discourage them."

"I don't even know who I'm shooting at!"

"Best not to ask, I've found. If they're shooting at you, that's identification enough."

"I feel like a grave robber," Cuvier muttered.

"In case you haven't noticed, gentlemen, that's exactly what we are." The other three of us threw our weight on our pry bar, there was a cracking sound, and the lid shifted slightly.

"Yes!" Fulton said.

"Another heave, just enough to look!" With a grind and thump, we managed to shift the massive lid far enough to peer inside. It was dark, of course.

"Fetch a candle!" Despite myself, I always get excited when I delve. I still mourned the lost treasure of the pyramid, and secretly hoped I might find another.

Outside, there was a boom and crack as something crashed energetically against the church door.

So I bent and pushed the candle inside, illuminating the interior of the sarcophagus.

It was vacant as a trollop's wink.

And then Smith's blunderbuss went off.

CHAPTER 13

"They made a hole in the door and I had a look!" the Englishman cried. "There's a crowd outside with scimitars and muskets!" He backed to reload. A chunk of the door had been knocked loose by an ax seeking to chop an opening, and Smith had fired through that. The chopping had stopped. We heard shouts and yells outside and then muzzles were pushed through and shots fired blindly. Thankfully, they thudded harmlessly into the stone. The door was too thick to break easily, and the church windows too high and small to easily climb into. Of course, that made them hard to climb out of, as well.

"How many?" I asked.

"More than in Venice or Paris."

"Who are they?"

"How the devil should I know? I saw hoods, helmets, turbans, and scarves. You seem to make enemies with half the world, Ethan. Too many to fight for very long, at least. So what's in the sar-cophagus?"

"Not a blessed thing," Fulton said.

"Ah. So we're trapped in a Greek church on a bleak island at the edge of the Ottoman Empire for absolutely no reason at all?"

"It appears so," my inventor friend said.

"Maybe we just got the wrong sarcophagus," I tried.

"I wish I'd stayed in London. My mother warned me about Paris."

Now a dull boom began to echo through the nave as whoever was outside began to slam some kind of ram against the door. The wood bulged with each strike, the bar beginning to crack.

"Maybe there's a back door," I suggested. I could see the reflection of torches through the high, open windows.

"If we go through it and outside we'll be cut to pieces," Cuvier said.

"And you don't think that will happen when they get in here?" Smith glanced up. "You can't reach the ceiling as you did at the Palais, either." The dome peaked thirty feet above our heads. "I think Gage has led us into a dead end."

"We can make a fight of it," I said, sounding braver than I felt. "If it's just peasants, they'll back off."

"I saw uniforms. And enough cutlery for a palace kitchen."

"Ethan, if you give me a hand I think I can delay them when they come through that door." Fulton hefted his bagpipe, and again I heard the curious slosh. "It's the dragon I've been working on. It spits fire."

"Satan's brew, Robert?"

"It's a twist on Greek fire, the ancient combustible. If it works, they'll hesitate."

I thought frantically. "All right. We'll start a conflagration, and then we'll hide."

"Where?"

"Cuvier, unlock a back door or tie the altar cloth to a high window to make it look like we've fled. Then we'll secrete ourselves in the sarcophagus, and once they've run on by, we'll escape by running the other way. It's quite brilliant, really."

"You want to get in a tomb and close the lid?"

"Just for a moment, to confuse them. Do you have a better idea?"

There was a crash as the bar of the church door cracked through and splintered timbers heaved inward. We could see a boiling mass of men, some turbaned and some not, the glint of steel, and the flame of torches.

"There's no time!"

"Yes there is!" cried Fulton. "Ethan, take up that candle stand there!" He was steady as a fireman as he aimed one of the pipes of his instrument at the disintegrating door, and I noticed he'd screwed on a tubular extension extending it three more feet. "Even a wolf learns not to touch a hot stove." There was a technical grimness about him, a willingness to put deviltry to practical use, if it were for a good cause—or self-preservation.

The bar finally burst entirely, the doors flying wide. Hooded, caped men like the crew we'd encountered in Venice pushed into the narthex of the church.

"Now!" Fulton cried. "Hold the candle flame near the tip of my tube!"

He squeezed his bag and instead of song, a jet of mist sprayed from his new nozzle. When I held the candle stand to put a flame into the stream, it ignited into a cone of fire that reached out like dragon's breath. There was a whoosh as the flame flared out, licking at the broken door and igniting some of the Egyptian Rite minions pushing through.

Men screamed, capes catching fire.

Fulton aimed his pipe like a fire hose and that's what, I suppose, I should call it, since fire came from its tip instead of water. The bag shot liquid fire thirty feet, igniting the door, its frame, and several attackers. The mob heaved back in terror and confusion and collapsed into a tangle, companions beating at the flames. A preview for the wicked, I thought grimly. The fiery door temporarily protected us with a shield of flame and smoke. Shots came through the murk, bullets pinging.

"Back into the nave!" the inventor cried. He carried the bag with him.

We retreated to the main room of the church and slammed that door, piling psaltery chairs against it. Then we ran for the sanctuary. Cuvier had already sprung a side entrance as if we'd fled that way, and now we slammed shut the sanctuary gates, shoved the heavy sarcophagus lid to make a wider opening, and piled inside, dragging our weapons with us.

"What about air?" the French savant asked.

"Judging from my experience with my submarine, we have at least half an hour," Fulton replied. "If they're not gone, we'll have to come out and surrender. But Ethan's idiotic scheme is our only chance."

It was stuffed as a sausage inside, but the tomb was far bigger than the one I'd found in the City of Ghosts near the Holy Land—more the size of a horizontal closet than a coffin. We wrestled the heavy lid back over us, centering it as best we could, and cast ourselves into complete darkness. Then we waited, hoping they'd run by.

Dim sounds through the stone.

A crash—the nave door being forced opened. The faint sound of shouts and outrage. A closer clang from the sanctuary gate forced open, the pounding of boots on the floor, and then a rush as the side door was found opened.

Silence.

Had it worked?

"There could be more who are waiting," I whispered. "Let's give it several minutes."

So we lay half atop each other, sweating, our weapons clenched, our breath hot and close. I was ready to have a peek when we heard more sounds, and froze. There was talking that came to us as the faintest murmur, and then an odd rattle.

"Sounds like chain," Cuvier whispered.

Then a pounding, like something being driven into the wall or floor. More rattling, and the squeal of something being ratcheted tight.

"What the devil?" asked Smith.

Finally all was quiet again, and I waited warily, listening for the merest hint our enemies were standing by. But no, they'd gone. We were nearing the end of Fulton's half hour, I guessed, and I didn't want us swooning from lack of air.

"Out we go then," I whispered, "for better or worse." Lying on our backs for leverage, we lifted arms and legs to push against the heavy stone lid to rotate it out of the way.

It wouldn't budge.

"Harder!" I hissed. We grunted, pushing with all our might. All we heard was the clanking of metal link against metal link, chain grinding against stone.

"No, hard this time!"

It was as if the sarcophagus had been cemented shut.

"Bloody hell. I think they've chained the lid down," said Smith. "They've got us trapped and sealed, Ethan. They're just waiting for us to suffocate."

"They can't be that clever."

I pushed again. But we couldn't get out.

"Well, hang."

My plan had buried us alive.

◻   ◻   ◻

A pparently we didn't fool them," I said unnecessarily, speaking aloud now under the assumption that they knew they'd caught us like insects in a bottle.

"*Apparently*, this is the most damn fool thing we

could have done," amended Cuvier. "I thought we were in a race for some secret! They simply want to smother us?"

"Maybe they already knew the crypt was empty," said Fulton, with a trace of admittedly understandable bitterness. I think he was beginning to doubt my reputation as a gifted adventurer. "First you set our bordello on fire, Gage, then you get us arrested, then some paramour throws a grenade at the mere sight of you, and now you've condemned us to suffocation. Can anyone remind me again why we chose him as a guide to the Palais Royal?"

"She wasn't my paramour." I felt more than a little defensive.

"He was supposed to be an expert on trollops, too," Cuvier said.

"Maybe they just want to take the fight out of us," said Smith. "Hullo!" He banged on the lid with the muzzle of his blunderbuss. "We surrender!"

Nothing.

So we all yelled and banged, to no more effect. It was as if they'd buried us and departed to have supper, Fulton's liquid fire cruelly repaid. What is worse, burning or suffocation?

"Maybe we could shoot our way out," Smith suggested.

"If you set that blunderbuss off in here the balls will bounce until they kill us all," Fulton replied.

"Well, it's empty anyway. Fearfully hard to load when we're packed in like this."

"Try not to set off Robert's bagpipes, either," Cuvier said. "I'd rather not roast as well. And I'm getting a cramp."

"Aye, Ethan, can you shift?" asked Smith. "We might as well die comfortable. What's it like to smother anyway, Georges? You're the zoologist."

"I assure you I haven't tried it."

"I think it's more insidious than painful," Fulton theorized. "As our breath grows short, our brains will fog—that was my experience in tests aboard my submarine. Eventually we'll lapse into unconsciousness and die. Not much different from falling asleep."

"Not such a bad way to go," I said, trying to see the bright side.

"Then hold your breath first, idiot, so the rest of us have a few moments more," Cuvier muttered. I don't know if he was tiring of me just then, or was simply annoyed at the idea of him and me lying together for all eternity.

"Do you really think they know the box is empty of any secrets or treasure?" Smith asked.

"I'm guessing their plan is simply to kill us by waiting and then open it up again to look for themselves," I said. "Rather efficient, really. I mean, we're already buried, too. They don't have to do any work at all."

"I'm full of admiration."

"We'd better stop talking to conserve our breath while I think," I proposed.

"And when is that phenomenon to commence, exactly?" Cuvier inquired. Then he began kicking at the stone lid and yelling things like "help" and "parley."

That did no good either and at last, exhausted, he lapsed into silence. We lay crammed in the dark, blind, helpless, and doomed. I wish I could report I had some kind of profound insight while buried alive, but frankly, nothing philosophical occurred except that, as the others had concluded, I was a damn fool. I was just glad my companions hadn't thought to strangle me. And so we waited. And waited. And waited.

Silence.

It felt lonely.

"Gentlemen, are you dead?" I finally ventured.

"For God's sake, Gage," Smith groaned.

"But I'm not dead, either. Isn't that a curious phenomenon, Cuvier?"

"Maybe we *are* dead," Fulton said. "Maybe this is what death is like, especially after you've killed men in bitter violence. Maybe this is hell."

"No, there's air coming in here," I insisted. "Has to be. Not light, but air."

"What are you saying?" Smith asked.

"That there's some leak in this box. Feel with your hands to see if you can find it. Maybe there's more to this sarcophagus than we initially realized."

We scrabbled with our fingers but could find nothing. I looked in vain for a crack of light, but since there was none, the air, if it really was coming in, had to be from the unlit below. "I think there's a hollow under this box," I insisted. "Put your noses down and sniff for better air."

"Gage . . ."

"Wait," said Cuvier. "It does seem fresher here at this end."

"Maybe we can dig," Smith said. "Ethan, do you have your silly sword?"

"It's a rather elegant rapier."

"Let's try scraping and prying with the thing."

Getting it clear of its scabbard wasn't easy, given our tight packing. Then we had to twist it around to get the point to the head of the sarcophagus where Cuvier was breathing.

"Ow!"

"Sorry. If you angle it this way . . ."

"Which way? I can't see a damn thing."

"Don't poke my bagpipes."

"Just hold still a moment. There we go, steady . . . aw. Careful, Georges, here comes the tip!"

I began scraping the weapon at the joint between the sides of the sarcophagus and the floor, feeling above it with my fingers. Wait, was there a mark? I felt a diamond shape inscribed in the stone, small and shallow, but eerily recognizable. A diamond, or was it an overlapping compass and square, ancient symbol of Freemasonry? My, that fraternity got around! I stabbed at the stone beneath it, looking for an opening. Suddenly there was a click.

And then, before I could cry warning, we were plunging into a void of utter blackness.

CHAPTER 14

It was a miracle none of us were impaled by my sword. We hit a slope and slid in the dark, hardly knowing which way was up, weapons clattering, and Fulton's theory about us having descended into hell seemed all too terrifyingly true. Yet at last we, sword, blunderbuss, longrifle, and bagpipes rolled to some kind of bottom—just how deep I never knew.

There was air, dusty but breathable. And it was hot, just like an entryway to Hades.

"Georges? William? Robert?"

"It just gets worse and worse," one of them groaned.

"Is everyone still alive?"

"How do we tell?"

"Well, we're here, I think. So the ring showed something after all. The sarcophagus wasn't the treasure, it was only the trapdoor to it. All we have to do is keep our wits about us, discover whatever secrets are down here, and find a way back out."

"Our wits! We can't see a thing." I think it was Cuvier.

"Ethan, we fell several seconds straight down before hitting that slope," Fulton said. "I doubt we can climb back up to that tomb, and what good would it do us if we did?"

"When our enemies open it, they'll see which way we've gone," Smith added.

"Perhaps, or perhaps my sword tip triggered a spring," I said. "The bottom opens, but then springs back. They may open the sarcophagus to find us and, instead of our corpses, it will be empty once more. They'll think it a miracle or, more likely, that we were never in there in the first place and gave them the slip. Quite ingenious on our part, really."

"Why should they care?" asked Fulton. "We're doomed anyway. We've gone from one grave to a bigger one."

"No, I run around in these underground places all the time," I said with more confidence than I felt. "There's something down here, maybe something that hasn't been seen since medieval times. I think there was a Freemason mark where I triggered the collapse of the trapdoor. This may be a Templar tunnel, my friends."

"Templars?" Smith groaned. "What are you talking about?"

"Apparently that group of Crusader knights was on the trail of some ancient mysteries and succeeded for a time in finding some. I discovered one in the Near East, in a lost city, and another in the

American wilderness. They seem to have been systematically reassembling the past. After the Saracens drove the Christians from the Holy Land, the Knights set up strongholds in places like Cyprus and Malta. Perhaps they came here, too, and built that hidden door for later generations who never came. We may not be in peril, but in luck. We're on the cusp of rediscovering what Napoleon and Fouché really sent us to find, some ancient weapon of a lost civilization. Maybe we'll win a prize."

There was a long silence in the dark. Then the Frenchman spoke again, slowly, carefully. "You realize that we are all completely insane?"

"If so, then Napoleon is, too. Think about it. He's heard rumors of a weapon connected with Og and Atlantis, and takes a chance by sending us here. I didn't much believe the legends myself, when we saw the poverty and rawness of this island, but a tomb with a trap? With a Masonic engraving? Come, my friends, there has to be a reason. We've tumbled into a pit, it's true, but perhaps a pit with a reason for being. I know we're bruised, bloody, without food or water, and lost in pitch blackness without a clue where to go, but fortune may actually be smiling on us." I grinned in the dark. "I'm quite excited, actually."

Silence, again. I hoped they hadn't crept away.

"Before we can find buried treasure," I continued briskly, "we have to decide which way to go. My hope is the slope we just tumbled down leads to a tunnel we can follow without any junctions, caverns, or drops. We can hold hands, taking turns groping through the dark."

Groans. "I'm not holding your hand," Fulton said. "We'll light a candle."

"Candle?"

"I kept one when we ignited my fire hose."

"You had a taper?" Cuvier asked. "Why didn't you light it in the sarcophagus?"

"There was hardly a point. There was nowhere to go and the flame would use up the oxygen."

"All Americans are lunatics," the zoologist muttered. "Not just Gage."

"Well, I can make a flash in the pan of my long-rifle," I said cheerfully. "Let's gather some lint to have something to better catch the wick."

So we did, and some priming from my powder horn and a pull of the trigger produced what was in the darkness a blinding flash, which ignited a ball of lint we in turn used to light Fulton's candle. With no holder, we stuck the wax shaft temporarily in the barrel of Smith's blunderbuss. Then we inspected ourselves for damage. We were filthy, torn, and raw from scrapes in our tumbles, but surprisingly intact. The very tip of my rapier was bent slightly and our weapons knocked about, but nothing—including our bones—seemed to be seriously broken. The candle illuminated a steep dirt slope, down which we'd tumbled. The sarcophagus was far out of sight above. In the other direction was a narrow tunnel, just high enough to stoop in, that twisted through lava rock.

The tube led downward, toward Hades.

CHAPTER 15

Our underground way twisted like a worm. At times the ceiling was high enough to stand freely and at other times we had to crawl, always fearing we'd come to a dead end. The walls bulged in and out irregularly, casting doubt that medieval knights had carved it.

"They apparently used nature's casting," Cuvier said. "It's probably a lava tube. Volcanoes will sometimes have pipes through which molten rock flows. When this island was a volcano, this may have been a conduit from the central peak to the sea."

"The island is still a volcano," Smith corrected.

"Does that mean lava could flow through here now?" Fulton asked worriedly.

"Only if there were an eruption," Smith said. "But if there were, we'd be suffocated by gas or cooked by heat long before any lava came."

"I see."

"Or earthquakes could collapse the tunnel on top of us," added Cuvier.

"Heated water could boil us alive," suggested Smith.

"Or scald us to death with steam," agreed Cuvier.

"At Mount Etna, onlookers have been killed by flying rock."

"At Vesuvius, they've found corpses petrified by the ash."

The two savants seemed to be enjoying themselves. "I love science, don't you Robert?" I asked Fulton.

"It's much more sensible to work with things you can control, like machines."

And so we explored, bunched up behind our little candle. It not only provided light but gave us assurance, by burning, that there was still breathable air.

"If we're alive, there has to be an outlet drawing air somewhere, eh?" I asked the others.

"Yes," said Cuvier. "Perhaps the size of a door. Or, the size of your finger."

"Well, yes."

Twice we slid down rubble chutes, seeming to creep closer and closer to some kind of hell. I was hot, but how much was my imagination? I wiped my sweat and noticed how dry my throat was. Then we crawled over a sill and our horizontal path momentarily ended. We had come to a vertical shaft that led both up and down, smooth and round like a well. I looked up, but the top was dark and presumably sealed. There was no easy way to climb up there. I ripped a scrap from my shirt, lit it with the candle, and dropped it down. There was a dirt floor twenty feet below, and the tunnel led on from that.

"The shaft isn't wide," I said. "If we jam ourselves across, we can inch our way down. I'll go first, and when I get partway you can pass the blunderbuss and candle." The wax had already burned halfway.

Somewhat awkwardly, we made our way to the bottom of this well and came upon a surprising discovery. The tunnel that continued on from the shaft was braced with timbers! It appeared to be an excavated mine instead of a natural passage. The wood looked very old, dry, and cracked, but protected from rot by the dryness of the warm passageway. There was a pile of excavated sand and crude rusted tools.

"Somebody's been down here before us," I said. "And not thousands of years ago, either. I think this shaft used to be an alternate entrance from the surface." I looked up. "Too bad there's no ladder."

"Perhaps this foolishness is not altogether pointless," Cuvier admitted.

"The bracing hardly looks strong enough to hold up tent fabric, let alone the earth," Fulton warned. "This is crude engineering, very old and weak."

"But I'm guessing it's been here since medieval times," I said. "Why would it fall down today after hundreds of years?"

"Because we're here, causing vibration and noise," Cuvier said.

"So let's whisper, and not brush anything."

And so we went cautiously on, and came upon the street.

It was not a normal street of course—we were somewhere under the surface of Thira—and yet it was. Some kind of miners—medieval knights was my guess, probably Templars—had dug down to the flat, sandal-worn flagstones of an ancient thoroughfare. The mine ceiling was overhead, and our light was pitiful until Cuvier took the gray, paper-dry wooden handle of a medieval shovel, wrapped our handkerchiefs on the end, and lit them with the candle, giving us the flare of a torch. With this new light we could see that a slope of volcanic ash and rubble made up one side of the street, still covering part of whatever city had been buried thousands of years ago when the island exploded. On the street's other side, however, was the excavated stone wall of an ancient building, with a door and room beyond. Straight ahead, our flagstone lane dead-ended at a slope of sand and rubble that almost entirely plugged the tunnel, except for a small crevice at its top. Cool air blew through that crack.

"The men who uncovered this probably used the well shaft to lift the dirt they dug out," Smith theorized. "Then they lidded it and, to hide any hint of the location, used that lava tube to connect this place to a very distant one, the church. Perhaps there was no church then, and the holy place was built around the entrance with the sarcophagus-turned-altar constructed to disguise it. It looks as if they were planning to come back, but didn't."

"Another eruption drove them away, perhaps," Cuvier suggested. "Or some kind of attack or war."

"The Templars were crushed and scattered in 1307," I said. "Friday the thirteenth."

"And this buried room—probably a buried city—was lost and forgotten," Smith speculated.

"Until this race between you and the Egyptian Rite to uncover these old secrets," said Fulton.

This was not a race of my choosing. I'd been dragged into this mess by winning a medallion in a Paris card game more than four years before, and my life has been uncomfortably tumultuous, and annoyingly unprofitable, ever since. Yet I also felt swept up in something historical. The Knights Templar had been annihilated by a king and a pope desperate to learn the secret of their power, and their discoveries were scattered. Now interest in the past had been revived. We lived in an age of revolution and reason, and yet legend and the occult are a respite from the headlong scientific rush of 1802. The modern world was changing so fast! And was there really something down here that could tip the balance of power in the Mediterranean?

"From experience, I'd say it best that we now poke around," I announced. "Treasure tends to be found that way."

So we stepped through a doorway into one of the excavated rooms and encountered not at all what I expected.

There were no machines here, and indeed no furniture of any kind. But instead of the austere whiteness I might expect of Greek architecture, we encountered a garden of blazing color. The walls were covered with murals, and murals of an ethereal beauty that seemed like a memory of a paradise long forgotten. The vines of flowers wound sensuously toward an implied sun, the petals glowing in gold, red, and purple. Antelopes and birds were drawn with sinuous lines as perfect as the fall of a river, prancing and flying across ocher meadows. Monkeys leaped from twisting trees. Galleys as graceful as racing shells were hung with garlands. A naked youth posed with a bundle of fish caught from a pristine sea. A graceful maiden lovely as a cameo, serene as a dove and with a waterfall of dark hair, gestured delicately while clad in a complex layered dress of lovely colors.

How different from the dramatic, stern stiffness of murals in Egyptian temples! Or even the angular, white grandeur in pictures I'd seen of the ruins of the Acropolis in Athens. In Egypt, warriors had marched and trod enemies underfoot. But these people were not just peaceful, they displayed a peace that suggested they'd never known war at all. It reminded me of Magnus Bloodhammer's dreams of an Eden not yet poisoned by the apple and the Fall.

"If we're looking for ancient war machines, I think we've got the wrong address," I murmured. "This looks like a pacifist arcadia."

"Gorgeous, aren't they?" Cuvier said. "The life in these murals! How many modern painters could capture that?"

"Our portraits are darker," Smith agreed. "Northern Europeans overdressed and overfed, with moody skies and harnessed horses. What a little heaven these people must have had in contrast, before the volcano blew."

"Is this Atlantis, then?" asked Fulton.

"It's something very old and very different from

Greece or Egypt," I said. "I have no idea *what* it is. They don't just look happy, they look confident. But they don't look warlike at all. Why would the Egyptian Rite expect to find a weapon down here?"

"We still don't know we're in the right place."

"But that tomb, that trapdoor, that tunnel? It's all very deliberate."

"Maybe whatever we hoped to find has already been moved."

"I don't think so. I'm not sure anyone has been down here since medieval times."

"There are more doorways. Let's keep looking."

The building seemed mazelike, as illogical in its organization as it was beautiful in its décor. Room opened to room with no organizing hallway or unifying atrium. It was hivelike. We passed painted ships with oars splayed like the legs of water bugs, papyrus reeds clumped in the sun, athletes boxing, and girls running. And we were going in our little cone of flickering light from one room to another when suddenly Fulton called, "Wait!"

We stopped.

"I think I saw something peculiar in the last room."

We went back. The inventor pointed to a frieze near the ceiling. It was a horizontal, scrolling picture of a flotilla of ships, not very different from others we'd seen before. It suggested that whoever built this now-buried place had been sailors, which was logical for island dwellers. Had they been able to sail away when the volcano blew? Had they founded new civilizations elsewhere, even in America?

"There's something odd up there," Fulton said, pointing.

There was a shape like a crescent moon painted to one side of the gliding ships, and beams of sunlight or moonlight emanating from its concave side to illuminate the little navy.

"It's the moon, don't you think?" I proposed.

The inventor shook his head. "Look, it's attached to an elegant curved frame of some kind, as graceful as their murals of flowers, but attended by small figures. This isn't a celestial object, gentlemen. It's some kind of machine." His finger traced the rays emanating from the crescent and followed them to one of the ships. There was a blossom of color above the vessel that I'd assumed was a representation of a dyed sail, but Fulton, perhaps mindful of his peculiar use of his bagpipes, had discerned something else. "I think it's setting these ships on fire."

I felt a chill then, as if I'd seen the snake undergirding Eden. People had lived here in peace, yes. But perhaps their peace was sustained behind the shield of some kind of weapon so terrible that it could ignite any enemy vessel that approached too close.

"But this idea has been attributed to the great Archimedes," Fulton said. "Surely this is much too early for the burning mirrors."

"The burning mirrors? What are you talking about, Robert?"

"There are accounts from ancient history, originally written by Lucian two centuries after Christ and later relayed to us by medieval writers. Lucian wrote that during the Roman siege of Syracuse in 212 B.C., the Greek mathematician Archimedes constructed a mirror, or lens, that could focus the sun's heat on enemy ships. The Greek was a mechanical genius who also devised a giant pincer that could crush Roman ships like a monstrous claw. In the end the Romans prevailed and burst into the city, and Archimedes was killed by an ignorant soldier while he drew his mathematical figures in the sand. His genius was lost, but the legend of a heat ray persisted. Some called it Poseidon's spear, or Neptune's trident."

I startled. Such words had also been inscribed in the gold foil I'd found in North America.

"Many have dismissed it as fable," Fulton went on, "and nobody has attributed it to earlier times than Archimedes. But what if the brilliant Greek got the idea for his mirror from a place like this?"

"From Atlantis?"

"Perhaps."

"Could it work?" said Smith.

"Who knows? But if it did, and if you could find it today, it might have the ability to ignite modern ships that are even more vulnerable, thanks to their dependence on sails and gunpowder. They'd light like a torch, and blow up like a magazine. Here is a weapon that never needs to be reloaded, and is tireless as the sun."

"I barely escaped the French flagship *L'Orient* when she blew up at the Battle of the Nile," I recounted. "The blast was so titanic that it actually halted the battle for a quarter of an hour. It was the most terrible thing I've experienced. Well, one of them, anyway." I'd accumulated a lot of memories the past few years.

"So this could tip the domination of the Mediterranean, if it existed," Fulton said. "But a mirror would have to be huge to have the power to burn a ship. There's nothing like that in this hole, no room big enough, and no way to get it out if there were."

"So what *is* down here?" Smith asked.

We proceeded to look. There were eight rooms in all, dirt cascading into the two at each end of the complex as indication this old city had been only partially excavated. Each was emptier than a cell. Except for the murals, there was nothing. The floor was hard-packed dirt, and search as we might we could find no more traps or hidden tunnels. The ceiling was earth braced by mining timbers. When we poked at it, all we got for our trouble was grit in our eyes. The street stopped at that slope of dirt. To go that way we'd have to be like worms, and I didn't fancy getting wedged into some wormhole, wondering about hidden treasure as I slowly withered to a husk. Yet there was no way to retreat, either, unless we could levitate up the shaft. As my companions had complained, it appeared that I'd succeeded only in trapping us in a slightly bigger grave, as barren as the sarcophagus above.

"It's already been robbed," Cuvier theorized. "I suspect we're centuries too late. These knights, or whoever they were, got the mirror first."

"Then why is there no record of its being used?" Fulton asked. "And why are so many people after us? Are we all chasing a myth? That picture is of the burning mirror, gentlemen, and that *is* an ancient weapon. There has to be *something* to it."

Our light kept burning lower. I tried to think, always a difficult task. Why the church, sarcophagus, trap, tunnel, excavation, and persistent pursuit if there was nothing down here?

Then it occurred to me.

"The fourth room," I proposed.

I led them back to it and we shone our ebbing candle on the mural in there. At first glance it seemed no different from the others—flowers, birds, and brilliant color—except I realized the color was slightly *too* bright. The lines of the mural were less sinuous somehow, less assured, as if the artist who'd copied them had not shared the gaiety that comes from living in a sunny place of perpetual peace behind a death ray that warded off all enemies. A talented but sweating Knight Templar, perhaps, pressed into service to hide a critical clue in plain view. I thought of the stone tablet and rotting shield in the Dakota territory of North America that bore enigmatic references to this "Og." Or the misleading signal in the City of Ghosts. Or mathematician Monge's dismissal of my sacred medallion at the Great Pyramid. Always there was a distraction.

I took my tomahawk and swung at the mural. A crack appeared.

"Gage, no!" Cuvier cried. "This artwork is priceless!"

"On the contrary, Georges. This mural has no value at all. It's a medieval façade, a fakery." And I swung again and again, making a spider's web of cracks, and then chipped at the edges to pry the stucco off the underlying stone. "It's a ruse."

"What do you mean?"

"I don't think this was painted by the ancient people who built this place. I think medieval knights, or someone else, put it here to cover something up." I hoped I was right, because all I was uncovering was rough-looking stone.

But then I spied the edge of something leathery. There was a sheet of parchment sealed between stucco and rock! I fingered its edge and peeled it as much as I could.

Then we heard a murmur of sound, distant clanks and grunts, and Fulton darted out to listen from the buried street. "Someone's coming!"

There was Latin writing on the parchment behind the mural.

CHAPTER 16

Smith, buy me time to get this parchment pried loose!"

The Englishman darted away with his blunderbuss again.

The old document was surprisingly pliable, but the sheepskin had bonded to wall and mural like glue. It could only be peeled off a little at a time. Cuvier used my rapier to scrape from the other side, the false painting flaking away.

I heard the roar of Smith's gun, shouts, and answering shots.

"Hurry," the French scientist muttered unnecessarily.

Then we heard a whoosh and crackling. I sniffed. Something was burning again.

Smith rushed back in. "Fulton is as mad as you are, Gage. He's set the mine's shoring on fire with his bagpipes. There's so much smoke we can't see a damn thing. Neither can our enemies, I suppose."

Cuvier slid the rapier behind the parchment like a razor and at last the document, about eighteen inches square, came free. I'd no idea what it said, given that it was in Latin, and there was no time for us to translate in any event. I slid it inside my shirt and nodded. "What happens when the timber burns through?"

"The earth will collapse on all this beauty," Cuvier said.

"And on us," Smith amended.

We hurried out to the main street. Fulton had backed down it, coughing. Flames seemed to be racing along the network of dried supports as if they'd been soaked in oil, and there was a merry popping and crackling as our roof burned. I could hear shouts of consternation from the other side of the smoke.

"Who followed us down here?" I asked.

"We didn't get a clear look at them," Fulton said. "William let them have it with his blunderbuss, and then I used the last oil from my pipes. I'd hoped it might collapse just a section to buy us time, but it appears the whole lot of it is catching fire. I think I'm going to bring the entire cave down on us, Ethan, and I don't have a gambling salon above to help us escape this time."

"I'm not the only idiot," I said, with more than a little sincerity.

"For the timber to burn vigorously like this means it's being fed by air, my savants," Cuvier put in, holding a handkerchief over his nose and mouth. "We still haven't found the vent that kept us from suffocating in the sarcophagus, so there's hope."

We backed away from the flames to the end of

the ancient street, where there was that small crevice at the top of a slope of rock and sand. When I put my face to it I got some grit from wind being sucked by the fire. The breeze was rushing through as the fire sucked, pushing the worst of the smoke toward our enemies.

"Help me dig! Maybe there's still a way out."

We threw sand like terriers. The crevice widened, more air pouring through, as behind the fire ate timbers that hadn't seen a drop of rain for seven centuries. This new hole was another lava tube, I saw, or perhaps a continuation of the one we'd already negotiated, this time just wide enough to crawl into. Ahead was complete blackness, with no clue if the geologic pipe would continue as a pathway or shrink to something we couldn't squeeze through. I took stock. Our stub of candle had blown out and our torches were too long for such a confined crawl. The only light we had was coming from Fulton's fire.

"I've no idea if we can get through here."

Then there was a roar and the ceiling back toward our attackers came down with a crash and an eruption of dust, thousands of tons of dirt snuffing out much of the fire and burying many of the rooms we'd just been in. They were lost forever, unless someone figured a way to dig down from above. The tunnel and the shaft that led toward the surface were plugged, separating us from any pursuit. Had it buried our enemies?

"It's not like we have a choice," said Cuvier. "Lead the way, Ethan, in the dark."

"What about the candle then?"

"I'll hold it in my teeth until we get to the place we most desperately need it."

"Don't leave your weapons. I've got a feeling we might need them, too."

"Given our luck so far, I wouldn't be surprised."

So we crawled. The tunnel was rough basalt, just wide enough for our shoulders. I took the lead, the others coming as best they could. I shifted the parchment and rapier onto my back, to protect them as much as possible from scraping, while using my longrifle to probe ahead for obstacles and falls. I hated the clang and clack that I knew was scuffing my armaments even more. No fine lady would be impressed.

The only encouragement was the breeze that blew around us, coming from somewhere ahead and blowing toward the fire behind. The discouragement was how warm the tunnel was getting from the surrounding rock.

There were more crashes to our rear as timbers burned through, and the last of the light winked out as the earth slumped. We were in blackness as profound as death itself. I could hear the quiet curses of the others as they crawled behind me, and the rattle of the weapons we doggedly kept. At least Fulton had let go of his empty bagpipes.

I detest underground places. I haven't found a burrow yet that doesn't involve dirt, sweat, the occasional swim, and precious little treasure. If I ever have a proper house I think I'm going to put it on stilts to get as far from the earth as possible. Or maybe I'll live in a boat, in a tub-sized pond too small to have any waves.

Even in the dark I could feel the rock seeming to press on us as I thought about the cave-ins behind. Suddenly the floor disappeared and I reached down with my arm in the dark, tensing in case I somehow touched something that could touch back. But I felt only air. I reached ahead and the tunnel floor we were on seemed to continue across a gap of only two feet. My vision seemed pink, and I blinked a moment. There was the faintest of glows far, far below, I realized, the merest murmur of hell. Heat wafted up from the hole.

I shouted back to the others that I was going to wriggle across the gap and continue on, and warned them to be ready for it. Then I dragged myself across the void, stomach clenching, and went on.

The tunnel kept getting narrower, however, squeezing down toward my head. I scraped several times, and could feel the trickle of blood from my crown. It was getting hard to breathe, the air stale, and finally my shoulders wedged and I could go no farther. Utterly dark, no hope ahead, and as I patted with my hands I could feel nothing but enclosing rock. I probed with my rifle, which only confirmed the passage constricted still more, far too small to wriggle through. Cuvier bumped up against the soles of my boots and grunted.

"What's wrong, Ethan?"

"I'm stuck!" I couldn't get the room to even go backward. "This isn't the way out, there's no air. We have to go back to that little chasm we crawled over and go down."

"Go down? *Merde*, I'm longing to go up."

"We don't have a choice. Collapsed behind, and too narrow ahead. The only way out is descent, I think."

The others groaned, but what choice did we have? Cuvier had to drag me back a couple of feet by my ankles to free my shoulders enough to wriggle backward, and then we all inched laboriously the way we'd come, sweating and panting, our weapons occasionally catching and jamming us. Fulton's feet were now leading.

"I'm going down the demon hole!" the inventor finally announced. "At least I feel a current of air! Hot as a bellows." And so we followed, one by one, my own legs slipping into the unknown chasm and my body following. Once again, by bracing my back on one side of the shaft and my feet on the other, I could descend.

"Now I smell sulfur!" Fulton called.

"The mouth of Hades."

"Maybe we *did* suffocate in that sarcophagus."

"No, this is worse than the real hell, I think. There, we'd have the devil to guide us."

Down I went, groping for a grip, worried that I'd slip and fall on my companions. My sword and rifle were a constant trial, but I refused to leave them. Then the shaft began to pitch at an angle and we felt a floor of sorts, sloping steeply downward. We slipped down it blind, bracing with our feet, this time with me in the rear.

"It's getting hotter," Fulton reported.

"Look!" Smith said excitedly. "Is that light?"

We did see a glow. In a normal night we wouldn't have even noticed its feebleness, but after what seemed an eternity in complete darkness, it shone like a reddish beacon. Yet when we came to the source we cringed.

There was a crevice giving a view far below, and from it came the reflected glow of something red. We were very hot now, and realized we were in a venous system tied to the heart of this ancient volcano.

"Hell's front door," Cuvier muttered. "We're peering into the bowels of the earth."

"We're seeing what few men have ever seen," Smith added.

"Pray we just see it, and not feel it as well."

"We need to light the candle to take a look," Fulton said. "There's more than one way to go here."

So we balled up more lint, struck sparks—a mighty flash to our light-starved eyes—and got it burning long enough to reignite the wick of our stub. How hope flooded back from even that tendril of feeble light! We were in a junction of sorts, one crevice leading down to that eerie glow, and two tunnels going on, one level and one aimed up.

"For God's sake, let's climb," said Smith wearily.

Cuvier sniffed. "No. This middle one has the breeze of air. We must take it."

He blew out the wick on our precious candle, put it in his mouth once more, and this time took the lead by crawling on.

How long we spent in Hades I can't really say. It seemed like forever, though was probably only hours. My hands were raw, my mouth cotton, and my clothes in shreds. On and on we crawled, blind mice, hope kept alive only by the whisper of air.

Almost imperceptibly, however, the tunnel began rising again. In places we squeezed through like corks in a bottle, and in others our arms thrashed out into voids we couldn't tell the extent of. Our fear was that we might pitch headlong into some new chasm, but that didn't happen, either. And at length we finally heard noise ahead, like wind blowing through trees.

"Is that a machine?" Fulton asked.

"The sea," said Cuvier. "We're coming to a sea cave, I think. I see a glow, if I haven't gone crazy."

"I'm not a good swimmer," warned Smith.

"At this point, drowning is preferable."

For the last two hundred meters we could hear the echo of rolling waves, and a slow blue light grew like a turquoise dawn. And then at last the tunnel opened up and we came into a high domed cave, illuminated from below by the glow of water and from above by a crevice in the ceiling. It was from there that the air we'd been breathing since the sarcophagus presumably came. A pale dawn glowed through the crack. Its opening was unobtainable, however, thirty feet overhead in a vaulted roof we had no way of climbing. Beneath it was a pool from the sea, the water breathing in and out like a sleeping giant. We splashed in the salty coolness, but it was only momentary relief. We were all very thirsty.

"How can we get up there?" I asked.

"We could shout for help," said Smith.

"Shout? They're as apt to shoot us as send a rope down."

"We've come all this way to be stuck in a pot?"

"It's too bright in here for that crack of light alone," I said. "Look—you can see more light at the far side of this pool. The open Mediterranean is just beyond this grotto, lads, and all we've got to do is swim through the underwater part and pop out the other side."

"How far is it?" asked Smith.

"Well, I don't know."

"Maybe we should just shout for help," he tried again.

"No. Look—dawn is coming, it's getting brighter. We need to be out and hidden before our pursuers see us. I'll swim first. If I don't come back, I'll either have succeeded or drowned."

"Well, there's reassurance!"

"Drown there or die of thirst and hunger here," I said, and shrugged. I'd faced this dilemma before. "Let's go while we have strength left to die swiftly." And so I dove.

It was probably a dunking of only about fifteen or twenty meters, but it seems twice that when you don't know. My rifle was an anchor, the sea dark, and the wave surge pushed me backward. But I held my breath, swam with all my might, and finally saw the surface silver from the sky beyond. I broke clean in a wave-churned inlet at the base of red lava cliffs. Air! I grasped a rock, floating and gasping, and at length Cuvier and Fulton popped up, too.

"Smith's hesitant. Doesn't like the water much, for an Englishman."

"Here, hold my rifle. I'm rested now." So I swam back through the cave to the grotto, the distance seeming a fraction of what it had been before, and took his blunderbuss from him. "It's just like being born," I coaxed. "The whole world is on the other side." I led the awkward geologist to the edge of the grotto, taught him to take deep breaths, and then we dunked and swam through, me leading him by the arm, and coming up just as the sky was pinking to our left, which must be east. Smith blew like a whale and coughed. I glanced around. From the direction of the sunrise, we'd come out somewhere on Thira's southern coast.

"Now what?" asked Fulton. "We can't even climb up."

"We go home," Cuvier said. "Look—isn't that our ship?"

CHAPTER 17

Dragut's xebec appeared to be anchored in a most unlikely place, off the steep unprotected stretch of Thira's southern shore. Had our luck finally turned? The vessel was quiet, the sun just breaking the rim of the sea, and no one spotted us as we swam the hundred meters to its bobbing hull. Fulton cupped his mouth to shout, but I instinctively cautioned him. I wanted to get on board first, with our weapons.

I caught the anchor line, wrapped my feet and hands around it, and pulled myself up to the bow. The crew was curled amidships, asleep, and the lone watchman, our helmsman, was focused primarily on getting seeds out of a pomegranate. At a signal my companions followed me up. I handed Fulton my soaked longrifle, pulled out my nicked and blunted rapier, and whispered to Smith and Cuvier to brandish their weapons. I trusted no one at this point. Then we lightly ran for the wheel, the helmsman turning just in time to find the tip of my weapon at his eye. The other Muhammadans came awake when we stood over them. Dragut instinctively reached for a pistol. As my sword dipped to stay his hand, he stopped, looking at us in confusion. We stood like a cluster of half-drowned rats, dripping, filthy, torn, and menacing, Fulton holding my rifle, Smith his blunderbuss, and Cuvier his dueling pistols. The fact that none of our wet guns would fire did not immediately register.

"You come out of the sea?" our captain managed.

"Aye," I said. "It's been a long night. And we're in a bit of a hurry."

"But I don't understand. Wasn't I to pick you up back at the quay, on the other side of the island? Why are you here, with weapons drawn?"

I looked about. "Here's a better question: Why are you anchored here in the open sea, away from any sheltered harbor?"

Dragut looked to the shore, as if an answer might be found there. "The weather was calm, so we anchored for the night to wait for the morning's breeze," he finally said. "If you were a sailor, you would understand." He blinked. "But where did you come from?"

"We've been poking about. We need to get back to Venice as soon as possible. Can you take us there?"

"Ah, then you have found what you were looking for?" He sat up eagerly, his eyes flicking from one to the other of us, looking for some sign of treasure. The man was a mercenary like me.

"We hope."

Now he seemed to gain more certainty. "Then of course. Abdul! Constantine! Up, up, come you lazy dogs, let us raise the anchor for our passengers!" He glanced to the shore again. "There is no time to lose!" He looked back to me. "But why do you hold your sword on your friend Hamidou?"

"Greece makes me nervous."

"You are under Dragut's protection now! Come, come, take your ease, have some dates and wine. Get out of your sodden clothes! You look exhausted. You can sleep in the sun."

"There're some ships on the other side of the island we should avoid, I think."

"And no one is swifter and more elusive than Hamidou! Come, put your weapons away, get some rest, and then you can tell me your adventures! Out of the sea. Ha!"

I had my sodden shirt half off before I remembered the parchment pasted by seawater onto my back. I hesitated about showing it, but there was no privacy aboard and if I was to salvage anything I had to dry my artifact out. Cuvier peeled it off my skin and we examined the old document. The writing had smeared, but was still legible. Dragut glanced our way as we uncurled it, but made no comment. The anchor came up, the sails filled, and we began to move.

Our captain had turned to watch the cliffs of the island.

"What are you looking for?" I asked.

"Shepherds who might betray our direction for

a coin." He snapped an order and a long red-and-green pennant was raised, unfurling and flapping in the wind.

"What's that?"

"A flag of the Barbary pirates. It will confuse anyone ashore about our purpose." And indeed, now I did see men, waving or shaking their fists as we gathered headway. "They will be confused by my cleverness. No captain is smarter than Hamidou Dragut! None swifter! Or more quiet! Yes, you are lucky that you are paying me."

I watched uneasily. "Are those the men pursuing us?"

"Who knows? Now they will report to their superiors, perhaps. But report the wrong thing, no?"

I didn't trust Dragut or anyone else, but the idea of getting away from Thira seemed a good one. His crew certainly seemed cheered by the idea.

So we staked our prize on the deck to dry, determined to keep an eye on it. I had some food, famished enough to gobble, and resolved to stand sentry while the others slept.

When I woke, it was dark again. I'd slept the entire day away.

A moon was up, lighting the sea, and the tops of the waves were silver. It was still warm, pleasantly so, and the rigging creaked as the xebec cut through the sea. I looked at the horizon but land had fallen away in all directions. I felt for the parchment. To my relief it was where I'd left it, so I rolled it into my ragged jacket. Then I drank to slake my thirst and crawled over my companions to find Dragut.

Our captain was standing by the bowsprit, studying the stars. I'm a poor celestial navigator and admire people who can make sense of the spangle.

"Where are we?" I asked quietly.

He turned, the whites of his eyes the most visible thing in his dark face. "On our way home," he said. "Look—the sea is as soft as a mother this night. The sail is billowed like a breast, and the moon is milk. A good sign, I think."

"Of what?"

"That we are all finding what we're looking for. You're a man who is always searching, no?"

"It seems so. And others always seem to be searching for me."

"Yes, in Venice and the island. Why is that?"

I shook my head. "I know nothing worth knowing."

Now a flash of teeth. "Yet you *have* things worth knowing, perhaps? Yes, I have seen your parchment, and noticed your urgency of escape. What is so important about it?"

"I don't know. I haven't read it. I don't even know if I *can* read it."

"Which is why you swim to my ship and climb aboard, sword unsheathed, guns displayed, wet and bloody? Well, I am a simple sailor, grateful for a calm night. Go get more rest, American, and tell me someday if our little adventure was worth it."

◘   ◘   ◘

Cuvier helped me decipher the parchment the next day. It was medieval Latin, as might be expected from a Templar document, and badly aged and smudged. Hamidou gave us paper and pen to write down our translation. I feared the sea-water had ruined it, but we made out just enough to come to a disappointing conclusion.

"This has nothing to do with Atlantis, ancient weapons, or Archimedes," the French savant murmured.

It in fact appeared to be an account of a Roman Catholic monk's pilgrimage to the Holy Land, as well as a series of standard prayers from the Roman church. There was nothing about secrets, Knights Templar, or underground tunnels.

"Perhaps it's a code," I suggested. "I seem to stumble across them all the time."

"Hail Mary is a code?" Cuvier replied. "I'm afraid, Ethan Gage, that you led us through the gate of Hades for a book of prayer." He gave me back the parchment. "Of interest to historians and theologians, perhaps, but no more remarkable than a hymnal."

I turned the parchment sideways and upside down, inspected the back, and held it up to the sun. Nothing. "But why would they seal this in plaster?" I asked in frustration. "That portion of the wall was newer, I'm certain of it!"

"Perhaps to reinforce their mud. There may have been something of *real* value down there they had removed and were patching. It was an interesting rumor, but we've investigated it and found nothing. *Fini!* That's how science works—the experiments that do not succeed are often as important as those that do. We've discharged our obligation to Napoleon and escaped with our lives, which itself is a miracle. Now we go home."

Empty-handed again! By the beard of the dwarf, I hate underground places. People dig them to squirrel away things all the time, but I rarely seem to emerge with anything valuable. Nor had I discovered anything on Thira that provided a clue to the fate of Astiza, which I'd been hoping for, given Osiris's wager in Paris. The entire expedition had proved pointless. All four of us were disappointed.

Fulton grew bored when Cuvier started translating the Apostles' Creed, and instead stood at the stern, looking about at the sea and then curiously at the sun. "What time do you think it is?" he finally asked us.

"Midmorning."

"And the sun rises in the east, does it not?"

"I'm hardly certain of anything anymore, but I'll hazard that," I said.

"And so our solar orb should be on our starboard side as we sail north, should it not? To our right?"

"Aye."

"Which by my reckoning means we are sailing due *south*, directly away from Venice instead of toward it."

We leaped up. "What?"

"I think our doughty captain is going entirely the wrong way."

"Hamidou!" I called to the bow. "Which way are we going?"

"Home, I told you!" he called cheerfully.

"Whose home? You've got us pointed south, you idiot! Don't you have a compass?"

Dragut looked at the sky in amazement and then shouted at one of his crewmen. An argument broke out. Finally, with a push, the man was driven to scamper up the mast like a monkey, bare feet climbing on the rings that held the sail, to scan the horizon as if looking for an alternate sun. No new course was set. He released a cord and a narrow white banner unfurled to wave in the breeze. What was that for? At last the man pointed excitedly and began shouting in Arabic. Then a chorus of shouts went up from all the crew, and they stood on the gunwales to peer at the horizon.

"What's going on?" Smith asked.

Dragut pointed off our bow and stern. "Pirates." And indeed, we now noticed dark sails cresting the horizon. "Many men, I think, very dangerous."

"What? Where the devil have you brought us?"

"Wait, I put about." He snapped orders and the helmsman turned, but then another crewman shouted and the wheel spun back. An argument broke out. The bow slid into the teeth of the breeze, and sails began to luff, and we coasted to a stop, wallowing in the waves. Now the crew was shouting at each other even more, while breaking out guns, swords, and pikes. Meanwhile we drifted, rigging creaking and banging.

My companions and I looked at each other, hope evaporating like dew.

"Look to your guns," I said resignedly.

Enemy sail were bearing down on us like boulders accelerating downhill.

Our own weapons had been dried and cleaned that morning and so we loaded, even as our crew seemed impossibly clumsy at swinging the booms and turning the rudder to get out of irons. At the time we needed them most they'd panicked into incompetence!

"I thought you were the best sailor in the Mediterranean!"

"It seems I am cursed by an incompetent crew," Dragut muttered.

"I thought you had fooled them with your Barbary banner!"

He looked aloft. "Maybe we still can."

"Do you think that's the bunch that was after us at Thira?" Fulton asked.

"How would they know to chase us here?" Smith said.

"My friends, I think it is wisest if we surrender," Dragut suddenly counseled. "They are drawing within artillery range, and we have no long-range guns to reply. My ship is swift and light, but it is small and can't stand up to a pounding."

"I thought you could outsail any ship out here!"

"Not a Barbary corsair. We're a Muslim crew. Perhaps they will have mercy?"

"But we're not Muslim! We're Christian! We'll be enslaved!"

"True. But we can save your lives. Thus does Hamidou look after his passengers!"

Smoke bloomed from the hull of one of the corsairs, there was a shriek of shot, and a waterspout erupted where a cannon ball dropped, just fifty yards off our stern. My heart began to hammer.

The trouble with sea fights is that there's nowhere to hide.

"No," Cuvier declared, looking more like a determined grenadier than a zoologist. "We're going to fight. Beasts of prey look for easy victims. So do bullies. But scratch the lion and he'll back off looking for easier meat. Let's crouch beneath the bulwark, wait until they draw near, and then give a broadside with your light guns and our arms. It will throw them into confusion. If we can cut up their rigging, maybe we can escape."

"You're willing to risk your life?" Dragut asked.

"I'd rather sell it here than in a slave market."

"You are mad, Christians. But very brave, too. All right." He snapped orders to his crewmen. "You Europeans take your place just by the bulwark there, where the protection is best. We will ready behind you, with matches for the cannon. I'll watch for the precise moment and we will rise as one and fire! Every shot must hit to throw them into disorder. Then you must help us with the lines to draw off and escape."

Ever notice how organizers put followers in the front rank, and them behind? But it didn't seem the time to argue choreography. The pirate corsairs were coming on fast, lateen-sailed vessels larger than the xebec but just as swiftly built, and crammed with men. As we crouched I could peek through a hawser hole at the mob of them, stripped to the waist except for earrings and armlets of gold. Some were bearded and turbaned. Others were shaved bald, muscles bulging, painted with tattoos or decorated with great mustaches. All of them were roaring and clashing steel for our maximum demoralization. Were these the ships I'd seen at Thira? The animal smell of them came across the water, plus oil and spices, the smell of Africa.

"Hold your fire until the last moment," Dragut counseled. "Remember, we get only one volley! We must wait until they are close as possible!"

"Damnation," Smith muttered. "I felt less confined in a canal ditch."

"Your blunderbuss will give them pause," I encouraged. "Georges, fire both your pistols at once. Fulton, you've lost your pipes. Do you need a gun?"

"I've got an ax to cut their boarding lines," he said. "And maybe we can swing the boom to knock some of them back. A pendulum can accumulate tremendous power."

"Just what Archimedes would advise." I turned back to Hamidou. "Ready when you are!"

He nodded encouragingly and laid his cutlass on the flat of his hand.

The nearest corsair loomed to fill all my view, its sails almost black, its crew balanced on the railing, twitchy as colts.

"Steady," I murmured. I'd already picked a target for my longrifle, a big brute of a pirate who looked to be their captain. Then, because of the time it took to reload, I'd slash at any boarders with my rapier. We'd sting like a scorpion. "When you give the word, Dragut." I tensed, ready to rise and fire.

It was then that I felt the annoyingly familiar press of a gun barrel at the nape of my neck. "And the word is 'surrender,' Ethan Gage," he said cheerfully. I realized I'd never told him my whole name and yet he knew it, the devious bastard. "Take your finger from your trigger, please, and lower your longrifle to the deck, so that I do not have to shatter your spine."

I glanced sideways. My companions also had guns to their heads, held by our own crewmen. We'd been betrayed, from beginning to end! Had the Venetian gondoliers simply been herding us to this treacherous vessel from the start? Our arms thumped on the deck.

Then there was a crash of wood as the two ships mated, and a shout as a rank of half-naked, unwashed pirates poured across, their bare feet lighting like cats. In seconds we were yanked backward, our arms wrenched and our feet bound.

Dragut looked at me with amazement. "You didn't get off even a single shot. I expected more from the hero of Acre and Mortefontaine."

"When I finally do, I'll aim at you."

"Alas, I think the time for that is past."

"What base treachery is this?" cried Smith.

"I believe, gentlemen, that we have once more been led into a trap by our esteemed guide, Ethan Gage," said Cuvier.

"But why not just seize us yourselves back at Thira?" I asked our captain.

"It was you who had the rapier to my eye, not vice versa. We didn't really expect you to escape from the island."

"And because I wanted the pleasure of seizing you myself!" cried a new voice. A lithe new pirate swung on a line from the enemy poop and lightly landed on ours, this one beardless and dressed in sea boots, greatcoat, and bloused trousers that were a century back in style, as braided and gaudy as a Caribbean buccaneer's. The newcomer wore a magnificent broad-brimmed plumed hat and held a jeweled sword in a fine-fingered hand. A broken, ominously broken second sword was tucked in a wide leather belt, along with twin pistols. As the buccaneer hopped down to the xebec's main deck, some of the other scoundrels flinched as they made room, and we soon saw why. With a leap a black hound cleared the gap between the two vessels and followed his master onto our deck, landing with a heavy thump with feet skittering for new purchase. This muscular beast was a short-haired, thick-snouted mastiff, ugly with slobber and hanging jowls, a dog that bristled at the sight of us and growled with the purr of Hell's Cerberus. Its eyes were yellow, its flanks scarred, its tail chewed, and the whole package was uglier than the fleas that inhabited it.

The owner plucked off the feathered headgear and gave a sweeping bow.

A torrent of auburn ringlets cascaded down around our captor's shoulders—a woman!—and she gave a seductive smile I remembered all too well, even as my heart fell like a barometer in a hurricane. "I told you we weren't through, Ethan."

I gaped in shock, revulsion, and fear, frozen by that still-beautiful face, that athletically graceful figure, those long, white fingers holding a blade that sparkled silver. How vividly did I now remember the broken sword tucked in her belt, which her brother had shattered on my longrifle. She was as bewitching as I remembered, too: the high cheekbones, the feline gaze, the wicked dance of her eyes. It was Aurora Somerset, the English aristocrat who had tupped and tormented me on the North American frontier.

"Aurora?" was all I could manage, stupidly.

My companions looked at us curiously.

"I've joined the Barbary pirates," she said, as if that weren't obvious enough. "I thought it would bring us together."

PART TWO

Aurora Somerset was one of the loveliest women I'd ever met. She was also one of the most dangerous, the most perverted, and the most insane, a murderess who killed my Indian lover, Namida, tried to slay my voyageur friend, Pierre, and left me alive in the North American wilderness only because she wanted to follow me to new secrets.

As threatened, here she was, fully recovered from her trauma and apparently in charge of an ill-tempered dog and several shiploads of feral pirates, most of them pledged to a religion that dictated women stay subservient and out of sight. Well, nobody is consistent.

My companions were merely dumbfounded. I knew enough to be terrified.

I'd met Aurora on my journey west to seek Norse artifacts with the late Magnus Bloodhammer. I was predictably blinded by her beauty and made a fool of myself, as men are wont to do. The upshot was my capture, near torture, escape into the wild, and final showdown in which I killed the man who was both Aurora's half brother and her lover, Lord Cecil Somerset. She and I did our best to kill each other, too, but in the end I was wounded and she was insane, and the only solace I had from that nightmare was the likelihood that the wilderness would swallow her up and I'd never see her again.

Time and distance had let me believe that.

Now, as inexorably persistent as the Rite itself, she was back.

One might expect trauma to rob her of her prettiness and harden her features. Instead, she was as physically alluring as ever, an ocean goddess of tumbling hair, green eyes, pursed lips, and a cleanliness out of all proportion to her environment: Venus, emerging from the sea. Had she been primping before she swung aboard? There was an eerie changelessness about her that made me suspect some pact with the devil, so perfect was her skin, so athletic her grace as she whirled on deck, so bright her maniacal eyes. She was immortal, I feared, an Antaeus who only grew stronger with every defeat.

Aurora Somerset was the reason I'd reformed.

"I thought you'd tired of me," I managed. She'd had nearly a year to dream up fresh torments, and Lord knows the girl had a better imagination than I did. I felt sick at what this reunion would lead to.

She walked to me, cutlass lifted like a serpent's silver tongue to hover under my chin as the ship rolled in the waves, her lips curled in a twist of faint contempt, her eyes intense as a jaguar's, while her dog eyed me for breakfast. "You're a hard man to forget, Ethan Gage. So durable. So ruthless. So careless. So stupid. I've been following you, anticipating you, marveling at you, and got that signet ring I discovered into the hands of the French and Fouché with the expectation they would turn to the wayward American to determine what it means. You are ever so predictable! Well, you can give the ring back. And now you've brought company!" Her eyes danced with calculation as she eyed my savants, and I didn't know if she was dreaming of bedding them or torturing them. Probably both. "You read something in North America that brought you to Thira, and now you've found something, I'm betting, that I and my allies are looking for."

"Allies? *You* have friends?"

I'd managed to annoy her. "More than you know."

"You must mean the lunatic Egyptian Rite."

"That, and the Tripoli corsairs, our newest comrades. Their bashaw saw the advantage of ancient secrets long before Bonaparte and Fouché." She nodded to the assembly of pirates, as motley a bunch of thieves and miscreants as can be found outside a parliament. They had the hygiene of sewer rats and the disposition of a wounded bull, but then I'm used to bad company. She turned to Dragut. "What did they find?"

"A manuscript, my lady." So our captain had been in her employ from the beginning: ready to pluck us from pursuit in Venice and from caves at Thira. This rendezvous had been planned for months. Why get dirty when Ethan Gage will crawl through the mouth of Hades for you?

"A manuscript? What does it say?"

"I wouldn't presume to read it before you." He pointed. "The American has it."

"Where is it?" she demanded of me. "Give it up!"

"Your manners haven't improved since our last time together."

"Or your impudence! Come, turn it over! The ring, too!"

Her monster of a dog started barking with the volume of a wolf pack, and I flinched despite myself. Why do people insist on bringing along their pets? I considered trying to hurl the parchment into the sea, but given what it said, what was the harm? "Here: What you've followed me for seven thousand miles for. It might improve you."

There is something to be said for the upbringing of the high bred. She was, it seemed, literate in Latin. Apparently young ladies of the English nobility learn more than just shooting and sadism. She read for a moment, her pirates shuffling like a restless classroom, and then looked at me in disbelief. "Are you trying to make me a fool?"

"That's all we found, Aurora. Dig down yourself if you don't believe me, but the ancient rooms under Akrotiri were as empty as a beggar's stomach. Except for this. I hoped it was a treasure, too—this is hardly what I came for—but I could have saved myself the trouble by simply buying a preacher's pamphlet outside the Palais Royal. If there was ever anything of value down there, I sus-

pect Knights Templar took it centuries ago. We're
both chasing ghosts."

She stood a moment, debating whether to believe me. Finally she threw the parchment at my
feet. I picked it up. It was, I supposed, a souvenir
of Thira. She kept the ring. "Very well. And, yes, a
wasted trip for you and your friends, but not necessarily for me." She turned to her shipmates. "We'll
sell them as slaves!"

To that they gave a hearty cheer, which meant
they got a share from hocking us. Everybody loves
a profit.

"Where's his gun?" she then asked. There
was some discomfort among Dragut's men as my
longrifle—the same one that had killed Cecil
Somerset—was brought out. "That weapon is
mine," she snapped. "You can have the others."

"It's scuffed and nicked but a fine piece," one of
the pirates objected. "It's ours to take, not yours,
under Barbary law."

"It slew my brother. Give it over."

The sailor, with the scars of more than a few
fights, wasn't about to buckle easily to this woman's whim. He turned to his captain. "Hamidou,
we captured them! She has no right!"

Dragut was shaking his head.

And as the poor sailor turned back in anger, debating just how truculent to be, Aurora's monster
dog sprang. It was a blur of black, snarling like a
lion, and the man was down yelling as the dog bit his
hands and face, pinning him with furious weight.
The rifle skittered away but no one dared touch it;

the other pirates instinctively jumped back. The poor victim writhed, his thrashing arm trying to get to his knife while the other hand clawed at the dog's face, but then the hound got past his guard and plunged his snout at the poor devil's throat. Its big black head thrashed as if it had been given a rag doll, and blood from a severed artery made a jet that shot three feet in the air. Men were at once shouting, pleading, betting, and laughing, ill-bred ruffians that they were.

The pirate twitched and jerked a final time, and died. A red pool spread like a blot.

"Sokar, heel!"

The mastiff backed off, jaws foamy with blood and saliva. It was growling, looking at me with its yellow eyes.

Trembling slightly, Dragut stooped to pick up my rifle and gave it to the demented woman. "His weapon, my lady."

She hefted it with the same air of possessive ownership I remembered from America, ignoring the baleful looks of the dead man's friends. "We set course for Tripoli," she told Dragut. And then back to me. "We'll talk again, after you've time to ponder your situation while locked in the hold. And if you don't renew our partnership, then Omar the Dungeon Master will make sure that this time, now that I truly own you, you'll not hold anything back."

"Omar the what?"

"He's one whose name is best not spoken aloud," Dragut said, and shoved me toward the xebec's shallow hold. "Or ever experienced."

He turned to the others. "The blunderbuss and dueling pistols are mine!"

◻   ◻   ◻

I and my three companions were hurled from our pampered position in the stern down into the sail and water locker amidships. Our bed became hemp sails, and our furniture the water casks lashed atop the greasy bilge. The only light checkered down from the wooden grating overhead. Our momentarily helpless xebec swiftly got under way, the lean and the rush of water announcing we were on the way to Tripoli. The afternoon sun soon turned our cell into a stuffy oven. We'd gone from seeming triumph to certain doom.

Piracy and slavery might seem an odd base for an economy, but in fact have worked so well for the Barbary States (so-named for the barbarians who occupied North Africa after the fall of the Roman Empire) that they've had little incentive to develop anything else. Why work when you can steal with impunity? By raiding the weakest fringes of the Mediterranean Basin, the Barbary corsairs keep city-states like Tripoli supplied with cheap male labor and pretty harem women. Their richest captives can be ransomed off to buy whatever else is needed. The ships and towns of the most powerful nations such as Britain, France, and Spain are avoided out of wary fear: in 1675, the English admiral Norborough had burned Tripoli's fleet as a warning. Weaker nations, however, find it more cost-effective to pay tribute than to try to catch the swift corsairs or assault their heavily fortified African cities. That tribute is not just money, but ships, cannon, and powder that turn North African ports into bristling hedgehogs of defiance. Cuvier might hope for ransom from the French government that had elevated him, but Smith, Fulton, and I had neither rich families nor high rank. That meant we were almost certain to die manacled: overworked, underfed, and rotten with disease.

I explained all this as gently as I could.

"What if we defy them?" Fulton sought to clarify.

"Their favorite discipline is the bastinado, where they tie the ankles, hoist up the feet, and flail them with two hundred strokes. Some slaves are crippled for life. If the beating is severe enough to render a man useless, he's suspended from hooks on the city walls to die of exposure. Then the pirates sail out to capture more."

"There's no mercy?"

"Sometimes you can gain better treatment by conversion to Islam, a cultural surrender called 'taking the turban.' "

"Then give me a Koran to swear to!"

"Unfortunately, you have to prove your submission through circumcision."

Fulton studied me to see if I was joking, which I was not. "Every time I think you can't make things any worse, your leadership becomes even more incompetent," he finally said.

"All is not entirely lost." I was, I suppose, our morale officer.

"What do you mean?"

"We have the American navy on our side."

I crawled to the grating and stood as upright as I could in our cramped chamber, my face checkered by the light shining down. "Hamidou, I must give you warning!" I called.

The captain came over to stand on the grate, casting a shadow. "Silence, slave, before I cut off your tongue and more besides!" He was not at all the jolly skipper who'd sailed us down the Adriatic, and once again I remembered that I needed to modify my habitually optimistic appraisal of people. I noticed he'd tucked Cuvier's dueling pistols in his belt, and no doubt was polishing Smith's blunderbuss as well.

"The United States has sent a naval squadron in response to Yussef Karamanli's declaration of war!" I warned. "Robert and I are American citizens. If you're caught with us aboard, it could mean the gallows or worse. I'm only trying to warn you!"

He laughed. "So you think I should let you go?"

"It might be best for you as well as us. We could put in a good word."

He pretended to consider. "No. If an American frigate could catch me, which it can't, I will throw you Americans to the sharks, cut out the tongues of the two other infidels, and swear that Yankees were never aboard. This is more satisfying, I think."

"Hamidou, we put our trust in you!"

"Yes. Better to trust in *me* than your own navy. Your ships draw too much water to get close to the shoals of Tripoli, and we slip in and out of your blockade like laces through a corset. Accordingly, the new commander, Morris, has abandoned the attempt and is hiding behind Britain's skirts in Malta. Your squadron is already a failure, Gage, and all of Barbary is laughing at the United States—and soon, they will laugh at you as well! Allah rewards the faithful, and punishes the coward, as you can now see. Do not waste your time threatening me! Try to think of something useful to say to lessen your torment from Omar the Dungeon Master!" He translated our conversation for his crew, with enough editing to provide hearty comedy.

Why the prospect of my torture arouses such amusement I've never understood, but it seems a universal reaction among my enemies. I am, as I've said, affable—except when I have to shoot particularly horrid people—and don't, in my opinion, deserve the rejoicing that always seems to accompany my capture.

"That didn't seem to work," I reported to the others unnecessarily, since they'd heard every word.

"We weren't exactly counting on you," assured Smith.

I took out the parchment I'd kept after Aurora threw it back. "This book of prayer hasn't reformed these Muhammadans in the slightest." I held it under the grating to look at its Latin script again, still puzzled why anyone would conceal it in the wall of buried ruins a hundred feet underground. Had I missed some kind of code, of the kind we'd deciphered amid the Dakota Indians in distant North America?

The dimness of the hold and pocks of light forced me to peer even more intently at what seemed a worthless old scrap of animal skin. It was then that

I detected the faintest of curved lines like a whisper beneath the Latin script. Moving the parchment beneath the grating, I began to notice other tracings, almost invisible if you blinked.

"Cuvier, could you take a look at this? I think there's something more to this parchment."

The French savant sighed, heaved himself up from where he had slumped between the barrels, and crouch-walked to join me under the grating. Following my finger, he squinted at the script, bored at first, but then more intent. He took the scrap in his own hands and held it this way and that under the light.

Finally he pulled me away and whispered in the shadows. "I think it's a palimpsest."

"Thank God for that. A what?"

"In the Middle Ages, writing material was in short supply and parchment durable. To reuse it, they'd scrape off the old writing and copy some new text over it. Perhaps what the Knights meant to leave was not this list of prayers, but whatever was first under them."

I began to have a glimmer of hope. Knowledge is power, and we'd need all the power we could muster against Aurora and her pirates. I scratched with my nail at the parchment, smearing some ink. "Then how can we get the new writing off?"

Cuvier stayed my hand. "Let me think for a moment." He exhibited that look of pursed concentration that made him look so smart. Then he turned to the others. "Gentlemen, biology teaches that we must breach a water cask so we can drink all we can hold."

"Why?" asked Smith.

"Because we have to do our very best to urinate on Ethan's discovery."

◻   ◻   ◻

Slave masters aren't in the habit of letting their captives drink their fill of anything, so we had to take matters into our own hands, or feet. We had no way to open the cask bungs, given that we'd been robbed of tools, but Fulton felt in the gloom until he found a water keg wet from slight leakage. He had us quietly shift its companions until we could bring the barrel out. "If three of us stand on top and push off the deck beams above, we might be able to compress the staves to the point that they leak. The fourth can catch the flow."

"Catch it with what?" I asked.

"I suggest our boots," said Smith. "I had to bail a leaky canal boat once and found my footwear quite adequate for the purpose."

"I can hardly bear to put my feet in my shoes, let alone drink from them."

"Then we can forgo the experiment and spend the rest of our short lives in slavery and torture."

"You have a point. Bottoms up."

We balanced on the barrel, pressed down, forced a leak, collected the overflow in each of our boots—we weren't friends enough to share, trust me—and drank as much as we could. It was satisfying to steal from Dragut, even if it was only water. We drank until we were bloated and could make our own water, a time-consuming task in the heat.

"Whose shoe should catch the piss?" Fulton asked.

"Ethan's, of course," Smith replied.

"Wait," I objected, "why not yours?"

"Because I didn't concoct this expedition. Besides, you're the one who found a palimpsest."

I did persuade them to take a vote but it went unanimously against me, so our production of urine was collected in my footwear, my companions taking great satisfaction in draining their bladders there. Then we began to scrub the parchment with urine, slowly sloughing the medieval ink away to reveal whatever was underneath.

It was a map, I saw, with a cross-hatching of lines and symbols atop a chart that looked like the outline of a coast. A bay with a narrow neck was shown, and an arcing line like a fence or boundary crossed the interior. The Templars, or whoever had plastered that wall, had left not a book of prayer but a guide to something, or somewhere. Just possibly it had something to do with this ancient weapon—this heat ray of Archimedes—that we'd seen painted. Unfortunately, there were no words on the map, giving no indication what it depicted. I'd produced a urine-soaked treasure map of a place we couldn't identify.

"Why are there no words?" Fulton asked.

"It's for men who already know where they're going," said Cuvier.

Smith studied it in the dim light. "It looks familiar, somehow."

"You're our map man, Smith."

"I'd say volcanic terrain, by the look of the coast-line, but that bay could be anywhere."

"Not Thira," said Cuvier. "There are no bays like that."

"I think you've actually found something, Gage," Fulton said. "Decipher it, man!"

"I'm fairly certain those lines and numbers mean something."

"Yes?"

"Unfortunately, I'm quite poor at puzzles. I really shouldn't be a treasure hunter at all."

And then a shadow fell on the grating. "Gage! Aurora will see you now!"

CHAPTER 19

I've been known to positively scamper to the side of an inviting woman, but I left our dank hold in dread at the thought of conversing with Lady Somerset. Beauty she might be, but I still bore the calf scar where she'd stabbed me with an Indian spear. Her new pet looked ready to chew on my other shank, and I was in no mood for witty repartee about our past. Nonetheless, her flagship was tacking to pick me up, and apparently I was expected to leap aboard with lusty panache. But Dragut took one whiff of me and yanked me back to wash. "By Allah, did you miss the bucket, or piss yourself in fear?"

"I just smell like a pirate, Hamidou."

I was stripped and doused with bracing seawater. Then I pulled my tired clothing back on, combed my hair with fingers as best I could, balanced on the rail while the two ships drew abreast of each other, and seized a line swung from a boom on Au-

rora's vessel. I did feel some pirate dash, and saw
how the trade had its attractions. But then I looked
about the flagship.

Aurora's vessel, *Isis*, was bigger than Dragut's,
with heavier artillery and a larger crew, but exhibited the housekeeping of an Ohio flatboat. Lines
were uncoiled, brass had curdled green, canvas and
crates were lashed haphazardly, and bits of food
and empty bottles rolled in the corners. Off-duty
pirates snored next to gun tackle. Chickens pecked
at grain scattered under a lashed longboat.

An American frigate would turn this to match-
wood in minutes, I decided. Too bad there wasn't
one about.

"I know it's not your habit to eat pork, but have
you thought of keeping pigs?" I addressed my captors. "You've already built a marvelous sty."

"Silence, slave!" I got lashed across the shoulders
for my wit, and then a pock-faced bosun shoved me
to the door of the stern cabin, guarded by flanking blacks with the muscled bulk of buffaloes. The
sentries were haughty as Mamelukes, and regarded
me with disdain bordering on disbelief. They must
have thought their mistress could attract better.

"Didn't have time to dress."

They wrinkled their noses, checked me for
weapons, and shoved me through.

"I'll tell you what she's like," I called back to her
goblins.

The corsair's cabin, high enough to stand upright
in, was pleasantly cool. The stern window glass was
open and a breeze filtered through grilled wooden
shutters. A Persian carpet covered the deck, and

more carpets and pillows were piled in the peripheries to provide some Oriental opulence. Aurora herself lay like Cleopatra in a hammock that swung to the rhythm of the waves. She'd shed her fighting clothes for a linen shift that did little to conceal the voluptuousness of her figure. An emerald necklace of Spanish design draped her fine neck, and the matching earrings picked up the color of her eyes. Her fingers were bright with rings, and enough bracelets, armbands, and anklets hung on her limbs to make her a candidate for an anchor, should we have an emergency. Despite my knowledge that she was a hateful harridan, her seductive allure persisted, her lips pursed as she sipped from a golden goblet. Damnation, I felt aroused. But Aurora also held a pistol, and was as different from Astiza as a cobra from a nightingale.

It didn't help that her mastiff watched me suspiciously from one corner, its growl distant thunder.

"Sokar, be quiet," Aurora ordered. Sokar, if I recalled, was another Egyptian god of the underworld. This waist-high monster fit the part of nether demon.

"The hold I threw you into is a preview of one way our new relationship can continue," she began without preamble, always the brisk dominatrix when the veil slipped. "I can assure you the dungeons of Tripoli are far worse, and the life expectancy of a Karamanli slave is shorter than that of a fleet sailor during a yellow jack plague. You never have enough food or water as a slave, it's impossible to keep clean, and your weakened body breaks out into hideous boils and pustules. Whips and canes raise welts that grow red and leak pus, and your hair falls out in clumps. Your joints ache, your teeth rot, your tongue swells, and your vision goes milky."

"Sounds like the clap after a night in bed with you."

Her goblet jerked, hand whitening, and I could tell she wasn't accustomed to candor. Any pirates who challenged her were probably at the bottom of the Mediterranean, and I suppose I risked that, too. Yet in some strange way I fascinated her. I had no idea why.

"Or, we can rule the world," she finally managed.

"Aurora, you've done well for yourself since our last meeting—I believed you entirely mad and likely to die in the North American wilderness and yet here you are, a regular admiral—but I don't think you're on the brink of ruling the world. Capturing me is not on the same level as outdueling Nelson or Napoleon."

"But capturing you is a step toward finding the mirror of Archimedes."

"That's what this is all about? The mythical toy of an eccentric old Greek?"

"That toymaker invented an early form of calculus almost two thousand years before Newton! Calculated the value of pi closer than the pharaohs! He was so excited when he discovered the principle of displacement in his bath that he cried 'Eureka!' and ran naked through the streets."

"Most famous people have a flair for publicity. I'm too modest to ever succeed."

"His mirror, if harnessed again, could incinerate any battle fleet sent against it. It would beam its death ray endlessly, never needing to be reloaded. We could pillage the merchant fleets of any nation and they'd be helpless to retaliate against us. In time we could mount the devices on ships and burn any port or fort we went against. Batteries of guns would explode. Ammunition wagons would be torn apart. Sailors and soldiers could be flung, screaming and burning, into the sea."

"Such imagination, Aurora. But all that was two millennia ago. Ancient history, eh?"

"Unless the mirror was saved and eventually stored by someone like the Templars, in a place like Thira."

"It wasn't. I checked."

"Maybe you didn't look long enough. Or maybe you know more than you admit. Come, lie beside me, Ethan." She wiggled. "It's a broad hammock."

"Actually, I've sworn off women. I think you'll understand why better than anyone."

"You begged for it once!"

"That was before you killed all my friends. And I did shoot your cousin, I believe. I mean brother. Or half brother . . . by the end, I wasn't quite sure what to believe about Cecil. All in all, we haven't had an easy time of it."

"Those people would be alive if you'd shared your mission as I asked at the beginning! We'd be partners, making the world a better place with the wisdom of the Egyptian Rite. Have you noticed, Ethan, that every time you try to do the right thing, it accomplishes the wrong thing? You have no love, no money, no home. Yet I can offer all that, and more! Tell us what you know and join a cause bigger than yourself! *Make* something of your life!"

Sokar rumbled again, just to remind me what the choice really was. Then he went back to gnawing and cracking a bone, probably from the last sailor who turned Aurora down. I walked to a small sea desk, piled with books and scrolls about ancient history, alchemy, and magic. Say what you will about the Egyptian Rite, they were certainly readers. "Aurora, I'm as useless as I always was. You saw what we discovered on Thira: a medieval prayer guide. We found old ruins as vacant as Versailles, and managed to cave in the ceiling. You're entirely right, I'm a complete failure, and you'd save yourself time and trouble by chasing someone more successful for once."

"Yet you're the one always one step ahead of us—in the pyramid, in Jerusalem, in the American frontier, and now on Thira. You want to know as fiercely as we do, Ethan!"

"And just who is this 'we'? How do you get membership in such a cabal of lunatics and scoundrels anyway? Do you have to apply? Is it a question of genealogy?"

"We are serious seekers of the past who by possession of ancient wisdom deserve to rule. We choose to defy convention, and elect to follow occult knowledge anywhere it might lead. We trade ordinary conformity for wisdom. Perfect harmony will be achieved by having everyone in the world answer to *us*. To you and me, Ethan!"

There was something odd here. Why would Aurora Somerset, English aristocrat and renegade explorer, want anything more than to pick up on the tortures where she'd left off? If I honestly possessed some useful knowledge I could see her pretending temporary interest, until she got whatever she needed and could safely slit my throat. But why suggest we had a chance of partnership? I couldn't stand the girl, and certainly she had no warmer feelings for me. She'd already seen my parchment of prayers, and didn't know yet that it might contain something of value. No, there was something else going on, some wickedness afoot I couldn't even guess at. "If there's one thing I'm poor at, it's harmony."

She was becoming impatient, her recline in the hammock no longer languorous, her eyes eclipsing from the seductive to the dangerous. "You'd rather rot as a slave?"

"Let my friends go. Then maybe I'll try to help with this mirror of yours."

"My crew has to be paid, Ethan. Your friends are a type to ransom. But you can save yourself. Think of yourself. Escape by yourself."

It was annoying she thought so little of my character that she assumed such a course would appeal to me—and even more annoying that she was half right. Here I was, single, rootless, an expatriate from my own country in the employ of another, caught up in the web of my old lover; and peeing on grubby sheepskin in hopes the latest sojourn underground wasn't entirely worthless. What did I ever do but think of myself? And yet it sounded hollow and ashen to hear it come from Aurora Somerset: the kind of craven self-preservation that came from men not yet grown up. The rare times I'd shown character and backbone I felt better for it, so maybe it was time to make it a habit. Not just to reform outwardly, but to start a construction project on my soul! Lord knows I'm good at resolutions, if not always quite as fine in carrying them out.

"But I'm not by myself, am I? I've got three good friends captive on Dragut's ship, and they're imperiled solely because of my unfortunate history with you. No, Aurora, I think I'll choose their company in that stifling hold over yours in the hammock, and enjoy it better, too. The fact is, you've captured impoverished savants, not merchant captains, and we aren't worth the trouble of a ransom note."

"Then you'll die as slaves!" She'd rolled out of her horizontal throne now and stood, trembling with frustration, her eyes green fire, and by Venus the form she cast in her linen shift would tempt a pope. I don't know how those who vow celibacy do it, frankly. The translucent gauze seemed to make her even more naked than if she wore nothing at all, and I wanted that flesh despite myself. Yet she was a devil's temptress, a fire I dared not touch.

"You'll never get Archimedes' mirror. It would be like giving a keg of gunpowder to a pyromaniac. You won't get your weapon, you won't get me, and you won't get whatever twisted goal you're after. You'll get this cabin, a crew of Muslim cutthroats, biscuit, bilgewater, and a lonely life seeking the peace you threw away."

"You know nothing!" Her dog jumped up and barked, making me jump again, and I longed for my tomahawk to play fetch with the mastiff.

"Exactly," I managed. "So sell me, drown me, or jail me, but please just let me be."

A wish that neither of us could keep, as it turned out.

CHAPTER 20

From the sea, Tripoli looked inviting as a lion's mouth. Dragut brought us up to the deck to watch our approach so that we could fully understand the futility of rescue. The heat of North Africa clawed as we neared land, the sky yellow above the desert and milk blue over the gardens and date palms that surrounded the city's walls. The forts and towers of the strongest pirate lair in the Mediterranean wavered in the heat like a bad dream. The lion's jaws were the reefs that girded the city as we approached, emerald and gold amid the darker blue of the Mediterranean, and the teeth were the cannon that jutted from embrasures in the ramparts: hundreds and hundreds of cannon, it seemed. Beneath their protection, the corsairs, xebecs, and feluccas of the Barbary pirates bobbed placidly, huddled like cubs.

I'd hoped to see the proud black frigates of my

own navy by now, given that I'd sailed back to Europe with the powerful American squadron. But any blockade was nowhere to be seen, and Dragut's taunt that the United States flotilla was hiding at Malta seemed dismayingly true. If Tripoli was truly at war with my own infant nation, it was hard to see any sign of it.

"See," said Dragut, as if reading my mind. "Your ships draw too much water to even come close."

Midday heat and sun were dazzling, adding to the hallucinatory effect of what Napoleon's savants had labeled "mirage." The land scent was of sand and spices, excrement and oranges, the wool of piled carpets and stink of drying fish. Tripoli is on a green plain that gives way to desert waste, and in the shimmering light its flat-roofed houses are whitewashed ice blocks that gleam like snow. This glacier is crevassed with winding streets so narrow and confused that they seem more like natural channels than planned thoroughfares. The city's flatness is punctuated by the bulbous domes of mosques and upright stalks of minarets, topped by conical green roofs like witches' hats. At the city's southeastern edge, near the harbor, is the squat, massive, crenellated castle of the bashaw, Yussef Karamanli. Beyond is a rocky outcrop with a fort that commands both city and sea: a fine place for a mirror.

Karamanli, Dragut told us with pride, was as ruthless a prince as Attila the Hun. "He came to power seven years ago when he drove out the pirate Ali Bourghal. Before that he murdered his brother Hassan in the palace harem, shooting off his mother's fingers when she raised her arm to try to protect her eldest son. Yussef dragged Hassan's pregnant wife off the dying body of her husband by her hair. Then he cut off Hassan's privates and threw them to his dogs."

"No wonder you joined up with him."

"And yet he is also a pious man—he wears scripture from the Koran, written in strips, wound into his turban."

"Now there's a commitment."

"When Yussef took the city from the pirate Bourghal, his other brother Hamet agreed to exile in Alexandria. However, Hamet's wife and children remain as hostages. Yussef views Hamet with contempt, and controls him by terrorizing his family. Yussef himself has two wives, a fair-skinned Turk and an ebony black."

The white Madonna and the black, I thought, remembering my adventures beneath Jerusalem with Miriam and my teachings from Astiza.

"Plus a harem of concubines. Yussef is a stallion. He also has a pet leopard, an Italian band to serenade him with music, and jewels the size of robin's eggs."

"I still can't see him winning an election."

"He doesn't have to. He is loved and feared because his rule is Allah's will. We Muslims are content with our lot because, as the Prophet said, 'It is written.' Christians are tormented because they don't really believe in fate and are always trying to change things. We faithful are happy with oppression if it is God's will. Tripoli is tranquil in tyranny."

"So you put up with a lunatic who murders his brother, wounds his mother, and drags his pregnant sister-in-law by the hair?"

"All the world pays tribute to Yussef Karamanli."

"By God, England and France don't," Smith put in.

"This is as it should be. The English and French keep other navies weak. Did not Nelson just destroy the Danish fleet at Copenhagen? We cannot fight their battleships, nor can they close in with our shallow coast. So we leave their flag alone and they leave ours alone, while allowing us to prey on the merchant ships of their commercial rivals. Shippers learn there is safety paying extra to sail under the English or French flag. Here again we see the wisdom of God, with each nation assigned to its rightful place. The only people who do not see reason are the Americans, but look—do you see their frigates? They bluster but hide."

"It was Yussef who declared war on us."

"Because your baby nation doesn't understand the way of the world and pay rightful tribute! The United States should give us what we demand. It will be far cheaper than senseless defiance. You'll see."

"I can't say we have faith in your advice, Dragut, given that you've lied, betrayed, and enslaved us."

"Ah! You are lucky that Hamidou Dragut is the one who captured you, and not a truly hard man like Murad Reis!"

"The traitor Scot?" Smith asked.

"He took the turban, but is dour and gloomy like his homeland. I will put in a word for you but he is not merciful like me, Hamidou. Murad chose valor under the Crescent over slavery under the Cross. Now he is captain of all our corsairs, renowned for his courage, cleverness, and cruelty. Every slave has that opportunity! In your backward nations, slavery is a life's torment, the work of Negroes you despise. In our enlightened nation it is but a step to wealth and even freedom for those who convert to Islam! Our Christian slaves live the life of the damned, but Muslim slaves can rise as high as their masters. Such is the wisdom of Allah."

"Not one of us will ever become a Mussulman," Cuvier vowed, "even we savants who question Scripture."

"Then you must be ransomed to bankrupt your families, or sentenced to the quarries, or given over to Omar the Dungeon Master. Are you savants not men of reason? Listen to me well: Only reason can save you now."

Cannon fired salutes as we neared the city. Aurora's flotilla answered in turn, each puff of smoke from the forts followed a second or two later by one from us, the bangs echoing across the lovely turquoise water. Swarms of dockworkers, slavers, soldiers, and veiled wives assembled on the quay as we glided between the reefs. Horns blew from the city walls and drums beat out a tattoo. Our ship tied up and great rattling chains, each set as heavy as two pails of water, were dragged aboard by starved-looking slaves and manacled around our ankles and wrists, the weight holding our arms down and our hands cupped as if we were trying to cover our privates. This forced pose was not entirely inappropriate because our clothes were ragged after the caves of Thira. Dirty, unshaven, and thin, we looked like the wretched slaves we'd become. My scientist companions gloomily surveyed the churning mob waiting to escort us to the slave markets. Reason! We had one card left, but didn't dare play it. We thought we knew the place to which the palimpsest map referred.

◘   ◘   ◘

It was Smith, with his love for geography, who'd figured it out. He told me when I'd been returned to the hold of Dragut's ship after meeting Aurora. "We had it backward, Ethan," he explained in a whisper as we made for the African coast. "This inlet here isn't a bay, it's a peninsula, as if the map is drawn in a mirror. And once I realized that, everything else became plain. I know of one harbor in this part of the world with that shaped protrusion, and it is Syracuse on Sicily, where Archimedes did his calculations and wielded his mirror. This curved line here is not drawn on land, but on the sea. Fulton suggested what that detail might represent."

"I think that's the limit of the mirror's effectiveness," the inventor said. "Within that line, the mirror's rays were strong enough to set attacking Roman galleys on fire."

"The symbols may refer to places on land the makers of this map wanted to record," Smith went on. "The hiding place, perhaps, of the mirror of Archimedes. Caves, forts, a church."

I looked. There was a cross on the peninsula, and a castlelike symbol a good distance from town. A line was drawn from cross to castle, but it angled at a horseshoe-shaped mark. Where the line bent, there was a wavy line like a symbol for a river. Nearby was an oval, little humps that could mark huts or caves, and arrows with odd symbols and meaningless numbers.

"I think the Templars drew this after they redis-covered the mirror," Smith whispered, "and hid it on Thira in a place only they knew: some under-ground catacombs, perhaps."

"So we have something to bargain with!" I ex-claimed.

"Absolutely *not*," Cuvier countered. "Are you going to help turn a terrible weapon over to pirate fanatics?"

"Not turn it over. Just use what we know to get out of this fix, somehow."

"I'd rather be enslaved than give the barbarians a clue that might result in the destruction of the French navy," my friend vowed.

"Aye, and the British navy, too," said Smith. "Come, Ethan, your own nation is at war with these devils. We can't tell them where this death ray is."

"Where is it?" I peered at the map.

"We don't know exactly, but sooner or later they would figure that out. Just pinpointing the city makes discovery far easier. Your frigates would become infernos, and your countrymen would fry. We can't trade that for freedom. Death before dis-honor, eh?"

"Of course." I swallowed. "Still, a little hint might not hurt."

Fulton shook his head. "Any modern inventor could probably improve on the Greek design. We dare not even tempt them."

By the whiskers of Zeus, I'd fallen in with honorable men! That's always a risky thing—not to mention novel. "But they'll take the palimpsest from us and maybe come to the same conclusion," I tried. I'm not craven, just practical.

"The only thing to do," Cuvier said, "is memorize this scrap to the closest detail and then destroy it. Then the key will be in our brains, not an underground tunnel or a piece of animal skin."

"Destroy it how? We can't throw it into the sea from down here."

"No, and we can't bring the obscuring prayers back, either. The only thing I can think of, my friends, is to eat it."

"After we've washed it in piss to see the design?"

"Nothing wrong with a little urine, Ethan," the scientist assured. "Less toxic than bad well water. Maidens used it to wash their hair. Besides, the palimpsest is long dried now. Seasoned, you might say."

"Eat a palimpsest?" I looked with dismay. "How?"

"A little at a time, I suspect. It's not like we have salt and pepper."

And so we did, and by the end I had a sore jaw from chewing and a knotted gut from too much parchment and not enough vegetables. Why can't I find normal treasure, like gold doubloons or a queen's tiara?

Our morose chewing of this cud did put us in a philosophical mood, and when men ponder the mysteries of the universe the first thing that comes to mind is women.

I'd explained my unsuccessful audience with Aurora Somerset and given hints of our unhappy history, which seemed to surprise no one. Females, we agreed, were more bewitching than a treasure map and explosive as a keg of gunpowder.

"It's odd how dangerous they are, given that men are so clearly superior," Smith said with honest puzzlement. "In strength, in courage, and in intelligence, the evidence of our gender's advantage is indisputable."

"Not entirely," Fulton cautioned. "I know many a man who'd quail at the prospect of childbirth."

"Certainly women have strengths of their own," the Englishman allowed. "Beauty, to cite the most obvious. My point is that despite our own male brilliance, the hens seem to get the upper hand over the peacock. Quite baffling, really."

"Upper wing," I corrected. "If the metaphor is peacock."

"It's really a product of natural history," Cuvier opined. "Now the male, it is true, has the instinct to be unfaithful. While monogamy is advantageous for the survival of children, in terms of procreation it's in a buck's best interest to mount as many damsels as possible."

"Here, here," I said.

"So that should keep men in a position of superiority," Smith said. "If his heart is broken by one mate, he simply transfers his energies to the next.

Look at Gage there, a perfect example of serial infatuation, faithlessness, and poor judgment."

I opened my mouth to clarify but Fulton cut me off.

"Fighting stags risk dying in combat, but the winner gains a harem," the inventor agreed. "The bull rules the pasture, and the ram his ewes. Male superiority, gentlemen, is the rule of the barnyard, and it should be the rule of the salon."

"And yet it is not," Cuvier cautioned. "Ethan, for example, is the kind of man who has endless problems with women, given his flealike frenzy, inability to plan for the future, rank opportunism, and hapless disloyalty. In his case, the advantage is to the fair sex. When does one hunt a stag? In the rutting season, when the animal's brain is positively addled by lust and he can't get anything right."

"Ethan again," Fulton agreed.

"The woman, in contrast, has a far weightier task than simple copulation," Cuvier went on. "While a loose bull like Gage might charge around the pasture, wearing out over this skirt and that, the female has but one chance to get it right. Just a single man will impregnate her, and so her choice of the stud is crucial to her own well-being and that of her child. As a result, she approaches relationships with the acumen of an Alexander and the strategy of Frederick the Great. Her brilliance at this dance is honed from earliest childhood, and faced with her ruthless strategy and judicious selection, we men are but helpless pawns. It is she who controls our success or failure, she who maneuvers to bring the right mate to her boudoir, she who calculates not just physical attractiveness but money, intelligence, and power, and sets in place a bewildering set of flanking maneuvers and ambushes that turn the hapless male to befuddled acquiescence. At the same time, she must convince the male that the entire affair is his idea."

"We are no match," Smith agreed with a sigh. "We are rabbits to their fox."

"Or at least hapless romantics like Ethan are," said Cuvier.

"They weigh our inheritance, our reputation, our prospects, and our hygiene," Fulton confirmed. "It's little wonder Gage here has such trouble with his Astiza and this Somerset, to just begin the list. It's a hopeless mismatch."

"I am hardly a victim, gentlemen." My pride was being stung.

"Perhaps not," said Cuvier, "but the farther you stay from women, Ethan Gage, the safer all of us will be."

CHAPTER 21

So here I was on a stone quay at the edge of Africa in the hot midday sun, dragging an anchor's worth of iron, appalled at the idea of trying to rekindle passion with Aurora Somerset, and facing the fate they whisper about in Mediterranean taverns. Our captivity was Muslim payback for their expulsion from Spain, the blood of the Crusades, and their whipping at Lepanto and Vienna a couple of centuries back. Every war breeds the next one. The four of us might be the despair of any parish prelate, given our rather liberal views on religion and Scripture, but to the pirates we were Christian dogs, about to get a preview of the hell we'd earned by not converting to Islam.

Someday I was going to learn not to go on errands for Napoleon Bonaparte.

"What is our plan again?" whispered Fulton.

"Well, I was going to ransom us with what we

know, but an outbreak of moral rectitude among the four of us put an end to that scheme. I see only two ways out. One is to run like the very devil when we have the chance."

Fulton looked down at his manacles. "I think they've anticipated that."

"The other is to appeal to reason. I don't trust our pirate queen for a moment, lads, and so we need to see the king of this place, one Yussef Karamanli, and convince him just how important we really are."

"Isn't he the one who shot one brother and exiled another on his way to the throne? The one who's declared war on our own United States? The one whose grandfather had his janissary guards strangled, one by one, as they came in the door of a thank-you banquet?"

"He's no George Washington," I allowed. "In the end, however, pirates are always businessmen. You savants represent the brightest minds in Europe. We'll figure out some harmless task to impress him, earn his gratitude, put him in our debt, and then be sent on our way. With presents, perhaps."

"Your optimism is ludicrous," Smith said.

"If we prove truly useful, he'll never let us go," Cuvier added.

"Maybe Napoleon will rescue us then."

"Napoleon has no idea where we are."

"Then look for any chance of escape, gentlemen."

"Punishable by excruciating death, I've read," Smith warned. "We really don't have a chance, if I recall."

"Well," I said doggedly, "I'll think of something."

They sighed.

With that and the crack of whips we shuffled forward, bunched with a second group of captives pushed off another ship. Some of these were sobbing women. Our vine of chain was locked together and we were pushed, stumbling, past hogsheads of sugar, pipes of wine, and casks of nails into the city proper, passing from blinding sunlight to the canyonlike shadows of a street of Africa, awnings casting them in shade. We were lashed through crowds of jostling soldiers, shouting merchants, shrouded women, braying donkeys, and snorting camels. We shuffled with bare feet on the manure-spotted sand of the street to the blare of horns and beat of drums. High overhead the red, green, and white banners of Tripoli floated to taunt anyone dreaming of freedom. From the alcoves, the poorest Muslim beggars made sure to strike and spit to ensure that our mood was even worse than theirs. We were jeered until we shrank into ourselves like the intimidated spirits we were. Our weapons were gone, our boots stolen—I made sure Dragut himself took my urine-soaked shoe—and half our buttons plucked off. We were thirsty, starved, sunburned, and whipped, and as pitiable a lot as you'll see this side of a cannibal campfire. I kept looking for opportunity, and finding none.

Tripoli did bring back memories of Alexandria and Cairo. Here were the coffee shops, the old men squatting at the entrance to puff at six-foot hookah pipes as we stumbled by, the air heavy with hashish and incense. There were taverns, too, run by freed

Christians and patronized by Muslims who sat in dark shadows to imbibe forbidden alcohol.

The Turkish and Arab women we passed were veiled, their robes shapeless, so that only the beauty of their almond eyes hinted at the charms within.

Tripoli also had a large colony of Jews who'd been expelled from Spain in Columbus's day. By decree the Jews were dressed in black, and forced to go barefoot if they crossed in front of a mosque. Most of the beggars were missing hands or arms, their extremities having been chopped off and the stumps dipped in pitch after conviction of some crime. Street urchins ran with us, too, yelling taunts and laughing at our shackled misery. High above, the eyes of more women peered down at us from the grilled windows of harems and apartments.

I preferred Philadelphia.

"There's a hierarchy in Tripoli you would do well to memorize," said Hamidou as his sailors jabbed us forward. "The rulers and janissary soldiers are Turks, answerable to the Sublime Porte in Istanbul. They are the ones allowed to wear the red fez wrapped with muslin. Below them are Arab merchants, the descendants of the desert warriors who conquered North Africa more than a thousand years ago. Beneath the Arabs are the Moors, the Muslims driven from Spain by the Christian knights. Then the Levantines, the Greeks and Lebanese who do menial jobs. The Jews are also refugees from Spanish intolerance, and they are our lenders. And finally, at the bottom, you slaves make up a fifth of our population. The government language is Turkish and Arabic, and the street talk is the Lingua Franca of the Mediterranean, a mix of all the dialects from around that sea."

We clanked by a market. There were ranks of silvery fish, mounds of bright spices, carpets, cloaks, leather, silks, figs, raisins, olives, grain, and oil. There was brass and iron cookware, finely tooled saddles, sweetly curving daggers, oranges, pomegranates, grapes, onions, anchovies, and dates. Everything was for sale, including me.

"How much am I worth, exactly?" I asked. "As a slave, that is."

He considered. "Half the price of a pretty woman."

"But you can't just mean to auction us off like common sailors," I reasoned. "We're learned men."

"You're Christian dogs, until you convert."

◘   ◘   ◘

The slave market of Tripoli was a stone platform under the wall of Yussef's central citadel, and perhaps his entertainment was the lamentation that rose from the hopeless. We queued next to its steps while a mob of bidders inspected us, since we represented a potentially shrewd investment. Our sale price would go to our pirate captors, but there was a chance a buyer might turn a profit not just from our labor but from ransoming us to higher-bidding relatives in Christendom. The bashaw's own representatives were resplendent in jeweled turbans and upturned slippers. They were there to take the prettiest for the harem and the most able for whatever household duties needed filling after the last purchase had finally expired of overwork and disease. Other buyers included swarthy Berber chieftains from the hinterlands, military overseers needing brute labor to complete battery work, galley masters looking to replenish their banks of oars, carpet makers who needed quick fingers and fresh eyes, and dyers, water carriers, wheat growers, tanners, drovers, and masons, all with whips and manacles of their own. The system was built entirely on coercion instead of free enterprise and I'd announce in a second that it couldn't work, except that the Barbary kingdoms had been defying the navies of Europe for three hundred years. My own United States depended on slavery in its south, and by all reports its most enthusiastic practitioners were quite wealthy.

The captives ahead were auctioned like cattle. Muscles were ordered tightened to judge strength, mouths forced open with wedges of stick, bellies prodded, feet lifted, and clothes rudely ripped to hunt for boils, rashes, or other signs of disease. We were all forced to prove, by prancing, that we didn't suffer from gout. In some cases trousers were tugged down to judge the size of the genitals, as if the poor captive was to be put to stud.

One Sardinian sailor reacted to this indignity with such shock that he shoved an auctioneer and kicked out at a soldier, his chains clanking. At this outburst, the crowd roiled and churned like an ant nest poked with a stick. I braced for the beating, and indeed guards leaped forward to rain blows on the poor man until he was curled like a baby on the auction platform, sobbing in Italian for mercy.

The savagery seemed disproportionate and wildly unrestrained, and yet this was but a preview of his real punishment.

There was a stir behind us and I turned. A man had appeared on a snow-white horse, surrounded by a troop of janissaries. He was in his thirties, I judged, handsome and fit, and dusty from some pleasure hunt that morning. Retainers had raptors hooded and tied to poles. When he halted, Negro slaves ran up to fan him with long-handled plumes.

Behind on another horse, her auburn ringlets cascading nakedly down in a display some Muslims would consider obscene, was Aurora Somerset, her lips slightly parted in excitement. She was watching the beating, quietly thrilled.

"It's Karamanli," Cuvier whispered. "Look at that emerald on his turban."

"Big enough to pick him out in a crowd," I admitted. "And give him a headache."

"He likes order in his markets," Dragut said. "This Sardinian will be made an example."

The bashaw said something sharp to one of his officers and the message was relayed to the auction overseer. This man winced at the thought of lost profit, but then issued orders of his own. In an instant the groaning, bloody sailor was unlocked from his chains, hauled semiconscious to the edge of the platform, and then held by both arms while a huge iron hook swung down from the shadows above. Fortunately, the victim was too dazed to know what was about to happen to him.

We gasped, jerking the victim to attention, and then the implement was jammed through his back and shoved out through his belly like a gigantic fishhook, its point obscenely dripping blood.

He howled then—screeched as if in the very grip of demons.

And then he was hoisted, flapping frantically, blood sluicing down his nakedness while his eyes rolled back in their sockets from the unbelievable pain.

"For the love of God!" My companions were sobbing.

Twenty feet above the auction platform his ascent stopped. The sailor thrashed and squirmed, eyes bulging as he regarded the hook jutting from his guts, bloody droplets spattering the stones. Finally the convulsions slowed and he fainted, and then I noticed that he was not alone in hanging in the shadows above. Other cadavers, half rotted and dried, hung from similar hooks to warn what would happen if we resisted.

Certainly my own will collapsed. Escape? I could barely breathe.

I turned to look back at Aurora and Yussef. The woman licked her lips. The ruler of Tripoli nodded with grim satisfaction and then kicked his steed toward his castle gate, the pirate queen and his retinue following. "Now catch his eye," I croaked desperately.

But my companions were in no mood to court this monster's notice, and in any event we were too ragged and anonymous to gain his appreciation anyway. He passed into the shadows of his fortress without a glance, Aurora ignoring us as well. Then we were left, helpless and humiliated.

And yet our shame at being exhibited like animals was nothing compared with the infamy visited on the women. If old and shapeless they were bustled off to the laundries or bakeries with cursory bidding and swift transaction, but if young and at all lovely they were stripped naked to a roar of approval from the throng of sweating men. Then they were turned like a piece of glassware, propriety forgotten. If bidding lagged the auctioneer would lift a breast or bring a cane up between the thighs while the assembly roared and the shouted numbers went higher. It made no difference how much the damsels wept or shuddered, one even wetting herself in fear and mortification: they were lasciviously inspected before being bundled off to the buyer's harem to be cleaned for his rape and enjoyment. We burned to avenge them, but what chance did we have? And if some of the women wailed at their fate, some of the captive men wept at an even worse future, knowing their existence would not be the dull luxury of the harem, but a monotony of dry bread, senseless beating, and crushing labor until death became sweet release.

We were dizzy from heat and angry excitement, swaying from thirst and hopelessness, and blinking against flies that swarmed to drink our last sweat. Finally our quartet of savants was shoved and whipped up the steps and onto the platform, the remaining buyers groaning and hooting at our lack of fitness. We did not appear to have half the endurance of a normal seaman. Who wants a scientist as a slave? The auctioneer began with a sigh of determination, barking and singsonging to the assembly. They shouted insults and mockery, hoping to drive our price down. The betting was that we'd go to the quarries and expire in weeks.

"We're finally in hell," Cuvier said, eyes closed against the mob. "Not Thira, but here."

"No," said Fulton. "Hell is coming."

I looked where he was staring. The crowd's noise abruptly hushed as a giant breasted the bidders with the heavy, swaying gait of an elephant. His shoulders were wide as a door, his bald head gleamed, and his torso was a crosshatch of tattoos and scar tissue. There was an odd paleness to him, like a cave being who rarely sees the sun. His eyes were tiny in his brutal and rumpled face, but they had the look of dull cunning the vicious sometimes muster. His hands and wrists looked capable of bending steel, his nose mashed, his lips heavy like a grouper's, and his muscles swollen as if pumped full of bile. There was a muttering of fear as the crowd hastily parted, and then it was quiet enough to hear the creak of chain as the impaled sailor, still dripping blood, made his last instinctual twitching above this ghastly scene.

"It's Omar," I heard the pirates breathe. "The Dungeon Master."

"Too ugly for a mother to love," I whispered.

"Too ugly to have been born at all," Cuvier amended. "He emerged, I'm guessing, like maggots from the dung."

The giant pointed at us with a finger thick as a small pistol, and we realized we'd been noticed after all.

"Yussef Karamanli says the little ones are for me."

CHAPTER 22

If the hold of Dragut's ship had been claustrophobic, and the slave market of Tripoli wretched, Omar's dungeon was infinitely worse. Its tunnels had been hewn by Carthaginians, Romans, Visigothic barbarians, Arab jihadists, and Turkish overlords over a score of centuries: a labyrinth of sorrow gnawed by generations of jailers and prisoners like termites into wood. Each tyranny had added a descending level, so each sin and cruelty could be hidden farther from the light. We were not marched but dragged to this hive in the bowels beneath Yussef's palace, and were not thrust into a cell but pitched into a pit, a rock well slimed with dripping spring water that made its sides too slippery to climb. The bottom was ankle-deep in mud and sewage. We mostly felt this instead of saw it, because there was no light except the reflection of torches somewhere far overhead. The pit's smell was peculiar, an odor of carrion and reptile, stale and prehistoric, so perhaps animals were sometimes kept there. No creature was in the pit now, which is just as well because we probably would have eaten it, killing the beast bare-handed and chewing it raw. The sweat from the rock was our only drinking water—we had to lap it like dogs—and our first food did not come for two days. We finally heard the shuffle of a troglodyte guard above and saw something tumble down in the dimness. We had the wit to catch what was a stale, weevil-infested loaf of bread, enough for two or three mouthfuls for each of us. The worms represented more nourishment than the rancid flour they'd fed on.

We wolfed down our share without tasting.

Our quartet barely said a word in our despair, so the primary sound was the screaming and begging of Yussef's enemies being tortured somewhere above. Omar himself had been immensely strong and immensely silent, flinging us into our misery without a word of explanation. He'd seemed not so much cruel as indifferent, as if the suffering he oversaw never registered on the animal lobe of his brain.

All of us were sick. Humans cannot live long in a wet, stinking pit without inhaling from its vapors all kinds of pestilence, as any doctor will tell you. Our occasional shouts to summon help or explanation were ignored, and we wondered at times if we'd been entirely forgotten. When the future is uncertain, the present is misery, and time creeps like a slug. Even had we wanted to betray our navies, there was no opportunity to do so. In any event, the four of us pledged again not to betray the secret of the mirror as a way of fortifying our spirits.

"Better this pit than dishonor," Cuvier said heavily.

"No Englishman would imperil his navy," Smith added.

"Nor an American betray his nation's cause," said Fulton.

"Well said," I confirmed. "Though a little negotiation wouldn't hurt, if we could get out of this slime hole and properly pay them back." They didn't respond to this, given that they hadn't much use for my ideas anymore.

We did try standing on each other's shoulders to reach the lip, but even with a precarious pyramid that had Cuvier, the lightest of us, reaching for the top, we were still too short. There was no shovel to pile sand, and no sand to pile in any event. There was, in short, no possibility of escape, and no communication. Didn't they want ransom? Had they given up trying to corrupt us to betray the secret of Archimedes?

And then they did break my will, but in an entirely unexpected way.

◻   ◻   ◻

Time had disappeared, and existence in the hole had become synonymous with eternity. Then, without warning, a chain rattled down, rusty and thick. Omar shouted in a deep voice, "Gage, alone!"

"What's this?" Cuvier asked, with just a hint of suspicion.

"Perhaps I'm the first to be shot." I could think of worse things, like staying where I was.

"I read they decapitate," Smith said.

"Oh."

"It's very quick."

"Ah."

"Maybe they want to torture you," Cuvier speculated.

"Remember our pledge, Ethan," Fulton warned. "We dare not help them."

"You remember it, too, when you hear my screams." And with that I grasped the chain, wrapped my legs around its links, and shouted. Omar hauled me up the slimy walls of our well, with me rotating so I was thoroughly smeared with filth. I was weak by now from lack of proper food and water, and had a hard time even holding on. My companions feared for me but also followed my ascent with envy, as if I'd been given leave to levitate to someplace that wasn't just an endless, hopeless *now*.

I knew better.

The Dungeon Master seemed to fill the pit's tight chamber, his teeth yellow, his breath stinking, and the skin of his palms thick and hard as boot leather. He clamped his paws on the back of my neck as if it were the scruff of a kitten, half lifting and paralyzing me, and I'd no doubt that should I not go where he pushed, my head would be snapped from its stalk. He began shoving me up a rock passageway.

"Torture doesn't work with me," I tried in Arabic.

He used his other hand to cuff me with the power of a bear, the blow leaving my ears ringing. "Silence, pretty one. Time enough for noise."

I saw no advantage in following his advice. "I have powerful friends, Omar, with money to buy not only the escape of us savants but a life for you, too, if you go with us."

Now he stopped, holding me at arm's length, and regarding me with squinted disbelief. "Look at me. Where else could I possibly be?" And then he slammed me back against the tunnel wall, my poor head bouncing, and dragged me even more roughly than before. "I told you not to talk. It makes it worse."

I was taken past horrid iron machines stained dark with blood, and heavy doors with small barred windows from which insane gibbering escaped. How can people invent such places, let alone administer them? Then we turned into a side rat hole and he pushed me ahead down a tight spiral to a new chamber lit by a tiny slit far, far above. The single ray of light just emphasized the grotto's darkness, its vaulted ceiling stained black by the smoke of two millennia of torches. There was a rude wooden table in the chamber's center, with manacles at each of its corners. To one side was the glow of a forge on which sat a bubbling pot, giving off noxious fumes. Iron implements were thrust into the coals. My courage, never all that vast to begin with, was starting to shrivel.

I was slammed down on the table and chained helplessly in place, my throat and belly and privates exposed to whatever deviltry this dim monster could invent. Never had I felt so helpless! The tiny window made things worse, reminding me there was a different world beyond. From a beam overhead swung metal implements designed to pierce, pinch, and cut. I wanted to scream already, and nothing had yet been done.

"Soon you will talk more than you believed possible." Omar, clinical as a doctor, pumped air into the coals with a bellows, sparks dancing. He slipped on a heavy leather glove and lifted out an iron bar like a fireplace poker and brought it over to where I helplessly waited.

He held it above my eyes, letting me see its glow. "Each time I do this, I learn ways to prolong the pain. Victims can live for days. Yes, Omar is not as clumsy as he once was!" The hulking brute nodded. "By the time I've had the last of your friends, I will make it last a very long time indeed; so long that I will become bored before they finally die."

"We wouldn't want that," I managed. My throat was dry as dust, my muscles cracking from tension. "Finish us quickly, is my advice."

"You are lucky you are first, while I am still learning. We will experiment with pain. And a handsome man like you needs a mirror, so I will bring one after my branding so that you can weep at the ruin I make of your face. My goal is to make you even more hideous than me. You will blister and infect, but I keep maggots to eat the corruption. It makes you last longer."

"Thank goodness for maggots." It was a wheeze.

"I am told you pride yourself with women, so I have tools to mutilate those parts as well. The groin is a locus of agony, and always elicits the greatest screaming."

I was near to fainting. "Can't you just kill me? Beheading, Smith read."

There was a hiss and I jumped, the poker thrust into a pail of water and then reinserted in the coals. "Why would they need the skill of a Dungeon Master to do that? Anyone can hack off a head with a sword. It is torture that is an art. The shame of mutilation. The peeling of flesh."

"Omar, please, I'll pay anything . . ."

He was rummaging about, clanging and clattering his tools of torment. I squeezed my eyes shut. I could hear the scrape of coals, and smell the fumes. Something hissed like acid. Then there was a long silence. I tensed to wait for the first excruciating assault.

"Of course," Omar said as if the idea had just occurred to him, "there is one other way."

My eyes opened. "What? What?"

"Perhaps you would once more speak to the mistress."

"Mistress?"

"The pirate queen, Lady Somerset."

I was sweating. "Yes, yes! To her and Yussef! We're the kind of men who should be ransomed, not tortured! Omar, let me see them, please! I'll explain it is all a misunderstanding! We are really quite valuable!"

"I think they will find you as annoying as I do, and give you back to me to do as I wish. Unless you please them very much."

"But that's exactly what I do! I please people!"

"While you talk with them I will think of new ways to hurt your friends, in case you can't come to agreement. I would like to hurt your friends very much." He grinned like a maniac.

"No, don't hurt my friends! Let me talk to Aurora!" By thunder, I'd tup the girl sideways and upside down, clenching my teeth while I did it, if that's what it took to get off this torture table. No need to talk about ancient mirrors when I could just rely on my charm . . .

Suddenly janissaries entered and the manacles were unlocked from my shaking limbs. I felt utterly depleted, even though not a scratch had been inflicted. Omar lumbered off to attend to some other wretch while the Tripolitan guards hauled me upright with looks of disgust. I was shuddering. None of *them* called me pretty.

"Strip off your rags, American," they ordered.

My hands were shaking so badly that they ripped my garments for me. Then they sluiced me with buckets of water again, the same rude bath I'd had on Dragut's pirate ship. Filth streamed off until I finally stood abject and naked, shivering, ashamed at my weakness, and terrified of what might come next.

"Put these on."

I was dressed in Moorish bloused trousers and a sleeveless vest, my chest bare, and given sandals for my raw feet. Maybe I'd have to turn Muslim after all! Then four of the soldiers formed a little box around me and we went up a flight of stairs. Realizing it must lead to the castle, I began to take note of where we were.

My escorts didn't speak. The passage grew less gloomy as we climbed, arrow slits giving light, and I couldn't help but have my hopes soar, even as trepidation grew. What was the point of seeing Aurora again? What could I agree to without betraying my country? Why had I been hauled out of the pit instead of someone more famous and reputable, like Cuvier? Because I was the weakest? But I had a reputation as a hero of Acre! None of it made sense. I blinked against the growing light, realizing just how dark and troll-like our lives had become. I felt confused, exhausted, and desperate.

A door opened, small enough that we had to squeeze through. Two soldiers filed before me, two behind. This corridor wasn't much broader than my shoulders and again had no light except from an oil lamp. Was this a secret passageway? We came to an iron grill at the end that my escorts unlocked and then locked behind. Then we climbed a winding set of stone stairs. Yet another door was unbolted, this one wood, and at first I thought beyond was more darkness. But no, it was simply a tapestry covering the door. The cloth was swept aside and I was pushed through into some kind of reception room, this one brilliant to my eyes even though the sunlight was filtered through wood-grilled windows. I blinked. There was blue sea and sky beyond, and my heart quickened, even as I tensed for a sudden blade or shot. Were my captors simply giving me a last cruel glimpse of this sweet earth before sending me off it?

Not yet.

Aurora wasn't there. Instead, I was face-to-face

with Hamidou Dragut, our traitorous sea captain. He lounged on a cushion in what I realized was the richly decorated throne room, picking from a bowl of figs. My stomach growled at the sight of them. The room's floor was strewn with thick Persian carpets and its marble walls were decorated with incised Arabic script that quoted the Koran. There was a gilded throne chair, the cerulean silk of its cushion embroidered with gold and its legs and arms studded with jewels. In one corner of the chamber was a leopard, lying on the cool floor and held to a pillar by a golden chain. Behind was its brass cage. The cat looked bored.

I'd come from hell to an odd little heaven.

Dragut looked me up and down. "She will be very disappointed. The pit has not improved you."

I worked to keep any quaver from my voice. "Aurora Somerset is always disappointed. It's her nature."

"Don't let your tongue betray your last remaining chance, American."

Sometimes I can't help myself, and my grit was slowly coming back. I was jealous he had figs and I was starving. "To be a slave to that woman, like you?"

He darkened. "I am no slave, and would die before becoming one."

I took breath. "Tripoli is a nation of slaves. I could tell that much just marching from the harbor. Endless castes, each man quailing before the other, and your women bagged and hidden as if they carried the plague. You've never tasted freedom in your life, Dragut."

"On the contrary, Monsieur Gage!" It was a new voice and I swung around. A door to the throne room opened and in strode the man I'd seen in the slave market on his white horse, Bashaw Yussef Karamanli himself. He was, as I've said, fit and handsome, a dagger in his sash and a sword at his side, and carried with him that confidence that comes from being born to royalty. Two powerful guards, one blond and one black, flanked him. His sword belt was studded with diamonds, and his turban had that jewel the size of a robin's egg—emerald enough, I guessed, to put me in high style the rest of my life if I could ever find a way to snatch it. He also had the ruthless look that is inevitable to men who cling to power in dangerous places. He plopped onto the European throne chair while a janissary gave a blow to the back of my legs, forcing me to my knees before him. My head was wrenched down in obeisance.

"In this country each man enjoys the freedom of knowing his place and role, unlike the chaos of democracy," Yussef went on with a scholarly air. "And our women have a freedom yours can't imagine. Yes, they are covered, but that means they can go anywhere in the city without being recognized, meaning they are free from malicious gossip and disapproving eyes. Behind the veil they have a liberty no American or French woman enjoys. They are mistresses of their houses, and in the cool of the evening they emerge on the screened roofs to talk and sing in a world free of harassment from men. No woman can keep secrets more readily than a Muslim woman, no woman is happier, and no woman is better protected by her husband. You will see if you take the turban. We have a harmony, a serenity, unknown in Europe."

My head came up. "I've experienced Aurora's serenity."

"Ah. Lady Somerset is . . . unique. And no Muslim."

"And she has nothing to say to you, at least not yet," Dragut said. "That will await some sudden birth of reason on the part of yourself and your companions. No, I brought you up to confer first with someone quite different, to see if we cannot be partners."

"We have nothing you want to know."

"From four savants? I'm skeptical of that."

"And if we did, it will die with us. I insisted on honor." I'm inclined to exaggerate, if nobody is around to correct me.

"Did you?" He licked his fingers of the stickiness of the figs and suddenly sprang up. He wore, I saw, Cuvier's two pistols in his sash. The guards were similarly armed, and looked ready to spring. Everyone had weapons enough to rob a mail coach, meaning I was not exactly trusted. "I appreciate men of honor," Dragut said. He rapped on the door Yussef had come through. "They can be trusted to do the right thing."

There was the sound of a lock being turned, a creak, and the heavy door swung open. A pale, corpulent, hairless slave—a eunuch, I guessed, the gelded men allowed to attend a harem—marched into our meeting place with pretentious authority, as if his rank exceeded that of the pirate captain and soldiers before him. But he fell before Yussef, his forehead touching the floor. And then another figure came through to slip around the eunuch and stand in a shaft of dazzling sunlight, like the apparition of an angel.

All sense left me then, and I heard a roaring in my ears. My knees went weak.

It was Astiza, my lost love from Egypt, as beautiful as ever.

With her, dressed like a little sultan, was a boy of just over two years. He looked at me with bright, cautious curiosity.

"Hello, Ethan," Astiza said. "This is your son, Horus."

CHAPTER 23

Astiza was as striking as I remembered. She's a Mediterranean beauty, Greek and Egyptian, her hair silk and piled for this reunion, held in place with a golden pin. She has eyes to drown in, dark and deep, and they shone with a bright intelligence that might frighten some men but captivated me. She was not as conventionally beautiful as Aurora Somerset but had a thousand times more character, the set of her lip or the waiting question of her eyes hinting at a depth of emotion the English noblewoman had no knowledge of. There was bright steel in Astiza, but vulnerability, too, and while she always seemed ready to slip away (that independence!) she once had need of me as well, as baffled by her attraction to me as I was by my longing for her. We had electricity. We understood each other's hopes in an unspoken way I'd never shared with another woman. Slim, poised, draped in Arabian finery, her sandals silver and her jewelry braided gold, she seemed a dream after the ghastliness of Omar and the horror of his dungeons.

Yet my appraisal was done hurriedly because my stunned stare necessarily went to the wee creature beside her. This was a lad not much beyond the nursery, shorter, I guessed, than Napoleon's Little Red Man, with a shock of unruly hair that mimicked my own in a way both enchanting and disturbing. My son! I wasn't aware I had one. He had Astiza's hypnotic eyes and upright stance, and my own cheekiness. He didn't shy behind my old lover's skirts but looked at me with that optimistic wariness children use with strange but promising adults. I might have a present—or, I might be of no use whatsoever. And damn if the tyke's face didn't look a bit like mine, too, a point I registered with both apprehension and pride.

"My son?" It came out as a croak.

"I suspected pregnancy when we were in Temple Prison in Paris."

"You didn't share this rather momentous information?"

"I didn't want it to dissuade you from bringing me to help stop Alessandro Silano and his Egyptian Rite treachery. And later, when Napoleon spared us . . . you're a man who's destined to go his own way, Ethan. I knew we'd have a reunion. I just didn't expect it to be like this."

"What are you doing in Tripoli?" My questions were thick, my mind reeling, my purpose confused. I was a father? By Thor's thunder, was I supposed to marry the girl? And was I supposed to be pleased, or disturbed? I couldn't remember old Ben Franklin having anything to say about this.

"I was captured, like you."

"What kind of a name is Horus?" She hadn't conferred on that, either.

"A quite noble name of an Egyptian god. You know that."

"I just always imagined having a Jack or a Tom or something." I was rambling, while I tried to take it all in.

"You weren't around to consult." Her tone was cool, and tarnation if I didn't feel guilty about the entire situation. But I hadn't planned this or wanted it! I just wanted her, and I still did, didn't I? Of course I did, I wanted to leap the gap between us, but a child gave new gravity to the situation. New purpose to every glance and word. What was my duty here?

Dragut and Karamanli were looking at me with amusement.

"How were you captured?"

"Kidnapped in Egypt. I'd returned to Dendara for my studies of the past when Bedouin raiders took us. Ethan, all this from the beginning—with Silano and the medallion, the Book of Thoth, your mission in North America—has been an attempt by our enemies to reconstruct the power discovered in the Middle Ages by the Knights Templar. They are reassembling the lost powers of a very ancient world, a world that preceded the one we know and that started our own civilization. Secrets lost for millennia are being bent toward evil."

"That's not true," Dragut said.

"The more I studied in Egypt the more I understood the vastness of their design, and I hoped the hieroglyphs of Dendara would reveal how all this secret history came about. But before I could work, Horus and I were kidnapped. We were ridden into the desert by Bedouin and I thought we'd be ransomed from there, but instead we were sold in a slave market to men who wore medallions of a pyramid entwined with a snake. It was Apophis all over again. They took us to the coast, threatening to harm Horus if I tried any witchcraft. Then we were chained to a corsair and sailed here, where I was brought to Karamanli's harem."

"My God. Are you a concubine?"

She shook her head. "I wasn't captured for him. I was captured for you."

"For me?" I was more confused than ever.

"To persuade you, if you failed to cooperate. All this has been planned for many months, Ethan, by some pirate captain who has some scheme I don't understand. A devil in league with Hamidou Dragut here."

"A devil-ess," I corrected heavily. "The pirate is a woman."

"A woman!"

"We have some history."

Her look was less than happy. "I see." In an instant many things had become clear to her, such as why she was in this predicament at all.

I swallowed. "Perfectly horrid, I assure you. The plague, Inquisition, and Reign of Terror were holidays compared with Aurora Somerset. I was asking about you in Paris, Astiza, really I was—I wrote Ashraf about you, too—which is how my friends and I got into this mess. I came to find you. And now, to meet you here, with . . . Horus." I blinked at the boy. "I'm more than a little astounded."

"Who that?" the boy piped up.

"It's your papa, I told you."

"He come stay?" His voice lifted at the end of each question, and he seemed quite the proficient talker for his age, which I was swiftly calculating must be just over two. I couldn't help but have some satisfaction at the precocious little prodigy I'd spawned, as well as new alarm at the question he raised. I loved Astiza, yes, but a family and domesticity? Everything was happening too fast.

"No, my sweet. He's going to save us by going away."

"Go where?"

"Where other people tell him to go."

"*Now* what are you talking about?" I interrupted.

"As we've explained, we need your help and partnership, Ethan Gage," Dragut said. "We could let Omar the Dungeon Master explore what you know, but one is never certain if the information elicited through torture is entirely honest. Much better for all, we think, is your voluntary help in achieving our mutual ends."

"Mutual ends!"

"Ethan, this was not my idea," Astiza said. "I'm as helpless as you. But these cultists, these fanatics, are as ruthless as the pirates they employ."

"You have two choices, Monsieur Gage," Dragut explained. "You can return to the dungeon and let Omar have his way. He, at least, will enjoy it. Perhaps we'll learn something useful, and while by the end you'll be broken and insane, Aurora and I can investigate whatever clues he has wrung out of you. Should you make this choice to end your life in hideous pain, Astiza will become a concubine to the highest bidder, and your son will be sold into a harem of a different sort. There are beys who run to that taste, and are always looking for young boys to initiate. We will put Horus there."

"Where, Mama?"

"Hush, baby."

"Mother and son will both be concubines until her master tires of his latest toy and turns Astiza out to more menial slavery. I think Somerset intends that it be the worst kind of crippling labor. And so your little family ends, you in a torture chamber, she as a scullery slave, and Horus, perhaps, as eunuch after his service to pederasts. Your courage, if you want to call it that, will have destroyed everyone around you."

"What about my friends below?" My tone was hollow.

"They will never emerge from the pit. Since Bonaparte sent them, we dare not risk his wrath by trying for ransom. We take care not to capture people from nations with powerful navies. Better that they simply disappear, presumably lost at sea, unfortunate casualties of a doomed treasure quest with the unreliable Ethan Gage. They were last seen fleeing Venice and, poof, they are gone!"

"You bastard. You will fry in hell!"

At that a guard sprang forward and lashed at me with a whip, which stung like the very devil. Worse, the crack of the lash terrified poor little Horus, who now did duck behind his mother's skirts, whimpering. My own eyes watered from the pain but I was damned if I was going to cry in front of my son. Family has a way of giving spine to a man.

"The other choice," Dragut went on smoothly, as if nothing had happened, "is to do what our federation has suggested from the beginning. There was something on that sheepskin you collected because it had disappeared by the time we took you out of the hold. You found a clue, Gage, and then destroyed it. Admit it."

"No more than a city, which you could guess anyway."

"Syracuse?"

I nodded as if it didn't matter. "Where Archimedes lived."

"But then why destroy the parchment? And how did you do it?"

"We ate it."

He smiled. "Which means it held more than a city. Take us to the mirror of Archimedes, Gage, and save both yourself and your family. Astiza and your son will be released to go back to Egypt if they wish, never to be molested by us again."

"And my companions?"

"They will be released and put on a ship back to France before today's sunset. You will not have to meet them, and they will have no idea what bargain you made. Their nightmare will become an adventure they will recount at the supper table for the rest of their lives. Napoleon will probably reward them for having tried, and praise Yussef Karamanli for his mercy."

"And me?"

"You will make your own choice, and it will be a real choice, not coerced. If the mirror works, you can join an alliance that is seeking to re-create the magic and power of the Knights Templar and dominate the world for good. I assure you the Egyptian Rite could run our planet far better than the grasping princes and warlords that rule it now. Mark my words, men like Bonaparte will wreak havoc! The mirror will make Tripoli impregnable to naval attack by even the greatest of powers, and behind it we will build a new utopia."

"Like the murals of Akrotiri," I murmured.

"What?"

"Nothing. Something I saw once."

"Or, you can throw away the opportunity to remake the world and go back to your old corruption, where you will be regarded as traitor to your country and all civilized nations. You will be despised and friendless. The best you might hope for is impoverished exile in Egypt with Astiza. Once we have the mirror, what you choose is of no moment to me."

By the beard of Solomon, wasn't this a fix? Condemn the son I hadn't known I had to slavery and rape, snuff out not only my own life but that of Astiza and my three savants—or, betray my nation when it was at war with Tripoli. I couldn't remember old Ben offering any advice on this kind of dilemma, either, except his comment about patriots hanging separately if they didn't hang together.

It was as if Yussef read my thoughts. "Do not flatter yourself that you hold the key to victory or defeat, Monsieur Gage," the bashaw spoke up. "We will find what we seek one way or another—the Rite assures me of that. You simply speed things along and, by doing so, spare your family. If your nation really has a chance in its war with me, why are its ships hiding in Malta?"

Why indeed? Where in hell was that incompetent commodore, Richard Valentine Morris?

"It's not treason to embrace the idealism of the Egyptian Rite," Dragut added.

Aurora's odd patience with me at sea was now explained. It had been planned from the beginning for me to turn traitor to the United States in order to save my young son. The slave market, the pit, the torture chamber—all were to soften me up for this unholy bargain. They sensed I knew more than I'd admitted, and had given me the one choice I couldn't refuse.

It didn't help that I felt guilty for putting the woman I loved (and our child!) in utmost peril. If I had the fidelity of a flea I never would have gotten entangled with Aurora Somerset in the first place, and she wouldn't be plaguing us now. There would have been no kidnapping of Astiza, and no devil's bargain. "Beauty and folly are old companions," Ben Franklin said.

Well, the pirates were a long way from having a death ray and the only possible plan was play along. If I said no we were doomed, but if yes? Maybe my luck would turn. I'm a gambler, after all. I began to fantasize about turning this death ray on them.

"All I have are rather vague clues. I'm not very good at puzzles."

"But you could help, no?"

"Yes. What do I have to do?"

"Find the mirror for us."

"And Astiza and Horus?"

"They will be released unharmed, as promised. But not until the weapon is in Tripoli. Until then, Astiza remains in the harem as a prisoner."

"How do I know you'll keep your word if I help?"

"You'll watch from a palace window when your savants are taken from the dungeon and put on an outbound ship this very evening. We'll fulfill the first part of our promise before you've had to do yours. We of the Rite are honorable, loath though you may be to believe it."

"And Horus will be kept safe?"

"I hope so, but that is up to you, Ethan Gage. Your son is going on our treasure hunt with you, to ensure your good behavior."

"Horus with *me*? But I know nothing of children! Astiza?"

Her eyes had lowered. "I dread this even more than you. I don't want my son taken away, and I don't trust his care to his father. Not yet. Not when your relationship with this woman started this tragedy. But I have no choice. *We* have no choice."

Not exactly a ringing endorsement, but how could I blame her?

And now Aurora Somerset stepped into the room, in sea boots and greatcoat, a cutlass on her waist. "There's no need for concern, because I will be a mother to that boy," she announced.

Her great black dog, Sokar, padded in with her,

yellow-eyed and slobbering. The leopard hissed at the sight of the beast.

And Aurora smiled, infuriatingly, at Astiza.

Oddly, it was Aurora's sneer that stiffened me. It was just the arrogance to remind me exactly where duty lay, and to which woman I owed every ounce of my loyalty. I recognized the desperate trust Astiza was extending to a lover who'd done little to deserve it. By Isis, I loved the mother of my son, loved her with a depth that sent all the old emotions flooding back, and it was time to save her or die trying!

"The hell you will," I told Aurora Somerset. "His mother is here, and I'm the boy's father. Astiza, I'll take care of our son, I promise."

Astiza nodded, as afraid of this moment as any episode in her life. She picked up the lad and stepped over to me, little Horus clinging like a squirrel. He looked at all of us with anxious suspicion, which was another confirmation of his uncommon intelligence. I caught the scent of my old lover as she leaned close, acacia and lotus, and felt the electricity of her hair. I reached out.

She put Horus in my arms.

"All is destiny, Ethan," she whispered.

"Destiny and determination." The boy was straining away, leaning toward his mother, as frightened of me as I was of him. "I'm having a hard time with 'Horus,' though. Maybe I could call him little Harry? You wouldn't mind, would you?"

"Love him as you love me."

And as Astiza was pulled by the eunuch through the door to the confinement of the harem, my new son burst into tears.

CHAPTER 24

I've been terrified many times in my life. I've been trapped in the Great Pyramid, hung upside down over a snake pit at Jaffa, tied to a stake in a fireworks display, and forced to run an Indian gauntlet on the edge of Lake Superior. Few experiences, however, have unnerved me as much as setting sail as guardian of a two-year-old son I didn't know I had.

Quite unintentionally, I had fathered responsibility! While I was aware that conception was theoretically possible when I dove for the bed, somehow the eventual likelihood always slipped my mind in the heat of the moment. I hadn't the faintest idea what one does with a child. Worse, I had fathered a bastard, and unless I somehow rectified the mess I'd made, he'd live his life with the stain of illegitimacy—that is, if he managed to escape slavery and rape. Indeed, thanks to me, the boy was in the clutches of a clan of half-mad Barbary pirates out to trump my own navy with a devil's device that dated back more than two thousand years. The only good news is that I'd watched as Cuvier, Smith, and Fulton had indeed been set free, no doubt wondering what odious deal I'd struck to get them hauled out of the pit. They sailed the same night I'd met with Astiza. Then Dragut, Aurora, young Horus, and I set to sea the next morning, while his mother wept and the boy wailed.

I'd hoped to get some time alone with my Egyptian love, but once I'd made my devil's bargain our audience was over. It occurred to me after we were separated that I might have said something more eloquent than dazed questions, but I'd been too discombobulated by Astiza's reappearance with a son to do much more than stutter. Even a simple, "I love you!" would have been gallant, but how often do we waste our lives saying things of no importance at all, only to neglect the eloquence that life's surprises demand? I knew Astiza was unenthusiastic about our bargain, given that I had no training as a father, but she knew the alternative was worse. At least I didn't mean to harm the boy.

That couldn't be said of everyone and everything. When we boarded Aurora's ship, the *Isis*, some of the crew muttered my tyke was bad luck. And then there was the hulking black mass of Sokar, Aurora's mastiff, who rumbled a growl as if inspecting us for dinner and then—as my son shrank against my leg—giving a loud, annoying bark. Horus jumped and cried.

"Damnation, do we have to take your dog? It will give him nightmares!"

"Sokar only kills when I tell him to. Your whelp will be all right."

Oh yes, Aurora Somerset had quite the mothering instincts. I realized then that she was above all a bully, who used growling mastiffs, pirate goons, or her own rapacious sexuality to intimidate and torment. Like all bullies she looked for the weak or helpless, like an innocent two-year-old or—yes, I had to admit it—his occasionally hapless father. I'd played victim to her sexual charms, giving her a taste of dominance that I'd been paying for ever since. She wanted to rule me again. Coming from a perverse aristocratic father and an utterly corrupt brother, Aurora had lost at an early age any capacity to love or even to enjoy a normal relationship, and assuaged her own wounds by picking at the vulnerabilities of others. That didn't make me feel any more charitable about it.

"I've also brought Horus a guardian for when we're busy," she added in her best airy manner, as if we were conversing from saddleback in Hyde Park.

There was a clump on the deck and at first I thought the man who peg-legged out from her cabin was simply another Mediterranean pirate: strapping, shaved bald, with a scar that cut across cheek and mouth and the usual murderous look I get from landlords, creditors, or jilted mistresses. But there was something familiar about the set of those broad shoulders and the penetrating glint of those dark eyes. What unholy reunion was this?

I finally groaned in recognition. "Osiris?"

Yes, it was my riddle master from Madame Marguerite's Palais Royal brothel, looking considerably more tanned now that he was in the Mediterranean, but none the happier for it. I glanced down to his foot, which was missing. The thump of his peg was coming from the leg I'd run over with the fire wagon. His facial scar, I realized, was where I'd slashed him with that medallion of pyramid and snake. I thought it gave him character, but doubted he'd agree.

"I told you we'd go on this journey together, Gage. But you hurried off."

"I thought it was that you couldn't keep up—say, did you have an accident with a fire wagon?"

"Accidents happen to us all," he prophesied. Just to add to his demented ugliness, it appeared he'd filed his front teeth into something resembling points. I should have checked the passenger registry.

"Not that I'd ever discourage partnership, but I don't know if our relationship is entirely working, Osiris. Just to look at your face and leg and all."

"And no man has the devil's luck forever, Ethan Gage. You're one of us now, to do with what we will. So is your boy."

"Unwilling hostages, you mean."

"I suspect you're susceptible to surrendering to the ecstatic revelations of my order."

"The Egyptian Rite? Don't you mean its corruption and degeneracy?"

"We could have killed you many times over, but mercy stayed our hand. Now your life is about to change profoundly. And should you refuse this opportunity? Well." He smiled with all the charm of a blood-sucking bat. "There's always the boy to initiate, if the father fails to accept rebirth."

"I'm having trouble enough with this first life, actually. I don't know if I'm up for being born into another. It's all a lot of bother, don't you think?"

"Don't disappoint us again. When the saw took off my mangled foot I had all kinds of visions of what I might do to you. Best not to tempt me."

"And you stay away from Horus, or you're going to be sawing the other ankle."

"Bold words for a man with no weapons and no friends."

"Maybe my friends are closer than you think." That was hogwash, given that my three companions were halfway to France by now and the American navy might as well be in China, but my instinctual reaction to arrogant people is to be cocky. It's usually a mistake.

"I don't see them. And someday, when you aren't necessary anymore, we'll discuss our business once again." And he sneered and limped off, which did little to reinforce his menace. I did wish for my rapier or longrifle, however, and wondered if they were locked in Aurora's cabin.

◘   ◘   ◘

Not surprisingly, Horus spoke Arabic, with a smattering of English words that Astiza had taught him. While I worked to expand the tyke's vocabulary, I wondered if his mother had said anything much about distant Dad. Had she simply pretended I never existed?

"Where Mama?" he asked as we worked our way

out of Tripoli's reefs and set sail for Syracuse, on the island of Sicily.

"Well, Harry, she said I could take you on a boat trip. We'll get to know each other and then all go back to Egypt together."

"I want Mama!"

"We'll see her soon enough. It might be fun to be a pirate, you know."

"Mama!"

And thus began our relationship. When he began wailing Dragut threatened to throw us in the hold if I didn't shut my bastard up, so I took him to the bow and managed to calm him down by pointing out light ropes he could play with. He was soon absorbed wrapping loops around my arms and legs, and in a short time had me pretty well trussed, being perfectly content with this mischief. As we played, the ship pitching in the waves, I noticed Aurora silently watching us from the door of her stern cabin and felt a familiar chill. Even if this ancient weapon still existed, or had ever existed—and I doubted both—I had a feeling the agreement I made would not be as simple as Dragut had promised. She had yet to add her own amendments. The more I tried to escape these Egyptian Rite rascals, the more deeply entwined with them I seemed to get. The more I dreaded Aurora Somerset, the more determined she seemed to make me her partner. We had become—as I'd concluded in America, after I wounded her brother—married in hate.

As baffled as I was at the prospect of taking care of a child, I found that Harry had practicality I admired. He was, in predictable order, hungry, sleepy, or bored. Addressing these issues came to be my primary responsibility. He was in the habit of one nap per day, but also subject to awakening in the night and crawling into my hammock for comfort. At first I found this startling and then, after a while, oddly natural and even reassuring. Certainly he slept better than I did, accepting his immediate environment with a child's equanimity, even though he did keep asking about his mother. On food, he stated his likes and dislikes plainly. The bread, dates, and fruit I fetched him were fine, but he had no use for olives, chickpeas, or pickled fish. Fortunately he was both weaned and trained to the toilet, though it took some persuasion to accustom him to the ship's bucket we used as his boy-sized head. With cheerful curiosity, he'd follow pirates to the vessel's real head under the bowsprit, watching them do their business above the pitching waves with a scientist's concentration. Bodily functions had unending fascination for him, and I gave long and learned lectures about the relative merits of privies, latrines, necessary houses, heads, buckets, bushes, and the tavern wall. He took enormous pride in mastering his own bucket, and I daresay it's a more useful skill than most of what we give medals for.

Keeping him entertained and out of mischief was my biggest challenge, since I had to warn him off the gunwales, ratlines, and guns, and away from swinging booms and finger-pinching halyards.

The dog he avoided on his own.

Fortunately, some of the pirates, after their initial apprehension, adopted him as a kind of pet.

They amused themselves by teaching him quick games. I found he could be kept occupied for an hour or two with a few musket balls and a belaying pin to knock them about. I created a simple dice game he took a liking to—the point was to jump the joints in the ship's decking to the count of the dice, and I always let him win. I was oddly proud, and worried, that he'd inherited my gaming instincts.

"Where you live?" he asked.

"A lot of places, actually."

"Where Mama?" It was his favorite subject.

"I met your mother in Egypt," I told him. "She was helping a man take a shot at me, but then I claimed her as a slave of sorts and it all worked out in the end. She's very clever."

"Mama say you brave."

"Did she now?" I couldn't have been more flattered if I'd been inducted in Napoleon's new Legion of Honor, even if Harry wasn't entirely certain what "brave" even meant. "I think I'd say resourceful, and occasionally determined. The real grit is in being a mama, Harry. It's a real commitment, being a mama."

"And papa!"

"Well, yes. I suppose I should have been here, or there, had I known about you. But my original home is across the ocean in America, so I visited there. I was looking for woolly elephants, I was. Have you ever seen an elephant?" I mimicked the beast, using my arm for a trunk.

"From castle! It hurt a man."

"My goodness! Was it an accident?"

"Mama wouldn't let me see."

"Well, that shows we have to be careful, don't we? If we get in a scrape I'll take you down to the hold and tuck you among the spare sails. You absolutely must stay there, you hear? When it's safe again, I'll come get you."

"What's a scrape?"

"Oh, just some unpleasantness. I don't think we'll have any."

"Am I pirate?"

"I think you are, Harry. A boy pirate, anyway, if you're on a pirate ship."

"Who pretty lady?" He pointed to Aurora.

"Why she's a pirate, too, and not one you want to get close to. She's not a nice lady like your mama."

"She gave me sugar."

"Did she now?" That little bit of favoritism annoyed me. I didn't want Aurora making friends with my son. "If you get hungry, you come to your papa."

"Dog bad. And bad man walks funny."

"Remember—find a hiding place in the sails."

CHAPTER 25

I'd half hoped we might run into an American frigate on our way to Syracuse, given that Malta was on the way, but I didn't see our flag anywhere. If Morris was fighting a war he had an odd way of doing it. We breezed past the British outpost as if in a regatta and pointed for Syracuse, that ancient city on Sicily's eastern shore that had been fought over by the Athenians, Romans, Vandals, Goths, Byzantines, Arabs, Normans, Germans, Spanish, and just about anyone else who happened by. It was founded more than seven centuries before Christ, about the same time as Rome, and was presently ruled from Naples by the Bourbon king Ferdinand under the protection of the British navy. Syracuse, in short, was a place so thoroughly besieged, shelled, occupied, surrendered, and liberated that I had a hard time believing there was anything left to find there but recycled rubble. With luck we'd poke about, realize the whole thing was a myth, and Aurora would good-naturedly grant us all our freedom.

I knew better, of course.

The old city of Syracuse is on an oblong island that is connected by bridges to the mainland. There's a fort called Castello Maniace at the city's outer tip, its guns commanding any ship trying to enter or leave the harbors. This island, called Ortygia, is what we'd initially mistaken for a narrow bay on the palimpsest map. There's a large harbor on the southern side and a smaller one to the north, and then the new town and villas run uphill on the mainland, occupying a pie-shaped wedge of land that culminates at the Epipoli plateau. It's a perfect, centrally located place for a city, and the ancient Greeks had built eighteen miles of walls (long since dismantled and stolen by farmers and contractors) to enclose all its suburbs and estates.

Now, in 1802, the buildings of Ortygia are three- and four-story houses of honey-colored limestone with red tile roofs, the old town dominated by the spires and domes of its primary cathedral, the duomo. There is more gay color in Syracuse than in Muslim Tripoli, more whimsy and more charm. Bright blue fishing boats bob at its quays, painted stucco has hues of yellow and pink, and the homes have wooden shutters of ivory, green, blue, and lavender. Wrought-iron balconies allow the city's damsels to step out to water fringes of flowers and pose above the chaos of cart, donkey, prancing cavalier, farm wagon, and fancy coach.

I saw all this playing the English tourist, Sir Ethan Gage, in the company of my cousin, the

Lady Aurora Somerset, both of us kept in European costume from clothes the pirates had pillaged and stored in Barbary. That this brought back memories of Aurora's incestuous relationship with Cecil Somerset is an understatement, and the charade made me queasy. Aurora treated it as a grand joke. We pretended this pairing because our pirate corsair couldn't very well tie to the town quay, so instead we were rowed ashore at a bay down the coast. Dragut took pirates to do some preliminary scouting at an old Greek fort called Euryalus, and came back reporting he found no mirror but that it was a ruin perfect for "the necessary rendezvous."

"What rendezvous?" I asked.

"If we find the mirror we need help getting it and reassembling it," the captain said. "But first we have to find it, somewhere in or around this city. Correct?"

"As best as I could tell."

"For your son's sake, I hope you're right."

"Assuming we find it, how are we going to take it without having half of Sicily at our heels? Castello Maniace will blow your corsair out of the water if it comes to fetch the mirror."

"An interesting problem you should apply your mind to, if you want to save your son's life. Remember, Ethan, our fate is your own."

Aurora hired a carriage that took us to Syracuse in style, all of us pretending to be on holiday during the European peace. Harry came along as my son, with me widowed should anyone ask. Osiris was our "servant," a limping ogre vowing quietly to hurt Horus should I voice a wrong opinion or fail to endorse their latest skulduggery. Dragut was Aurora's manservant and bodyguard, lest I be tempted to try to strangle the girl. Fortunately, our tight little contingent of domestic bliss was able to leave her slobbering mastiff behind. I hoped Sokar choked on a sailor's femur by the time we got back.

We were to search the city for clues and then rendezvous with more of the pirates in that ruined ancient fort of Euryalus, Greek for "nail head." This castle, reputedly designed by Archimedes himself, had nonetheless fallen to the Romans in record time, which made me wonder again if the mirror was simple myth. But how to explain the peculiar mural at Akrotiri, on Thira?

The new Italian city of Syracuse had long since buried the ancient Greek one, and there was little sign on Ortygia that Archimedes had ever walked there. One clue of continuity, however, was built into the city's cathedral on the central piazza. The duomo had a baroque façade, erected after one of the periodic earthquakes that ravaged Sicily, but its sidewalls incorporated the pillars of an ancient Greek temple to Athena. It was a pragmatic recycling of faith and architecture that reminded me how new beliefs entwine with old.

"It's said that the gold of her statue would catch the morning sun and serve as a beacon to sailors when they were miles out to sea," a waiter told us on the piazza as I kept trying to keep Horus in his chair instead of crawling around on the pavement. I don't know how mothers keep track of their scamps. "While our duomo is closed in, the Greek temple was open to the air."

"Maybe that's where Archimedes got his idea for his mirrors," I theorized.

"What mirror, Papa?"

"The brightest mirror in the world. That's what we're looking for!"

His little face beamed with delight. Aurora looked bored, her halfhearted attempts at acting matronly reminding me of a folktale witch who'd just as soon pop a child into the oven.

To be playing the English squire with Aurora, Dragut, and Osiris was more than a little bizarre. I supped with a woman I loathed. She was absolutely imperturbable to my hostility and gloom, acting as if ours was the most natural reunion in the world. She knew this annoyed me, and enjoyed the annoyance. Hamidou searched me periodically to ensure I carried no weapon, and made certain I was aware of Cuvier's dueling weapons in his own belt lest I try something rash. Osiris loomed over Harry. Cain and Abel had a cheerier partnership.

At least propriety required that Aurora and I have separate rooms, given that we didn't pretend to be married. Otherwise I was forced to fake fond union; there was no question of escape. "Your son's fate rests with our success or failure," Aurora said quietly over glasses of port in the evening, after little Harry had been packed off to bed in my room, Osiris standing guard like a golem in a nightmare. "Find the mirror, or condemn your family."

"All we had is an old map showing the city. It proves nothing."

"Then think! Where would the Greeks or Romans hide it? Where would the Templars find it? How has it been hidden for two thousand years?"

I sighed. "Well, Archimedes got the idea from the Atlanteans, perhaps, or whoever it was that lived behind the mirror's protection on Thira. Maybe the Greeks even found a mirror already ancient, ten thousand years old, and brought it to Syracuse. Who knows? But the Romans adopted every military idea they could find, and would have taken that one if it had worked—unless Archimedes hid it away."

"The Roman commander claimed the scholar's death was an accident," Dragut said, "an impulse by a common soldier who didn't recognize the famous Greek. But maybe the mathematician really died for not telling them where the mirror was."

"It could have been melted down. Or thrown into the sea."

"Not destroyed," Aurora insisted, "or the Templars would never have been interested. Think like Archimedes, Ethan! You know more than you're telling us. The Romans had an army to find it. What did they miss?"

"How the devil should I know?"

"Because your son's life depends on it."

"You think it helps when you keep threatening my innocent child?"

"You're the obstinate one, not me. I've asked for partnership since our beginning."

I sighed. "And now you have your wish."

She smiled, cold as an iceberg. "Exactly."

I actually had an idea. Above the city were the old Greek theater and the Roman arena, half buried now. I remembered a horseshoe shape on the map; could that refer to the old amphitheater? And then there was that angled line from the old Greek fort to a cross on the island of Ortygia. This meant something to the men who'd drawn it.

There were also stone quarries from which the ancient city had been built. We hired a schoolteacher for information and were told that invading Athenians had been imprisoned there, many dying a ghastly death from hunger, exposure, and thirst. These limestone cliffs above the city were also riddled with caves. It was no place for a two-year-old, so I reluctantly agreed that Osiris could keep my lad occupied playing with the ducks at the Fountain of Arethusa, a freshwater spring that emerged near the edge of the sea in Ortygia. The ancient pool had been abandoned as a watering hole and recolonized by birds that Harry squealed at every time we passed. The ducks made up for his instinctual distrust of Osiris.

The rest of us purchased lanterns and explored the quarries as if enthralled by ancient atrocities: there's something ghoulish about tourism. The grottoes were pleasant escape from the heat of summer, the quarry pits shady from orange groves and musical from the trilling of birds. I kept my eye out for obvious burial places or hiding spots, but it seemed to me this was the first place any invader would look. We separated to make the task go faster, Dragut satisfied by now that I intended to cooperate to safeguard Harry. I explored one quarry cave after another, each as empty as those rooms on Thira. There were no murals, either.

By midday I'd wearied of the task and took a

break. I was trying an orange in the high grass under the cliff walls, wondering where the mirror might really be, when a sound crept into my depressed consciousness. Music like songbirds, I realized, but this was human, an ethereal melody that seemed to be floating off the cliffs. A woman was singing with a voice of angels, and the sweetness shook me out of my lethargy. Here was grace embodied by sound, sweet deliverance from my depressing captivity and this ancient quarry prison. I had to discover who the source of such loveliness was!

I made my way toward a towering cave in white cliffs shaped like a gigantic pointed ear, its opening a good hundred feet high. This was the entrance to a deep cavern with a flat, sandy floor, and it was from there that the haunting aria came from. The sound was amplified by the walls, giving it a depth like a heavenly choir. The song was Italian, a strain from an opera.

I walked in, my eyes adjusting to the dimness. What magic in a woman's voice, given the right place! Yes, there she was in the rear of this excavation, lost in reverie, her voice lifted like an offering. Who could it be? And so I stealthily advanced, she turned, and . . .

It was Aurora.

I stopped, confused. The idea such music could come from my archenemy had somehow never occurred to me, nor the notion that she'd ever sung in her entire twisted life. Yet there she was, a little flushed, lips parted, eyes alight, and I was suddenly jolted with memory of my initial attraction to her on the Canadian frontier. She had an over-powering, bewitching beauty, a sexual power that swamped the senses and blinded the mind. I still hated and feared her, but I still wanted her, too—and silently cursed myself for it.

There was a moment of silence. Then:

"I don't often sing, but the acoustics were irre-sistible."

"You surprise me again, Aurora."

"We don't know each other, Ethan, not really. Everything went badly too quickly in America. But we could."

"You killed my lover, Namida."

"You killed my brother. People die, Ethan, for all kinds of causes. But the quest for knowledge is eternal. That's what we have in common."

"Why do you want to pretend that?"

"Why do you resist it? It's no different from your attraction to Astiza. When you wanted me, on Lake Superior, you couldn't have me. Now that you can, you repudiate me. Which of us is con-fused?"

How lovely she was, and how dangerous! I shiv-ered, and hoped she didn't see it. I did want her, but I also wanted to kill her, and would do so in an instant if Horus and Astiza weren't at risk. Why hadn't I insisted on staying with Astiza in the first place, three years before? Then none of this would have happened.

Aurora stepped close, her scent a mix of perfume and sweat from the day's exertions. "I could learn to be a mother, too. Do you think I've never wanted children? Do you think I don't have feelings, like you?" She grasped my arm. "I could be like other women, Ethan. I could!" And for just a moment I glimpsed the desperation beneath her steel.

I shook free. "Aurora, the last thing you're like is other women. Harry has the good sense and instinct to be afraid of you."

"He'll feel different when I make him a prince." The stubborn yearning was pathetic, the determination unnerving. "You both don't know me. Not all of me."

I knew enough, and looked away. "We should find Hamidou and decide what to do next," I said, for lack of anything better to say.

"The mirror is here somewhere, I can feel it," she said. "Some great bronze thing, as bright as the sun, bringing fire like Prometheus and remaking the world."

"Somewhere."

"We're going to find it, Ethan, and possess it together."

CHAPTER 26

Dragut's appearance saved me from having to continue that disturbing conversation. We gave up on the echoing cave, its walls too smooth and featureless to hide anything. Outside we climbed through tall grass and the hum of insects to the crest of the white quarries and looked back at the city below. The Mediterranean was dotted with sails, and I tried to imagine some mirror harnessing the sun's power to set them all afire.

"If this ancient invention worked, why did Syracuse lose?" I asked.

"All weapons have vulnerabilities," Dragut said. "Perhaps the Romans came at night, when there was no sun. Perhaps it didn't work in the rain."

"And perhaps there was treachery," Aurora said. "There is always someone willing to bargain away a city to save his own life." She gave a glance as she said it, which annoyed me.

"Or bargain for the life of his innocent family," I replied. Did even my captors hold me in contempt for helping them?

"But for medieval knights to be interested, the mirror must have somehow survived," Aurora went on. "Somehow Archimedes knew the city must fall and he hid his machine. There is no record of the Romans capturing it. He secreted the mirror and either the Templars never found it, or they did so and hid it again. You saw the map, Ethan. You're the key." She smiled again, as if that might forestall any mutiny.

But the map didn't show anything obvious, not even a picture of the mirror itself. These pirates were chasing a pipe dream of opiates and legend. I tried to remember the parchment we ate, its taste all too vivid. "Well, there's the cathedral." I pointed downhill toward Ortygia and the towers and domes of the duomo. "There was a cross on the map at that point."

"I believe we could have found that landmark without your help," Dragut said drily.

"There was also a castle or fort on the map, probably this Euryalus: the one that Archimedes supposedly designed. Where is that?"

"This way." Dragut led us up a ridgeline past a tall, blocky mill to a plateau above the quarries. He pointed to a ridge in the distance. "It's up there." I saw a ramble of broken stone, with farms on the hill below. There were also the ruins of an old aqueduct that appeared to lead toward the mountains.

I considered a moment, and then held my arms out with my thumbs pointed skyward. One was aimed at the fort, the other at the cathedral several miles away. That line from one to the other should be the roughly angled line I'd seen drawn on the old map. I walked to the lip of a low cliff and looked down. Below were the ruins of a Greek theater, built into the limestone hillside. This was the horseshoe on the map, I figured. The nearby caves might be the humps drawn on the old parchment. Numbers might be measurements. But where was the squiggle that was the river? This was dry country.

"What is it you're seeing?" Aurora asked. "What are you looking for?"

I ignored her. "Listen," I said to Dragut. "Do you hear water?"

"It sounds almost under our feet."

We climbed back down to an earthen platform that formed the top rim of the Greek amphitheater. At its rear was a limestone cliff about forty feet high, again pocked with caves. The largest of these was directly behind the center of the theater, a half-moon with a stream issuing from a dark tunnel in the back. The water fell into a pool contained by a stone wall. The rock behind the little waterfall was bright green with slime.

"Explain this, Hamidou."

"A spring," he guessed. "Perhaps that's why they built the theater here. The citizens would make their hot climb for a performance and at the top have fresh water to drink."

"They didn't bring the theater to the spring," Aurora said. "They brought the spring to the theater. This is below that aqueduct we saw. It feeds a tunnel that leads to this pool." She pointed. "The water probably goes on to power that mill there, and then flows downhill to the city's fountains. Clever."

"Water power is just the kind of thing that would have fascinated Archimedes."

"Yes," Dragut said. "He invented a screw to lift water into irrigation canals."

"So perhaps he engineered this. Which means he might have known this aqueduct and tunnel intimately." I studied the cave mouth the water was pouring out of. "Not big enough to hide a ship-burning mirror, however."

The other two watched me ponder, not sure if I was onto something or deliberately misleading them. I wasn't sure myself, but I enjoyed that they were forced to trust me as much as I distrusted them. "Well. There was a line on the map that angled at this stream. I don't have the slightest idea what it meant, but I think it might be worthwhile to take a look inside. The very fact that Roman soldiers would most likely *not* look inside a giant water pipe intrigues me."

"You're going to climb in that hole?"

"Yes. Hand me a lantern when I get up to the entrance."

"How do we know you aren't going to try to run away through the tunnel?" Aurora asked.

"Because your henchman holds my son, my dear. Your perfidy, your greed, your cruelty, and your ruthlessness are all keeping me perfectly in place." I smiled sweetly and hopped over the low wall to splash across the thigh-deep pool to the little waterfall. As I expected, it was slippery, but by working up one side I was able to pull myself the ten feet up to the tunnel mouth, black as a nun's habit. I squatted, water running past my boots, and called back to the others. "Now, a lantern!" I don't like underground places, but I do have a certain expertise. There's pride in having a skill besides cards, women, and wine.

Dragut handed me up a lamp and I began duck-walking into a passageway four feet high. Water splashed to my knees. The tunnel seemed wholly unremarkable, carved for the sole purpose of delivering what I was wading through. I was exploring because I didn't know what else to do.

I left daylight behind. The others shouted but I ignored them, squatting and thinking in the dark. It was good to be by myself for a moment. But this cave crawl seemed pointless—until I saw a sign in the lantern light and my heart jumped.

A fat Templar cross, etched into the stone. No Archimedes did that, two and a half centuries before Christ was even born. Some medieval knight had crawled in here, too.

For what?

Now I went more slowly, looking carefully. The limestone was slick, cool, and featureless. Finally I saw a glow ahead. Was the aqueduct ending already? No, there was a shaft of light from above. I awkwardly made my way to it, thighs aching, and looked up. There was a carved crevice in the rock about one foot wide, extending across the ceiling of the tunnel. It rose, a vertical pocket like the sheath of a sword, toward the surface of the plateau we'd stood on earlier. At the top, stones had been placed to close most of this shaft so that the opening to the sky was only a foot square, too small for people to fall into or climb out of. So why make the pocket so big? There was nothing in it.

I crawled on and in a hundred feet there was another slit, same as the first, carved upward in the ceiling. And another, and another. I counted six before finally stopping. The shafts served, I assumed, to equalize air pressure and encourage water flow in a channel that barely sloped. They also let in light for maintenance. Yet each one had been hollowed to enormous size and then closed back up at the top. It made no sense.

Unless it did, to Archimedes.

I reversed course and crawled back out the tunnel, skidding down the waterfall and landing in its pool with a splash. I climbed out, soaking, dirty, and puzzled.

"You took a long time."

"It's a long tunnel." I poured water out of my boots. "There are man-made crevices in there that might have hidden something." I drew a circle in the sand, and lines across it. "Suppose you divided the mirror into sections, like a pie. Perhaps you even cut each section into two or three lengths."

"Not cut," said Aurora. "They were hinged, to catch and focus the sun."

"The result would be narrow slices. There are air shafts in the tunnel in which the pieces of a dismantled mirror might have been hidden."

"Might?" Dragut asked.

"There's nothing there now. I did see a Templar

Cross chiseled into rock. This medieval order you want to emulate got here ahead of us, I think. We may be too late."

"No," Aurora said. "Then why hide a map in such a secret place on Thira, and make a signet ring marking it? The knights found the mirror but had to conceal it again, until their investigations were completed. Perhaps they didn't know yet how to reassemble it, or were waiting for a military base to deploy it from."

"Perhaps they decided it was such a terrible invention it ought never be deployed."

She ignored me. "If the mirror had been reassembled and used, there would be a medieval record of it. If it was destroyed, there is no need to draw a hidden map. If it was shipped away to another city, they would not have drawn Syracuse. It's here. I can *feel* it here."

"Not at Euryalus, the abandoned Greek fort: we searched there," said Dragut.

"No, some place more accessible than that, from which the mirror might be more easily shipped. Yet somewhere it would never be disturbed. Somewhere sacred, somewhere sacrosanct, somewhere unsuspected." She walked to the edge of the ancient theater and looked at the city below. "Somewhere like a temple to Athena, the Greek version of Egypt's Isis, built in 480 B.C. after the Greek victory over the Carthaginians at Himera. The continuity of temple into cathedral would appeal to the Templars. Why else mark its location with a cross on the map?" She turned to me. "Ethan, I

THE BARBARY PIRATES 259

think our weapon is hidden in the city's cathedral, its duomo."

"Where?"

"I don't know."

"How will you ever get it? Or get it out of town?"

"I told you to ponder how we might slip by Castello Maniace," Dragut said. "How can our ship get safely away?"

I shrugged. "Any lateen-rigged corsair is going to be a primary target. You need a decoy. No—you need a second ship, a Sicilian ship, with your own as a false target. You've got to allow the Sicilians to sink the *Isis*, so you can escape with the other."

He considered and nodded. "Sly. See? We *are* becoming partners, Ethan Gage."

CHAPTER 27

The piazza in front of the Syracuse cathedral is one of the loveliest in Europe, elongated and artfully irregular, its slope following the natural contours of Ortygia. Its border is fine three-story stone-and-stucco buildings that provide a harmony of grand entrances, high windows, and iron balconies. The façade of the duomo itself is a baroque confectionery of pillars, statues, arches, scrolls, angels, eagles, and enough additional architectural frosting to decorate a wedding cake. The cathedral's side is much plainer, a largely blank wall interrupted by the old Greek pillars of what had been in turn a pagan temple, Christian basilica, Arab mosque, and ever-evolving cathedral.

Inside, the hodgepodge continued: Greek columns, Norman arches, and baroque side chapels. A circular window with a thick-limbed cross, reminiscent of the muscular signature of the crusading knights that I saw in the aqueduct cave, shone in the sturdy wall above the vestibule. I had a feeling most any prayer would work in here, thick as the place was with the ghosts of intertwined faiths.

"What this place, Papa?" Harry and Osiris had rejoined us.

"A sanctuary." I hoped it really was.

"What's a sanry?"

"Where bad people go to be better, and good people go to be safe."

"Are we bad?"

"Not you, Harry. You're a good boy."

He nodded solemnly. "And safe."

A few old women sat in the pews, waiting for the confessional and the one person, the priest, who had to listen to them. An old man desultorily swept dust with a stick broom from one corner to another, and then back again. Except for its mix of architecture, the duomo seemed grand but unexceptional.

"The mirror must be long gone, Aurora." Without even thinking about it I whispered.

"Then your little family will be destroyed." Crossing herself with holy water—an act of blasphemy, given her character, that I half expected would be answered with a bolt from heaven—she played the English tourist again, slowly circuiting the side aisles while counting pillars and arches. She sauntered as if a cathedral was her most logical environment in the world, and smirked at me as she did it. Every intimacy had become an act of reprisal.

But even she had respectfully murmured, I noticed.

Light filtered in through small stained-glass windows, its dim glow supplemented by votive candles burning as offerings to the saints. The place had that church smell of old wood, wax, dust, incense, and water used to mop down the flagstones.

"There is no crypt, I asked the priest," she whispered as we followed along. "We can see the roof beams ourselves, eliminating an attic. The walls are as thick and plain as a fortress. But this sacred site is what the Templars would have chosen, I'm certain of it. The spirit of a dozen religions is here. The knights would applaud the continuity of faith. But where, Ethan? Where? You're the one with the knack for finding old relics."

My only knack is for getting into awkward situations like this one, but I didn't say that. I wandered about with Harry looking for who knows what, struck by how the Norman plainness contrasted with a central white altar that seemed spun out of sugar. The three other chapels were jewel boxes of marble and gold. Castles and cathedrals are where men put their energy, I've found: war, and the afterlife.

But I saw no hiding places for mirrors. Just angels, saints, and miracles on the ceiling, everyone up there floating about in flowing robes and pointing portentously. If only real life were so weightless! I was tired of old legends, and would give this one up in a moment except for Harry. He toddled along holding my finger, awed by a place so big and shadowy. So I looked, counting the old Greek columns—ten on one side, nine on the other—and marveled at the craftsmanship of the artisans. One chapel had steps of rose granite, a silver altar that glowed like the moon, and velvet tapestries like the raiment of Apollo. High above, painted on the ceiling, were cherubs and bearded patriarchs, half of them looking like Archimedes. It was all quite grand and meaningless; I recognized no particular Christian story. My eye was about to skip on when I noticed the central oval in the design, highlighted by a small ocular window that let in a cone of light.

Cherubs floated there, four baby heads looking down on three more full-bodied angels. The trio looked as uncorrupted as little Harry, their naked bodies strategically draped with red ribbon. I'd seen the same in a hundred churches, and would have paid no more attention except for what they were holding. There was a sun in this painting, beaming down with yellow rays, and it was being caught by what looked to be a hand mirror or magnifying glass.

A mirror, radiating its own rays.

I remembered the ring Fouché had shown us, with a second dome on the inside and the letter "A." *Angelus.* Angels. I squinted upward, trying to make sense of the scene.

A white-bearded notable of some sort was pointing with a staff toward a wall, or was he pointing beyond it? I looked down. On the rococo marble masterworks that made up the walls, I suddenly realized, was a most peculiar inlaid piece of art. A dagger was crossed with a palm leaf, represented by different shades of stone. Above was what looked to be a chalice, but a chalice with two eyes of the Greek kind—the solemn almond-type they painted on their ships—looking across in the same direction. Looking at what? I saw nothing in this chapel to hide a mirror. But then I remembered the chapel next door, where the old man was pointing. I walked to it. Unlike the first alcove, this one had a dome like an upside-down saucer, painted not with cherubs but adult angels smoky from centuries of soot. A dome like any other, except it had the diameter and depth of a parabola reminiscent of the shape Cuvier had guessed Archimedes' mirror might take. I looked up. A dome to hide a fearsome weapon? Could it be?

I beckoned to Aurora. "Imagine," I whispered, "if the Templars built the mirror into the ceiling, to hide it until the time was right for retrieval."

"The ceiling?"

"Encased up there, bowl-side down. Look again at the signet ring."

I showed her the cherubs and staff and eyes. Her face brightened as she paced rapidly from the one chapel to the other, and then back again. "Ethan, I think you have it!" she hissed.

"Too bad the Templars were clever enough to hide it in a place from which it could never really be taken. Built right into the skin of a sacred church, in the middle of Syracuse. Hidden in plain sight. They must have done it after an earthquake, when the duomo was being repaired. They put the entire power of the Church to work protecting their discovery, Aurora. Quite brilliant, really. Impossible to steal."

"Sandwiched in a false ceiling," she murmured.

"Yes. Well, we've done our best. It's too bad,

I'm sure the weapon is all very interesting, but the knights have always been a step ahead, haven't they? Since it's safely sealed away, can Harry and I go free now?"

"Young Horus?" She smiled. "But he's going to help get this for us!"

◻   ◻   ◻

The baroque chapel with silver altar and red tapestries had two low and narrow doors at the back. Casting a quick eye about for any priest, Aurora darted to one, shielded herself with the rich fabric, and tried its latch. It was locked. So Dragut brutishly forced it, the pretty wood splintering in a wound that would have made Gabriel weep. A narrow passageway behind the main wall led sideways, toward the rear of the church. That would do us no good.

"The other. Hurry!"

The pirate snapped that latch free, too, and this time there was a spiral staircase going upward.

Aurora reached for Harry but he shrank against my leg. Frowning, she then beckoned to me. I hesitated, hoping we might be discovered and rescued by a mob of angry monks, but we'd deliberately chosen a time in the somnolent afternoon when no masses were scheduled. I picked up my son and quickly crossed to the broken door and the stone stairs.

"Where we go, Papa?"

"Up. I'll hold you."

He thrashed his way down out of my arms.

"No. Walk!" And he led us all, happy as a monkey. Just behind him, the votive candles that Dragut, Aurora, and Osiris had snatched threw a wavering light.

We came to a crude attic above the chapels. We were at the edge of the adjacent dome, with room only to crouch where a roof eave came down. It was a cat's cradle of old beams and buttresses, dusty, cobwebbed, and spooky. I wondered again how long before a priest or prelate discovered our trespass and roused all of Syracuse against us. It was creepy enough that Harry lifted his arms to be held again.

"I knew we'd need your whelp," Aurora said, peering into the dark crevice between interior dome and exterior roof. "Give me the boy."

"Certainly not."

"Hurry, or do you want to spend all day up here, waiting for a prelate to discover that broken door?" She pried my son from my grasp and set him on the floor, taking out a stick of sugar. "Now, Horus, do you like candy?"

He nodded solemnly.

"I think you should have some, but there's something clever I want you to do to earn it. Only *you* can do it because you're small enough to wiggle where big people can't. I want you to crawl up the space here and scratch what you find with this little knife." She held out a penknife. "Then bring the knife back to me, and you can have your candy."

"He'll cut himself!"

"Not if the urchin does what he's told." Her voice gentled to speak to the child. "Only big boys are allowed to handle knives, but I think you're very big for your age. I want you to carefully crawl up this little slope on top of the ceiling here, and when you can go no farther, then rub this knife on whatever is blocking you."

"Dark!" my child said, perfectly reasonably. He was as confused as I was.

"You won't have to squeeze far, and I'll hold the candle to light your way. It will only take a moment."

"Aurora, are you insane?"

"Think, Ethan. If the mirror is hidden in the dome, it must be sandwiched between ceiling and roof. But before I start taking this cathedral apart I want to make sure it's actually there, and I can't squeeze into the sandwich to see. Horus can. It's not unreasonable for your bastard to be useful for once."

"What if he gets stuck?"

"Then we'll jam you in there to pull him out. Stop complaining and help me!"

I sighed and squatted. "Harry, this edge is sharp." I showed him the knife. "You have to be careful. Hold it like this." I formed his fingers around the handle. "Rub the blade against whatever stops you and then crawl backward to Papa. Can you be brave?"

"Will I get candy?"

"Yes."

"Will dog bite me?"

I sighed. "No."

He smiled, rather excited by the importance of his task. He took the knife, held it ahead like a probe, and wriggled up the narrow space between the ceiling of the dome and the rafters of its tile roof overhead. I could still see the soles of his shoes when he called, "It stops!"

"What can you see?"

"Dark." It was almost a whimper.

"Rub the blade and come back for your candy!" Aurora called.

Nothing happened, and she swore.

"It has to be there," Osiris said, with more hope than proof.

"We have to be sure."

"Eyes!" It was a yelp and Harry's little feet kicked. I roared and reached in to grab his ankles but Dragut gripped me and then there was an animal squeak and my boy was still again.

"Harry?"

"Remember, rub the blade on the dark part for your candy!" Aurora called.

After a moment's hesitation we heard a raspy scraping and then he was wriggling backward. Dragut let go of me and I caught his ankles and helped pull him out.

Harry held up the knife proudly. Its edge gleamed yellow, with scratched flakes of bronze or gold.

"It's here," Aurora exulted, her eyes a glaze of greed.

"Wait, there's something more," I said. The blade had hairs on it. "Horus?"

He beamed then and pulled from his shirt, where he had tucked it, the dead body of a slain mouse. He had stabbed the little monster to death. By thunder, my son was an Achilles!

"Candy?"

I handed it to him, hands shaking. My boy had the makings of a fine treasure hunter, I realized— the worst curse I could think of.

"Get the Rite," Aurora told Dragut, "and then ready the ships as Ethan suggested. Thanks to him and his bastard, we're going to blow this ceiling apart."

CHAPTER 28

The crumbled ancient Greek fortress of Euryalus sits at the crest of the Epipoli plateau at the apex of the old north and south walls, its battlements pointed west like the prow of a ship. We rode rented horses to the forgotten ruin after dark, Aurora having changed from traveling dress to riding clothes. "We'll get help, and then you'll save your son." As if I could believe anything she said.

The ruins seemed deserted when we approached. Warm wind blew off the mountains to the west, bending the tall grass, and dogs barked from farmyards far below. In the distance we could see lamps from the city and anchored ships, six miles away. Bats flew against the last glow of twilight, and the first stars were faint in the evening haze. I wondered where one would make a secret camp here, when suddenly the ground opened like a mouth.

"This is the old moat, one of three that fronted

the fortress," Dragut said. "There's a ramp over here."

We were swallowed as we rode cautiously down, passing through a short tunnel to the bottom of the old Greek excavation. Fires reflected from a tier of arches on the side of the moat, and I realized that my captors' confederates were waiting here in the fort's underground chambers, out of sight of any Sicilian peasants above. We stopped, the tails of our horses flicking, and then a hooded man came from one of the caves and grasped Aurora's bridle.

"Greetings to our Astarte, our Ishtar, our Freya! Lady of moon and womb, the risen eastern star, our dove and our lioness!"

Well, that was a little much.

"Greetings, Dionysus. I bring the Fool, as prophesied. And his pup has indeed played a role, as foretold. All is happening as it should, and soon we'll begin to inherit the true powers of the ancients."

I startled at the introduction because a gypsy fortune-teller had once called me the Fool who sought the Fool, the primitive wisdom of Enoch and the long-lost god Thoth. Here the label was again, like that long-ago tarot card.

"May the gods grant us the courage to grasp such power, the will to wield it, and the ruthlessness of true conviction!"

"Isis and Osiris are listening to our prayers even now, Dionysus." She swung down from her saddle as dozens of other hooded figures crowded the mouths of the fortress tunnels to greet us. Pagans again, and if I tripped over many more of them in these bizarre adventures of mine it would be enough to take holy orders. This bunch was lunatic to a man and woman, I guessed, but none the less dangerous for that.

Dragut took me into the arcadelike tunnel that ran the length of the moat and gave access to caverns behind. Tunnels led deeper into the ancient fortress, and torches flickered back there. In ancient times, I guessed, these passages allowed soldiers to move from one part of the fort to another out of sight or catapult shot. Now they served as a dandy warren for bandit clans like ours. There were at least a hundred of Aurora's confederates gathered, a few of them Muslim pirates but many more European. These newcomers wore black, gray, and white robes over the more conventional dress of their nations.

Harry clung tight as a limpet. "Who these people, Papa?"

"The local asylum."

A hundred candles illuminated the grotto with smoky light. Animal-headed gods had been placed in niches, and pentagrams were drawn in the sand. There were muskets, pikes, cutlasses, and axes stacked in corners, and pipes and ram's horns for music. Great coils of rope were stacked along with kegs of gunpowder and twists of fuse. The cloaks and hoods gave a sinister anonymity to the gathering, as if nobody wanted to be recognized as part of such foolery.

"Where did these people come from, Aurora?"

"You told Osiris in Paris that you were curious about the Egyptian Rite," she replied. "Here we are, drawn at my summons from the lodges and temples of Europe. This is a rebirth of Templar and Pythagorean wisdom, Ethan, of Babylonian astrology and Cabbalistic mysticism! These men and women are some of the finest minds in Europe, and unlike other scholars we are open to new ideas and experiences. We have dukes and duchesses, savants and theologians, merchants and sea traders, highborn ladies and brilliant courtesans. They are here by merit. We induct tradesmen as readily as aristocrats, if they have proven themselves in the study of hermetic lore and the willingness to undergo ceremonial trials. There are English, French, German, Italian, and Spanish, united by their thirst for knowledge and reform."

"What kind of reform?"

"The kind that comes from establishing our own rule. We're a superior order, as far above the common man today as judges among the apes. It is our privilege, and our burden, to reform this planet, and to exterminate as many of the unilluminated as necessary."

"Unilluminated?"

"Ancient truth is there to be rediscovered, but some turn their back on it or refuse to recognize what must be changed. The obstinate will be disposed of. The Rite will initiate a pure society, where everyone agrees on truth."

"By eliminating anyone who doesn't."

"That's a basic principle of governing. One achieves harmony by unanimity. There is nothing more chaotic, or inefficient, than people who question their rulers. Doubters by definition are not part of the exalted race. Those commoners who survive will serve as slaves to our priesthood."

"I see. And am I exalted?"

"That remains to be seen."

"And you're going to achieve this consensus by burning all the world's navies?"

"The world will be better without any navies, except ours."

"A pirate navy."

"A navy of entrepreneurs, mystics, and seekers of the light."

"And what are all these fanatics doing *here*, Aurora?"

"They are not fanatics. They are the holiest of the holy, the ones who adhere most faithfully to our cause. They are patriots, Ethan, patriots who want to rediscover the secret powers of the civilization that came before our own, and bring back a lost golden age. We want to walk as the gods walked, with their powers and sensuous freedoms. We will do whatever we wish, with whomever we choose, and our slaves will rejoice that our tyranny is a thousand times sweeter than any liberty in today's myopic world! When we finish our investigations, we of the Rite are going to be incapable of wrong, and will rule with perfect understanding. We'll have visions through our opiates, and enlightenment through our ecstasies. We will be gods ourselves, perfect beings! And you can still join us! You and young Horus!"

"And Astiza?" I had to put a brake to Aurora's fantasies.

Her lips narrowed. "If you still want her, after having seen the light."

Here it was, then. Bored aristocrats, passed-over scientists, shunned deviants, bankrupt merchants, indebted gamblers, poxed libertines, the eccentric, and the wicked: all had finally found family in this monstrous perversion of Freemasonry founded by the charlatan Cagliostro more than a generation before. This bunch wanted magic and technology, yes, but even more they wanted to persecute every man and woman who had ever snubbed them. How sublime to be convinced that everyone who disagreed with you was your inferior! How satisfying to deem yourself a chosen race, without need for the scruples of lesser men! It was audacious and ludicrous, and yet what if we did find some death ray from old Archimedes? What if my own nation's small navy was about to burst into flame because I, Ethan Gage, was helping this menagerie of megalomaniacs along? I dare not do it, except that little Harry was clinging to my neck, eyes instinctively wide at these robed conspirators. And then there was the dark snuffing shape of the attack dog Sokar padding in the shadows. How could I get us safely away?

By playing along until chance offered escape.

"We're going to return to Syracuse," Aurora said. "Dionysus will lead a parade of penitents, our own Egyptian Rite army, into the city to aid us. They'll pose as pilgrims coming to celebrate the Feast of the Assumption, when Mary rose into heaven. Hamidou will have the new ships ready and bring them to the city at the precise moment. We'll break the mirror loose, even if we have to bring the entire duomo down to do so."

"You're going to blow up a church during a Catholic holiday?"

"Just part of it, as quietly as possible."

"This is balmy, Aurora. Give it up! Even if it's there, you can't get at it, or you'll be sunk if you do."

"We'll get at it. You already suggested a way to get past the castle's guns so that your child is not stung with flying splinters. You can plot the details with Hamidou while we conduct the Ceremony of Baal here. Then you're going to help me steal the fire of Barbary." Her eyes gleamed. "We'll erect it in Tripoli, Ethan, on Karamanli's ramparts, and when it is ignited by the sun we'll have taken the first step toward world harmony!"

She turned from me to start readying some age-old occult ritual, the Muslim pirates eyeing this blasphemy with disquiet.

Harry whispered in my ear, "I want Mama."

"So do I, son. So do I."

CHAPTER 29

Once more I was breaking into a church in the middle of the night, committing so many sins on this quest that I feared I'd find the mouth of Hades in the most literal and unpleasant way. In addition to common sacrilege, I was assisting pirates and fanatics, I had dragged my son into the worst kind of danger, I was betraying the interests of my country, and I had gone back on my pledge to my three friends to keep our map secret. And this was my record when trying to do the right thing. If I ever consciously turn to infamy, my soul will be so threadbare that it won't fill in a gale.

We used a bar to break in through a side door of the duomo from the Via Minerva, Aurora's monstrous dog coming with us this time on an iron chain. Other Rite members passed through the city's dark streets like a procession of pilgrims and then hid in the shadows of the duomo's vestibule, crouching to wait by its twisted pillars entwined with carved grapevines.

Inside, the church nave seemed even higher and plainer in the midnight gloom, while the silver altar of Saint Lucia glowed like ice in starlight. Every footstep seemed like a transgression, every foot-step a heresy. The dog's huffing wheeze was like an invasion of older beasts from demon times. We crossed to the chapel and the door that had led us upward. Its lock was still shattered, but a wooden bar had been nailed to close it.

Dragut took out a pry bar and pulled, the nails a shriek in the night.

Suddenly there was a shout. "By the grace of God, stop!"

An elderly priest was hurrying toward us from the shadows of the main altar, half dressed and agi-tated. One arm was lifted either in supplication or anger, and his shouts echoed in the vast space.

"What are you doing, blasphemers?"

Aurora froze for only a moment. Then: "Sokar, strike!"

The dog's chain was dropped and the animal whipped away, running silently at the frantic holy man dashing toward us, its metal tether skipping on the floor. I tried to cry warning but Dragut's hand clamped over my mouth. The dog leaped, a blur in the dark, and then the priest yelled and went down, sliding backward on the stone floor as the animal's momentum carried them toward the sacristy. There was a savage snarling, muffled screams, and the sounds of bones snapping under powerful jaws. The priest thrashed wildly, his agony muffled by the animal's gnawing of his head, and then the poor man was still. The dog trotted back with a self-satisfied growl, its jaws bloody.

Little Harry clung, terrified.

"That's not a dog, it's a monster." My voice was shaking. "You're damned for all eternity, all of you."

"Sokar protects an older, finer religion. It is men like that who will be labeled sacrilegious and eliminated."

"That's it." Sokar was snuffling as Osiris patted his head. "I quit. I'll have nothing to do with this. I resign, before we all go to hell."

"You can't resign, or I'll sic my dog on your son. You know you can't quit, not now and not ever. You're one of us, and the sooner you help us the sooner we can leave Syracuse so nobody else has to die."

"Aurora, please!" I groaned.

"Someday you'll see the beauty of our desecration."

There was a click as Dragut held one of Cuvier's pistols to my head, to reinforce the point, and a growl as Sokar shook his massive head, blood and spittle flying.

"We're all partners, now," the pirate reiterated.

¤   ¤   ¤

For a band of sybarites, perverts, addled mystics, and amateur magicians, the Egyptian Rite proved frighteningly efficient at rigging the demolition of a sacred chapel. With the priest dead,

Dragut opened a main door and Aurora's confederates swept in like a silent tide, pulling ropes, gunpowder, and wrecking tools from under their robes. Directly beneath the dome was a small shelf running around its circumference, high above the chapel. The heretic monks daringly crawled out on this, oblivious to the thirty-foot drop, to string ropes and place charges of gunpowder. A web of stout line was tied horizontally to form a net to catch whatever was blown free. This was no attempt at delicate surgery; it was a quick snatch and run before the good citizens of Syracuse realized we were sabotaging their principal place of worship. Banks of votive candles were lit to provide lurid illumination. The work was done in choreographed silence. There was a last scramble up, fuses were unreeled to the chapel floor, and the hooded men waited for her order, each holding a candle.

Aurora walked to the middle of the chapel, looked upward at the placed gunpowder, and pirouetted beneath the dome and its dark angels, arms outstretched as if to catch the mirror herself.

"Now!"

The fuses were lit, sparking and smoking, and the Rite members backed into the main nave. Aurora was the last to come. Points of fire danced upward toward the chapel dome and a low hum rose up from those assembled, a hivelike chant.

"What if you destroy the mirror as well?"

"Our readings say it's sturdy as a shield. Besides, there's no other way. We don't have the men to seize and hold this city while we chip it out."

"This won't just wake the town, it will wake the dead."

"Then they can wave good-bye to a relic they didn't even know they possessed."

The light from the fuses disappeared, and there was a moment of suspense while we waited. Then a staccato roar as the circle of charges went off. Even Sokar jumped. Plaster and stone erupted downward, destroying the grimy angels in the ceiling, and a stinking cloud of smoke and dust rolled out from the chapel into the main church. Then, with a screech, something clanged and fell.

We ran through the choking fog and peered upward. Through the haze a disk vast and round was lying on the net of ropes that had been strung across the chapel. It was bronze, twenty feet in diameter, and bright where its metal had scraped as the mirror came loose.

My heart hammered. Two thousand years after Archimedes was slain by a Roman sword, his most terrifying invention—or was it a copy of an even earlier invention—had suddenly been rediscovered.

"Hurry, lower it!" Aurora shouted. "Every moment counts!" Bells began ringing in the city. Some of the Rite's monks pulled pistols and muskets from their robes and crouched by the main cathedral entry, looking out at the dark piazza beyond. Others clambered up to the mirror. Ropes were cut and slowly the makeshift hammock and its burden were lowered to a marble floor covered with debris. High above, the joists of the domed ceiling jutted like broken branches.

The prize was about half an inch thick and shaped like a shallow upside-down bowl. Nestled inside this bowl were more bronze panels, hinged inward from the rim so that the mirror looked like an upside-down folded flower. The Rite's henchmen lashed a hawser cable around the rim to make a crude tire. Then more ropes to pull the mirror upright onto its edge. Some of the monks were dancing with excitement, and their chants rose in volume. The brass weighed a ton, at least. It trembled, a giant wheel, men on both sides helping balance it. Like a wobbly plate, it was rolled out the duomo doors—just fitting!—and down the steps to the piazza. A dozen of the Rite's hooded monks had to corral the mirror just to keep it from careening away.

While attention was fixed on the rolling mirror, I crouched in the ruined chapel and hastily scratched a word on the dusty floor.

Tripoli.

I straightened before Osiris noticed, picked up Harry, and followed the crowd outside.

Torches appeared where the Via Santo Landolina debouched into the square, and we heard shouts to stop. The city's constabulary guard was coming, and no wonder: We might as well have brought an orchestra for all the noise we were making. We'd desecrated the city's duomo, had a dog eat one of the local priests, and were trying to steal something too big to fit on a hay wagon. Shutters were banging open all over Syracuse. The Rite's monks halted for a moment, hesitant, guns half raised, looking to Aurora for an order.

Then there was thunder. Grapeshot rattled down the length of the piazza and into the advancing Italians. A number fell, torches winking out.

Dragut had hauled a cannon from one of the ships and fired it down the length of the Landolina. "Come, do you think you're a frozen sculpture!" he shouted to the robed pilgrims. "Roll the mirror, roll it!" He was waving Smith's blunderbuss, the muzzle of which was smoking as well.

"Give me a weapon," I told Aurora. "I need my rifle back."

"You'll get it when you prove yourself."

We retreated as the monks did, the Rite's members pushing the giant disk so that it began to wheel downhill toward the eastern end of the piazza. That street led to the Fountain of Arethusa, the natural spring where Horus had played with his ducks. There was a quay adjacent, two ships waiting there.

Dragut turned to me. "Now we'll see if your plan works, Gage."

There were more shouts behind and gunfire began to chase us, bullets pinging and passing by with that peculiar hot buzz. The breath of their passage makes survival exhilarating. One Rite member yelped and went down, others pausing to help him.

"Leave him!" Aurora shouted. "The mirror! The mirror!"

"It's Anthony!"

She pointed a pistol at her wounded follower and fired, the man jerking and then lying still. "None can be left alive to betray our plans."

The others began pushing the mirror even faster.

I sprinted ahead, holding young Harry. Sokar's baying had started dogs barking all over the city and the child clung to me in confusion, bewildered by the excitement but intrigued, too. Yes, there the new ship was, just as I'd suggested and Dragut had promised! I bounded aboard a square-rigged brig the Barbary ruffians had captured, its crew set adrift in its boats. *Zephyr*, its name was. And, as I'd proposed, Aurora's *Isis* was in tow behind for sacrifice. I looked back and heard the pirate cannon go off again, keeping pursuers at bay. Like some vast coin, the great bronze mirror came rolling down the street, chased by the monks as if it were a child's hoop. Its weight and bulk made a grinding noise as it turned.

Just beyond us at the Castello Maniace fort at the tip of Syracuse, torches were flaring as that garrison came awake. It would be their guns we'd have to slip past to clear the harbor. If I wanted to keep my son from drowning, my trick had to succeed.

I stood by the stern rail as the mirror was wheeled across a wooden gangplank and maneuvered between main and mizzen. A dozen men gently lowered it to lie on the deck, the platter so big that its rim extended over the gunwales on either side. Once the Rite members and their pirate allies piled on board, Dragut had the gangplank rotated and lashed to make a bridge between main deck and poop so sailors could get across the top of the mirror. Lines were cast off, sails blossomed, and oars crabbed the merchant vessel away from the dock. Fortunately, there was a night breeze and the canvas bellied, even as carabinieri, soldiers, and outraged priests charged the quay where we'd been moored. Two cannons went off from the corsair being towed, scattering our pursuers again. Our ship broke out the flag of the Kingdom of the Two Sicilies, while the pirate craft unfurled the banner of the Tripolitan pirates. It was a ruse I prayed would work long enough in the dark to keep my boy from harm.

"Harry, remember when I told you to go hide in the sails in a scrape. Now is the time!"

"No! Watch!" He was spellbound.

"Too dangerous! More sugar if you're a good boy and go below!"

It was a few hundred paces down the seawall of Syracuse to the fortress we must get past, and I could see more and more torches flaring there. Men ran back and forth on the ramparts as the great land guns were run out. They were 24-pounders, capable of ripping the bowels out of our tubby ship and its ancient cargo. As we gathered speed, sliding past the shallows at a brisk walking pace, I turned to Dragut.

"*Now*, if you hope to fool them."

He waved.

Behind us Aurora's corsair, connected by a tow-rope that was invisible in the dark, unfurled its own sail. A bow gun loaded with nothing more lethal than old rags gave a sharp report as if shooting at us, and we fired with equal pretense from light stern guns, both of us banging away as if the pirate corsair were chasing the *Zephyr*. Bits of burning rag flew in the air. The monks and pirates who'd jammed aboard the merchant vessel sank behind the gunwales to make us look lightly manned, while behind us the scarecrows I'd suggested for the corsair were propped up by the handful of brave pirates left aboard the *Isis*. In the dark, the impression was of a preying craft crammed with eager buccaneers.

The scheme was to make our ship look like a desperate, fleeing merchantman and to concentrate the Sicilian fire on the nearly empty corsair.

I looked anxiously at the fort. The excited shouts within the Castello died down as officers applied discipline. Door after door of the fortress gun ports banged opened. We heard the groan of tackle as each behemoth cannon was hauled out, its muzzle pointing at our vulnerable hull. We tensed, waiting for a barrage of fire that would gut us, but none came.

Now the corsair was coming abreast of the fort's guns.

Its tiny crew slipped into a cutter on the side of the ship and pushed off with oars in the dark.

Finally there was a cry of command and a ripple of cannon fire thundered from the fortress. Metal screamed and punched through the towed pirate vessel as though it were paper, heeling the decoy.

Aurora swung her cutlass and chopped the tow-rope away, even as Dragut winced at the pummeling of the graceful flagship. Its rudder had been lashed, and it began ghosting on a course of its own.

"*Fuoco! Sparare!*" The excited commands to fire and shoot could be heard from the fort.

More cannon balls crashed into the pirate craft's hull, sending up showers of wood splinters. The sail was slashed to ribbons, ending the ship's motive power, and then the entire rigging cracked and crashed down, spilling tackle and shredded canvas over the side. The corsair began to drift and wallow. Cheers began in the fort.

Not a shot had come our way.

Another command, and another roar of fortress artillery. Pieces of Aurora's old ship erupted, a barrel of gunpowder went off, and the vessel began to burn. The flames made it an even easier target, and more shot struck it solidly amidships. A mob had formed on the city's shoreline and a fusillade of musket shots came from there, too, the crowd peppering the empty vessel and its scarecrows with bullets. The corsair's stern began to settle.

We'd slipped by the tip of the fort and were gaining speed, on our way to safety.

Aurora looked from the *Isis* to the mirror. "A fair trade," she murmured. "You destroyed my vessel, Ethan, and I salute you for it. That's the kind of ruthless wisdom we'll bring to all affairs."

Perhaps they expected our merchant vessel to stop fleeing and turn around upon our apparent rescue from the destructive pirates. Perhaps they expected us to slow, or dip our flag in acknowledgment, or light a lantern, or give a cheer to our saviors.

Instead a score of pirates and monks clambered silently up our rigging to unfurl yet more sail.

Faster and faster we slid into the dark, the mirror of Archimedes rocking where it balanced. The brightest light was the burning corsair, and it drew the eyes of fort and town ever more hypnotically as we faded into the night.

By the time the Sicilians put out in small boats and realized they'd battered an empty target, the skeleton pirate crew that had abandoned the corsair had hoisted their own cutter sail to race to catch up with us. We hoisted them aboard and were out the harbor mouth, reaching down the coast of Sicily without so much as a bullet in our hull. The island's greatest prize was ours, to be resurrected in Tripoli.

"If the gods didn't want this, why would it be so easy?" Aurora told her followers.

They laughed.

Now the Barbary pirates could set the world's navies on fire.

CHAPTER 30

We sailed south across the Gulf of Noto, apparently having confused any pursuit. Once we cleared Syracuse, I went below and found Harry in the sail locker just as the sun was coming up. Both of us curled into the folds of canvas, the little lad cradled in my arms, but despite my exhaustion, sleep eluded me. Having performed my part of the bargain by finding the mirror, would Astiza, Horus, and I be allowed the freedom to try to find peace while the Rite reassembled its diabolical machine? My only hope was that I could warn the world in time to make up for the bargain I'd struck. Yet Aurora, Dragut, and Osiris seemed more convinced than ever that we'd become partners.

I eventually dozed fitfully. I got up by late morning to see that despite their tumultuous night, the "monks" couldn't keep away from the mirror. They were inspecting it more closely and speculating how it might work. The crew rigged an awning over the weapon as the sun climbed, because even covered in dust and tarnish it was blindingly bright. The pirates feared it might accidentally set their own rigging aflame.

We anchored that evening off Sicily's south-eastern tip, at a small, flat island called Capo Passero. As the sun descended behind the Sicilian hills to the west, the Rite members worked to better secure the mirror and prepare a celebration in the hold below. Oddly, I found myself a pirate hero, thanks to my idea to sacrifice Aurora's corsair to enable our escape. Even my young son, cheerful after his sleep, was celebrated as a swashbuckler in the making. The attention pleased Harry because they gave him a hat.

There was no pursuit from Syracuse. Chances were that the city's ministers and priests were uncertain just what it was we'd even taken. So we risked some lanterns as the mirror was lashed more securely. Carpenters cut out a section of each gunwale so it could sit firmly on the deck, while members of the Rite began to sketch and measure the ancient contraption. It was more complex than we initially imagined. The main surface was shaped like a huge shallow bowl, but it had been forged or hammered with a complex system of hexagonal facets like the pattern of a honeycomb; a thousand small mirrors linked into one. Then there were hinged sections that folded like a closed flower over the main mirror. If unfolded, they would double its diameter. They pivoted as well. There was also some kind of engraving on the back,

Dragut announced after crawling underneath. It showed a complex scaffolding to support and turn the device, with lines suggesting how to orient the mirror and its "petals" in relation to the sun.

"It's as simple as a magnifying glass and as complex as a watch," he said. "The Rite's savants will have a challenge mounting this properly. There are more ropes than on an opera stage."

Hard to operate, easy to sabotage, I thought, but didn't say that.

"Osiris will figure it out," Aurora said, looking exultant. She'd finally slept, too, and emerged radiant. Her Egyptian Rite lieutenant limped around the circumference of the mirror to calculate and draw. "Osiris and Ethan together, masterminds of a new age!"

"Not the most natural of partnerships, given that I crippled your engineer," I commented.

"A wound of battle, no different from the one I gave you in America," she said cheerfully. "Wounds heal, minds forgive. Right, Osiris?"

"We'll see what your electrician has to contribute."

"Yes, my electrician!"

"Your helper, your sycophant, your lover, your slave."

"I'm not any of those things," I told him. "I and my family are free, now that I've done my part of the bargain. Right? And what's your real name, when you're not made up like a eunuch in an emirate? Is it Dunbottom? Lord Lack-Purse? Prince Preposterous?"

"You're not entirely free," Aurora interrupted.

"Come. You said if I helped you find the mirror, you'd let Horus and Astiza go. There the bronze platter is, to incinerate whom you wish. Now keep your part of the bargain."

"Oh, young Horus will not be sold into slavery. And your Egyptian wench can wander wherever she wishes. But there is one thing more you and I must complete before we give her final leave from Yussef's harem. There's still unfinished business between you and me, as I told you in America."

"What? I've done exactly what you asked."

"I've decided that we're going to be married, Ethan."

"Married!" I was as dumbfounded as when presented with my son. I thought she would break into laughter at her joke, but she looked quite business-like.

"Marriage will give Horus a proper mother and legitimacy. I will raise him as an acolyte of the Rite, and when he comes of age he'll be a prince ready to inherit the world."

"But we hate each other!"

"That's a crude, simplistic way of explaining our relationship." She fingered the edge of the mirror. "We repel, and yet we attract. We extinguish, and yet we ignite. We loathe, and yet I will make you a little king yourself because I know how much you'd dread such responsibility, even as you long for me. Don't deny your longing! I saw it in that cave of echoes in Syracuse. I saw it in my cabin on the *Isis*. We're bound, Ethan, and the success of this quest only proves it. We're chained by destiny. I'm going to marry you and weld you to me forever, and if you're unhappy with that, as you watch me indoctrinate your son—well, so much the better!" Her eyes flashed. "You will marry me so you must serve me!" All good humor had disappeared. "You will marry me so you can never escape again!"

No wonder I've never galloped to the altar. "I'm a poor bet as a husband."

"If you don't marry me tonight, on this ship, Horus and Astiza *will* be sold into the worst kind of slavery you can imagine, and you'll be given back to Omar the Dungeon Master to break. But if you *do* marry me, and help us erect and operate the mirror, you'll rule by my side and your son will inherit powers that not even Bonaparte has ever dreamed of. King George and Jefferson will be his minions, and the emperors of Austria and Russia will prostrate themselves."

"That makes no sense. From one weapon?"

"This is but the beginning of the ancient secrets we are working to relearn, and just the first mirror of a million—if we need them! We will set nations on fire like your Norwegian's Ragnarok, his end of the world. And you and I, Ethan, will be freed of all law, all hypocritical rules, all morals, all restraint. We'll do anything we want with anyone we want to, because we will have acquired the magic of gods who once walked this earth. We will be perfect beings, because it will be us who define perfection."

I knew she was balmy, but not to the extent of this megalomaniac ranting. She was a cult courtesan on a merchant tub of pagans and cutthroats, and yet boasted like she was Queen of Sheba. I wasn't on a pirate ship, I was in a house of the addled. I closed my eyes in frustration. "I won't marry you, Aurora. You're not the mother of my son."

"You *will* marry me, this midnight, or I will give your son to Dragut's Moors this very night to begin to use as they will! You will marry me or hear his screams, and then you'll explain what you've done to your Egyptian slut of a harem whore before Yussef sells her away to the worst kind of degradation!"

"This wasn't our bargain!"

"You never asked what the full terms of the bargain were. And I couldn't tell you, because you're too stupid to grasp the chance to be a king. So I'll force it on you, and force you into my bed, and in time you'll worship me as I deserve."

She certainly had a high opinion of herself, which is a problem with lovely women. Admittedly, I'm sometimes guilty of the same vice. I stared out at the sea, thinking furiously. No union consecrated by this rabble would be recognized anywhere as either holy or legal. Should I go along with this sham until I could finally get Astiza and Harry away from this treacherous bitch? She wanted to marry me to torment me, to keep me close enough to make every day a misery of regret for what I'd done to her brother. Climb into a bridal bed with a woman who'd slain my friends? I couldn't even pretend to function. And yet what choice did I have with little Harry still a hostage? I was surrounded by a hundred hostile fanatics and fantasists, and my former friends probably believed I'd betrayed my own country.

"I will make it as hateful for you as it will be for me."

"I don't think so, Ethan. No, I don't think there is any chance of that." And she turned to Osiris. "The ritual, at midnight! Bring the boy so he can see!" She smiled back at me. "I'm ever so certain I can corrupt you both."

CHAPTER 31

The moon rose orange over the desolate island, as big as the captured mirror itself, and then as it climbed and brightened, the sea and ship turned silver. The Egyptian Rite contingent had commandeered the hold below the main deck, and its hatch glowed orange as well. The pirates drew uneasily toward the bow and muttered to each other about serving under the shadow of Satan, pagans, and Christian blasphemers. Cutthroats they might be, but Aurora and the Egyptian Rite unnerved them. These self-styled exalted ones seemed more ruthless than any buccaneers, and the Moors were nervous.

I wasn't about to reassure. "These men and women are the disciples of hell, Dragut," I told my captor. "You're dooming your own souls to consort with them."

"Silence, American. No man is more confused about good and evil than you."

"Do you think they'll use their mirror solely on Christian enemies? Aurora wants to control the world, and the Ottoman Turks are closer than Europe. You're equipping a diabolical monster who will prey on your own people."

"I have no people. I, Hamidou Dragut, rely on myself."

"Nonsense. You've sold your manhood to power-mad pagans."

"As you are about to sell yours!"

"I have no choice. My God, to use my son to blackmail me into marrying her? So she can play harridan the rest of my life? Where's the sense in that?"

"Those people obey a different law. There's nothing we can do when we're in their world, and down that hatch is their world. Like all of us, you made the bargain you must. Aurora promises she can give Tripoli victory. Perhaps, as they said, it is written."

"I don't think it's written for a bundle of blasphemers to turn the planet on its head. Tripoli is going to infuriate England and France into a war against it, Dragut. This woman you've allied yourself to is going to pull all of you down with her."

"No, she promises we'll be rich. You can't see a future even when it's a temptress!"

"I see the future, and it's all on fire."

And then Osiris appeared, stumping across the deck with that limp that continued to give me some satisfaction. Maybe I could chop away at other body parts, too. He looked at me with distaste. "It's time, American. I'm to take you on a trip through the underworld to judge you worthy, as dictated by the Egyptian Book of the Dead."

"Underworld?"

"When the British cornered Blackbeard in the Carolinas, he forced his crew into the hold and lit matches so the smoke and stink would give them a preview of hell. He wanted his sailors to fear the afterlife so much that they'd never surrender to the gallows. The inferno caused them to fight like demons, out of terror. We of the Rite have a different kind of journey, to purify and inform. It will prepare you for Aurora."

"What, I'm to be a vestal virgin now?"

He gestured toward the hatch with its lurid light. "Virginity, I presume, is out of reach. What we weigh is your courage and your soul."

"Weigh my soul! Your own is a lump of coal!"

"This is about you and Aurora."

Sometimes the only thing to do is play along and look for the odd chance. So I went over to the opening, considered the haze of incense and smoke drifting from the hatch, and decided to take a stroll in Hades after all. With Osiris behind me, I descended to the deck below, hot and smoky from a hundred flickering candles.

What I encountered was a dreamworld, populated by creatures from a pharaoh's nightmare. The Rite's members—I assumed that's what they were—had donned the heads of a witch's bestiary. Their robes were white, black, and scarlet, and their heads were of jackals, hawks, serpents, dogs, and lions. The eye sockets were blank cutouts, utterly unrevealing, and their cloaks so shapeless as to leave me uncertain if the wearer was man or woman. Beaks and white teeth gleamed in the haze of this hell, and fingers decorated with long, artificial talons clacked and tapped as they reached out for me, pulling me down and in. I coughed, eyes streaming, while they turned me in dizzying circles. Odd music, pagan and primitive, came from their pipes and drums. Some potion was pushed upon me and I drank, increasing my disorientation.

Finally I was pushed to stumble deeper into their gathering, the man-beasts pulling at my sleeves. A gypsy crone loomed, and whether a noble lady in costume or some witch from the Carpathians, I know not. She held a tiny brass scale. "Shall we weigh your sins on one pan, and a feather on the other, pilgrim?" she asked with a glassy gleam to her eyes. She laid a fluff of down. "The crocodile consumes those whose good deeds don't tip the scale in their favor."

"I did my best."

She laughed, shrill and disbelieving.

And then a dragon lurched out of the throng and grunted, brought up short by a bright yellow leash.

Not a dragon, exactly, but the biggest and ugliest lizard I'd ever seen. It was some kind of primeval monster a good eight feet long, with darting forked tongue and bright pink mouth lined with bloody teeth. He was terrifying as a crocodile! The beast lunged at my crotch, nostrils flared, and as I fell backward the assembly shrieked with delight. This was a real animal, its feet armed with wicked claws, but nothing like I'd ever seen or imagined.

Its skin was made up of glittery scales as dry and hard as chain armor, and the monster smelled of rotted meat. The beast was medieval nightmare come to life, its tail swishing on the deck.

"The dark forests of the world have all kinds of creatures that men have half dreamed of," Osiris whispered in my ear. "We brought this one from the jungles of the Spice Islands, where the boundary between world and underworld is not as firm as we think. Nor is the barrier to heaven as absolute as established religions would have us believe. Strange beings watch us, and sometimes can be summoned. Demons can give power."

I thought of Napoleon's Little Red Man and shivered, despite myself. The animal-headed denizens of this hazy hold were murmuring at my hesitation, and I was determined not to give them the satisfaction of seeing me retreat.

"It's just a damned lizard."

"Give your soul to us, Ethan, and we'll erase the boundary between hell and heaven. You'll live in an eternal now of endless power over all men, and all women, and worship magic and depravity. Fiends and angels will be your slaves. Nothing will be forbidden, and no whim denied. Evil will be indistinguishable from good, and justice will be what you decide it to be."

"Isis and Osiris!" the bizarre throng cried.

"Come with me past the dragon, to a new kind of light!"

We pushed toward the stern of the ship, the great lizard regarding me with pitiless gaze as it yanked against its tether, its tongue testing the air for carrion. The animal was something from those depths of time that Cuvier longed to discover.

I think the bestial past should sleep.

Now filling my dazed sight were the costumes of ravens, bears, toads, blind moles, sharp-toothed wolverines, and horned bulls, nostrils wide. Hands pawed me. People chanted my name. Hands horny and scaled slid over the torsos of other costumed animals, and snouts sucked on pipes of pungent smoke. Monsters caressed, and turned in little dances. And then I was being pushed up another companionway, still choking on the swirling mist, and into the ship's stern cabin.

Aurora Somerset waited.

Here another hundred candles blazed, the cabin dancing with light, hot and close. Shimmering silks had been hung to turn it into a Persian pavilion, the deck paved with the arabesques of intricate carpets. Corners were stuffed with pillows and bright scarves. There were figurines of long-forgotten gods watching from the shadows: a jackal-headed Anubis, a hawklike Horus, a hideous gaping thing I guessed might be Baal, and of course a sculpted snake with gold and green scales that must be my old friend Apophis, serpent of the underworld and counterpart to the dragon Nidhogg of Scandinavia. Aurora stood erect, draped with a blue velvet robe trimmed in gold, the tumble of her red hair aflame in the candlelight. Her throat and ears and fingers were arrayed with Egyptian jewelry, and her eyes lined with kohl and her lips with vermilion. She was regal as a queen and disturbingly exotic, like some false copy of Astiza. I realized there was a half circle of men in the cabin who had formed behind me, naked to the waist and wearing counterfeit Masonic aprons below that. They shuffled to push me forward, Osiris directly at my back. And then I saw a small, overdressed child to Aurora's left, who stood in recognition as I came into the light and gave a half-hopeful, half-fearful smile and squeak.

"Papa!"

Harry was dressed like some kind of midget potentate, with silly turban, baggy pants, and jeweled vest. The absurdity broke my heart. We were props in a play, tools of an occult fantasy, and I knew all this must end very badly. Thank the ghost of George Washington that Astiza wasn't here to see all this! Or old Ben Franklin, either, who had little use for mysticism or folderol, although he did like a good party.

"Come over here, Harry," I tried, swaying from my disorientation.

"No," Aurora said in a tone of imperious command. "Stay, my son."

The boy hesitated.

"Your father must come to us."

So forward I went, as Osiris slipped around to stand behind Aurora and take the cloak off her shoulders with his own jeweled fingers. The intake of breath by the men in the room was audible, for the diaphanous shift of Egyptian linen she wore, cinched at the waist by a linked belt of solid gold, left nothing to the imagination. Aurora was as beautiful as ever, ripe as a peach, and some trick of the light seemed to give her white-gauze body an odd glow, as if she were supernatural. She smiled triumphantly, her look possessive.

"Behold, Isis and Athena!" Osiris cried. "The black Madonna and the white, goddess of the earth, queen of the sea, bringer of the light! We elevate her to replace the fallen, and consecrate to her a new husband and new son, so that she might take her place as leader of the Egyptian Rite and founder of a sublime tyranny! All princes shall someday bow before her, and all knights of the Rite shall be glorified as she is glorified, and rule in her name. She is mother, she is harlot, she is priestess, she is seer, and her mate shall be her servant for all eternity!"

Well, the harlot part I could agree with, but I was damned if Aurora Somerset was going to go around without proper underwear pretending to be Harry Gage's mother, or my master. I was snapping more awake. This entire ceremony was not just illusionary, it was ridiculous. It didn't surprise me that Dragut's Barbary pirates were nowhere to be seen. They knew blasphemy when they saw it, and my guess was they were perched on the bowsprit waiting fearfully for Allah to put a quick end to this ludicrous affair. Except no divine lightning bolts sang down, and no false idols toppled. I was stuck in a nightmare for which there seemed no awakening, with a pack of enthusiasts who seemed several thousand years out of sync. Now a woman who first spurned me and then speared me was proposing permanent matrimony, so long as it was certain that I'd be utterly miserable till death do us part.

"Shall we unite the sacred"—Osiris pointed at Aurora—"and the profane?" You can guess where he pointed next, and I was none too flattered by it.

"It is prophesied!" the men in the crowded cabin shouted.

"Shall we unite the Wisdom and the Fool?"

"It is prophesied!"

"Earth mother, do you take this seed?" The bald-headed bastard pointed at me.

"I do."

I waited politely for the question to be put to me so I could spit back. And waited. But I was of no consequence, you see, which was Aurora's point.

"Then I pronounce this union made when it is consummated on the Altar of Apophis below and witnessed by the Heir of Unity here." He gestured at Harry.

"Now just a damn minute . . ." I began, not at all amused at the notion I was supposed to perform with this witch in front of one hundred of her closest friends, not to mention my toddler son! Even barristers make more sense than that. But then a wooden bit was slapped in my mouth before I could object further and its leather thongs twisted tight against the back of my head: a wedding custom different from most, I'd wager. Aurora stepped near, gorgeous as the moon, repulsive as a serpent's fangs, and whispered her particular brand of venom in my ear. "This is the start of your eternal degradation, my dear. You will copulate with me before our assembly and our dragon to seal our marriage on an idolatrous altar. If you don't, I will hurt our son."

There's a way to put you in the mood.

"You'll see," she continued. "I'm going to make you love me."

And then she passed by to begin to descend to the hold I'd come from, and where people seemed to be losing clothing of their own in a heretic's idea of Mass and matrimony.

I was doomed to some kind of new humiliating captivity just marginally better than Omar's.

And then a voice called warning from the deck outside.

"American ship!"

CHAPTER 32

My would-be bride and her as-sortment of Satanists and miscreants momentarily froze, giving me time to duck past the Oriental draperies and glance out the stern windows. There my savior was under the moon, black hull, white ports, gently pulling sails, and a glorious fifteen-striped, fifteen-starred United States flag bigger than a bedsheet that glowed with luminescent glory. Somehow the war-ship must have been near Syracuse and gotten my dusty clue that Tripoli, to the south, was our desti-nation. Now here she came after us, guns run out, and I couldn't help but silently rejoice at the prospect of this whole lot being blown to flinders. That would end my marriage!

Then I remembered innocent little Horus.

My boy and I had to get off this pirate tub, and fast. I began wheezing and mumbling past my wooden gag, and at Aurora's sharp, irritated command, someone pulled the bit free. I coughed, taking breath. Above, bare feet were hammering on the deck as the Barbary pirates ran to loosen lines, drop sails, and raise anchor. Our few guns were run out, but all knew our captured merchant vessel was no match for even this small American schooner.

"You've got to let Harry and me go," I said. "The boy has no part in this."

Her response was to snatch up my child. "He's in this by your blood, and his deed. You'd better think how we can escape that schooner, Ethan, because our son's life depends on it."

"*My* son."

"I told you in America. We are nowhere *near* the end." Her smile was a grimace, clenching my child to her with the determined greed of a child clutching a doll. He squirmed against her body and its thin shift, tired at last of the silly clothes she'd dressed him up in, but her grip was like iron. Outside there was a splash of a cannon ball, and an instant later the report of the American gun that fired it. They were seeking the range.

So I charged her.

I rammed Aurora as if she were a stout oaken door, my head deliberately butting into hers and poor Harry screaming as we collided and went down, silks ripping down with us. The idols of long-forgotten gods toppled and rolled on the deck. Flames ignited as some of the fabric caught from the candles, and men began yelling and beating at the sparks. I grabbed Harry and tried to pull him away from the squirming woman beneath me, but she clung like a cat ready to bite and scratch, hissing hatred.

I'd bloodied her nose, which gave me immense satisfaction.

Then someone was lifting me off her and hurling me across the cabin. I hit the bulkhead with a grunt and went down.

It was Osiris, looking murderous. He wanted to hurt me for running over his leg, and finally had his excuse. I could feel our own ship beginning to move, hoping to get distance from the American schooner.

Dragut appeared in the companionway. "We'll lure them on the reef!"

Another splash and thud of a ranging cannon ball, and then the roar of one of our own guns. Where was Harry! Aurora had picked herself up and retreated into a corner to hold him like a shield, looking hateful. It was the only honest glance she'd given me all evening.

Suddenly I realized that the collapse of the silk trappings had revealed a rack of arms, including my confiscated rapier. I snatched it up, smiling at its remembered balance. Maybe my fencing lessons would do some good after all!

Osiris grinned as well, evilly, and stepped back to fetch from behind a settee his own sword, a thicker cutlass. It was shorter and more efficient in the tight killing ground of a ship's cabin. I'd given him an excuse to gut me, and he intended to take full advantage. By the same token, I needed to get through him to save my son.

We sprang and fenced. The blades rang and I let

mine slide off to keep it from breaking against the heavier sword, sidestepping in the narrow space and trying to remember what I'd been taught in Paris. It was more formal there, the spacing neatly defined, rules spelled out, and without low ceiling, swinging lanterns, and little fires burning in the corners. I stumbled over a statue of Bastet, the cat goddess, and tried a strike at my opponent's thighs, but he parried.

Then Osiris came in after me, trying to box me in a corner so his cutlass could do its work. He chopped back and forth, driving me backward, but I was quicker than he and got in a jab toward his eyes that made him recoil. As he arched backward I squeezed away, trying to catch Aurora. She'd picked up a silver knife to hold near my son's throat.

"Just give me the boy!"

"Only wound him," she instructed Osiris. "I want to make it last."

"Papa!" Harry was screeching. Barely weaned and he was in a duel and a naval gunfight? What kind of father was I?

Our waltz continued, only the speed of my fencing keeping the bigger Osiris and his heavier sword at bay. He was beginning to pant and sweat. I feinted, again and again, to force him to swing. He was frustrated, but no less dangerous for that.

So I stooped and threw Baal at him. It banged off the cabin wall near Aurora.

As he ducked, there was an opening to pink his sword arm. He cursed, spitting, and hopped back on his good foot, blood running down to the hilt of his cutlass now. He looked frustrated, the two of us circling while overhead the pirate crew was attempting to claw out of the anchorage. He was tiring—cutlasses are heavy—so he came at me thrusting hard, wanting to end it. The heavier weapon took a moment more to swing, however, so I checked and parried, getting more confident as Aurora began calling for help. Finally I exaggerated his parry of my sword, letting it slip sideways farther than I needed to, and the riddle master who'd taunted me in Paris risked raising up his cutlass for a final blow. It was just enough exposure. As his blade started down I whipped mine back, got underneath his stroke, and took him through the heart. He was a dead man before his cutlass sang past my ear and sank uselessly into the deck.

I leaped over his toppling form with my bloody rapier and rushed Aurora. "Just give me my son!"

The cabin door burst open and Dragut was there with what I realized was Smith's blunderbuss. I lurched backward and fell flat on the carpets as the big gun went off with a roar, kicking the pirate backward. A ball or more hit my blade and yanked the hilt from my hands, while more bullets shattered the stern windows, glass spraying out over the water. I was stunned by the wind of the shot blowing over me, the bloody heap of Osiris beneath. Now I was weaponless.

Aurora lifted a naval pistol and cocked.

She wanted me alive. She aimed for my head at first, and then shifted to my splayed middle, aiming at that tender spot men prefer to protect at all costs. Then, thinking better of it—well, the girl *had* experienced me in bed—shifted yet lower to blow off one of my knees and merely leave me shankless, her mouth a cruel curl.

And then she shrieked and danced.

Little Harry had stuck her foot with her own silver knife!

The pistol went off, its ball embedding itself in a bulkhead, and even as she snatched my son by the hair in howling rage, ready to do who knows what, I leaped up with Osiris's cutlass in hand. I'd run the harridan through!

Then there was a black blur, a snarl and leap, and Sokar the dog from hell was crashing against me to bite, even while a cannon ball blasted through the sidelights and screamed between Aurora and me, crashing into the opposite wall in a spray of splinters. The dog was spun away from the wind of its passage, and I was kicked by the concussion out the shattered stern windows to fall, end over end. Before I understood what had happened, I plunged into the sea.

"Harry!" It was a thought, because I was underwater and couldn't scream.

I came thrashing up, desperate to get back aboard to learn the fate of my son, but the *Zephyr* was already going, sails full, gathering momentum, the savage dog up there barking madly at me from the broken stern windows. The American bow chasers were throwing up spouts where the ship had just been. My son, if he was still alive, was sailing away from me. I'd lost the mirror, lost my family, and probably lost what little reputation I had by consorting with a witches' brew of Barbary pirates and cultists.

And then there was a crunch I could hear from five hundred yards off. I turned, sickened, to watch the pursuing schooner lurch as it slammed into the reef where Dragut had led it. The collision was so hard that men pitched out of the rigging. The foremast snapped at the top and came down in a tangle. There were shouts, curses, and howls of frustration.

The Americans had grounded and Aurora and her acolytes were drawing off into the night, headed for Tripoli.

I hadn't stopped them from getting the mirror, and I hadn't saved my own son.

I treaded water, ashamed by my own impotence, and then with no other choice began slowly swimming for the grounded schooner. It took me a full hour to work my way there but it hardly mattered, since the ship wasn't going anywhere until it worked off in the morning. The wind had died, and the flag that so excited me hung limply, as if in defeat.

I came close enough to shout. The ship had already lowered longboats to sound the reef, so men hauled me aboard a cutter.

"You a pirate?"

"I escaped them."

They let me clamber up the ship's ladder to the deck.

There I came face-to-face with Lieutenant Andrew Sterett, whom I'd heard about on the Atlantic crossing. As commander of this ship *Enterprise*, he had scored the only unambiguous victory of the war the year before by capturing the corsair

Tripoli, killing or wounding sixty of its crew. The *Enterprise* had returned to Baltimore last winter so the exploit could be trumpeted. Now here he was, back in the Mediterranean.

"Lieutenant Sterett," I gasped. "I trust you remember me: we met in America and I sailed for Europe with Commodore Morris. Ethan Gage, the American envoy?"

He looked me up and down in amazement and distaste. I dripped water like a dunked cat and my skin was spotted with cuts and splinters. "Where the devil did you come from?"

"I was blown off the pirate ship. It's imperative we catch them."

"And how am I to do that, caught on a bloody rock?"

I looked over the side. "Wait for tide and wind, of which there is very little."

Another voice suddenly came from the dark that I recognized with a start. "That's the one!" it shouted. "He's the one I told you about!"

And Robert Fulton, inventor and fellow adventurer, rushed up to see me.

"Robert, you've saved me!"

"He's the one! Ethan Gage, the traitor who needs to hang!"

PART THREE

PART THREE

CHAPTER **33**

My admiration for the military discipline of my nation's small navy was dampened by the crew's efficiency in rigging a hemp noose. The sailors, frustrated by their grounding on the reef, seized with enthusiasm the idea of throttling at least one passenger of the escaping pirate ship. Sterett, I remembered, had become famous for running one of his own crewmen through with a saber as a response to cowardice, during a 1799 battle between the *Constellation* he served on and the frigate *L'Insurgente*. This was an episode in the undeclared naval war with France that I'd helped put a stop to. Republican newspapers had clamored for Sterett's punishment, but he'd coolly replied, "We put men to death for even looking *pale* on this ship." Of course the Navy liked that so much, they gave him a promotion. Now he was to be my nemesis as well.

"Fulton, explain to them who I am!"

"I already have. He's a scoundrel American who

threw in with the Barbary rogues like another Benedict Arnold. I don't care how badly Omar tortured you, Ethan—how could you go back on your pledge to keep the mirror secret? Are you coward, or traitor?"

"Likely both," Sterett said, sizing me up.

"Dammit, man, who do you think got you sprung free from that Tripoli hellhole?"

"By a devil's bargain! Didn't you just aid yonder pirates in stealing an infernal machine from Syracuse, when we expressly promised each other not to?"

"I did it to save your life!"

"Death before dishonor, Ethan. That was our pledge. It's your bad luck I volunteered to help these brave Americans intercept your mission, and my bad luck we were a few hours late." He turned to Sterett. "Hanging may be too good for him. He has very few principles at all."

"Then the devil will finish the job for us."

I struggled against the sailors holding me. "I'm stuffed full of principle! I just fall in with the wrong kind of women! And spend a little too much time looking for treasure, since I don't have what you'd call a proper career. I drink, I gamble, I scheme, but I do know something of electricity and firearms. And I mean well." It seemed a feeble defense even to me.

"Do you deny you're a turncoat to the United States of America and every man on this ship?" Sterett had his sword out and looked like a farmer who has cornered vermin in a larder. Excitable people should never be armed.

"On the contrary, I'm trying to be a hero!"

"By throwing in with pirates?" cried Fulton. The rope cinched against my throat.

"By trying to save my son!"

That stopped them.

"My boy, who I didn't even know I had until a few days ago, is still aboard that pirate ship and in the clutches of the weirdest bunch of cultists, fanatics, magicians, mesmerists, and megalomaniacs this side of the House of Representatives. His mother is captive in Yussef's harem, and if I hadn't played along they'd both be sold into the worst kind of slavery. And you, Cuvier, and Smith would already be dead! While you were running for the reef, I just killed one of the more annoying of the bunch, that Osiris I met in Marguerite's Palais Royal brothel. I gave Aurora Somerset a bloody nose, and was plotting how to sink their whole scheme when one of your cannon balls knocked me overboard. You and I and the fiery lieutenant here are the only ones who can fix things now, but only if you stop pulling on this damned noose!" It was getting hard to talk.

"You and us how?"

"By using your genius and my pluck, Robert, to slip back into the heart of Tripoli and destroy that mirror once and for all!" I nodded eagerly, as if going back to that den of slavers and extortionists was the brightest idea I'd ever had.

◘   ◘   ◘

The crew was grumpy about having no one to hang, but at length I got Fulton and Sterett settled down enough to hear me out. By the time we kedged off the reef there was no chance of catching Aurora and Dragut anyway, and the ambitious lieutenant was interested in any proposition to erase the ignominy of running aground, which is a mortal sin for any captain. The navy reasons that with so much ocean, it shouldn't be that hard to avoid the shallow parts.

"How are you going to get into Tripoli?" Sterett asked skeptically. "Commodore Morris won't risk our squadron in those reef-strewn waters for the exact reason we've seen tonight."

"It's time we harnessed the ingenuity of our new nineteenth century," I said, my clothes stiff with salt as they dried. "I've been thinking about how to defeat this peril for a long time, but it's really Robert here who offers the solution." Actually, I'd only been thinking since they put the noose around my neck, but the prospect of execution does focus concentration.

"What solution?" Fulton asked.

I addressed Sterett. "My scientific colleague here has invented a vessel so revolutionary that it threatens to make all other ships obsolete," I began.

"You said that's not the way to sell the thing!"

I ignored Fulton. "It's called a submarine, or 'plunging boat.' It sinks deliberately, like Bushnell's *Turtle* during our American Revolution, and could deliver a crew of intrepid saboteurs directly into Tripoli harbor."

"The *Turtle* failed to sink any British vessels," Sterett pointed out.

"But Fulton has advanced the technology a full generation. Why, he told me he stayed underwater off Brest a full three hours!"

"This submarine really exists?"

"It's called the *Nautilus*, and is so remarkable that it may someday end war entirely."

Sterett looked skeptical, and Fulton bewildered that I had stolen his sales pitch.

"Or make wars more terrible than ever," I added.

Suddenly, Fulton saw his opportunity. "Ethan, this is the way to prove myself to Napoleon!"

"Yes. I remember you told me the French want to break the *Nautilus* up, but you couldn't bear to and sent the pieces to Toulon to test in the quieter Mediterranean. Here's your chance, thanks to me." I could still feel the abrasion on my throat where the rope had cut, but I don't hold grudges except against true villains. "We pack the *Nautilus* down to Tripoli, sneak into the harbor beneath Yussef's palace, and rescue Astiza and little Harry." I nodded. "All we have to find is a set of adventurers willing to risk their lives in a metal sausage and cut their way through an army a thousand times their number."

Sterett was looking at me with new respect.

"That, at least, is no problem at all," Fulton said.

"You have some volunteers in mind?"

"Cuvier and Smith, of course. They're reconditioning my plunging boat. They decided to wait in Toulon in hopes of hearing news of your hanging, before daring to face Napoleon again."

"Ah. It's good to be remembered."

"And me, gentlemen," Sterett said. "You're not going to romp among the pirates without my ship in support. My bully lads will say the same."

"We may have to have a lottery," I predicted. "Just how many can we squeeze into this craft of yours, Robert?"

"Three, if we want room aboard to get your wife and son out. Of course some of us will most likely be cut to ribbons when we venture ashore, so we might want four or five to start. But then we need room for explosives, too."

"Explosives?" I massaged my throat.

"To blow up the mirror and the navy of Tripoli. Maybe that damned dungeon, too."

"Five against the janissaries and cutthroats of the bashaw of Tripoli!" Sterett said. "Perfect odds! By God, gentlemen, I am heartily tired of lurking at Malta with Commodore Morris, and positively thirsting for action. Gage, I'd heard you were quite the hero, but didn't quite believe it until now."

"I have a hard time believing it myself." My plan had been to sneak quietly about, but Sterett and Fulton apparently wanted a noisier demonstration of American might. Well, a battle tomorrow was better than hanging today. "If you don't mind, I'll get my family out of the line of fire first."

"It is fire that will *save* your family, Mr. Gage," the lieutenant said. "We'll so light up Tripoli with hell and pandemonium that you'll be able to rescue half a harem if you want to."

That didn't sound bad at all. But no, I had Astiza, hang it, and no more business with harems except to get her out of one. By the devil, it's complicated to be a father and suddenly responsible! Oddest thing in the world, really.

But not entirely bad to have someone to rescue.

CHAPTER 34

I'm not sure what I expected of Fulton's beloved *Nautilus*, but the copper coffin he unveiled in a Toulon warehouse did not inspire confidence. It looked like a patchwork of green plating, odd bits of dried seaweed, and conspicuous holes where the leakiest of the iron bolts had been removed for replacement. The contraption was twenty-one feet long, six wide, and in cross section was the shape of a "U" with a short keel. A propeller projected from the rear of the craft, and a folding mast with booms and odd, fanlike sails was lashed to the flat deck on top. A round turret three feet high, with thick glass windows, jutted from the top. Its roof was a hatch allowing entry. From inside the vessel came an unholy banging.

"I've no doubt your invention will sink as planned, Robert," I said. "The question is whether it will rise back again, as prayed for."

"It worked splendidly on the Channel coast. We might have torpedoed a British frigate or two, if they hadn't slunk away." He glanced at Smith. "Sorry, William."

"No offense taken," the Englishman replied cheerfully. "Our nations are at peace now, and here we are united against infamy and extortion. And the day a British ship waits around to be sunk by a contraption like *this* is the day we might as well start speaking French."

Our quartet had been reunited when Sterett, not waiting for orders from his unaggressive commodore, rushed us to Toulon to pick up Fulton's secret weapon. Cuvier and Smith began as suspicious of me as Fulton, but eventually I persuaded them that I'd been faced with an impossible choice. Now we were cautious allies again.

"It was destiny, perhaps, which left Fulton unsuccessful at Brest so he had the chance to prove himself at Tripoli," Cuvier said optimistically. "And perhaps Bonaparte had the foresight to predict we four would make an effective fellowship?"

I thought it more likely Napoleon had been happy to get rid of four eccentrics on a mission with slim chance of success, but opportunity has a way of turning into inevitability. "Your vessel does look a little worse for wear," I judged. "Are you sure it's going to be ready?"

"I've got a clever little fellow working on it," said Fulton. "Said he was something of an expert on all things nautical. He even mentioned that he knew *you*, Gage."

"Me?" I knew no submarine mechanics and tend

to stay away from people capable of honest work, lest they make me feel inferior. "He probably heard you say I'd gone over to the pirate side and figured he could claim anything he liked, since you'd never see me again. Let's catch the look on his face when he pops up and spies me in the flesh!"

Cuvier stepped over and banged on the hull. "Foreman! Your old friend has shown up after all!"

The hammering stopped and there was a long silence. Then a shuffling inside, and finally a head with dark, wiry hair raised above the lip of the little tower like a mole.

"Donkey?" He inspected me critically. "They told me you'd turned pirate, or were dead."

It was I who was thunderstruck, not this "mechanic." In fact, I was so shocked that I took a step backward as if seeing a ghost. "Pierre?" First Astiza, then a son I hadn't known I had, and now this?

"But why am I surprised?" the little Frenchman said. "Here I am readying a cylindrical death trap, a perfectly absurd excuse for a boat, and I have been asking myself, who would be crazy enough to set out in an anchor like this? And I thought, well, Americans, because I have met Americans on my journeys to the wilderness and not encountered a snuff of sense in any of them. And which American do I know who is the craziest of all beyond Fulton there, who is already the laughingstock of Paris? And of course such an imbecile would be my old companion Ethan Gage, who conjures calamity wherever he goes. Yes, a metal boat designed to sink? It sounds absolutely like something donkey would be involved in."

"This is no mechanic," I sputtered.

"More of one than you!"

"This is a French voyageur from Montreal's North West Company! I last saw him in St. Louis, on the Mississippi River. He's a canoe man! He doesn't know any technology more complicated than birch bark and beaver tail!"

"And what do *you* know, besides thunderbolts you can't control and sorcery you can't perform? Plus the worst taste in women imaginable?"

So we held each other's stare, and then began to grin, and finally at last we laughed, and he sprang from the submarine so that the two of us could lock arms in the kind of dance the North West Company's Scots do over crossed claymore swords, chortling over our mutual resurrection. We'd survived, and were together!

This was a good omen.

Cuvier cleared his throat. "This confirms, then, that you have met before?"

"On the American frontier. Pierre was my companion when I searched for Norse artifacts and explored the West. He's the only man I know impervious to bullets."

"Well, one bullet." A ball from Aurora Somerset's gun had been stopped by an Egyptian Rite medallion that Pierre Radisson had stolen from her sadistic brother, Cecil. He'd seemed to have risen from the dead then, but later disappeared from our room in St. Louis. I'd assumed he'd gone back to the wilderness but here he was, thousands of miles from where I'd left him. "I may have used up my luck," he said.

"But I've not used mine, given that I meet you again. What are you doing in Toulon? By Poseidon's spear, this is sweet chance beyond anything I expected!"

"You made me curious about the world, donkey. It was too late in the season to catch the fur brigades, so I decided to paddle home to Montreal. Then there was a ship that needed a hand, even though depending on sail is a woman's way. So I found myself in Europe. Peace gave me the chance to get to France, and by the time I learned where you'd gone, you'd already gone there. Ah, I thought, but donkey has a way of drawing attention! I decided that if I got to the Mediterranean coast I'd hear of you soon enough. And indeed, a Barbary ship deposits three ex-slaves in the middle of Toulon, cursing a mixed-up American. And I think to myself, 'This sounds like the donkey.' So I go to work for that sorcerer there"—he pointed to Cuvier—"and suspect you'll be along, too, by and by. And here you are."

"Why does he call you donkey?" Cuvier asked.

"Because Gage can't properly paddle, although the great Pierre was beginning to teach him. You're a donkey, too. All men who can't paddle a North canoe are donkeys! And this craft! *Mon dieu*, only sorcerer donkeys would come up with an idea as lunatic as going underwater!"

"And hire a French voyageur to reassemble it," I said. "If this boat wasn't a sarcophagus before, it certainly is now."

"No, I've been plugging the holes that the rust has left, and using brass and copper instead of silly iron. Even better would be birch wood, if we had proper trees. Yes, Pierre and his donkeys, out to revolutionize warfare. It makes perfect sense."

Fulton was walking around his craft. "Actually, his work is not entirely awful. We can finish making it seaworthy on the deck of your *Enterprise*, Sterett."

"We're in a hurry then?" asked Pierre.

"I have a woman in danger," I said.

He raised his eyebrows. "Of course."

"And a son, not yet three years old."

"I told you to think about what you were doing."

"And we've got to stop an ancient machine that could give Aurora Somerset power over all the world's navies."

"Aurora Somerset! That harridan is here, too? Is this another Grand Portage rendezvous?"

"She followed me, like you. I am oddly popular."

"And how long do we have to rescue this new woman and son of yours from that witch?"

"Once we draw close, only before the sun rises, I suspect. For when it does, they can set the *Enterprise* on fire."

CHAPTER 35

By the time we repaired and loaded the *Nautilus* on the American schooner and approached Tripoli, it had been more than a month since Aurora had escaped Sterett in Sicily, taking little Harry with her. Time enough, in other words, for the mirror to have been erected and tested. Could something two thousand years old, possibly inspired by Atlantean designs thousands of years older yet, actually work? We didn't want to be surprised by a beam sweeping out to sea.

Confirmation came a different way. As we approached the African coast we spied a wisp of smoke in the distance and cautiously closed, realizing that some ship had been burning. What we saw was a small brig low in the water, her rigging gone and her masts blackened like trees from a forest fire. The smoke drifted from a charred hull.

"Fire can start from a hundred reasons," Cuvier said uneasily.

"And be put out in a hundred ways," Sterett said, "unless the entire ship ignites at once."

We lowered a boat and rowed across, confirming what we suspected. There was an awful smell of ash, putrefaction, and roasted flesh emanating from the vessel, with burned bodies on the deck. The name, *Blanca*, suggested Spanish origin, although jack and staff had been incinerated. On the starboard side was a circular hole, three feet in diameter, where the fire had eaten entirely through the wooden hull and caught the inner decks and timbers. Nothing stirred, inside or out.

"So it's true then," Cuvier finally said.

"By Lucifer, the mirror cuts like a cannon ball," Fulton added.

"Rather than test their infernal machine on a derelict they aimed it at an innocent merchantman, crew still aboard," I guessed. "It must have gone up like a torch and then drifted out to sea. Look at the helmsman there, welded to the wheel. He died where he stood."

"This is utterly barbaric," Smith said. "There's nothing more painful than to die by fire."

"So our timing will be critical," Fulton said. "We must sail my submarine in under cover of darkness, dive, propel ourselves into the harbor, make the rescue, and then retreat underwater to Sterett's schooner offshore. If the sun rises and we haven't destroyed the mirror of Archimedes, the *Enterprise* will ignite like this ship and we'll all burn, drown, or be enslaved again. Gentlemen, we must assault the most impregnable harbor in the Mediterranean, slip by a cabal of determined fanatics, disable their most closely guarded weapon, rescue a woman and child from the central harem of the ruler's palace, and slip out like a fish."

"Jolly good!" said Smith, infused with that mad English enthusiasm that has given them an empire. "I'm for paying that Dungeon Master back, I am."

"Or we can just sneak about, doing our best," I amended. I'm all for valor, but cautious about suicide. "My experience is it's easier not to shake the nest when going for the honey. I've had the sailors help in making us some makeshift Muslim garb for disguise."

"You're a clever sort, aren't you, Ethan? But a regular Lion of Acre if it comes down to a fight, correct?"

"Certainly." I blinked, wishing I still had my longrifle.

"Our small numbers must be our advantage," Smith went on. "The Barbary scum won't be expecting an attack from a handful of men, emerging out of nowhere. Little Pierre here may be able to slip into places or unlock gates the rest of us couldn't hope to."

"Who are you calling *little*, Monsieur Beefeater?"

"It is the littlest men who have the greatest hearts. Look at David versus Goliath. Look at the Little Corporal, now first consul of France. We are each blessed in our own way, and must use our skills to advantage."

"Well put," Cuvier said. "Ethan, with his head for women, can head for the harem. His voyageur friend can help free helpless prisoners. Smith with his blasting expertise can make a sortie toward the mirror. Fulton will steer and I'll crank to create chaos in the harbor. Surprise, confusion, and darkness will be our allies, and revenge and disruption our goal!"

He seemed quite the bloodthirsty buccaneer for a biologist, but then the French do have élan. "You agree we have a chance, then?" I clarified. If I was going to lead my friends on a rescue mission of my old paramour and illegitimate son, I wanted success to at least be possible.

"Oh no. But patriotism, love, and your own folly, Ethan, dictate that we must try."

◘   ◘   ◘

We hoisted *Nautilus* off the American schooner's deck with block and tackle and lowered it over the side. It rocked in the waves like an ungainly copper log, banging against the wooden hull. The vessel seemed about as seaworthy as the bearskin coracle we'd fashioned on the American frontier, and three times less buoyant. But it didn't immediately sink, and Fulton was brisk as a bunny as he organized our war party.

"The voyageur will man the rudder because it's tightest in the rear," he said. "Then Gage to keep him company and crank the propeller when it's time. Smith and Cuvier will counterbalance in the bow. I'll stand in the tower to con the boat and shout directions to Pierre. We'll sail to the harbor mouth, dive, and creep. Now: Do any of you have a problem with claustrophobia in a dark metal cylinder heaving up and down in a restless sea?"

We all raised our hands.

"Well, bring along some cards then, Gage. To a new way of warfare!" We all took a slug of grog, the only way to get up the courage to drop into the contraption, and then climbed down to the submarine's flat, slippery deck. We pushed up the mast and fitted its boom, extended the bowsprit, and turned our metal coffin into a little sailboat. The mainsail was peculiar, a rigid fan-shape like the arm of a windmill. Its color, like that of the jib, was brown.

"The narrow shape is more easily lashed down when we dive," Fulton explained.

"I'll sail in close tomorrow morning to pick you up," Sterett called as we cast off. "You must destroy their weapon! You saw what happened to the Spanish ship."

"If you don't find us," said Fulton as he waved good-bye, "then save yourself."

And off we went to Tripoli, sighting the gray coast of Africa just as the sun went down. I was pleasantly surprised that not only didn't we founder, but that the submarine actually sailed on the surface like a smart little fishing smack, more buoyant than I expected. Its tubelike shape gave it a tendency to roll, but it had a fine bow for going into the seas and a rudder sufficient to set our direction. The problem was that we were confined to the stovepipe that made up the interior of the craft. While it had a flat floor, it was still like voyaging in a sewer pipe. The only daylight came from the open hatch and thick glass windows in the little tower where Fulton perched to navigate. The boat corkscrewed in the waves, and the motion soon had Smith vomiting, the smell of which added to our own nausea. For a Brit, he seemed to have an aversion to all things watery and nautical.

Pierre considered our situation and, as always, offered his opinion. "While I am happy to go along with you because you are a complete idiot without the great Pierre," he announced, "it seems you have made the usual ill choices, donkey."

"I'm just trying my best."

"First, I've pointed out to the crazy American inventor there that metal does not float. Yes, we are somehow bobbing, but I hope this craft does not leak like a canoe because there is no pine pitch to repair it and it will plummet to the bottom in a very short time."

"It might be better for morale not to speculate on such a possibility," I said.

"Second, you have thrown in with savants, whom I told you in Canada have very little practical use. I have noticed these here seem to carry a great deal of useless information about rocks and extinct animals, but very little expertise in assaulting a fortified pirate city."

"'A learned blockhead is a greater blockhead than an ignorant one,' Ben Franklin used to say. Just to give you the point, Pierre, if it will shut you up."

"Third, I see no cannon or rockets aboard, or even your old rifle and tomahawk."

"I've been reduced to borrowing American naval boarding arms, a pistol and cutlass. And we have some of Fulton's mines, or what he calls torpedoes."

"Fourth, you are to proceed, if I understand the plan correctly, to a guarded harem to rescue a female friend who happens to be the mother of your child, suggesting not a lot of foresight into that matter, either. Harems, I am informed, are full of women, and there is no group more difficult to govern or direct. Cattle you can corral and buffalo you can stampede, but women? It is like making a file of cats."

And he sat back, his argument at last made.

"But it seems," I said agreeably, "that I've rectified my bad planning by enlisting my old friend Pierre Radisson. Not only can he point out my faults, but I'm certain he'll find solutions for all the difficulties he just listed. No one knows better than Pierre the evil character of the enemies we're up against, and no one is happier riding in a copper sarcophagus to seek revenge against the very woman, Aurora Somerset, who shot him in the back."

He considered, and nodded. "All this is true. So. I will put my mind to keeping you out of trouble, donkey, and doing so before the sun rises too high. I do have a question for Monsieur Fulton, however."

"Yes, Monsieur Radisson?"

"Locked as we are in a cramped chamber, and unable to emerge without drowning, just how do you propose to sink an enemy vessel?"

"Ah. It is quite clever, if I do say so myself. On board are three copper bombs, each containing one hundred pounds of black powder and a gun lock to set them off. Protruding from my turret is a spear like a narwhal's horn, its butt end coming inside through a stuffing box, as you can see. Oakum packing around the shaft keeps leakage to a few drips. Now: We creep under the bottom of an enemy ship and twist the shaft by hand to drill it into the enemy's bottom. Near its pointed end is an eye, threaded with a lanyard that also comes back to the tower here. After the 'horn' is screwed into the victim's hull, we back off, pulling the lanyard. At the rope's other end is tied a copper mine. As the lanyard threads through the eye of the narwhal horn, the mine, or torpedo, is pulled with it until it is jammed fast against the enemy ship. Then a jerk of the lanyard sets off the gun lock and the explosion. By that time we have backed sufficiently away to survive the concussion."

Pierre looked dubious. "And if the torpedo goes off prematurely? Or the horn doesn't stick? Or the enemy hears us fumbling about underwater?"

"Then we are probably sunk ourselves," the inventor said. "It is fearfully important to get things right. I'm sure we can all muster the proper intensity."

"Certainly we have motive for doing so," the Frenchman agreed.

Fulton turned back to look out his tower. "I see the evening lights of Tripoli. A little to starboard, Frenchman."

"Do you think they might see us?" Cuvier called up.

"Our sails are small and dark and our hull barely above the water," Fulton said. "We can tack close before submerging."

So we neared the port. While Tripoli is on Africa's northern coast, its bay faces northeast, formed by a protective spit, islands, and reefs. The westernmost entrance is a gap in the reef just two hundred yards wide. We sailed close enough that we could hear the breakers and Fulton could judge our position by their creamy white. Then the inventor had Pierre rudder us into the wind while he popped up through the hatch to swiftly drop and lash the sails and mast. Then he came down, closed and locked the hatch, and turned a handle. There was a hiss and gurgle as buoyancy tanks filled.

"Archimedes himself discovered the principle of displacement that suggests how a boat may be made to sink or rise," Fulton said.

"Fish use the same principle in their swim bladders," Cuvier said.

"And humans sleep in a feather bed," I put in.

It grew even darker, so we lit a candle. "We are now below the surface, gentlemen, and about to make history with an undersea naval attack."

"Without being able to see where we're going?" Pierre amended.

"Yes, we are somewhat blind. My compass is illuminated with bioluminescent fox fire, an innovation first suggested by Franklin for the American Revolution's *Turtle*, so once again we benefit from the wisdom of Ethan's mentor. From here we'll navigate by compass, and then rise just enough to peer through the tower windows. Ethan and Pierre, start cranking our screw propeller. Cuvier and Smith, look to our guns and powder."

It was humid and close inside the submarine.

Pierre and I were soon sweating as we cranked away.

"How long can we stay down without any air?" the voyageur asked, panting.

"With this crowding, three hours," Fulton said. "But I brought a copper container from Toulon pumped full of two hundred atmospheres, which was suggested to me by the chemist Berthollet. If released it should give us oxygen for three hours more. If the candle begins to gutter, we'll know we need more air."

There was no sensation of progress. Occasionally Fulton, peering at his compass, would call a slight course correction. Once we heard a scraping on the starboard side, as we grazed a harbor reef, and we steered away. Finally the inventor told us to rest and he began pumping a lever that emptied water from the ballast tanks. The faintest glow came from the tower windows as they cleared the surface of the water.

He waited a moment for the water to sheet away and then turned in all directions, looking about. Then he dropped down to grin, excited as a boy.

"Gentlemen, we're in the middle of Tripoli harbor and no alarm has been raised." He nodded to Pierre. "Good job, helmsman." And then he clapped his hands, once, with a pop. "Now. What do we want to blow up first?"

"The castle, then the harbor," I said. "Smith can carry one of your explosive torpedoes, and you can time your submarine assault for dawn. Blow up at least one corsair to create confusion, with a final torpedo in reserve. Cuvier to crank, and you to navigate, Robert."

"But it is America that is at war with these rascals, and we are Americans, are we not? I'm afraid that, as hopeless as this assault is, Ethan, I must insist that I join you. Smith can crank and Cuvier can steer the submarine. I'll carry a mine ashore because I'm the one who built it and know how to fuse it."

"You're willing to give over command of the *Nautilus*?"

He smiled. "If I let the French play captain for a while, maybe they'll buy her! You'll put in a good word for me with Napoleon, won't you, Cuvier?"

"And why does the Englishman have to crank for the Frenchman?" Smith interrupted.

"You're stronger, with more endurance than our biologist. You know as well as I do, William, that it is almost impossible to get a Frenchman to do anything he doesn't want to do, while an Englishman will volunteer for almost anything, particularly if it is arduous and disagreeable. We must all recognize our national traits."

"And what's the American trait?"

"To get into quite unnecessary trouble through idealism, pride, and the need to rescue helpless women. Right, Gage?"

"Astiza is anything but helpless."

"At any rate, you two savants are the best to figure out how to attack enemy shipping in this harbor. Pierre has worked with Ethan before, and I'm a Yankee as well. Our nation has declared war, and now we're going to execute it, or die trying." He swallowed, and by God I liked him, eccentric inventor or no. I always admire a judicious man who masters his fear more than an enthusiast with stupid courage.

"I'll pick you up when you have the woman and the boy, and you can put in a good word with Napoleon yourself," Cuvier promised. "We leave nobody behind."

"And can England and France cooperate?" I asked Smith.

"Let this be a new beginning, under the Peace of Amiens," the Englishman said. "I'm betting that Bonaparte never goes to war with my country again."

"Perhaps France and England will even be allies," Cuvier said.

"Don't speculate too ludicrously. But at least we can man this casket together."

"To peace!" Pierre said. "Except for this little war here."

"Dawn is when our work must be done," I reminded, "lest the mirror be used against us. When the sea lightens, surface slightly, and listen. When chaos begins ashore, try to strike in the harbor. If everything is timed perfectly, we might have the slimmest chance."

"Nothing goes perfectly in battle. You know that."

We were all quiet a moment.

"But not for the other side, either," I finally said. "In gambling, you don't have to be perfect, just good enough to win the game. Let's put on our Arab robes."

CHAPTER 36

We maneuvered to the outer-most boat in a line of docked feluccas and Fulton, Pierre, and I crawled out onto the fishing vessel, clambering from one to another until we were on the stone platform of the harbor. The *Nautilus* sank out of sight.

Yussef's palace was ugly as a chopping block, and everywhere there were ramparts with the black snouts of artillery poking toward the sea. Up on a fortified platform just north of the castle, facing the harbor, was a shrouded round disk that was a deeper black against the stars. That would be the mirror, I guessed, and very likely a thousand pirates and janissaries were between it and us.

Pierre looked at the looming walls. "We have to climb these? Perhaps you are not a donkey, but a spider."

"I propose that we drink our way into the dungeons instead, and make our way upward from our old home by the stairs. Do you remember the taverns, Robert?"

"Aye, the ones run by the Christian slaves and prisoners for Muslims forbidden to sell alcohol on their own."

"I thought Muhammadans weren't supposed to drink, either," said Pierre.

"And cardinals aren't supposed to have mistresses," Fulton said, "and yet half could give lessons to Casanova. All men are pious, but find a way around their strictures. Have they repealed human nature in Canada?"

"We men of the woods have limited experience, but not that limited. So we're to become pious drunkards?"

"To get ourselves in the door," I said.

He looked up. "A cleverer idea than scaling this fortress."

Like all cities in all cultures, Tripoli had made accommodation between what men were supposed to do and what they want to do. Islam frowned on usury, so the Jews exiled from Spain had become the bankers. Alcohol was forbidden, so Christian slaves could make an extra living by quietly providing it. The practice had spread to the prisons themselves, where entrepreneurs also provided the chance for the devout to obtain a prostitute, pawn booty hidden from taxation, or buy literature more stimulating than the Koran. The Muhammadan town might be more orderly than a Christian city, but sin could be found among the jailers and janissaries as easily as at the Palais Royal. Accordingly we crept along to the courtyard that abutted Yussef's prison and slipped into one of the grog shops on its periphery. I ordered in Arabic while scouting for our chance to get beyond the dungeon gates.

Two guards in a corner were very quietly becoming inebriated, and once I was sure they'd become sufficiently muddled, I approached to refill their cups and propose a sale of opium. Drugs go with prisons like hand to glove, with the cottage industries of the inmates devoted mostly to paying for the narcotics needed to make hopelessness tolerable. A dishonest jailer can make more money selling to thieves than a thief can ever get stealing, and guarding the miserable bagnios of North Africa was a sinecure as valuable as being bookkeeper in a treasury. These guards didn't trust me, of course, but they sensed opportunity and were greedy enough to beckon me to a locked door. When passing through I jammed the keyhole with a nail to prevent the latch from closing. And when the jailers bent to inspect my narcotic—flour and ground tea I'd brought from Sterett's schooner—my companions crept in and clouted the drunken fools with socks we'd filled with sand from the streets.

We hesitated then, silently debating what to do with the two unconscious guards, until I reluctantly drew my naval cutlass from under my robes and thrust it through both their bodies, finishing them. Fulton gave a little groan.

"We are at war, gentlemen, with fanatics who are holding hostage my innocent son and who hope to declare war on all civilization," I said. "Steel yourselves. It's going to be a long night."

"They won't show us mercy, either," Pierre said.

"Certainly they haven't yet."

"Let's get on with it, then," said Fulton, swallowing as he looked at the dead. Apparently practicing war close-up was not the same as designing its machines, and the deadly consequences of his genius were just occurring to him. I wondered if Archimedes had discovered that, too? Had the old Greek ordered the dismantling of his mirror to not just keep it from the Romans, but from mankind itself? Could his own king have killed him in frustration?

"But first we take their pistols," said Pierre. "With the mood Ethan's in, I have a feeling we're going to need them."

"And their keys," I added. "Help me drag the bodies out of sight."

I felt nauseated as we crept back into the labyrinth of dungeon tunnels under Yussef's castle. The smell of earth, sewage, and lightless corruption came back like a slap, triggering old fear, and we could hear moaning and the occasional insane scream. Then I reminded myself of Astiza and little Harry, captive somewhere in the harem far above, and resolved to blow this mouth of Hades permanently shut by bringing Yussef's fortress down on top of it. Let slip the dogs of war!

We passed several iron corridor gates, locking them again to discourage interference or pursuit. Then a flight of stairs upward that I recognized as the way I'd been taken to Yussef's palace to meet Astiza.

"I think our army of three needs to divide at this

point," I said. "Robert, somehow we've got to get your torpedo, or mine, to where the mirror is and set it off."

"Archimedes might have used a catapult," he said. "Perhaps something similar will occur to me. How do I get within view?"

"If we can get you to the roof of Yussef's storage rooms you may be able to look across. Follow this tunnel and hunt for stairs, if you don't meet a sentry."

He drew his own cutlass. "Or kill one if I do."

"What is your assignment, donkey?" Pierre asked.

"Go to the harem where the women are."

"Of course."

"That's where Harry and Astiza should be. I'll slip in, find them, and bring them down to go out the way we came."

"And brave Pierre, who never seems to be given the job of rescuing harems of young, nubile, enticingly captive women?"

"Brave Pierre has the most important job of all. Take these keys and release as many prisoners as you can. When we retreat, their escape will create confusion while we make for the plunging boat. Beware, Pierre, an ogre lives in these tunnels. He's a brute known as Omar the Dungeon Master and we want to avoid him."

"A presumptuous title. Is he big and ugly, like you?"

"Bigger. And uglier, I dare say. Even homelier than our late giant friend Magnus Bloodhammer."

"Then I shall be David to this behemoth's Goliath. I am the great Pierre Radisson, North Man and voyageur, who can stroke twenty hours in a single day and travel a hundred miles before sleeping! None can portage more weight than I, or drink more, or dance more splendidly, or jump higher, or run faster, or more quickly charm a woman! I can find my way from Montreal to Athabasca with my eyes closed!"

I'd heard all this several times before. "Then you'll do fine in the darkness down here. Quickly, Pierre, and quietly, and run like a deer if Omar hears you. We need you in our submarine to remind us again of your prowess."

"Of course you need me! Those two savants you left there, while they have undoubtedly concocted eight new harebrained theories of the history of the earth, have probably by now lost all sense of direction, if they haven't sunk already. Well, Pierre will do all the real work as usual, and meet you at the gates that lead out of this dung hole. Then we will work on your reform!"

And so I turned to climb the castle steps and rescue my son and the woman (I realized with a jolt that I had unconsciously come to think of her this way) who was, for all practical purposes, my wife.

◘   ◘   ◘

The climb was familiar, taking me up to the reception hall where I'd met Astiza. I passed with disquiet a side tunnel that I remembered led to Omar's torture chamber. Then I opened the wooden door, pushed aside the concealing tapestry, and entered the throne room. This, I guessed, was close to the harem. The royal chair and pillows were as I remembered them, shadowy in the darkness. Even the African cat was there, locked for the night in its brass cage. I could see the fire of its eyes as I quickly passed through, and the beast made a rumbling purr. I wondered if Dragut's dragon was lurking about, too, a lizard with the appetite of a polar bear.

In the rear of the cage a third eye gleamed, and I realized a smaller cage held Yussef's turban and emerald, ably protected by his cat. Even the leopard earned his keep.

At the far end I slipped out into a quiet hallway hung with old brass medieval shields. There was a forbidding stillness to the castle as if the building was waiting, and I puzzled that I hadn't encountered more guards. It was midnight, yes, but was I really this lucky? Where was everyone?

Up a flight of marble stairs—I must be at the top of the palace now—and there a eunuch doorman, conveniently asleep in the depth of night. There was a flask nearby, and if he was caught in this dereliction he'd no doubt be bastinadoed on the soles of his feet, or hung from a hook on the castle wall. I hesitated, thinking of killing him, but couldn't do it to a man already cruelly castrated. Instead I tore a drapery and jumped, clouted his head, gagged him, and tied him tight. Another sharp clout put a stop to his squirming.

Then I went to the wood and brass harem door and listened. No trill of female laughter; the harem was asleep. I was ready to smash its lock with a pistol ball if need be, but instead this door opened, too. Clearly, Yussef was either not expecting an imminent American attack—or had faith in his eunuch guards. I slipped inside cautiously, not wanting to risk a riot by startling the girls. Could I find the duo I was looking for? If we could just creep away, I hardly cared about the mirror. It couldn't *really* work after all this time, could it?

But it had, burning that Spanish ship. As it could burn ours.

The harem was empty, too.

I passed through an antechamber and entered the lovely harem court, far more opulent than the merchant's attic I'd once broken into in Cairo. This room had a central pool and a domed roof pierced by inserts of colored glass. In daytime, a rainbow of colors would filter down. Pillars ran around the chamber's periphery to form an arcade beneath and balcony above, and doorways opened to what I presumed were the separate bedrooms and kitchen of the women who lived here. Flowers filled a score of vases, and lotus petals floated in the pool. The place smelled of perfume and incense. What would it be like when the concubines lounged and laughed, the beauties of a dozen nationalities just lightly clothed? Limbs dangling in the pool, breasts casually exposed, gossiping as they brushed each other's glossy hair, smooth shoulders, sweet hips, their great almond eyes lined with kohl, their lips picked out with . . .

Focus, Ethan!

You're worrying about just one woman now.

And suddenly I had company. There was the

light tread of a slipper behind me to which I might have turned, but at the same instant there was a growl ahead, the bass rumble of a heavy muzzle flecked with saliva and blood. Sokar! The grip on my pistol was suddenly slick as I realized why the castle was so quiet. I'd walked into a trap.

"Ethan, Ethan, so predictable," Aurora's voice came from the shadows where the dog regarded me with its piss-yellow eyes. "We've been waiting for *weeks*." And there emerged the wolflike bulk of her brutish mastiff, head lowered, shoulders bunched.

"We were going to let you turn the mirror on your own navy," another voice said behind me. Dragut! "You could have proved yourself to us, Gage. But now, we'll just try it on you." His tone was anticipatory as a gun muzzle as wide as a dog's mouth nudged my back. "Please don't move, because I'm holding your friend's blunderbuss. If my finger slips, the blast will cut you in two."

"Hell of a mess in this pretty pool."

"We've slaves enough to lick it clean, if necessary."

CHAPTER 37

Aurora stepped into better light, holding my longrifle in a hand that also grasped Sokar's leash. In her other fist was a second leash, this one tied to two figures coming miserably into view. The line led to a leather collar around the neck of Astiza, whose eyes were flickering to search for a means to fight back. And then from her to little Horus, who was walking with a limp and looked tearstained and traumatized.

He brightened a little as he recognized me across the pool. "Papa! Dog bit me!"

I wanted to shoot the damned beast right then, but if I did the blunderbuss would go off and Astiza and Harry would be finished. My naval pistol was damned inaccurate at that distance anyway, and the one I'd taken from the dead guards no better. I might shoot and miss.

"Serves you right for stabbing my foot, you wretched cretin," Aurora snapped.

Her foot still bore a bandage, I saw, and I

couldn't help but smile. The apple didn't fall so far from the tree, did it? Less than three and Harry already made me puff with pride. First he'd stabbed a little mouse, and then a bigger rat!

"That dog won't frighten you much longer," I called.

"No, it won't," Aurora said, "because you've doomed your bastard to the most hideous kind of slavery. This slut who spawned him is going to be roasted by the reflected rays of the sun. You can watch her catch on fire, Ethan, just before we test the mirror on *you*. That's what you get for killing Osiris! Then we'll let whatever boat dropped you here come in close to rescue your blackened husk, and set them ablaze as well. Bright as a bonfire."

"You really should have been a dramatist."

"A month ago I offered you the world and myself. And now? We only had to wait for you to come. Omar sent word that he had intruders. That eunuch you trussed was playacting. Janissary guards let you stupidly slip by. Any friends foolish enough to accompany you should already be dead. Everything you touch turns to disaster, and every person you befriend comes to grief. You do not control the lightning but are lightning yourself, a bolt of misery everywhere you alight."

"Which explains why I'm more than a little baffled by your attraction to me. Of course, you're not exactly a Saint Nick yourself."

"Oh, I will be revered, never doubt. Winners are always honored by posterity. The most powerful become gods and goddesses. It's the ruthless who are worshipped."

"Brave words when you sic a mongrel on a near infant and have me outnumbered a hundred to one. You've never been anything but a bully, Aurora. Too much the tart to ever win a real man, a dabbler in the wilderness dependent on her brother, a female with the mothering skills of a Gorgon, and a sportsman with the shooting expertise of an English fop."

She stiffened, her habit when hearing the truth. "You saw me shoot this gun in Canada!" And she held up my own beloved rifle. It had traveled perhaps fifteen thousand miles since its forging in Jerusalem, and my heart quickened when I saw it. "I can outshoot any man in this fortress!"

"You can't outshoot me. Remember what I did to your brother, twice."

She flushed. "The one shot at Cecil was lucky and the other almost point-blank."

Astiza had gone still as deep water during this exchange, waiting for me to make a miracle. I saw one, or at least a tiny chance.

"I'm still better than you."

"It's my rifle now, Ethan."

"Let me prove it. You've never shot against me."

"You propose a competition?"

"I'm just saying it's easy to boast when your opponent has a blunderbuss in his back and a hundred soldiers stalking him. But at anything like fair terms, you'd never win. Especially in a shooting match."

She laughed, and Sokar barked. "Pick a target!"

"Aurora, we've no time for this nonsense," Dragut protested.

"Now that we have him, we have all the time in the world. Pick a target!"

I looked, and pointed upward. "That glass pane in the dome, no bigger than a hand. I'll hit it before you, and when I do . . . you have to give us a minute head start."

"That's so absurd, given your situation, that I'd spit on it and you if I wasn't so certain I'm the better marksman! Let's make it interesting, instead. I'll bet the head of your son."

"No! Leave Harry out of this!" But I secretly knew this monstrous idea of hers that I'd triggered was our only hope.

"Yes," she said, almost speaking to herself, "his terror from your absurdity. Hamidou, keep your gun on Gage because he's full of tricks! Ethan, we're going to put a glass flute on your little monster's head and aim for its stem. I'll go first, and I guarantee I will completely miss the boy and clip the stem if his mother holds him still enough. Then you can have a turn, and if by a miracle you break the glass more times than I do without blowing off the head of your child, I'll give you your little race, with Sokar in pursuit. It will be amusing to watch him run you all down and hear the screams, since I had to hear my brother's."

"I like a girl with enthusiasms."

She tied my family's tether around a pillar with the assuredness of a sailor, testing its tightness. "Whore, crouch and hold your child like a statue," she ordered Astiza. "If he twitches an inch, one or the other of us might miss."

Trembling, her expression toward Aurora exhibiting the purest hate I'd ever seen, the woman I loved kneeled, noose at her neck, and took our two-year-old darling into her arms. "Horus," she whispered, "you must be very, very still. Mama will hold you to be safe."

My boy was crying again, completely confused by what was going on. Aurora put the goblet upon his head, which wobbled as he snuffled, and walked around the bathing pool to where I waited, bringing my rifle. She brushed my cheek with a kiss—it was like the lick of that reptile in her satanic ship's hold—and took my pistols from my belt, tossing them into the pool. With a plonk, they sank out of reach. Then she turned and raised my gun with the assurance of the trained marksman. The muzzle of my weapon was steady as a rock as she aimed.

I held my breath, terrified that Harry would bolt into the path of the bullet. There was a flash, roar, and a high ping as the glass stem was clipped in two by the ball. The cup of the goblet fell and shattered while poor Harry screamed and wept. Astiza clung to him even tighter, whispering in his ear.

There were shrieks and cries from the harem's concubines, no doubt jammed into the back of this complex by their anxious eunuchs. The bullet had ricocheted above them.

The woman I'd once lusted after slammed the butt of my rifle onto the marble floor, took out a cartridge of powder and shot, and reloaded with the efficiency of a deadly huntress. Then she handed my weapon back to me, first drawing her own pistol to aim at my head.

"Put the next glass on his head!" she called to

Astiza. Then she turned to me. "I warn you, if that rifle barrel strays even minutely away from your wretched offspring, we'll kill you in an instant and turn the two of them over to the slavers."

"What's the matter, Aurora? Afraid I might equal you and that you can't get lucky a second time?"

"Just shoot and miss. And then beg for my mercy."

Astiza and Harry had absolutely frozen, mother murmuring into her son's ear. The glass flute was bright as a diamond.

"Remember, if you do miss, the game is over," Aurora said.

I aimed as carefully as I ever had, drawing breath, holding, and then letting a slow hiss escape as I pulled the trigger, the gun aimed at a target I could barely see in the gloom.

I fired, the flash and bang cacophonous in the marble chamber. The harem women screamed.

And the leash of my loved ones snapped, cut in two by the ball as I intended! The end of their collar flapped loose in the harem air.

Our ears rang with the report of the gun. For the briefest fraction of time everyone was frozen, surprised at my shot.

Then I popped the stock atop my shoulder and rammed my rifle backward, catching Dragut full in the face with its butt. He reeled, his blunderbuss swinging away. I twisted to grab it and deliberately fell to the floor as Aurora's pistol went off, the ball singing over my head. I then swung my own piece like a scythe to try to break her ankles. She jumped and fell, both our guns empty now.

I scrambled up, wrenching the blunderbuss from the stunned Dragut. "Run!" I cried. I longed to use the gun on our tormentors, but guessed I'd need it on the stairway outside. The blunderbuss in one hand and the longrifle in the other, I waited for my lover and son.

◻   ◻   ◻

Astiza tucked Harry, frozen and mute, under one arm and dashed past us, the end of her tether flapping. Then I was up and after her before Dragut or Aurora could recover their wits. My longrifle felt as if a lost limb had been restored, even if the weapon was empty. In my left hand was Smith's loaded thunder gun. We burst out the harem door, slammed it shut, and hurdled the tied eunuch. Janissaries sprang up from where they'd waited in ambush on the marble stairs and I cut loose with the blunderbuss. The gun bucked, there was a spray of bullets, and the gang of them parted like the Red Sea, men screaming as they somersaulted down the stairs. I swung my rifle for good measure, knocking aside a couple of obstinate ones like tenpins. Then we were plunging down the stairs past them to the royal reception room below, even as all the eunuchs began screaming.

Behind us came Aurora's sharp command: "Sokar! Kill!" And then to Dragut: "Get to your ship, idiot, and cut off whatever boat they have to escape!"

I could hear the baying of the mastiff and the skitter of its nails on the marble flooring as it chased after us. I slammed the throne room door, threw its light latch, and watched the wood stretch like canvas as the big dog slammed against the other side, howling and slavering. I'd little time to reload, but I could buy a few seconds. "Save our boy! Past that tapestry is a stair to the dungeon! A companion waits there!" I had just time to pour powder, but not yet ram patch and ball. Then there was a gunshot, the edge of the door exploded into splinters, and the frenzied dog burst through, howling for blood.

My longrifle club met the dog midleap. The animal grunted as I knocked it to one side of the room, and I prayed I'd cracked a rib.

Aurora burst through the doorway after her pet, hair flying, mouth wide as a banshee's, a pistol smoking and Dragut's sword held high. "I'll kill you all!"

But Astiza, instead of fleeing, had thrust Horus in one corner. Now she grabbed the edge of one of the carpets and yanked. Lady Somerset fell, cursing like a sailor, and Astiza pounced, wrestling for the sword. The women rolled, bit, and scratched. They were a blur of struggling limbs and tangled hair, fighting at a pitch of wild fury. The dog came at me again as I fished for a bullet and this time it leaped to catch my rifle in its teeth, chewing and growling. I was knocked backward, landing on the pillows, and the beast was astride me, one hundred pounds of quivering malevolence, breath hot, flecks of foam flying, its growls primeval. I tried to use the weapon to twist his head away from mine, but its neck was as strong as my arms.

"Mama!" It was poor Harry, crying amid the chaos. I could hear a frenzied snarling and realized that Yussef's leopard was banging against its own cage, frantic at the sight of the black mastiff that had invaded its domain.

Aurora used the hilt of her sword to clout my woman, stunning her, and then tried to pry her wrists free of Astiza's desperate hands so she could run her through. With the ferocious protective instincts of motherhood Astiza twisted back and with a cry from both women the sword suddenly flew free, ringing as it fell on marble tiles.

Then the real havoc happened, a blur of animal reflexes.

With a yowl the spotted leopard suddenly shot free of its cage and the dog launched itself off me to meet it. The mastiff was as big as the cat and probably expected it to bolt, but instead the leopard twisted and the two collided at the apex of their leaps, spinning in the air. If the dog was powerful, the leopard was swift. They writhed, dueling with their jaws. Then the mastiff yelped, suddenly terrified as the leopard caught at its throat. The two animals tumbled over each other on the Persian carpets, the leopard hissing and tearing. The dog frantically pawed the air, its legs no match for the cat's lethal claws.

"Sokar!" Aurora screamed and heaved Astiza to one side, my lover's head striking a marble pillar. Harry's mother slumped, dazed. "Your bastard let the leopard out!" Aurora crawled for her sword and then turned toward little Harry, her eyes completely mad as the boy shrank in the corner. I finally fed a bullet in the muzzle and began ramming the shot, but squeezing the lead down the tight barrel takes an eternity. Aurora rose like a crazed Valkyrie, wild with frustration as she aimed to stab my son, and now I was scrambling to stop her, trying to think of a distraction.

"Save your dog!"

At my cry Aurora twisted, confused, her purpose momentarily incoherent, and then suddenly stepped toward the fighting animals, presumably to kill the cat. It was the only sacrificial thing I ever saw her do.

So the leopard sprang, ten feet through the air in a perfect gyration of predation, and flew past her sword arm to land against her body, claws gripping flesh and jaws splayed wide to close over her face.

Aurora didn't even have time to scream. There was a sickening crack of bone as the leopard bit, and her head disappeared under the animal's.

Behind them the ugly dog was in ruins, its throat and flanks pumping blood.

Aurora thrashed frantically on the floor, Yussef's pet leopard on top of her and pinning her down. The beauty that had transfixed me in America was being clawed to ribbons, each swipe leaving parallel red streaks and ribbons of flayed flesh. Her feet slid frantically on the rugs and marble, heels making streaks of blood. Then the cat was at her throat. Her face had already caved, her eyes gone. I finally reloaded, but there was no need to waste a precious shot as leopard and victim twisted. Her head flopped loose, her neck bitten half through.

Finally she went limp, the big cat batting at her and growling, and then there was a bustle at the door as eunuchs and janissaries crowded to see. They halted abruptly at the sight of the freed leopard, frozen by the bloody tableau.

I shot the biggest one, a great goon of a mulatto guard, and then the angry animal leaped again, there was a shout as the guards surged backward in terror, and the cat disappeared through the door. We heard a fusillade of shots, punctuated by snarls.

I picked up the dazed Astiza to shove her toward the rear tapestry and escape, but she staggered away from me and nonsensically grabbed an antique shield from the wall. It was a carved and filigreed thing of polished bronze and probably quite valuable, but the last kind of anchor we needed at a time like this. Had the blow to her head left her daft? But then I saw my own souvenir—Yussef's headdress from the back of the leopard cage! I grabbed, picked up little Harry, pulled Astiza again, and finally we staggered past the tapestry and through the hidden dungeon door. I slammed home its locking bar before tumbling down these narrower stairs with my longrifle and blunderbuss, shaken by the wild fierceness of what I'd seen. Astiza's chest was heaving with exertion and shock.

"Papa, I let lion out," Harry confessed.

"Good boy! You saved your Mama. And me."

"Will it eat us?"

"It's dead. And so is Aurora," I told Astiza, who'd finally set the shield down. She was shaking with exhaustion and excitement.

Above, we could hear guards pounding on

the door I'd barred, and then shots as they fired through it. It would hold until they fetched axes or gunpowder.

Astiza closed her eyes and took little Horus to hug even tighter. By thunder, the boy had pluck! He was a clever little tyke, too, given to my rather improvised luck. I'd just have to keep an eye out that he didn't copy the side of me I'm trying to reform.

"I could hear her face breaking inside its jaws," Astiza said. She shivered. "She was the wickedest woman I've ever met. The old demons possessed her, Ethan. The ones I thought had been banished to the deepest part of the earth. The Egyptian Rite summoned the succubus back and they took over her soul and her mind."

"Bad animals, Papa."

"There's wildness in fierce animals no human can come close to," I said. "But unlike people, they kill without sin."

She hugged me, the three of us a tight cluster. "Ethan, I wasn't sure you'd come back. To have Horus return and not you . . ."

"And leave my family?" I grinned. "I'm a papa now!"

"I didn't know what you were aiming at with that shot."

"I didn't know what I'd do if I missed the tether."

"If Horus had been hurt, I didn't want to live."

"He hasn't had an easy time of it since he met me, has he? Which is why I'd like a little more payback before we leave. There's a mirror, Astiza, big as a courtyard, and they're planning to turn it against the American navy. Have you heard about it in the harem?"

"All of Tripoli has heard of it. Yussef is beside himself with pride. We've watched its erection from the harem windows."

"We have to destroy it before we go or it will burn the schooner coming to rescue us. Its reach is longer than a cannon shot. Is there a way to get inside the fort where it is?" I untied the collar from around her neck and cast it aside.

"No. There's a warren of streets between palace and fort, and hundreds of soldiers and Somerset's fanatics. Please, Ethan, for Horus's sake let's go! How much more can a child take?"

"We can't go. The sun's almost up and they'll set us afire. We have to fight it through. I've got a companion below who can help look after you and Harry, and another with a bomb to destroy the mirror. Robert Fulton is eccentric, but he's smarter than Lucifer. If we can get close enough, we'll blow it to flinders."

She bit her lip. "I don't know if a bomb will do, but I have a different idea. It's why I took this shield. If light can be focused by one disk, why not reflected by two? Maybe we can block the ray."

"And then what?"

"Turn it against them. You carry the shield, I'll carry Horus. Let's find these friends of yours and give the Egyptian Rite a taste of their own terror."

CHAPTER 38

I feared we might have provoked uproar in the tunnels below, given the shooting and tumult above, but the prison corridors were eerily quiet. Pierre had managed to release hundreds of men, sharing keys with those captives fit enough to unlock still more comrades. As the prisoners were freed they overpowered the guards not blocked off by the gates we'd closed. Now they crouched silently in their oppressive hive, trembling from anticipation, waiting for the right moment to rush the entrance. This, Pierre had instructed them, must be just before we attempted to destroy the deadly mirror and escape ourselves for the harbor. The chaos, all of us hoped, would shield each other's flight.

True criminals were usually executed or trimmed of hands or feet, so these men were mostly captured Christians awaiting ransom or auction. We didn't know if we were giving them a chance of freedom or hopeless riot. We simply knew we had to do all we could against Tripoli. Some of the prisoners were too weak and tortured to move, but even these were carried into the passageways by their fellows, the wretches blinking and disheveled. Their cellmates would not leave them behind. The crippled looked at us with wan hope, and their mere presence was inspiring. In the only way we had, we were striking back at slavery.

"There's a deep pit in the dungeon's deepest level where I and the savants were kept," I told Pierre. "Is it empty of victims?"

"I've been rather busy with these others, if you would care to count."

"I'm going to see. I'll not leave anyone in that hellhole."

"We don't have time!" Astiza said.

"It's like being buried alive. Come, Pierre, let's finish emptying Hades!"

"I had no idea Hades was so big, donkey."

"This is what happens when no one fights the devil."

I reloaded my weapons, giving Pierre the blunderbuss. To Astiza I loaned Pierre's pistol to watch over Harry. Then Pierre and I descended farther, finding a few more cells and sending saved souls stumbling past us toward the light.

"Have you encountered the Dungeon Master?" I asked.

"I picked up a rock in case we meet your Goliath. But at some point the surviving guards thought better of it and withdrew, I think. Even your troll doesn't want to face a hundred men he tortured."

We reached the small cavern at the prison's lowest level and its rancid pit, its stench making me want to vomit. Had I really survived down here? I heard a clank of chain and leaned cautiously over the edge to see. It was dark, of course, and I saw only an odd unblinking eye looking up at me.

"Hello?"

No answer.

"Pierre, I need a torch."

Then there was a sudden agitation in the pit below, mute but frenzied, and suddenly a leap up the side. I got a glimpse of scale and lizard claw and then a chain yanked tight as the monster fell again into the blackness. I lurched backward. It was the nightmare from the ship's hold! We'd found the dragon again.

Then my companion yelled. "*Mon dieu!* Even homelier than you!"

"The lizard?"

"Your jailer!"

I spun around. It was Omar, filling the doorway to this chamber like a swollen bull and holding my friend with a forearm the thickness of a log locked around Pierre's chest and arms. The Frenchman was purpling. A heavy steel chain hung from Omar's other fist, his bulk making its links look almost delicate.

"I wait for *you*," the Dungeon Master rumbled. "I woke because the weeping stopped. Something is very different in my lair, I sense." He sniffed the rancid air with his brutish, broken nose, as if freedom had a smell. "So I think, maybe the one they wouldn't let me have has foolishly come back as they promised. Do you remember my table, pretty one?"

"We're not as helpless this time, Omar," I said as I raised my rifle. "Let my companion go."

"All right." He hurled Pierre at me to spoil my aim, the voyageur sprawling at the edge of the dungeon pit, and then quicker than a cobra strike—unbelievable speed for such a large man—the chain lashed out and caught my rifle muzzle. I fired, but my bullet just seared his shoulder. The chain wrapped my barrel and yanked the weapon from my hands, slamming it against the dungeon wall and snapping its neck. My precious longrifle fell into dust, the butt hanging like a broken hinge, held at the trigger by a single screw.

"You monster!"

Omar laughed, picking up the broken longrifle. "You miss, little man."

"Little man!" Pierre cried in indignation.

He tossed my gun past us down into the pit and I winced as I heard it scrape and clatter. It was the gun I'd labored on for long days in Jerusalem with Jericho and Miriam, the weapon that had carried me through Acre and Egypt, the rifle that had defended us during the relentless chase of the Ojibway and Dakota on the American frontier. It made a greasy splash at the bottom. "You can share with dragon." Then he laid his chain on his shoulders and picked up Pierre's fallen blunderbuss. The torturer loomed like a titan, tendons inflated, his eyes a squint of hatred and triumph, his mouth a pitiless smirk as he stepped toward us. "This gun can hit both."

A bellow came from that damned monstrous lizard, no doubt waiting for dinner. Yussef Karamanli had assembled a satanic zoo! The agitated animal bounced off the pit walls, trying to process in its primitive brain why the shattered rifle had fallen from our struggles above.

"You can jump into the pit and try your luck against the dragon," Omar said. "Or you can let this shotgun knock you in."

"Let us go, Omar," I tried, "or there are two hundred prisoners that will take vengeance on you if they know you've harmed us."

"What will they know? You will be in the lizard's belly. Besides, the Christian dogs will be running the other way to escape. Yes, Omar has long planned this. I am not stupid like people think." He gestured impatiently with his head. "Jump." He fingered the links on his neck. "I do not like guns because they are too quick. If you don't jump, maybe I will drive you in with my chain."

"Don't give the bastard the satisfaction, Ethan," said Pierre, his eyes bright and watchful. "Make him shoot."

"That gun will kill us instantly."

"Exactly. A mercy." Pierre's eyes scanned the floor of the chamber and he picked up a chunk of stone. "You think us little men, giant?" He hefted the rock. "This is what a little man can do, Goliath!" And he threw with perfect aim, the missile bouncing off the Dungeon Master's forehead. Omar actually stepped back, his eyes squinting in pain and confusion. Then another rock, and another.

"How many little men have you bullied in your lifetime, ogre?" Pierre challenged. Another rock, this one on Omar's cheek, and I saw the white spark of a piece of tooth flying. There were roars below as the lizard thrashed and spun.

"How many have you never given a chance to fight back?"

Omar howled and lifted his fat gun. Blood was running from his forehead as he squinted at Pierre. The mouth of the blunderbuss looked wide as a cannon, and I tensed for the spray of balls.

Pierre seized me. "Turn away!"

There was a boom, flash, and crack—and the blunderbuss blew up. Pieces flew in all directions and Omar shrieked, hands to his blinded face, staggering in shock.

"Now, seize his chain!" We'd been stung with fragments from the explosion, but not seriously wounded. Each of us desperately seized the end of the chain draped on the Dungeon Master's shoulders and threw a turn around his neck and pulled. He lurched and stumbled past us, blind, bleeding, and crying. The other end of the chain rattled down into the pit.

The lizard, enraged, leaped to take the metal in its jaws and fall back.

The weight jerked Omar over the lip of the chasm.

The ogre fell yelling. There was a thud and muddy splash as the Dungeon Master struck the bottom of his well, and then cries like the ones he elicited from his victims as the bizarre beast, ravenously hungry, went at him. Omar howled, and the two thrashed and snarled in the darkness below, chain rattling as they wrestled.

"It would have been easier for him if he'd died from the backfire," the Frenchman said, peering over.

"My God, did you know the blunderbuss was going to explode?"

"Of course. I didn't have a sling to deal with Goliath, but when he seized me I jammed a rock tight in the barrel. Then more rocks to throw, to annoy him enough to fire."

"Couldn't you have confided? I just aged ten years."

"You're terrible at keeping a secret."

I staggered to fetch a torch, cautiously crept to the lip again, and looked over. Omar was sprawled on his back, eyes wide and sightless, face shredded, his mouth making faint mewing noises as the dragon fed on his torso. His hands had seized the barrel of my longrifle for a club but only bent it in agony.

"I've lost my gun again."

"And I do not care to fetch it back for you," Pierre added.

I watched the lizard tail thrashing back and forth as it gorged.

"The animal may eat his fill before the real monster expires," the voyageur predicted with the harsh experience of the wilderness traveler. "He'll chew out the soft parts first, the ones that kill slowly so the other meat stays fresh. The ogre will die in hours or days, but if not the muck will seep into his wounds and give him sepsis. That would be a more fitting end for a torturer, I think."

"You don't seem to like our Dungeon Master."

"He should not have called a North Man little."
Pierre watched the lizard feed. "They have truly
ugly animals here in Africa."

"I think it came from the East Indies. And a
leopard chewed a dog, upstairs."

"Probably a giraffe in a tower, and a warthog in
an antechamber. Too bad your zoologist friend,
Cuvier, did not come ashore to catalog it all."

I was recovering my breath and wits. "By the
sling of David, how did you learn to throw like
that?"

"A rock in the forest can save powder and gain
dinner, too. Indians learn to throw. I was going to
teach you, had you ever learned to paddle properly,
but I cannot instruct everything at once. You know
it remains amazing, donkey, how many unpleasant
enemies you seem to accumulate."

"I'm equally astounded. I try to be friends with
everybody."

"Yes, we are people of good will, you and I, but I
suspect that by now there are hundreds more here
in Tripoli hoping to kill us. If only everyone could
be like Pierre Radisson! Well, come. We have
many more things to destroy before we can make
good our escape."

CHAPTER 39

It was almost morning. We told the prisoners to make their break, hoping the exodus would distract the janissaries as the alarm was raised. As those released stormed and staggered out the tavern gate and soldiers began to shout and fire, Pierre showed us the side tunnel that Fulton had taken to try to get closer to the mirror. We followed, Astiza confirming we were going in the right direction.

Little Harry had sensibly fallen into exhausted sleep in her arms.

I felt naked again without my rifle or any other weapon, but carried Astiza's shield. There was a Greek Gorgon embossed on its surface, her hideous grimace and hair of snakes enough to turn any enemy into stone. The hero Perseus had used a mirrored shield so he didn't have to look directly at the monster, cutting off her head and ultimately giving the trophy to Athena for use on the goddess's armor. This piece, inspired by the story, might predate Arab manufacture and stem back to Archimedes' time or before.

We emerged on a terrace that faced away from the town's harbor and the coming sun. Yussef's blocky castle loomed high behind us. The sky was aglow with approaching dawn, the last pink flushing away. Across a gap of flat-roofed houses was that smaller fort on a rocky knob that gave a clear view in all directions. Atop it was the mirror, its edge crisp as a planet, men hurriedly pulling tarps from its glittering surface. The weapon had been shined to a little sun itself, and its petal-like extensions were being unfolded. It was a bronze flower, set to embrace and reflect the coming morning.

"Ah, my necessary counterweights," Fulton greeted. "Just in time!"

"Counterweights?"

"A way to prove useful." The inventor had lashed together a tall trestle frame from pole lumber being used to repair a roof, and across this at right angles was a beam some twenty feet long. It was lashed in the middle so each end could bob up or down like a child's seesaw, or a scale. One end was pointed skyward, aimed at the mirror. The other end, down on the ground, was being fussed over by the inventor.

"It would be most appropriate to build a catapult of Archimedes to combat the ancient Greek's own mirror," Fulton said. "But a true torsion device of the kind the mathematician most likely built against Roman ships would take far more time, tools, and craftsmanship than we can muster on this exposed balcony."

There was a flash, and the sun cleared the eastern horizon. Even lit from the side, the mirror across from us began to shimmer.

"As you can see, to reach the fort where the mirror is, we'd have to leave Yussef's complex, find our way through the winding streets of an aroused city, and somehow break into another fortress defended by hundreds of men. The only alternative I can think of is to hurl my torpedo through the air and have it fall at the base of the mirror. Fortunately, there seems to have been some tumult in the palace behind me and the sentries watching this terrace disappeared." He raised a questioning eyebrow in my direction. "If we time the fuse correctly, it will explode shortly after landing and, if in exactly the right place, will damage the mirror beyond repair."

"We're working with Ethan Gage," Pierre warned. "Do not expect precision."

"No, he improvises. But that's good, too. I see you have fetched your woman and child, Gage, and by the sound of it have woken half of Tripoli doing it, and maybe the dead as well. Perhaps the distraction will give us enough time."

"We emptied their prison."

"How helpful. Now, I've constructed a small version of a simple medieval war machine the French called the trebuchet. I attach the bomb to this end of my pivoting beam here, tie that end to the terrace floor, and weight the other end of the beam. When I cut the rope holding the lower end, the counterweight comes plunging down, the missile end goes flying up, and our mine with its fuse flies over these houses. We destroy the mirror, run to the harbor, and make our escape." He counted us. "I thought by now that one or two of you would be dead. It's going to be very crowded in my submarine."

"My son doesn't take much room."

"Well, I'd include him before you in any event—and your pretty woman, too." He grinned. "But we'll squeeze in Ethan Gage as well! Now, the sun is climbing. Are you ready? They haven't spied us yet."

"Ready for what?"

"Notice that the opposite end of the trebuchet has no counterweight. Nothing came readily to hand. Then I realized three adults represent a good five hundred pounds. So what you must do is climb up to grasp the very end of my makeshift catapult. When I cut the rope from this other end you will crash down, the bomb will fly up, and my experiment will be completed."

"Crash down?"

"Think of it as fun."

Sunlight was flooding the rooftops of Tripoli.

"What about Horus?" Astiza asked.

"I'll hold him," Fulton said. "I'm good with children."

She looked from one of us to the other. "Absolutely not. Not one of you men has been good for him yet. And this is just the kind of stupid device boys would invent. *You* three climb up there and *I'll* cut the rope. I've already had to leave my son with his father, and he's had so much misadventure it will be a miracle if he doesn't grow up as disturbed and incorrigible as Ethan."

"I'm not incorrigible. Just improvisational."

"I'm heavier anyway," Fulton conceded. "It's as you say, Gage: your wife is smarter than any of us. Here, let me cut the fuse to length."

She glanced at me. "Did you call me your wife to your friends?"

I swallowed, and grinned. "Possibly." Had I? I couldn't remember.

"Without informing me?"

"Just as you neglected to tell me I was a father."

She considered our mutual miscommunication, her expression inscrutable. My grin was growing anxious. I worried that I'd annoyed her—or the opposite, pleased her! Both seemed risky, even calamitous. It's easier for women, I thought jealously. In our world they need a provider and protector. So a man provides, giving up a variety of quim for one, and gets . . . what? Love, help, constancy, and a sum greater than its parts: a family. He gets a son, and a lifetime of pride, worry, and responsibility. He gets the half of him that's missing.

Not such a terrible bargain.

I swallowed, as afraid of Astiza as a janissary regiment.

So I turned to look at the mirror of Archimedes. It was dazzling, a beautiful golden sun in itself, a sight that must have terrified the Roman galleys by its brilliant sheen alone. I realized that if Lieutenant Sterett was returning for us as planned, the schooner *Enterprise* would already be in sight. The mirror would look like a glowing lighthouse. Would he dare come close?

"How will we ignite the fuse?" Pierre asked.

The inventor stopped. "I hadn't thought of that." He peered eastward. "Does anyone have a glass we can focus in the sun?"

"For the sake of Apollo, this is the nineteenth century," I said. "We're also in the shade. Pierre, prime the pan of your pistol. That will give flash enough to light the fuse."

"Of course," said Fulton. "Such a modern man you are, Ethan! All right, up we go! Gage, you're biggest, out to the end. Yes, yes, we'll hug each other, no time for squeamishness." I clung like a monkey to the end of the beam. Pierre wrapped around me, and Fulton half dragged himself on top of both of us while looking backward. "Astiza, light the fuse and then use my cutlass to cut the rope."

"You're certain of your aim?"

"I've spent the night in calculations."

"Then I'm ready." She carefully cradled our snoozing Harry on one shoulder and picked up Pierre's gun with her free hand.

"Hold the pan of the pistol next to the fuse and pull to let the hammer fall."

There was a flash but no sizzle.

"It didn't catch."

"Try it again."

The sun was climbing higher. Across at the fort, men were starting to yell and point at the spectacle we made, knotted at the end of a beam like an octopus. More figures appeared in long robes. Egyptian Rite! How would they react when they learned their intended queen was dead, her body mangled?

Astiza poured more powder on the pan of the pistol and pulled the trigger again. Another flash, and this time the fuse caught. The burning cord was very short, just enough for a quick flight through the air.

"Now, now, cut the rope holding the trebuchet arm! Hurry, before we blow up!"

She swung and the sword bounced, only chopping partway through.

"Saw it! There's a hundred pounds of powder there!"

She began desperately slicing the strands. We tensed. Now more men at the fort were yelling and gun smoke blossomed. Bullets thudded into the stucco around us. The fuse let off a bright hiss and wink of sparks.

"Please!" Fulton shouted. "We make a perfect target!"

Finally the rope snapped, we plunged, and the other arm of the fulcrum jerked up. The bomb shot skyward, leaving a thin trail of smoke. Men began shouting warning, and running from the mirror. The mine plunged down, a lovely parabola . . .

And fell just short of the mirror's parapet, landing on a lower ledge fifteen feet below.

We waited.

There was no explosion. We could see the bomb sitting impotently.

"Damn," Fulton hissed. "The fuse went out!"

"*Mon dieu*," Pierre groaned, picking himself up off the ground where we'd fallen. "Why do I get involved in the schemes of the donkey? I might also point out that you missed the mirror completely, Monsieur Inventor. Just what calculations did you make all night long?"

"If the beam were two feet longer . . ."

"Ethan, use your rifle!" Astiza said. "Maybe we can set it off with a bullet!"

"My piece was smashed in the dungeon. And Robert's pistol won't hit anything at that range, even if a bullet could by a miracle detonate the charge."

"We'd better retreat," Fulton said. "They'll signal the other janissaries to trap us here."

"Wait," Astiza said. "Look! They're turning the mirror."

And indeed the Egyptian Rite's robed warriors had run back to the contraption and were beginning to swing it toward the climbing sun and, coincidentally, toward us. Where before it had seemed to gleam, now it positively blazed, the petal-like arms beginning to twist and bend as they were hauled on tackle to help focus the power of the rays. They were going to aim Archimedes' death ray at our little party.

"Retreat!" I had my family.

"No, this is our chance!" Astiza seized the sword and began hacking at the cords holding the beam to the trestle.

"What are you doing?" Fulton cried.

"We need to hammer that shield onto the beam and catch the heat ray when it comes this way," she said. "If we hold the shield itself we'll be burned, but we can use the beam as its handle. Ancient records in Memphis and Dendara suggest just such a countermeasure."

"You want to reflect their beam back at them?"

"Yes, until they scatter. Then I want to aim it at your bomb."

"Ah!" cried Pierre. "It is the pretty woman who is the sorcerer, not you, donkey!"

"Well, I'm the one who found her." And I remembered just how much I was in love.

We fetched an iron nail and used the butt of Pierre's pistol to pound it through the shield onto the beam, crouching below the parapet. I glanced over. Ropes, gears, and pulleys were sharpening the mirror's focus. That would be necessary, I realized, to hit a moving target like an enemy ship. The Egyptian Rite savants had figured out the old design of Archimedes, and perhaps improved it.

"Stand! Let them aim at us!" said Astiza.

"And risk burning?"

"So we can burn them."

There was a flash and a ray of light pulsed across the rooftops and hit our terrace. The heat was instantaneous and terrifying. Astiza twisted away to shield Harry with her back, wincing, my son waking with a start. "Now, now, pick up the beam and use the shield!"

Grunting, we lifted our crude reflector into the path of the death ray, the head of the Gorgon flaming in the light. Immediately there was another flare of illumination, a counterbeam bouncing back as we struggled to aim, and then we tilted the shield just enough to run the reflection across the Egyptian Rite technicians at the mirror.

They screamed. Two robes burst into flames. Men began running from the controls.

"Now, now, the mine!" Fulton ordered.

Carefully tilting, we deflected the mirror's ray onto the torpedo we'd hurled. In seconds it began to smoke again. Flame curled. We waited, praying.

And at last a roar!

The mine and its hundred pounds of gunpowder blew up in a great gout of fire, smoke, and stone, the wall just beneath the mirror blown to pieces. The platform the wall had supported tilted and sagged, and the mirror lost focus and abruptly dimmed, as if there were an eclipse of the sun. Several soldiers and technicians on the opposite side had been knocked down by the blast, and one or two controlling ropes snapped.

But that was it. The mirror was tilted, not destroyed. Hurled chunks of rock clattered down on the city's rooftops, the smoke blew away, and our failure was plain. There was a gaping hole in the wall beneath the mirror and small fires burning inside the fort, but no serious damage.

"I should have brought a second torpedo," Fulton groaned.

"No," I said, "it's enough to keep them from roasting us and the *Enterprise* while we escape, if we go quickly enough. Let's run, and maybe we still have a chance!"

"A fulcrum of Archimedes can prop up that damaged rooftop in seconds," the inventor insisted. "Look, they're already running to fix it. Not only are we doomed, but so is Sterett."

"I'll go down fighting before I go into that pit with that lizard," Pierre muttered.

"As will I before I lose my wife and son to slavery," I vowed, realizing I'd said wife again without thinking. By the eye patch of Odin, was I making a commitment? Ethan Gage, rootless adventurer, tireless womanizer, who thought too often only of me?

"Ethan?" Astiza asked. Women do like to know. Yet what could we say when there was so much unsaid, because we hadn't had time to say anything yet?

And then there was a truly titanic explosion, a thunderclap that knocked us over and sent mirror, Rite, and the top half of Yussef's fort skyward in a monstrous fountain of fire and smoke. Glittering golden shards of an ancient weapon flew apart as if a rock had been hurled into a glass mirror, and they glinted like stars as they radiated. Bits of rock and metal and human beings flew in all directions, raining down on Tripoli. There was a rattle as bronze fell like hail. Our ears ached from the punch of air.

Fulton swayed to his feet, looking in stupefaction at the smoking stump of ruins where the mirror had been. "They stockpiled powder and guns to protect it," he said dazedly. "Our fires reached the magazine, and it went off." He looked at our shield, bent by the heat. "Medusa turned them to rubble."

CHAPTER 40

We escaped through chaos. The dungeon was empty, gates hanging wide, and in the streets escaped slaves and prisoners had fanned out in a frantic riot to try to break free of Tripoli before janissaries caught them again. A huge pillar of smoke was roiling up from where the mirror had been, and secondary explosions were still going off as kegs of gunpowder ignited. We ran in our Arab robes through confused, milling crowds without drawing fire. There were sharpshooters boiling on the roof of Yussef's palace and I thought I saw Karamanli himself, head bare of his jeweled turban as he shook his arms and furiously shouted orders. But he didn't spy us, or recognize yet what I must be carrying away in my pocket.

Just as we dashed through a water gate onto the harbor quay, there was another roar and a docked pirate corsair blew up. A geyser of water shot up from the vessel's bow and then it began to sink at its moorings. Its rigging and that of pirate craft nearby caught fire. Sailors spilled off the boats in fear and confusion, not knowing where the attack was coming from. As they did so, some of the escaped prisoners began stealing smaller feluccas.

"Splendid," Pierre said, marveling at the havoc. "Donkey, you've done it again."

We spied a ripple and shadow in the water as Cuvier and Smith steered the *Nautilus* away from the ship they'd stalked. For a moment I feared they were steering straight for sea, leaving us, but then the shadow slowed and Fulton's little windowed tower broke the surface. The submariners paused, no doubt peering out, and then the hatch popped open and fell back and Cuvier appeared. He waved cheerfully.

"Don't call attention to yourself!" I warned.

And indeed, muskets began to crack and bullets began to kick up spouts near the submarine. Cuvier ducked back down and the vessel turned hard to starboard and made for where we were standing. I longed for a rifle to answer back, but my piece belonged to a well-fed dragon. I felt naked.

Harry, whose moods flickered with each calamity, was looking around the harbor with bright interest. Apparently he was getting used to cacophony. People were running in all directions, smoke roiled up, and cannon balls were making splashes in the water. "Fire, Papa!"

"Bad men," I said. "You'll never play with fire, will you, Harry?"

"Can you play with it?" The idea intrigued him.

"Certainly not!" said his mother.

"Fire hot!" He held up his little fingers.

"Very hot," I said. "Very dangerous."

"No danger!" he said. He thought. "Bad big dog."

"The big dog is dead."

"Good."

"You give every indication that you are brighter than your father," Pierre observed. "Must be your mother's side."

And then with a bang and a clunk the *Nautilus* was at the quay. Astiza handed a squirming Harry to Cuvier to drop inside and then we four adults followed, filling the little craft to bursting. Harry began crying again at this confinement, quite reasonably, and the palace gunfire coming our way was increasing. A couple of musket balls pinged off the tower.

"We'll have to go underwater until we get out of range," Cuvier said. "How far will the mirror reach?"

"We destroyed it," Fulton said. "It was Astiza who figured it out." He seemed as impressed with her as he'd been dissatisfied with me, and was good-looking enough that his compliment made me feel a little jealous.

"My congratulations, madame," Cuvier said. "And allow me to apologize for the discomfort. Our American inventor here seems to have forgotten any amenities."

"Escape will be amenity enough." She looked uncertainly about the metal tube, sweating with moisture and stinking of confined men, but smiled bravely. "I'm sure this is just the first draft of his experiments."

"And the next few minutes will determine if it is to be his very last." Cuvier winked.

"I have a new design that will hold twenty men!"

"Let's finish with this one, first."

We submerged and Pierre and I took over from the winded Smith to crank the propeller. All too clearly we could hear the eerie whoosh of cannon balls as they plunged into the sea nearby. The garrison of Tripoli seemed to be firing at everything and nothing.

"Have you seen Sterett and the *Enterprise*?" Cuvier asked.

"Not yet," I replied. "We have to get clear of these reefs and surface."

We had no way to gauge our progress except by studying the compass and counting minutes, which Fulton was doing under his breath. With so many people and the hard exertion of the crankers, the air was quickly getting stale. Horus had solved the problem by nodding off to sleep again, and we all looked at him with envy.

"How about some of your compressed air, Robert?"

"I'm saving that for an emergency."

"Seven people crammed into an underwater craft designed for three, and being bombarded with cannon balls, is not an emergency?"

"I think we're already out of range." The plonk of the falling cannon balls had ceased. "Let's come up to reconnoiter and crack the hatch. Gage, I'll spell you on the propeller. Take a look when the tower breaks free of the water." We squeezed past each other while Cuvier pumped some of the water out of our buoyancy tanks. Our chamber lightened as we neared the surface, illumination glowing as the thick windows broke above the waves.

I looked behind us through the glass. A haze of smoke hung over Tripoli and several xebecs and feluccas had caught fire. The quay and walls were boiling with men, but the gunfire had stopped. We were either too far away or they'd lost sight of our shadow passing underwater. Fulton's submarine had promise after all.

So, could we see the *Enterprise*? I turned around to look toward open sea. And almost yelped! A Barbary ship was bearing down on us, sails bellied, spray dancing at the bow, and Hamidou Dragut balanced on the bowsprit, face bloody, pointing frantically at our form.

Pointing precisely at me! He was directing his ship to ram us.

A bow cannon was being run out to say hello with another cannon ball, and sailors were aiming muskets as well. "Down, down, down!" I cried. "It's Dragut, heading straight for us and trying to ride over the top of us!"

Fulton and Cuvier slammed levers and spun cranks and our tanks began to fill. The windows filmed with water as we dove, but now the brighter light of the surface was agony, suggesting we weren't descending fast enough. A shadow loomed, the Barbary pirate ship casting darkness like a thundercloud, and then we could hear the hiss as it sailed over us. There was a screech as it briefly scraped our conning tower with its keel, pushing us down. Then we kept sinking on our own, gaining acceleration as the light dimmed, and with a bump struck the harbor bottom, forty feet deep.

Harry woke up. "Where, Mama?"

"Safe." Her voice trembled.

A hiss of thin water streamed from one of the bolt holes.

"Wet!"

"Yes," she said coolly. "It is." Her eyes were wide.

"Can we wait Hamidou out?" Cuvier asked, looking upward.

"He'll luff and drift over us," I predicted.

"We're running out of air," Smith warned.

"Not if we uncork the container I brought," said Fulton. "I told you we should wait for a real emergency. Now it should buy us an hour, at least." He worked the stopper partly free and a new hiss joined that of the leaks. Fulton worked a pump a few times to keep the water streaming into the hull from deepening too quickly. Then he lit another candle. "We could use some cheer."

"Our rendezvous was to have been at dawn," I said. "Sterett will see the smoke and know we've done something, but how long dare he wait?"

"Let's use the screw to try to finish our journey out of the harbor. How far did we have to go, Gage?"

"I didn't have time to judge the reef."

"So we'll have to try it blind."

We pumped, and lifted off the bottom. Then there was a splash overhead, a few seconds silence, and then a clunk.

"Is Dragut anchoring?"

"Maybe he's dropping cannon balls on us."

"Blind?"

There was a boom and the *Nautilus* lurched, as if kicked from behind. We were all thrown forward and our candles went out, and then water began gushing through the packing around the propeller shaft as well, a cold jet that soaked us all. Harry began whimpering, climbing up his mother's bosom.

"The pirates dropped a fused keg of powder on the bottom," Fulton guessed. "Man all the pumps! We've got to surface before we sink!"

"I knew I should have stuck to a canoe," Pierre muttered. "Did God make us fish, to go about underwater? No, he said, 'Stay where you can breathe, Adam.'"

"Georges and William, do we still have that last mine?" Fulton asked.

"Aye, but it's not rigged."

"Can we turn the propeller?" I asked.

"It's bent, but it turns a little," the inventor reported.

Water was swirling around our ankles.

"I think we're going to have to swim for it," Fulton said. He glanced around his little cylinder, looking stricken. "I don't think *Nautilus* will make it back to *Enterprise*."

"The pirates will simply pick us off if we leave this boat," Smith said. "Or pick us up for prison."

"Not if we destroy them first," I said. "We've got that mine at the bow, even if it's not ready. How do you set it off?"

"The usual plan is to screw the charge into the ship's wooden bottom, back off with a long line, and trigger the torpedo with a lanyard," Fulton reminded.

"What if we just nuzzle up and blow?"

"It will sink both ships, and whoever is in them."

"Then that's what I'm going to do, after your companions are off the *Nautilus* and swimming for safety. I'm tired of this son of a bitch Dragut."

"Ethan!" Astiza cried. "You can't kill yourself now!"

"Quite right," Smith put in. "You're a father, man."

"With a boy I'm not putting back into slavery. Look, I got us into this mess. None of this would have happened if I hadn't been caught up with the Egyptian Rite, Aurora Somerset, and Napoleon Bonaparte. I've escorted all of you into Hades, because you've had the pluck and ill fortune to come with me. Now I'd like to buy you some time."

"By committing suicide?" the Englishman protested.

"Robert," I asked Fulton, "if I tied a line to the mine's lanyard and led it through the hatch, could I set it off in here where I'd have your metal hull between me and the bomb?"

"Well, yes, but the nose of the *Nautilus* is going to be crushed like a snuff tin. My plunging boat is going to sink like a rock."

"Maybe I can hold my breath and then swim free."

"Ethan, no!" Astiza pleaded. "Horus needs a father!"

"He needs to live first, which requires the sinking of Dragut's ship. This is what I get for not finishing that pirate off in the harem. Every time I fail to kill people, I regret it. Now"—I addressed them all like a lieutenant briefing a sortie—"when we get to the surface you have to get out before the pirates have time to see us and start shooting. Swim and scatter. Dive when you can, to make it harder for them to hit you. Meanwhile, I'll drive the submarine under their hull, trigger the mine, and swim away after the explosion. Make for the reefs, and maybe you can stand on the shallowest ledges and signal Sterett for rescue."

"That's no chance at all," Cuvier said.

"Which is just how the donkey likes it," said Pierre. "You forgot one thing, Monsieur Lunatic—how are you going to both drive the submarine and ready your bomb? I, Pierre Radisson, can crank harder and swim better and jump higher than any man, and so I will help in your scheme. I am, after all, in the habit of aiding you in all things ridiculous."

I bowed. "I take that as a compliment, voyageur."

"It's getting light!" Fulton warned. "We're nearing the surface!"

"Astiza and Harry first! Then the savants, for world knowledge! Men might read about your work someday!"

Not the most bloodthirsty of cries, but it was honest sentiment. If we had to choose between a geologist and a gambler, or a zoologist and a fur paddler, the ranking seemed obvious to me. I didn't think they'd get far, but by then I'd be dead and not have to worry about it.

"Ethan, not when we're finally together again," Astiza moaned.

"I'll catch up," I said with absolutely no conviction.

"And I don't like to swim," Smith groaned.

"Consider the alternative."

"Surface!" Fulton banged back the hatch, sprang out on a deck awash, and reached down to haul up Harry, the child mute again from all the adult anxiety around him. Astiza scrambled out, took her boy, and jumped into the water, sidestroking away as best she could.

"Go, go, so I have a chance!" I shouted to the other men. "Help Astiza!"

Cuvier and Smith hauled themselves out, too, the Englishman shaking.

"I'll help you, William," Cuvier encouraged, pulling him by the hand.

As they left Pierre began cranking the half-jammed mechanism to get the submarine moving. "It's hard, donkey! But the loss of weight makes us less sluggish!"

Fulton dropped back inside. "I'm going to help."

"No! The whole secret of this will go down if you do!"

"I'm not leaving my ship. Come on, Gage, tie on your lanyard! We're the Americans, at war with Yussef Karamanli!"

The inventor certainly had grit, which meant I had to muster it, too. I pulled myself up on deck. "Hard right so we come under her stern," I hissed. "She's stopped to hunt for us and just drifting. No one's looking behind." As we ponderously turned and gathered headway I untied one of the sailing lines and used a simple square knot to tie it onto the final mine's lanyard. The explosive was stored in a basket at the bow. Slowly we crept toward Dragut's ship, the morning sun making its planking glow as if lacquered. I could read the name of this vessel we'd used to escape Venice, *Mykonos*. Quietly, our deck awash . . .

Now pirates spotted our low form and began shouting. Men ran to the stern. Muskets went off, and I heard the rumble of cannon wheels as they tried to swing one around and depress its barrel enough to hit us. A bullet pinged off the hatch.

"All right, straight!" I shouted down. "Crank, crank, crank!" Now a swivel gun was aimed my way and I hastily backed away and fell back down the hatch. Water was knee-deep in the submarine. The swivel gun went off with a bang and there was a rattle of grapeshot topside, one fragment singing through the hatch and bouncing inside.

"Ow! *Merde*, donkey, close the hatch!"

"I can't and pull the rope! Besides, we're going to need a way out!"

"We'll most likely be blown to jelly," Fulton said mildly, "but if by some miracle we survive the bow will be gone in any event, so we won't need the hatch. But yes, don't jam the lanyard rope, Ethan." He seemed resigned, as calm as if pondering blueprints.

I looked up. Our hatch was drifting under the xebec's overhanging stern. There were bangs and thuds as the pirates dropped uncomfortably heavy things on us, making big splashes. Then there was a softer bump as we nosed to nest against the rudder and hull. I could hear cries of alarm in Arabic.

I said good-bye to my little family, yanked the rope and lanyard, and tensed.

A roar and concussion knocked all three of us hard into the stern of the submarine. There was a flash as the bow of our vessel cracked and gave way, and then a wall of cool seawater gushed in like the bursting of a dam to ram us even harder into the stern and shut off all light. Our air snuffed out. And then we were plummeting, my ears pained, all the way to the harbor bottom again.

The stern of the *Nautilus* hit hard on the gray sand, the bow completely gone. It was the jolt that made me realize that I was in fact still alive enough to feel, and that because of it I and my companions might possibly be saved.

Something floated past and I grabbed it. Fulton's kettle of air! It was now lighter than the water and floating like a buoy, bubbles streaming out. I seized the Arab robe of somebody with the other hand and kicked out from the destroyed front half of the submarine, aiming for the silver surface so far above. We shot upward and burst like porpoises, shrieking and coughing.

I had hold of Pierre, I realized, and he'd dragged up Fulton in his own grasp. Both men appeared at least half alive, dazed and spitting water as we drifted in a line with the kettle.

I looked wildly about. Dragut's xebec was nowhere to be seen. There was a fan of shattered timbers, broken pirate bodies, and floating spars with scraps of canvas.

We must have set off the ship's magazine.

I let loose of the air kettle and struck out for one of the spars, pulling Pierre and Fulton with me. We reached what I realized was the bowsprit of the *Mykonos* and saw there was another man clinging at the opposite end, a pirate survivor as dazed as we were. We floated, blinking, and I peered blearily at the villain we were sharing with.

It was Dragut, his face bruised and bloody where I'd slammed him with my rifle stock. His clothes were half gone from the explosion of his boat that kicked him off the bow, and his arms and shoulders were peppered with splinters and little burns. He returned my look with baleful eyes, making a calculation.

I groaned. Did I have to fight him again? I was as spent as a pauper's purse, weaponless, frantic to find my wife—yes, I'd thought of her again as that—and child.

But instead of attacking, he finally gave me a limp salute. "So you have won after all, American. Blown me off my own ship." He shook his head. "What kind of devil craft have you Christians made now? I couldn't understand Aurora Somerset's fascination with you, but it's clearer now. You are indeed a sorcerer."

"I told you not to go to war with the United States." I looked for something I could club him with.

"Here." He threw me something and I caught it: one of Cuvier's dueling pistols. He'd been tossed from his ship with the pair in his sash and now he drew the other and pointed. We aimed at each other the length of the bowsprit.

The hammers clicked on wet powder, the pistols harmless, and he gave a wry smile.

"You haven't beaten us yet." He dropped his gun in the Mediterranean, and I let mine go, too. All the weapons we'd acquired in Venice were gone. "I will avenge my ship. But not today, it seems." He pointed. "Your navy is closer than my cowardly own."

I looked and there to my joy was the *Enterprise*, luffed just outside Tripoli's reefs and banging away toward the harbor with her light guns. The flag was rippling sprightly in the morning breeze. A spray of splinters went up from a felucca that had put out to join the fight. It and others were turning back.

"Turn and fight, you cretins!" Dragut shouted to his own comrades. But they couldn't hear him, and wouldn't listen if they could.

"For just a morning, it seems we do have an American blockade," I said.

Dragut shook his head. "Good-bye, Ethan Gage. I don't think I will offer you passage on my ships again." And with that he let go of the spar and began wearily swimming, the last of his crew, for Tripoli and its retreating boats.

I was happy enough to let him go. He may have been Aurora's tool, but he was not Aurora.

"Well, Robert, it seems I have sunk your submarine, just as Pierre predicted," I said.

"I should have warned you at the beginning," the Frenchman explained to Fulton. "Ethan Gage is a walking calamity. I had to watch donkey so he didn't put his clumsy foot through my birch canoes. Or add green wood to a fire, or wet rocks to a fire ring, or flub a gutting job, or poison himself with berries."

"I can imagine," the inventor said.

"Every once in a while, however, he would perform sorcery. Like this."

"*Nautilus* worked, Ethan," Fulton said with tired pride. "I can go back to Paris and tell Bonaparte it succeeded. We sank two ships."

"No, you can't. Napoleon won't let you implicate France in an attack on Tripoli and jeopardize safe passage of its shipping. He has troubles enough. Besides, the submarine is gone. You don't have anything to prove it with."

"I have you, as eyewitness!"

"I will say what I saw, but how likely is he to believe me, Ethan Gage?"

The inventor looked crestfallen.

"Come, let's kick after the others and swim out to *Enterprise*. I see they're lowering boats."

As we slowly swam toward rescue, Fulton began to cheer up, displaying the dogged persistence of all successful inventors. "My steamboat idea he'll like better," he said as he kicked. "I'm sure he'll be won over by the next demonstration. And someday there will be fleets and fleets of submarines."

"Stick to your panoramic pictures, Robert. People like to be somewhere other than where they are."

CHAPTER 41

The pirates had had enough for the day, and did not try to pursue us. Nor did we have the naval firepower to duel Tripoli's batteries. Sterett set course for Malta and the American squadron. From there, my companions could catch ships to whatever destination they chose.

It turned out that Fulton was cheerier about my necessary destruction of his *Nautilus* than I expected, once he thought about it. He had every hope this first experiment would allow him to construct a second, and was already drawing sketches. "Imagine a dozen men cranking or, even better, a steam engine that operates underwater! Imagine living under the sea!"

"Wasn't it rather dark and wet?"

"Imagine floating over the canyons of the deep, and swimming with giant fishes!"

I smiled indulgently. "Will anyone believe, Robert, that five men—only two of them American—successfully attacked Tripoli?"

"Of course they will believe it! I will tell them! We can show, we have . . ." He looked about as if proof of his exploit was at hand.

"Not a weapon, not a prize, not a prisoner," I said. "Just be aware that men like Bonaparte hear many tales from men seeking favor, and learn to be skeptical."

"You'll back me up, Gage! We'll be partners, earning huge bounties from sinking ships of war!"

"The world is at peace, Robert. Look at the Englishman Smith and Frenchman Cuvier over there, getting on like old friends as they talk about rocks and bones. Why would Napoleon ever go to war with Britain again?"

"My steamboat, then. You have to help me in that convincing way you have, Ethan."

"I told Madame Marguerite in Paris that I was going to write a book."

"Then write one about our adventure!"

"Maybe I shall. And mostly tell the truth."

I visited with Cuvier. "And what's next for you, Georges?"

"Extinct animals instead of live pirates. It is a fine adventure exploring the Mediterranean, but I think I've had enough holiday for now, and prefer quiet bones. I'm also a bookish man, and supposed to reform education. Then there are all these interesting ideas about the origins of life! We found time at Thira, Ethan, depths and depths of time. And those pretty rooms down that tunnel: Was that Atlantis, or an arm of it? Who first invented the mirror? Was the idea bequeathed by mysterious ancestors, like your Thoth and Thor? I'll have to sift the records of antiquity. You've given me a hobby for the next several years."

"My pleasure. And you, William?"

"I think I've seen enough of the human world, too, and will return to England to continue my geologic mapping. Rocks don't shoot back. Such work could help others think about the mysteries of the earth. Scientific luminaries have ignored me, Ethan, but this little adventure of ours has given me confidence—confidence and persistence. When I see that even Ethan Gage can win at the end of things, I think that I might too!"

"Don't let the snobs discourage you, William. They know you're smarter than they are, and are afraid of you."

"I'm going to win them over," he vowed. "I'm going to map the earth, and they are going to invite me into their Society!"

Pierre said he missed Canada. "There are too few trees in Africa, and too many people in France. I've decided I want to see more of the North Country before I grow old, Ethan. I want to paddle all the way to the Pacific."

"I met a man named Clark who had the idea to do the same thing. And he was friends with Lewis, the secretary Jefferson wants to send that way."

"Well, maybe I will go with them."

And I? There was still the sale of Louisiana to persuade Napoleon on. Beyond that there was the little matter of a woman I loved, a boy I wanted to raise, and a life I still hadn't entirely worked out.

So as we sailed for Malta I sought out my love in the bow of the *Enterprise* and we settled against a cannon, watching the dancing waves.

"Did you know that I was almost forced to marry Aurora Somerset on a pirate ship?" I told Astiza.

"Almost?"

"We were interrupted by cannon balls from Sterett. As it turns out it wouldn't have mattered, because I'd be a widower by now. Aurora dead, you alive, and little Harry out of nowhere. It's amazing how life works out."

"Horus. And he's not out of nowhere, Ethan."

"We made him, didn't we?" It was a little presumptuous of me to share equal credit, but by the soul of Patrick Henry, I couldn't help but be proud. I rather liked being a father, given the spunk of my son. He might be the cleverest thing I'd ever done. "I think I want to settle down, Astiza. I want to find a place where nothing ever happens, and live there with you."

"Nothing? How long would that last, Ethan?"

"You can teach Harry about the stars and the goddesses, and I'll get a new rifle made and show him how to shoot. We'll live on an island, perhaps, and let the world have at it while we watch from the beach. Wouldn't that be the thing? I'll weave us hammocks, and write down this story for Harry, and never get mixed up with Napoleon again. Will you stay with me now?"

I won the slightest of smiles. "It appears that's what destiny intends. Together forever, and not a ripple in our lives." She sounded skeptical, but women usually do when I announce my plans.

"Yes!" So I kissed her, my first chance in nearly three years, and I was relieved we hadn't forgotten how. Then I leaned back, feeling breeze and sun as we danced across the Mediterranean. "To think I'm to be a gentleman farmer! Of course I know nothing about farming. Nor do I like grubbing in the dirt. So I'll be a philosopher, perhaps. Or maybe we'll hear of a treasure that is a little less exasperating. And I suppose I haven't given my son the easiest time of it yet, so I need to learn to play with him. As well as teach, of course. I've a lot of wisdom to pass on."

"I pity the boy already. And how are you going to support us for these dreams?"

"Ah, I almost forgot. While you were sensibly seizing a shield from Yussef's throne room, I went for something a little more frivolous, kept locked away in the leopard's cage." I fished in my pocket and pulled out my prize. It was the emerald from Karamanli's turban. "This will get us started. And send our child to school someday, to boot."

"Ethan! You finally saved something."

"I've got a family to save it for, now."

"And where *is* Horus, by the way?"

"Why, he's right . . . I thought he was with you. Didn't you put him down?"

"And I thought he'd gone to find you!"

We looked at each other with consternation. Gunfire, explosions, vicious animals, desperate fights, sinking submarines—we were terrible parents.

Now we couldn't even keep track of our only child on an eighty-foot ship.

"Harry?"

We began searching the deck, increasingly frantic. What if the tot had gone overboard? We blast our way out of Tripoli, pioneer a whole new way of warfare, and misplace the lad on our own navy's schooner? "Where sense is wanting, everything is wanting," Old Ben used to warn, always looking at me with particular intensity.

And finally I remembered something and took my love by the arm. "In case I forget, remind me to have Sterett marry us," I told her. "He's captain of the vessel, after all. That is, if you'll have me." My heart was hammering. Franklin said to have your eyes wide open before marriage, and half shut after.

"Of course I'll marry you! I can't get rid of you! But what about Horus?" She had a mother's panic.

"I know where he is. Right where I told him to be. Come with me below."

And indeed I found him below in the sail locker, curled fast asleep. His look was that of the angels, but he sleepily blinked as we watched him, and then looked at me.

"Hungry, Papa."

He'd crept off to nap in the one place where I told him he'd be safe.

H I S T O R I C A L
N O T E

America's conflict with the Barbary States simmered and boiled from 1784, when the new nation had won independence and lost the protection of the British navy, until 1815, when the United States sent naval forces against Algiers. The British navy launched another punitive attack in 1816, and the French conquered Algiers in 1830, starting the colonization of North Africa that finally ended Barbary piracy once and for all.

The American war with Tripoli in present-day Libya, immortalized in the Marine Corps Hymn line "To the shores of Tripoli," ran from 1801 to 1805, and was punctuated by victories and defeats on both sides. It ended after capture of the Tripolitan city of Derna by rebel forces aided by American Marines. Bashaw Yussef Karamanli agreed to release American prisoners and cease attacks on American shipping in return for a ransom of $60,000, an ambiguous "victory" that nonetheless marked the coming-of-age of the American navy.

And what of the daring and revolutionary 1802 submarine raid on Tripoli by the American adventurer Ethan Gage and three famous scientists—an episode missing from more conventional histories?

We do know that Georges Cuvier was one of the most prominent zoologists and paleontologists of his day. William Smith was the father of English geology, but unrecognized for his achievements until very late in life. Robert Fulton was a tireless inventor who marketed schemes to both the French and British navies, and who eventually returned home to develop the first commercial steamboat, the *Clermont*, on the Hudson River in 1807. His invention of the submarine *Nautilus* was a century ahead of its time.

Fulton came to France hoping that the revolutionary government might be open to new inventions, given the inferiority of its navy to Britain's. American David Bushnell had developed an even more-primitive submarine, the *Turtle*, which unsuccessfully attempted to sink British ships during the Revolutionary War. Fulton expanded on Bushnell's idea after plans for the *Turtle* were published in 1795, and proposed a submarine, or "plunging boat," to the French on December 13, 1797. The eventual design is described in this novel.

The idea languished until Napoleon seized power in France in November of 1799. With preliminary backing, by the spring of 1800 Fulton had built a working submarine, approximately twenty feet long and six wide. It was launched July 24, and on July 29 commenced sea trials in the Seine. Further experiments followed in Le Havre in August, where Fulton managed to blow up a barrel in a test. He actually tried twice to approach two anchored English brigs, but the British had heard of the experiments and, whether by accident or from alarm, raised anchor and sailed before Fulton could get close. Experiments resumed in the summer of 1801 off Brest. There the *Nautilus* dove as deep as 25 feet, stayed submerged as long as three hours, and traveled underwater about a half mile. The vessel also sailed adequately on the surface.

Unfortunately for Fulton, a new Minister of Marine was opposed to this secretive method of war and French support ended. While history records that Fulton told the French he broke up the *Nautilus* to prevent its being copied, Ethan Gage suggests the vessel's remains may actually be at the bottom of Tripoli's harbor.

Fulton subsequently demonstrated a steamboat to Napoleon in the Seine on August 9, 1803, and then, frustrated at the lack of French backing, went to Britain to propose submarine and torpedo schemes to defeat a French invasion fleet.

Equally revolutionary was the mirror, or death ray, of the great Greek mathematician Archimedes. Syracuse, a Greek colony on the island of Sicily, founded in 743 B.C., became one of the major cities of the ancient world, and was eventually caught up in the titanic struggle between Rome and Carthage. It was besieged and captured by the Romans in 212 B.C. Despite the orders of the Roman general Marcellus, Archimedes was slain by a Roman soldier who did not recognize the famed mathematician.

Legend has it that Archimedes invented ingenious machines to defend his city, including an improved catapult, giant mechanical claws that could crush Roman galleys, and a mirror that could set them on fire.

The first surviving biography of Archimedes is that of Polybius, written seventy years after the inventor's death. It does not mention the mirror. However, in the second century A.D., the historian Lucian wrote that the Greeks repelled a Roman attack with a burning glass, or mirror. This story was elaborated on by later writers, and has ignited the public's imagination ever since.

Modern attempts to replicate the weapon include a 1973 Greek experiment in Athens that set a plywood mock-up on fire, using an array of 70 mirrors. A 2005 try by Massachusetts Institute of Technology students set a stationary target on fire, but an attempt to replicate that deed for the television show *Mythbusters* was unsuccessful. Whether a genius like Archimedes might have done better—and whether a renegade American helped rediscover just such a device in 1802—we leave to the reader's discretion.

Certainly there has been a steady accumulation of evidence in recent decades that the ancient world was more technologically sophisticated than once supposed. Cicero recorded that Archimedes made an early geared "computer" to imitate the motion of heavenly bodies, and just such an ancient device was discovered by Greek sponge divers in 1900. Dubbed the Antikythera computer and on display in Athens, it calculated the movements of sun, moon, and stars.

Fulton's idea of a flamethrower is predated to at least A.D. 674, when Byzantium used a new invention called "Greek fire" to destroy an Islamic fleet.

The French legend of a Little Red Man is true, and recorded in some Bonaparte biographies. Also reported is Napoleon's habit of shooting at Josephine's swans.

The Palais Royal was the Las Vegas of its day, and the ruins, caves, and cathedrals of Syracuse are mostly as described.

Ioannis Kapodistrias, the Greek patriot whom Ethan meets on Thira, became the father of Greek independence from Turkey. Other characters taken from history include French secret policeman Joseph Fouché, American naval lieutenant Andrew Sterett, and Yussef Karamanli.

The gigantic lizard aboard Aurora's ship is the famed Komodo dragon of Indonesia. While not documented by Western science until 1910, the animals were most likely known to natives of the archipelago. History records that Yussef did keep lions and other cats in his Tripoli palace.

The Egyptian Rite was a real heretic offshoot of Freemasonry, founded by the con man and conjurer Cagliostro about 1777. Its reach, ambition, and longevity have been fictionalized in my novels.

The island archipelago of Thira is better known as Santorini today, the rim of a shattered volcano. In approximately 1640 B.C., the island blew itself apart in an eruption so violent that the tsunami waves that hit Crete may have toppled Minoan civilization. Some scientists believe that Plato's story of Atlantis was inspired by that real-life incident.

Minoan ruins were uncovered near Akrotiri, and some of the murals described in this novel can be seen at a museum on the island.

Was there ever really an Og, mysterious ancestors, and fantastic ancient weapons? History is just that, a story, and sorting fact from legend will occupy historians and archaeologists for centuries to come. What we do know is that legends once dismissed as complete myth, such as Atlantis, seem to have some basis in geologic truth—and that the more we learn about ancient people, the more ingenious they seem.

This novel was made possible by the research of scores of nonfiction authors who have written on the lives of its principals, the Barbary Wars, and the history of France and the Mediterranean. The book was also a wonderful excuse to visit lovely lairs such as Santorini and Syracuse. Special thanks to Huxley College and to Nick and Cynthia Zaferatos, who introduced me to Greece. Once again, my appreciation to the team at HarperCollins: my editor, Rakesh Satyal, publisher Jonathan Burnham, assistant editor Rob Crawford, senior production editor David Koral, publicist Heather Drucker, online marketing manager Kyle Hansen, foreign rights marketer Sandy Hodgman, and the designers, artists, copy editors, and marketers who make any novel a team effort. My agent Andrew Stuart adeptly keeps me in business. And, as always, my wife, Holly, remains as travel assistant, first reader, necessary skeptic, and muse. May the adventure continue!

CHAPTER 1

Berlin
March 21, 1938

First day of spring, and pregnant with the same expectancy that gripped Kurt Raeder at his unexpected summons from Reichsführer-SS Heinrich Himmler. The Prussian sky was cold, ragged sunlight dappling the German capital with that glitter atop iron that promised an end to winter. So might Himmler be the pagan sun to part the clouds of Raeder's stalled career. So might Raeder win his own expedition.

"We have read with interest your books on Tibet," the summons stated. With that simple missive the explorer had been yanked out of the ennui of his university teaching and the gloom of his wife's death, the opportunity like the twin lightning bolts of the SS Rune.

As Raeder walked from the U-Bahn into the heart of Nazi power, Berlin seemed to share his anticipation. The city was its habitual gray, buds swollen but little green on the trees yet. Yet the paving was bright from a night's rain and the capital seemed poised, purposeful, like one of the new steel tanks that had waited on the border for the *Anschluss* with Austria just nine days before. Now the two nations were united in a single German Reich, and once more public apprehension about a Nazi gamble had turned to excitement bright as the red swastika banners, vivid as a wound. All the world was waiting to see what Germany would do next. All Germany was waiting to see what *Hitler* would do next. His New World Order was improbably succeeding, and on Wilhelm-Strasse, marble blocks and columns were stacked to the sky where the Führer's imposing Chancellery was rising. Speer had promised completion in less than a year, and workers scrambled across the pile like frenzied ants. People watched, with pride.

Raeder was too much the academic to feel entirely comfortable in his black SS uniform. Entry into the new German knighthood in 1933, suggested by a politician friend, had been a way to establish Aryan ancestry and win a measure of grudging deference in a university system glacial in its advancements. Appointments had come quicker with the exodus of the Jews, but Raeder's brief fame had not solidified into quick promotion. Meanwhile, Kurt secretly liked the theatricality of the dramatic costume and the medieval ritual of SS indoctrination. It meant brotherhood, the satisfaction of being one of the chosen.

University intellectuals were snobbish toward the Nazis. At school, Raeder had mostly avoided the costume, preferring to blend in with high starched collar and restricting tie through years of brief celebrity, dull instruction, and finally private tragedy. But now the Reichsführer had somehow taken notice. Here was the hinge of Raeder's life. So the young professor had put on the *Schutzstaffel* uniform with its runic insignia, both proud and self-conscious. When his faculty colleague Gosling spied him from a café and joked about it, the zoologist managed the good humor to shrug.

"Even scholars have to eat."

Life, the Nazis preached, was struggle.

Raeder knew he cut a fine SS figure. Brown hair a shade too dark to be ideal, perhaps, but handsome and fit from his explorations: erect, wiry, what a German youth might wish to be, the new man, the Aryan prototype. Crack shot, alpinist, university scholar, hunter, author, and scientist for the Third Reich. Lotte's death had not been publicized, out of deference to his achievements. His self-doubt he kept to himself.

Almost unconsciously, Berliners swerved around his uniform on the crowded Wilhelm-Strasse, a caution he accepted as normal. The SS was not to be loved, Himmler had preached. But Untersturmführer Kurt Raeder, adventurer! His resolute gaze had been in magazines. Women swept by him, and peeked.

Pedestrians thinned as he walked past the sterile, massive headquarters of Göring's new Air Ministry, the power of the Luftwaffe implied by its modernist bulk. And then thinned still more as he turned left onto Prinz-Albrecht-Strasse and arrived at Number 8, the most notorious address in Nazi Germany. Here was the home of the Reich Security Ministry, which included the SS and Gestapo. Next-door was Number 9, the Prinz-Albrecht-Palais Hotel, also subsumed by the growing security bureaucracy. To Raeder's eye the home of the police was a more inviting structure than the plain severity of Göring's headquarters. With classical arched entry and Renaissance styling, the SS buildings harkened back to the more refined 19th Century. Only the black-clad sentries who flanked the door hinted at its new purpose.

There were rumors of Gestapo cells in the basement. There were always rumors, everywhere, of the very worst things. This was good, Raeder believed. Menace promised security to those who followed the rules. None could deny the Nazis had brought order out of chaos. While the democracies were flailing, the totalitarian models—Germany, Italy, Spain, Japan—were on the rise.

This building was the fist of the future. Raeder's future.

There was a hush inside, like a church. A grand stairway with thick balustrade, steps carpeted in red plush like a movie palace, led up a flight to a vaulted entry hall. The only decorations were three hanging swastika flags and busts of Hitler and Göring. Public depictions of Himmler were rare; his power was his air of mystery. Bare wooden benches as uncomfortable as pews lined one side of the waiting area, glacial light filtering in from arched, frosted windows. At the far end three steps led to another entry (like an altar, Raeder thought, continuing the church analogy) with black-clad guards presiding instead of black-robed priests. Himmler had modeled his elite on the Jesuits, and SS zeal on the discipline of the Inquisition.

Raeder's credentials were checked and he was admitted to a more private reception area, the offices beyond barricaded by a massive counter of dark-stained oak, stout as a dam. Now a more thorough check, this time by a blond-headed Nordic guard of the type the SS put on its posters. The officer scrutinized his insignia skeptically.

"An untersturmführer to see the Reichsführer?"

Raeder showed the letter that had summoned the SS lieutenant from his residence in the respectable Wilmersdorf district, the apartment haunted now since Lotte's death. "The Reichsführer expects all ranks to serve."

The comment drew no reaction from a man with the expressiveness of a robot. "Wait."

The explorer stood stiffly as the orderly spoke into a telephone and then returned it to its cradle. The guard didn't bother to look at Raeder again.

Long minutes passed. Raeder could hear the faint clack of heels on tile, the cricket-murmur of typewriter keys and code machines, the rumble of wooden file drawers sliding out and slamming home. Each muffled

BLOOD OF THE REICH

ring of a distant phone was answered before it could
jangle a second time. All was whispered, as if the ministry building had been selected to absorb sound. Was
noise from the basement muted too? The colors were
institutional green and cream, the lights a somber
yellow.

"This way, Professor Raeder."

Another SS officer, a sturmbannführer, thicker and
pinker, briskly led him into the maze of corridors
beyond. They wound one way and another, climbed a
flight of stairs, and wound again. Raeder was (perhaps
deliberately) lost. The office doors they passed were
shut, shapes moving behind obscured glass. The few
people in the hallways were male, hurried, boots drum-
ming, conversation a murmur. The walls were blank.
Floors gleamed. The calm efficiency, the monkish concentration, the paper-and-glue smell of a library . . . it
was admirable and disquieting.

Then more SS guards as strapping as Vikings
snapped to attention, a double door swung open, and
they came to a high-ceilinged anteroom paneled in
beech. Sentries checked Raeder for weapons and scrutinized his identification once again. No one smiled or
spoke more than the minimum. It was a wordless play,
the anteroom dim, windowless. He was in the middle
of a vast hive.

A knock on a side door, an answering buzz, and he
was ushered through.

Raeder expected another corridor, but instead found
himself in a modest painted office, with a lower ceiling
than the anteroom outside. A single window looked out
on a courtyard, the wall it faced blank stone. No one
from outside could look in. There was a large but plain
desk, left over from some Prussian ministry, and three
leather chairs in front of it. Behind sat the second-most
powerful man in Germany.

Himmler looked up from a manila file and gave
Raeder an owlish blink. With round spectacles, reced-

ing chin, and narrow shoulders, the Reichsführer SS was nothing like his praetorians outside. In fact, he resembled a bank clerk or schoolmaster. He had a thin mustache, pale skin, and white, fastidious, womanly hands. His hair was shaved close to the skull above his ears in the dull helmet shape of Prussian fashion.

A much fiercer portrait of the Führer looked down on them with burning zeal: that shock of black hair, that punctuating mustache.

The office was otherwise absent of decoration. There were no personal pictures or mementos, just a wall of books, many of them old, leather-bound, and cracked. Raeder couldn't read the faded titles. The Reichsführer's desk was neat as that of an accountant, stacks of files with colored tabs precisely squared and ranked. Either this was not Himmler's regular office, or the Reichsführer had no need of the baronial opulence of a Hermann Göring. The abstention was eerie.

Himmler closed the folder and turned it so Raeder could discern his own name and picture.

"Sit."

The zoologist did so, sinking into a chair. Its legs had been trimmed so that he almost squatted, looking up at Himmler. The Reichsführer smiled thinly, as if to relax his guest, but the chilliness simply reinforced the man's power. There was something oddly vacant about the personality he projected, as if Raeder was meeting with a facade.

Then Himmler abruptly leaned forward in a disconcertingly intense way, with a predatory glare like an insect, eyes obscured behind the reflection of the glasses, purpose ignited as if with a match.

"Untersturmführer," the security minister began without preamble, folding his hands on Raeder's folder, "do you believe in the importance of blood?"

CHAPTER 2

Seattle
September 4, Present Day

He was cute, he was checking her out, and he was a frozen foods guy.

Rominy Pickett believed a man's character could be divined by his location in the supermarket, a method at least as reliable as the signs of the Zodiac. She usually dismissed males spotted in the beer-and-chips aisle, on the theory they might represent the man-child-slob archetype in need of too much reform. Those in stock foods she suspected to be conservative and dull: only a Republican would buy canned peas. The wine section was more promising (she supposed that marked her a bit of a snob, favoring wine over beer) and fruits and vegetables were also possible. She didn't need a vegetarian, but a man who thought about his greens and took time to cook them might be thoughtful and slow about other things as well.

The bread aisle was a place to find solid whole-wheat types, but too many already wore wedding rings. Picnic supplies suggested an outdoorsman, while intellect could be gauged by where a guy planted himself on the magazine aisle: Was he browsing *The Economist* or *Truck Trend*?

But spices, condiments, and wine were best, Rominy believed, suggesting a fellow open to detail, experimentation, and taste.

Admittedly, this screening was far from perfect, given the tendency of grocery hunks to move from one aisle to another. But then the Zodiac was open to interpretation, too. Her criterion was at least as reliable, she maintained to her friends, as the arch fiction encountered on Internet dating sites.

Frozen food was a problem. The likelihood of meeting bachelors rose here, given the stacks of entrées aimed at singles. But the freezer cases also implied haste, microwaving, even (could you read this much into a grocery cart?) a certain lack of ambition. Defrosting was too easy.

True, *she* was in the frozen foods aisle too, with Lean Cuisine Cheddar Potatoes and Broccoli and a pint of Häagen Dazs. But this was about prospective life partners, not Rominy's own singleton existence as software publicist. She'd achieved a bachelor's in Communication, a gray forty-square-foot cubicle with industrial carpet and underpowered PC, two longish relationships broken off well short of real commitment, and personal resolve not to settle for competent mediocrity. Yet nothing ever *happened*. Grim global news, limping economy, girlfriends who only quipped, men who only wanted to hang out.

And shopping at Safeway. For one.

She was almost *thirty*.

Not that old, she reminded herself. Not nowadays. She was due for promotion soon. She was due for things to happen.

And yes, cute frozen foods guy was glancing again. Rominy caught herself instinctively and embarrassingly flipping her brunette hair as she imagined a thousand things about him: That his lingering by the pizza case made him interested in Italian food and renaissance art, that the way his left foot with trail shoes rested on the shopping cart gave him the athletic stance of a mountain biker or rugby player, that the pen in his shirt pocket announced not nerd-with-grocery-list but poet prepared for spontaneous inspiration. Unruly surfer blond hair, icy blue eyes, an intriguing scar on the chin: How delicious if it had been from reckless danger! (Probably a juvenile skateboard accident.) And there was a hint of a muscular physique under the denim shirt. Yes, Rominy was a regular Sherlock in the way she could scope out the human male at a glance. Too bad if the scrutiny took them aback—and damn them if they did too much of the same to her.

What *she* wanted was to undress their souls.

He wasn't approaching, however, just looking. Too much looking, in fact. Evaluating her with a curious, hesitant stare that was anything but coy, flirtatious, or even leering. He simply regarded her like a curious specimen. Creepy, Mr. Frozen Foods Guy. Or boring. Get a life.

On to the condiments! Rominy pushed her cart two aisles down and pondered the advance in civilization represented by squeeze bottles of ketchup. Her ambition was to invent something simple and practical, like the paper clip, retire to the beach, and try Proust or Pynchon again. Master Sudoku. Train for the Iron Man. Open an animal shelter. Build a kayak. Figure out her camera.

But then Frosty the Snowman idled into view, leaning on his own cart like a handsome cowboy over a saddlehorn, oblivious to whatever might be melting on his metal mesh. Still looking but not doing. Shy, or stalker? Not worth it to find out. Maybe she read too much Chick Lit, but she wanted a man who showed confident initiative. Who came up and said something funny.

So she wheeled around and took a quick dash to the feminine products aisle, territory guaranteed to ward off unwanted males the way garlic and crucifix could deter vampires. Rominy should never have returned his glance in the first place, but how could you know? She'd camp here until the lurker had time to move away.

But no, he'd peeked down the aisles from the broad corridor at the back of the store and tracked her to this new refuge. Now he turned his cart into terra incognita and looking questioningly at her, mouth opening like a fish, hopelessly uncertain what his first line should be. Next to the tampons? Did she know this dude? No. Why was he trailing her? Why hadn't he said anything? He wasn't just checking her out. He was *watching*.

So she pivoted and squeezed behind a middle-aged shopper who had her cart nearly athwart the aisle in that worst-of-Safeway rudeness. Now Mrs. Dumbo could unintentionally run interference while Rominy headed for the cash register. The fast-check-out lane, eight-item-limit-be-damned.

Escape! But no, Mr. Frosty appeared again, the front of his cart cutting in her direction like the prow of a battleship, his look anxious and his pace quicker. Would he make a scene? Where was pepper spray, or self-defense kick boxing training, when she needed it? Or was this klutz just socially inept, like so many men?

Calm, Rominy. Just another of your countless admirers.

As if.

But then his jacket opened slightly and she gave a start. There was something black on his hip.

Let the ice cream melt. She abandoned her cart, squeezed by the rump of another overfed matron tapping password numbers into a debit card reader, and headed for the door. Sorry, Safeway. No sale.

Rominy's experience (which included more than a few dead-end dates as excruciating as an IRS audit) was that intriguingly eccentric men turned out to be . . . weird. Politeness only encouraged them. Avoidance was a mercy.

Nor could she call for help.

Please, a man with a grocery cart is looking at me.

But instinct screamed that something was wrong.

Rominy had dropped some overdue bills in the mailbox at the lot's outer limits, so her car was parked a good fifty yards away. The vehicle was her pride and joy, a silver 2011 Mini-Cooper scrubbed bright as a new quarter, suddenly as distant as a football goalpost. It had taken the trade of her ancient Nissan, a diversion of funds that should have gone into her 401K, and the commitment to four years of monthly payments to buy the runabout, but my, how she loved its cuteness and handling. Now it represented refuge. She knew she was probably hyperventilating about Abominable Snowman, but she'd never had a grocery guy track her relentlessly as a cruise missile without first attempting a friendly hi.

"Miss!"

He'd come out of the store after her. Rominy quickened her pace toward her car. This clumsy come-on would make a snarky text message for her girlfriends.

"Wait!" Footsteps. He was starting to run, fast.

Okay. Get in the car, lock the doors, start the engine, engage the transmission, crack the window, and *then* see who this lunatic was. If harmless, it would be a story to tell the grandchildren.

So she ran too, purse banging on her hip, low heels hobbling her speed.

"Hey!"

His footsteps were accelerating like a sprinter. Wasn't there anyone in the lot who would interfere? Run, Rominy, run!

Her Mini-Cooper beckoned like a castle keep.

And then without warning the creep hit her from behind, sending her sprawling. Pavement scraped on hands and knees. Pain lanced, and she opened her mouth to scream. Then his weight crashed fully on top of her, a body-slam that knocked out her wind, and the bastard clamped his hand over her mouth.

This is it, she thought. She was going to be raped, suffocated and murdered in the broad daylight of a Safeway parking lot. Frozen food guys, it seemed, were psychopaths.

But then there was a boom, the ground heaved, and a pulse of heat rolled over them. Her eardrums felt punched. She lay pinned, in shock. A cloud of smoke puffed out, shrouding them in fog, and then there was the faint rattle of metal pieces clanging down all around them.

Her beloved Mini-Cooper had blown up. She still had thirty-nine months of payments, and its shredded remains were bonging down around her like the debris of some over-extended Wall Street bank.

Her assailant put his mouth to her ringing ear and she winced at what he might do.

But he only whispered.

"I just saved your life."